LESLEY THOMSON

The Detective's Secret

HEAD
of ZEUS

Stare. It is the way to educate your eye, and more.

Stare, pry, listen, eavesdrop. Die knowing something. You are not here long.

From *Walker Evans at Work*, with an essay by Jerry L. Thompson

413 The Thames is a tunnel.
414 The river is a tunnel, it's civil infrastructure.
415 The river is a tunnel with an uncountable number of entrances.
416 When you go into the river you discover a new entrance – and in yourself you uncover an exit, an unseen exit, your exit. (You brought it with you.)

From *Another Water: The River Thames for Example*
by Roni Horn

For the Nelson sisters who have had a profound influence on my life: May Walker, June Goodwin and Agnes Wheeler.

And for Mel with my love.

Prologue

October 1987

Clouds streamed across the sky. Street lights obliterated the stars; the moon wouldn't rise until midnight, four hours away. A fierce wind rattled reed beds on Chiswick Eyot and tore through the undergrowth. Cross-currents on the river made rib-cage patterns; patches of stillness in the black water resembled corpses.

The Thames was rising, a deadly confluence of tide and turbulence. Miniature waves broke across Chiswick Mall; water welled in gutters, covering kerbstones and lapping at the steps of St Nicholas' church. A storm was gathering force.

At night Chiswick Mall was outside time. Misty yellow light surrounding iron lamp standards might be gas lit, cars were carriages on cobblestones. On the foreshore of the Thames, the clank-clank of a barge's mooring chain against the embankment wall beat the passing of no time at all.

A shape reflected in the river was dashed by a squall; it resolved into a tower. Utilitarian, a cylindrical tank supported by stanchions, the water tower was built in the Second World War to protect riverside wharfs and factories from fires. Long in disuse, the wharfs demolished, the tank was empty, the pipes stripped out. Fifty metres high, it stood taller than the brewery and the church spire and dominated the west London skyline. Against streaming clouds and tossed boughs, the tower, designed to withstand bombs and tensile stresses, seemed as if forever falling.

A cage attached to one supporting column housed five

stairways connected by a platform; the last arrived at a narrow metal walkway that gave access to the tower. Violent gusts harassed the grille, testing steel rivets.

A man hurried through the church gates, skirting the water; he ducked into an alley between the brewery buildings and struggled up the staircases into the tower, head bowed against the wind. Minutes later, a woman emerged from the subway by the Hogarth roundabout and went into the alley. Checking about her, she pulled on the cage door and, both hands on the guard rail, began an awkward ascent.

'I hate this place.' Her voice rang in the concrete tank.

He watched as she zipped up her slacks, smacking at dirt although there was none; he kept it clean. Grimacing, she eased on brown leather faux-Victorian boots, doing up the laces with slick-snapping efficiency.

'You wanted secrecy.' The man pulled on underpants, his nakedness absurd as their intimacy of the afternoon ebbed. Her boots had heels. He had advised flat shoes for safety, but was glad she had ignored him. She was his fantasy woman.

He had put himself out to get the key from the engineer. The man had kept it after the developers went bust – as ineffectual revenge for non-payment – but there was no point in telling her of this effort: it would not convince her to leave her husband.

'*Come and be with me.*'

She had insisted that they leave no spending trail. No hotels, no meals out. No risk of meeting anyone they knew or being remembered by strangers. She had admitted that nylon sleeping bags on the tank floor, drinking wine from the bottle and feeding each other wedges of Brie on bite-size water biscuits spiced up the sex. Strangely there was no handle on the inside: he propped open the thick metal door with a brick and, once she was inside, he locked what he called the 'front door' after her. She'd surprised him by saying that the danger of being locked in made her feel alive.

'*You'd feel alive all the time with me.*'

She knew that, she had told him.

'The apartment has a view of the sea.' He had told her he would take a year's lease. Things had changed, she'd said as soon as she arrived. It had spoiled his performance.

'Another bloody excuse!' He shouldn't have said that.

He buttoned his shirt, saw he'd missed a button and started again. She was pouting and air-kissing into her compact mirror. Already she had 'gone', planning the kids' meal, back to her life that was death. The knickers he had bought her lay discarded beside the used condom – just the one this time. Last time she had agreed to leave; today she said her family needed her.

'I need you.'

'The flat does sound beautiful.' She appeased him, shrugging into her coat.

'Then leave!' He always tried to be everything her husband was not. Mr Perfect. He'd once let her know the other girls didn't need persuading. She knew there were no other girls.

She smoothed her skirt over her stomach and he was aroused all over again.

'You look lovely.'

'That wind nearly blew me off my feet,' she said again as if she hadn't heard him. 'There's a storm getting up.'

'It's not all that's "getting up"!'

She came over, put a hand on his crotch and whispered, 'Next week.' She didn't usually do this when she was about to go; he dared to hope it meant something good.

'I can't hear any wind,' he said. 'It's nothing.'

'You told me this place is soundproofed!' She looked about her as if she'd just arrived. 'It's like a prison cell.'

'Sea view versus a mauso-bloody-leum!' he snarled. Usually he toned down his accent.

'In my heart I'm yours, you know that.' An off-the-shelf response.

It frightened him that he could hate her. He saw why people killed their lovers. If she were dead, she would stay.

He tensed his jaw. 'Do you have sex with him?'

She was rootling in her handbag. She squirted perfume on her wrists – not for him, but to expunge him.

'You promised to leave.'

'You'd be horrified if I turned up with two kids in tow!'

He tortured himself with a vision of her with a leg over the blubbery husband, letting him pump away inside her. In his dreams there were no kids in tow.

'Bring the girl. Let him have the boy.' Unlike the husband, he played fair.

She laughed and looped her bag over her chest as he advised, for safety.

'I'm leaving on Saturday.' His palms tingled at the decision made there and then.

'You said we had a month.' As he had hoped, she was upset.

'I'll be at the station at three on Saturday. If you're not there, I'm going.'

'It's too soon.' She kicked the brick aside and stepped on to the spiral staircase.

'It's always "too soon".' In her heels he wanted her again.

'I can't just leave.'

Not a 'no'. His venom evaporated. 'Be careful in those boots, that wind is strong.' Too late he recalled he'd underplayed the wind.

'I climb mountains in these.'

Not with me.

He followed her down the staircase and stopped her in the lobby by the front door.

'Promise me you'll give it some thought,' he said, but really he wanted her to give it *no* thought, just to leave. 'I'll be there next Saturday at Stamford Brook. At three. You won't regret it!'

'Darling, don't—'

He cut across her: 'You owe it to yourself. We only have one life – let's make the most of it! When we're settled, we can get the kid. One step at a time. Your life now is like living in a coffin, you said so yourself!'

4

He went towards her, but she blew a kiss and turned away. The bottom door shrieked when she opened it. He watched until she reached the caged staircase, and then he returned to their room.

Without her the magic had gone; it was a just cold concrete tank. He stuffed everything into the holdall, anxious to follow her, to see her when she wasn't with him. She had left him the Brie, not out of generosity, but because she wouldn't want to explain how come she had it.

Footsteps. She was coming back. He grew excited and regretted packing up the sleeping bags. 'Hon, you came back. I knew you would!'

There was a deafening report.

The tank door had shut, he stared disbelieving at the grey metal. Beware the jokes of those with no sense of humour. The lack of handle wasn't sexy now. She was on the other side of the double cladding, daring him to lose his nerve.

'Good game!' His temples thudded from the alcohol and he needed a pee. This was her revenge for his ultimatum. 'Joke over!'

Wind fluted through vents near the ceiling – she was right about the storm. Daylight no longer drifted in; the street lights didn't reach so high. Bloody stupid to have said leave the boy, he liked him. The walls emanated chill.

'He's a good kid, I'll treat him like my own son.' His voice bounced off the concrete.

There was a distant vibration – the bottom door slamming. There was no keyhole this side; his key was useless.

'Maddie!'

In the dark, the man wondered if, after all, it was not a joke.

One

Monday, 16 September 2013

Forty-three minutes past eleven. Dead on time, Jack brought his train to a stop at Ealing Broadway Underground station. Late-night passengers decanted and straggled up the stairs to the street. As usual he had seven minutes and thirty seconds before his journey to Barking. He would stable the train at the Earl's Court depot and then the night was his.

Ealing Broadway was the end of the line. On autopilot, Jack strolled up the platform to what, with the 'turn around', was the front of the train, glancing into the carriages. There was one woman in the second car. She was leafing through a *Metro* and looked up as he came alongside her. He thought he saw a flicker of fear pass across her face and quickened his pace. At this time of night a woman travelling alone might feel vulnerable; Jack hoped she would see his uniform and know he was a driver and not a passenger who could threaten her.

He opened the front cab door. Being a driver he swapped between different, but identical cabs at each end of the train during the course of a day or night. Travelling up and down the District line, he was never in one place for long: he thrived on the mix of stability and change. As the proprietor of a cleaning company, Stella restored stability in different locations. Pleased by this tenuous link between their working lives, Jack considered texting her. He put his hand in the fleece pocket of his uniform for his phone. But Stella called a spade a spade. His whimsy frustrated her and at this time of night would worry her. When Stella worried about Jack, she allocated him cleaning jobs – he worked part-time for her cleaning company, Clean Slate. Thinking of Stella made him wistful because since her mother had gone on holiday to Australia, she hadn't been herself. The change was fractional: a pause before she replied, an arrangement misremembered, a minute late to meet him because she'd walked the dog. Stella cared about her mum more than she let on.

Her father too. Two years after his death she still cleaned his house, ate supper there and did her emails at his computer with no sign of selling the place. Jack had once asked her if she was maintaining it for her father's ghost. She had retorted that she was waiting for the housing market to pick up. But prices were rising and even next to the Great West Road, the end of terrace in Hammersmith would fetch a small fortune. He dismissed the lurking notion that it was not a ghost Stella was waiting for, but a real live man. When Stella ended a relationship – eventually she always did – the dumped partner ceased to exist. Except her last man, the one who she thought a David Bowie lookalike, had left her with a dog; undeniable proof he had existed for her once.

He felt something in his pocket and fumbling under his phone pulled out a folded slip of paper.

To Let.
Apartment in Water Tower.
A cosy home with detailed views.

If you crave silence and a bird's eye view – Jack squinted at the type in the watery lamplight – *then Palmyra Tower is your home. Guardian wanted for Grade 1 listed Water Tower. You will sign a year-long contract with no breaks and be available to take up residence as soon as your application is accepted.*

It was the flier he had found lying on the doormat when he left the house that morning. He had shoved it in his jacket pocket and, intent on getting to work, had thought no more about it. Reading it now, Jack was intrigued by the imperative *you will*. He touched his face to stop an involuntary twitch and, shivering, zipped up his fleece. The cheap pink paper didn't compete with Clean Slate's glossy brochure.

The style was a marketing ploy that Stella would reject as too obvious an attempt to be different. However the paper did carry an unnerving air of authority, so in that sense it had worked.

Beneath the text was a fuzzy photograph of the tower. It was functional, effectively a tank on stilts; a caged fire escape-like structure attached to one column gave access to it. It stood metres from Chiswick Eyot, an island in the Thames. As a boy, Jack had once tried to climb it, but couldn't open the cage. The steep aluminium staircases and narrow treads were not for the vertiginous.

There was no phone number on the flier. At last he found an email address in tiny lettering: *info@palmyra-tower.co.uk*. Regardless of the amateur appearance, Jack guessed there would be a deluge of responses. For many, the tower would be the dream home. He scrunched up the flier and stuffed it back in his pocket. Leaning back on the cab door, Jack gazed up at the sky.

This section of the District line was above ground. The moon was a waning crescent in the sign of Leo. Stella was a Leo, as his mother had been. Two women with attitude, courageous and strong-willed. Jack's mother had died when he was a boy so what he didn't know about her he made up; this meant she was his particular brand of perfection.

A plane cut below the moon on its descent into Heathrow, the rumble of its engine carrying on the night breeze. Jack thought of the moon as his friend; it accompanied him on his walks. Or it had until he promised Stella to 'stop all that', although he doubted she understood what 'all that' was. The second hand on his watch ticked towards three minutes to twelve.

As soon as he stepped into the cab, Jack had a premonition of what would happen when he turned the key – it had happened here before. The motor whirred, but didn't start. His train was going nowhere.

He reported the train out of service, activated the door at the rear of his cab and went down the aisle of the cars ushering passengers off: seven altogether. Vaguely he noticed that the woman he had seen earlier wasn't among them. Back on the platform Jack felt a pricking at his temples: like last time, this breakdown was a sign. Like all signs, its meaning had yet to reveal itself.

The coffee stand was shut; a metal box covered with stars, it might be a magic trick about to emit a cloud of doves and many wished-for things. The moon had gone behind a cloud and the temperature had dropped. Jack picked up an empty coffee cup from the platform and tossed it into a litter bin two metres away. *Bull's eye*. The tracks hummed. He returned to the top end of the platform and, as the train approached, tipped a hand to the driver. His greeting wasn't returned. When the train was stationary, he peered into the empty cab at the rear.

With no train, he had no set number. Set numbers were the means of identifying a train and allocating it to a driver, but to Jack the set number was a sign. This train's number was 126. The last time this happened, his set number was 236 and led him to Stella.

Jack was tempted to rush from the station to evade whatever fate 126 decreed.

Running away is no escape if you don't know which direction is 'away'.

Jack rubbed his temples to eradicate the voice. Recently it came unbidden, like the voices of a high fever, and uttered dictums like a seer. It didn't feel his own. He looked up and saw the driver walking the length of the train towards him.

'All right?' Jack nodded.

'You're Jack.' The man had acne and looked no more than sixteen. 'They said you'd be here.' He offered no clue as to what he thought about this.

'Yes.' Jack agreed.

'I wanted you as my trainer, but you were fully booked,' the driver continued in a querulous tone.

'Ah.' Jack smiled. 'No matter, we're all the same.' Not true. He knew he was the best trainer, as he knew, although Stella never told him, that he was her best cleaner. Fact. Jack climbed into the cab after the driver. The doors swished shut.

The driver gripped the handle, his every nerve directed to his task. This wasn't the first time Jack had witnessed the terror of a novice driver. For him, responsibility for hundreds of passengers had come naturally when he had settled into the seat for the first time. It had felt right. But Jack wasn't like others.

Hands resting on thighs, Jack gazed out at bunched cables and silver rails converging and parting as the train left the station and increased speed.

On Google Street View, Jack could travel with the roll and click of a mouse. As if operating it now, he zoomed in on Stamford Brook station and focused on the strip of platform a hundred metres away. Yet again he was reminded of the toy station he had bought as a boy. Grey and brown plastic with a detachable ticket office and a couple of sweet-vending machines, added for free because the toyshop man had felt sorry for him.

Jack's train slowed as it entered Stamford Brook station. There was one man on the westbound platform: he would have a wait: the information board was blank. Trains would be diverted to Richmond because of his dead train at Ealing Broadway. He felt a flash of poignancy that he had abandoned it to be shunted without him to the Acton depot. His concern for inanimate things frustrated Stella.

Jack's attention was taken by the headlights of a Heathrow-bound Piccadilly train lighting up the rails ahead. After Hammersmith, it wouldn't stop until Turnham Green.

Nervous of overshooting the platform, his driver was applying the brake too soon. The last time Jack's train had broken down at Ealing Broadway, he had been sitting in the cab of a novice driver. Everything about this man was the same as the other; both moved their lips as if silently talking. The Piccadilly train was nearly on them – its headlights flooded the cab. He braced himself for the slipstream after it passed his train.

Jack glanced again at the platform for Richmond: still no train on the board. No need to hurry, but the man on the platform *was* hurrying. The wheels of the oncoming Piccadilly line train clack-ety-clacked closer. A tinny announcement came through the platform speakers: 'Stand well away from the edge of platform two. The next train is not scheduled to stop at this station.'

Five metres to go until the end of their platform. Jack's sense of déjà vu was oppressive, as if the last time had been a rehearsal for tonight.

'Take it right up,' he said softly, using the same phrase as last time. 'Get your passengers off. We don't want them pitching on to the line.' The man shoved the handle forward. Jack smelled his fear. 'Keep connection with the lever, coax it. The engine is you and you are the engine.' Something was wrong.

All stories are the same.

Jack banished the unwanted voice and saw the man on the platform lit by the headlamps of the Piccadilly train. The man gave a backward glance and abruptly broke into a run along the plat-form. Did he think the Piccadilly line train would stop? He was looking at Jack – not a glance, a proper look as if trying to express something. Jack had seen the expression before. Then the man was in mid-air above the tracks, caught in the glare of light as the Piccadilly line train thundered into the station. The man's body hit the windscreen and rolled under the cab. All was over in a second. Carriages jolted along and blocked Jack's view. Both trains halted. Jack looked at his watch. Six minutes past twelve: *126*.

A haunting wail carried across the station. The Piccadilly driver was sounding the whistle for staff to assist trackside. The bleak marking of a life extinguished.

Jack's driver was a waxwork, his hand frozen over the controls. He had berthed their train perfectly, seemingly unaware of what was happening metres to his right.

Later, at the inquest, Jack found that his driver had indeed seen nothing. Only Jack and the Piccadilly line driver, a man called Darryl Clark, had witnessed the incident. The few District line passengers had been asleep or plugged into headphones in a private world and although the other train was packed, it was impossible for anyone to have seen the man go under the front of the cab.

'What's your name?' Jack touched the man's arm, intending to ground him.

'Alfred Peter Butler,' he replied as if reporting for duty.

'You did well, Alfred. We'll stop here, you need a break and I think they might need some help here.' Accompanying Alfred Peter Butler through the carriages, for the second time in an hour, Jack informed passengers that a train was out of service.

Like Stella, Jack was comfortable with emergencies, everyone acting according to their role. While the tannoy announced delays, he and his driver checked seats and gangways for abandoned possessions. In the past he had found wallets, handbags, a tatty London street atlas that he had been allowed to keep, even a Springer spaniel lashed to a pole by its lead.

Alfred Peter Butler escorted their little troop down the stairs and across the station concourse, Jack bringing up the rear. To their right, Piccadilly line passengers were streaming down the westbound staircase, there was the buzz of muted exchange, word had got around.

It was a 'One Under'.

Jack Harmon dubbed himself a *flâneur*; he walked the night-time streets of London, observing others unobserved. Unlike a *flâneur*, he cared about those he watched. Courting mortality, feeling the imminence of death, he hunted out those with darkness in their souls and minds like his own. Jack entered the homes of what he dubbed his 'True Hosts', those who had killed or would kill if he didn't stop them.

Jack was quite aware that he sought a re-enactment of the day his mother had died, a day that for him, as for many, was when his world stopped. As when a film is watched again and again in the vain hope that the next time the victim won't die. He drove in the tunnels of the London Underground to find his way back to *before*.

Affecting nonchalance, Jack strolled across the station, singing softly:

'*Humpty Dumpty sat on a wall,*
Humpty Dumpty had a great fall.'

His hair blown back from his face by a cold night breeze, Jack guided passengers through the gap in the concertinaed gate to the street. Even though it was after midnight, traffic on Goldhawk Road was nose to tail, slowing for those filing over the zebra crossing. Someone was watching Jack from the top deck of a 237 bus; he supposed it was a man – a baseball cap was pulled low over the eyes. The bus moved towards King Street and the reflection of the blue station fascia wiped the figure out.

In ten years of driving a train, Jack hadn't had a suicide. Some drivers had it twice, while others went their whole working lives without a person jumping in front of their cab. Jack could not shake the conviction that tonight's incident was the culmination of many signs.

The station office reeked of sour sweat. Alfred Peter Butler was huddled in a corner nursing a mug of tea, staring at his feet. The other driver was texting on a BlackBerry, thumbs skimming the tiny keys. Someone on the phone confirmed that the 'customer' was dead. Jack refused tea. He kept to himself that he felt nothing. He told himself that since his mum died, he had nothing left to feel. Jack fastened the grille and ran up the stairs.

There was no one on the platform where the man had been. Lights from the train cast bleak stripes of light across the tarmac. Jack could feel the dead man's presence in the deserted station.

Staff had rigged up lighting gear for the paramedics, due any minute. Confident that the train driver had dropped circuit breakers to cut the electricity, Jack vaulted on to the rails and crunched over the ballast. Sharp stones jabbing him, he peered beneath the train's underbelly.

A splash of red. A hand curled over the live rail. The man wore a wedding ring; the thick gold band spoke of status, hopefully of love.

'*Wake up,*' Jack had said to his mummy.

He leant in and touched the man's ring finger. It was warmer than his own and still pliant.

'*I will save you,*' he had told his mummy.

Blood was soaking the front of the man's shirt. Globules of blood seeped into the ballast. Jack trembled; his teeth began to chatter. The man's eyes – hazel flecked with green, the pupils dilated – fixed Jack with the impassive gaze of the dead.

Eyes are like fingerprints, they don't alter with age.

'I knew that!' Jack found himself retorting out loud. He clambered out from under the train and hauled himself on to the platform. A woman in paramedic green was fumbling with a body bag. He stayed to see the man zipped into the bag and laid on to the stretcher. He accompanied the crew back down to the ambulance.

'Go well.' Jack formed the words silently, touching his cheek to stay a tic that happened at certain times. He watched the ambulance turn on to King Street, heading for Charing Cross Hospital's mortuary. No blue light required.

In his statement about the incident, Jack didn't put that, before he died, the man with the ring had looked at him. It wasn't pertinent.

His shift declared over, he strolled down to King Street and into St Peter's Square as the church clock struck a quarter to one.

The set number was 126. The man died at six minutes past twelve. From the moment he had stopped at Ealing Broadway, his every action and interchange was a sign. For Jack, death was a beginning, it was a sign that something else would happen.

Eyes are like fingerprints, they don't alter with age. The voice got there first. Jack had seen the man before.

With no True Host to watch, tonight Jack went back to his own house. The building was dark; he never left a light on. A wind had got up – forecasters warned of a hurricane-force storm coming

– it battered the panes and shook casements swollen from the rain.

His door knocker was a short-eared owl fashioned from brass tarnished with age. Her burnished feathers flickered when she puffed up in greeting. Jack sang:

'All the king's horses,
And all the king's men,
Couldn't put Humpty together again.'

Two

'He left me!'

Stella was rubbing at an oily stain on a hearth tile with a dash of detergent on a damp cloth. The stain was lifting. The voice startled her; she thought her client had gone out.

'No warning.' Mrs Carr put her palms to her cheeks in a pose of desperation.

Jackie had briefed Stella that Mr Carr had walked out on his wife in September, but from how she was behaving now, Stella thought that it was as if he had abandoned her that day.

'I'm sorry.' Stella avoided commenting on clients' lives. Many would lay out their problems as if she could wipe them away as she could any stain. Jackie counselled that listening was integral to the job, but Stella was unwilling to put this in the staff manual: it invariably led to leaving a job not completed, which triggered a complaint. Jack had the right balance; he provided emotional support and did the cleaning within the allotted time. But Jack wasn't like other people.

'You don't expect someone you love to lie. You miss tiny signs. Hesitation when you suggest meeting, and when you arrive they end a call without saying "goodbye" and pass it off as a sales call or wrong number.' She did a smoothing motion with her hands as if rubbing in moisturizer. 'Blood is thicker than water, he said, then he tells lies about my family.'

'Ah.' Stella wanted to get on with scrubbing the tiles and washing the skirting. Jack was always seeing signs, tiny or not. The best advice she had about relationships was to avoid them. Blood was thicker than water and she was tempted to suggest it was best to start on a stain with water rather than use hydrogen peroxide, which could bleach the colour out of a carpet.

When she gave Stella the job sheet, Jackie had warned, 'It's a complete tip, dirty and neglected.' Often such scenarios were prompted by a friend or relative calling Clean Slate to halt the slide into chaos. But Mrs Carr herself had rung, which, Jackie and Stella agreed, hinted she would be co-operative, likely to pay promptly and let them get on with the job. Wrong, it seemed. However, she had been keen to get the job done, which included working on Saturday mornings.

Stella liked 'cleaning sites' where she could make a radical difference, but because of the estranged husband, she had judged this was one for Jack.

'He'll need to use the Planet vacuum. He'll like that, he thinks it's like a steam engine.' Jack was like a magpie around the polished chrome casing of the cleaner.

'He got himself one for Christmas – isn't that typical of our Jack!' Jackie had laughed.

As it turned out, Jack was doing day shifts for the Underground, so it was Stella who, fifteen minutes earlier, had parked her van in Perrers Road, a modest street of flat-fronted terraced houses close to Hammersmith Broadway. The little house was less dirty than Mrs Carr had described. It smelled of long-ago-cooked meals and fusty upholstery, but the Planet vacuum wouldn't be needed. Stella applied their basic cleaning package. The biggest issue was mess.

'I trusted him!' Mrs Carr sagged on to a sofa arm, the only clear surface. Piles of clothes, CDs and DVDs, shoes and electrical gadgets, an iPod, a couple of phone chargers, portable disc drives and a tangle of cables were scattered on the furniture, on the floor.

'It might help to move?'

'Why should I? There's no such thing as love. Water under the bridge now. I can't turn the clock back.'

Mrs Carr spoke as if she had physically tried to. Stella's gaze wandered to a clock on the wall, a replica of an old-fashioned train-station clock. When she left here she had to walk Stanley before going to her mum's flat and watering her plants. Over the last weeks she had got into the habit of dropping in on her way to Terry's. This would be the last time; her mum was due back tonight.

'He said we need "space" and bolted.'

Jackie said Stella did the leaving to avoid finding out what it was like to be left. Stella resisted pointing out that David being detained at Her Majesty's pleasure, where pet dogs were not allowed, was hardly her leaving him. It was difficult to miss that Mrs Carr, pale with aquiline features and dark brown eyes, was beautiful. Stella had liked David because he wanted deep cleaning and looked like David Bowie.

'Please take all this away.' Mrs Carr wagged a finger at Stella. 'Your company promises a fresh start. I want one of those.' She did a grand sweep with her hand and left the room. Stella heard the front door shut.

She went to the window. Mrs Carr was heading off down the street, shrugging into a padded jacket.

Happy to be finally alone, Stella filled six bin bags with all the stuff in the sitting room. This took longer than she expected because she opted to separate heaps of junk mail, newspapers and sweet wrappers from the clothes and electrical equipment which it seemed a shame to throw out. She wouldn't take her at her word. Jilted clients were apt to change their minds later and accuse Clean Slate staff of stealing.

Stella didn't consider it her business to tidy, unless restoring objects to places and positions designated by the client. She did arrange gilt silver candlesticks symmetrically on the mantelpiece and position a framed photograph of a man and a woman she guessed were Mrs Carr's parents – the woman looked like Mrs Carr – at one end, which, she hoped, would form a point of tidiness for Mrs Carr to model elsewhere in the room.

Mr Carr must have an extensive wardrobe because the clothes he had left would constitute many a man's entire wardrobe. He had favoured military-style clothes: camouflage jackets and trousers – for the desert as well as dense woodland. Sturdy walking boots, Dr Martens shoes. She rolled up a canvas belt with compartments for bullets. Into another bag went a pair of chinos, a selection of lambswool sweaters branded with the Stromberg logo and some polo shirts. Stella counselled against judging clients but, folding Ben Sherman shirts and Calvin Klein jeans into the bag, could not help constructing an identikit of the unfaithful husband. He was chisel-cheeked, cleft-chinned, with an army-style short back and sides, his looks less remarkable than Mrs Carr's. Several of Stella's clients were former soldiers; she worked contentedly alongside them, keeping their 'billets' tidy. No, none of them would leave their kit behind.

Not her business.

She hefted the bags of newspapers out to the van and lined up the bags of clothes in the hall to await Mrs Carr's final decision.

Someone was watching her. After Terry Darnell's death Stella had got the impression that her father was there when she was in his house. This had faded after she and Jack solved the Blue Folder case. Jack said they had laid his ghost. Stella said that it was because probate was completed. Terry couldn't be haunting her here.

She turned to the front door and stifled a yell. Mrs Carr stood perfectly still, staring not at Stella, but through her. She was so white that had Stella believed in ghosts she would have thought she was seeing one.

'I didn't hear you come back,' Stella said pointlessly.

'I asked you to take all that away.'

'I wondered, as it's all in good condition, whether you meant to give it back to your husband, if he could collect it, or perhaps a charity, a hospice or…' She trailed off. *Do what the client asks. Don't question anything.* This was why she allocated these jobs to Jack.

'I asked you to take it away,' Mrs Carr repeated.

Stella stowed everything in the van, pushing on the back door to close it. She returned to the house to confirm that the next shift was wanted as arranged, guessing it unlikely. Mrs Carr wasn't downstairs. Stella called up: 'See you on Monday, Mrs Carr.' The use of 'Mrs' seemed tactless, but she didn't know her first name and, besides, they weren't on those terms.

No reply. Stella ventured up three stairs and called again. Nothing. She gave up and banged the front door shut to signal her exit. She would warn Jackie to expect an email cancelling the contract.

In the van, she lingered over the job sheet to give the woman a chance to sack her in person. The upstairs blinds were down. The house gave no sign of life.

Passing Hammersmith's Metropolitan station, Stella pressed the button on her steering wheel. An electronic voice boomed through the car:

'*Name please.*'

'Jack Mob.'

'*Dialling.*'

'This is Jack, who are you? Tell me after the beep.'

Stella cut the line. The day could only get better.

Three

May 1985

The high garden wall cast a shadow over the single-storey prefab, a crude addition to the Victorian estate. The kitchens were built to cater for increased demand when pupil numbers reached their optimum in the 1950s. Tresses of ivy disguised much of the shingle cladding and were an aesthetic link to the mansion featured on the school brochure. Steam drifted from open window flaps and misted panes; the cooks inside might have been phantoms but for clattering dishes and pans and raucous chat. The afternoon air hung heavy with the smell of institutional meals, past and present: boiled vegetables, suet and sallow meat.

A diminutive boy, pale and thin, lingered at the corner of the building, gripping the drainpipe as if he would float away should he let go.

Simon had expected to find Justin sitting on the steps surrounded by the cooks in their white caps. The fierce lady who had told Simon to eat his cabbage would be mussing Justin's hair – they fussed over him like a prized pet. The kitchens were out of bounds. But Justin was not there. Simon had lost him again.

In the last months, one event had cheered Simon. Justin had arrived at the school.

Simon had been told to 'show Justin the ropes'. Proud to initiate him into the routine, he was dismayed when the new boy refused to do what Simon told him to. Simon had understood that abiding by the rules and working hard would endear him to the teachers and the other boys. But whatever he did or did not do, Simon was disliked. In a culture where physical perfection and prowess were valued, the fact that the first two joints on the middle finger of his left hand were missing, that he was clumsy and that he was too clever for his teachers assured his unpopularity. When Miss Thoroughgood had told him to look after the new boy, Simon had been happy. At last he had a friend all of his own.

A burst of laughter came from beyond the fogged glass. Illogically, because he couldn't have been spotted, Simon believed they were ridiculing him. Keeping low, arms hanging loose like a monkey's, he pattered past the building.

The path came to a dead end by a group of tall bins. Simon skidded on a scattering of potato peelings and turned his ankle. Tears pricked his eyes. Justin was missing, and it was Simon's fault.

There was a door in the wall opposite. Simon read the notice: 'Private'. Since the old man was found dead there on New Year's Day, the kitchen gardens were even more out of bounds. Simon had overheard Mr Wilson, the RE teacher, saying the 'gardener was lying dead as a doornail in the greenhouse'. He had written up this extraordinary piece of information in his notebook: 'dead as a doornail'. When he told Justin, the new boy had nodded as if dead gardeners were usual.

Simon should go back to the library and mug up on his Tutankhamun project for Mr Wilson, whom he liked, but then he thought: *Enter enemy territory and retrieve missing personnel. Evade capture.* It was his duty to rescue Justin.

A cloud hid the sun. The wall, spiked with flints as sharp as stone-age knives, overshadowed the boy. He stood at the crossways of three gravelled paths. Left, right and ahead, they separated raised beds in which tall weeds and nettles flourished. The gravel was blotched with moss, endive and rhubarb cloches made of clay peeped between cow parsley and thistle. Snails and slugs consumed bolted lettuces and once-prized dahlias. Fearsome fennel, gossamer foliage browning, towered over the herb bed, the geometric definition of which was lost to wooded branches of rosemary and clusters of sage. Garlic and thyme ran riot.

Simon marshalled facts. *Quarry last seen going to kitchens, doing his stupid hopscotch walk, like a girl.* Simon tripped on a bramble meandering across the path. He should report Justin to Mr Wilson. He liked Mr Wilson. His first name was 'Nat', not spelled with a 'G', but still the boys called him the Stick Insect because of it and because he was thin. The air was cooling. Simon had left his jumper on his chair in the library to make it look as if he was there. Mr Wilson would be cross that Simon had let Justin out of his sight.

He saw a greenhouse, beyond a rusting lawn roller. A crack. Simon dived behind the roller. Above his head a gull cried, derisive like the white capped cooks. The dead gardener groped at his leg. He shouted and scrabbled free. A cat, black with a white bib, was weaving about him. Simon liked the cat – although as Mice Monitor it had been his job to keep it away from the classroom. He put out his bad hand and stroked it; instantly it arched in appreciation, then it gave a start and darted away. Simon peeped around the roller.

The door to the greenhouse was open. The metal frame had buckled; slats of glass were missing. Shelves were filled with flower pots and seed boxes. No one was there, dead or alive.

He ventured further along the path, the weeds so high it was like a tunnel. Justin liked tunnels; he said he was going to be an engineer when he grew up. Simon had asked if an engineer drove engines and Justin had laughed and said he was stupid. Simon turned a corner and saw Justin sitting on the ground in the middle of a patch of sunlight.

'You're trespassing!' Relieved to find him, Simon grabbed Justin by the shoulders. He was surprised by the feeling of sharp bones.

'Let go!' Justin wrenched free. He was pouring water into a hole in the side of a pile of earth. The pool shrank as water soaked into the ground.

'I need to get more.' Justin spoke as if to himself.

'What are you doing?' Simon expected that Justin would be sorry and accompany him to the library where they were meant to be.

'This reservoir has to feed two towns. There's no need for a pump or a water tower, it's higher than the settlements, I'm using gravity.' Justin waved a hand. The ground had been cleared of weeds, earth flattened and marked with stones like a railway track. A gutter had been cut into the raised earth through which a tunnel ran. Justin had constructed it with lolly sticks and mud. Simon poked at the mound with his bad hand.

'Careful!' Justin grabbed Simon's wrist. 'It could collapse. I had to measure the sides, make sure the rolling stock can pass through.' Justin's father was an engineer. Simon's father worked with mad people and never smiled. Simon didn't want to be mad when he was grown up.

'Get off me, Stumpy!' Justin glared at him. 'Go away.'

'Your mummy's dead.' Simon said and was immediately horrified. He hadn't meant to say it.

'She's not. And anyway your mummy doesn't love you. That's worse. Mine loves me very much.'

Simon felt his eyes sting. Dashing at his face with his sleeve, he pulled out of the tunnel a red locomotive attached to three carriages.

'What's in here?'

The carriages uncoupled and crashed on to the tracks. He picked them up and peered in through the windows of one of them.

'Gosh, it's a dining car!' he exclaimed. 'Look, that's you and me having our lunch. Let's pretend we met there. I've got steak and French fries like the man in *Strangers on a Train*. Have you read it? It's my mum's favourite book. It's really for grown-ups. What are you eating?'

'I don't know what you're talking about,' Justin replied as if he didn't care either.

'Two men meet and become friends.' Simon chattered on happily, his mood recovering as he warmed to his idea. His mum had been impressed that he had read the book from beginning to end. 'Do you like tomato ketchup?' He imagined shooting it all over his chips like the man in the story.

'I am about to drive my train through the tunnel,' Justin said.

'I'll do it.' Brought rudely back to the present, Simon was terribly sorry to have made a mess, but this was all against the rules. He reattached the carriages and, lifting the engine, ran the wheels over his palm, making them spin. He pushed it on the impacted soil, wheels whirring, and watched with satisfaction as it sped into the tunnel. It shot out of the other side, carriages twisted and buckled, and veering off the tracks smashed into the watering can.

'You went too fast.' Justin rubbed his hand on his shorts.

Simon was horrified; he had wanted to help. He pulled on his bad finger and pretended he was a racing driver who didn't care about going fast.

'Can I have a turn?' Perhaps Justin had forgotten it was his own train.

'Unfortunately you cannot. I need to perform more test runs.' Simon pressed too hard on the locomotive and it sank into the earth. 'Stop doing that with your mouth,' he ordered.

Justin twitched his face on purpose to frighten him. 'I wasn't.'

'You were. I don't want to have to get cross with you.' The engine was stuck; soil clogged the axle and front wheels. 'There's nowhere for the passengers to get out.' Simon's palms were damp. Who had killed the gardener? *The enemy can smell fear.*

'I will kill you and bury your body so that no one will ever find you and then your flesh will be eaten and your bones will crumble.' Simon stuck his bad hand inside Justin's shorts and pinched him. 'I'll say you escaped again. Message understood?'

Simon tore the pin from the hand grenade and hurled it into the tunnel. He dragged Justin away as a blast tore into the mountain, pelting the enemy with clods of earth.

'You're mean.'

Simon pretended he hadn't heard Justin. He imagined radioing back to base. *Enemy camp destroyed. Mission accomplished.* He imagined being an entirely different person, someone who could make people do what he wanted. This idea faded before it had taken shape. Flushed with shame, Simon stared at his bad hand as if it were his enemy.

The boy hurried along the low vaulted passage, past the reception. Outside the cloakroom toilets he bumped into nice Mr Wilson.

'Hey, kiddo!' The teacher had a funny accent because he wasn't English. 'Have you seen your mate, Justin the Dreamer?'

Simon stopped, clutching at his bad hand.

Mr Wilson waited.

'He's in the library.'

'OK, Simon, can you make it your job to get him into dinner on time? We don't want him being late again.' Mr Wilson was smiling down at him.

'Yes I will, sir.'

Simon had lied for Justin. That meant he would like him.

Careful not to run – it was against the rules – Simon continued to the library.

Four

Saturday, 19 October 2013

Stella slotted the van behind a dented blue Toyota Yaris. It had been a long week, she could spend the evening on her own, catching up on emails. Jackie's street, tree-lined and spacious, was quiet considering it was close to a busy main road. Beyond the railings was a cemetery and, not for the first time, Stella considered she wouldn't like to live opposite dead people.

Her dad had owned a blue Yaris. This one's rear panel was a mismatch of replaced panels. Terry's car had been ten years old, but he had kept it immaculate. She could remember his car, but she couldn't conjure up his face.

A bus went by; its back draught rocked the van and light from the windows raked the interior, breaking her thoughts. There was a bleat. It came from the dog strapped into the jump seat behind her on the passenger side. She had installed the seat especially, because if he travelled beside her in the front, he risked being killed by the airbag. In the dim light the little beige poodle, the size of a cat, could be a ghost dog, a blurred shape with dark brown eyes. Stella had forgotten about Stanley. She wasn't cut out to own a dog. Just as well that she would be giving him back soon.

'We're here,' she remarked as she unclipped him. He climbed on to her shoulder and she manoeuvred them both out of the van.

On the way from her mother's flat in Barons Court, unsettled by the silent empty rooms, Stella had wished she could go to Terry's and empty her inbox over a microwaved shepherd's pie. Nothing personal, Jackie was a friend and Stella liked her husband Graham and their two sons, but she didn't fancy company.

However, the Makepeace family wouldn't require her to join in; they did the talking, leaving her free to eat, and then Jackie would let her wash up. Jackie was minding Stanley for the night while Stella went to fetch her mum from the airport.

'You like it here,' she said as the dog jerked the lead taut and snouted towards Jackie's gate. Stanley was left over from a relationship of the sort her mum called a 'wrong turning'. Stella had wanted to refuse, dogs were liable to cause mess, but months into minding the dog, she decided that relationships caused more mess.

The house next door to Jackie's was up for sale. Jackie was worried about this. The man living there now had been there since he was a boy and, Jackie said, he was a 'sweetie', kind and gentle; she hoped the new owners would be as nice. Stella thought again how living in a flat at the end of a corridor meant that, apart from the rare times she met anyone in the lift, she could avoid knowing her neighbours.

Clutching white wine, plucked from the chiller cabinet in Dariusz Adomek's mini-mart beneath her office, Stella took the dog over to a sycamore tree by Jackie's gate to lift his leg. The tree trunk was thinner than the others in the street. Jackie had told her the tree replaced one that came down in the 1987 hurricane and crushed their car.

She rummaged in her pocket and gave Stanley a biscuit as reward for peeing outside, to reinforce his toilet training as she had been told at his obedience class. Something fluttered to the ground. It was the paper she had found under a cushion at her mum's flat. Jack had cleaned the flat many times during her mum's six-week absence, but the paper was caught under the back of the sofa. The dog had been whining and when she gave in and pulled away the cushions, he had truffled out a bone-shaped biscuit. The paper was next to it. The writing was her mum's: 'Dale Heffernan, 38 Fisher Ave, Vaucluse. Likes sailing and B. Springsteen. Dislikes having time on his hands!'

During the first week her mum was away, Stella slept with her phone under her pillow expecting the call informing her Suzie was clinging to life. She had even looked up St Vincent's Hospital in Sydney. There had been no call. No call at all. Passing up Skype or email, Suzie sent two postcards to the office which Beverly, the admin assistant, stuck on the pinboard reserved for staff holiday messages. The sun was hot and there was a possum in her friend's attic. 'Love to Stanley.' In the second card she had wasted space with advice about the client database she had built, but had sent love to Stella.

Stella had told Jackie she didn't miss her mother. However, she found the comparative quiet at work uncomfortable; she missed the daily task list and the weekend calls informing her that Stanley wanted a walk in Richmond Park (as if her mum and the dog had conferred). Before Terry's death Stella might have welcomed the break from her mum's grumblings and demands. Now she wanted everything to be back to normal.

She stuffed the paper back in her pocket. Dale Heffernan was probably an ex-client.

Jackie and Graham Makepeace had lived in the 1920s semi for thirty years. Graham had made their gate; their initials, 'J' and 'G' intertwined, were carved into the beech struts. Jackie and Graham were still in love. Stella saw falling in love, like falling trees, to be fraught with the danger of crushed hopes and rearranged schedules.

'Heel.' She marched up to the front door, the dog trotting beside her.

Had Stella not met Jackie, the immaculate front door, gleaming window sashes and weed-free shingle path bordered by box hedging would have assured her she would like her. Jackie's mix of house-proud care and easy homeliness was apparent in the twisting branches of a laburnum, bracketed to protect brickwork, around the porch and the recycling bins corralled behind a trellis draped with honeysuckle.

The door flew open. The wine bottle slipped from her grasp; trying to stop its fall she kicked it on to the hedge.

'Hey, Stell!' A young man in a boxy leather jacket and hipster jeans was squatting at her feet submitting to a busy washing from the dog. 'Mum said you were coming. Sorry to miss you, I'm off out. They're all waiting for you.'

Gathering herself, Stella couldn't think of his name. She retrieved the bottle from the hedge. 'All?' she echoed.

Jackie's older son lived up north. Steve. Leeds. Teacher. This was Nick the dancer.

'Some guy Mum's got round.' Nick spun on his heel and leapt over the gate.

Stella froze. 'Is he staying to eat?'

'Sure he is – and there's candles!' Nick Makepeace grinned. 'He's your type!'

'On your way, Nicholas. Text if you're not coming home, so I can lock up.' Jackie pulled off an apron and popped a biscuit, magically produced, into the dog's mouth. She shook her head. 'Ignore him. In you come!'

Stella's last visits had met Jackie's promise of freshly cooked vegetables. Stella had forgotten there was sometimes another motive. Six months after one of Stella's 'wrong turnings', Jackie often launched a campaign to find Stella's Mr Right. It was six months since Stella had finished with David.

Always welcoming, the Makepeaces' kitchen, rich with the smell of roasting lamb, wine glasses glinting in candlelight, was tonight no exception. Graham Makepeace, mindful that Stella disliked kissing – for fear of germs – fussed Stanley instead.

A man stepped into the pool of candlelight and grasped Stella's hand, shaking it vigorously. 'William Frost, so pleased to meet you!'

Stella didn't need an introduction. An inch shorter than her six feet, in a dark suit and tie, this was Jackie's latest Mr Right.

Five

Saturday, 19 October 2013

'There is no step-free access at Hammersmith station until late November. Customers requiring step-free access should change at Earl's Court and use local bus services.' Jack shut off the public address channel and, as he drove out of West Brompton station, he sang under his breath:

> *'Little Jack Horner*
> *Sat in the corner...'*

Fulham Broadway, Parsons Green. At Putney Bridge station, about to close the doors, Jack consulted the driver's monitor and saw something on top of it. Someone had left a toy for the owner to reclaim; it must have been a driver because passengers weren't allowed beyond the gate. He leaned towards it.

It was a red steam engine. He felt a prickling at the back of his neck. It looked identical to the engine he had lost when he was little. Jack rose from his seat; he would hand it in at Earl's Court after stabling his train. Then he saw the time: he was running thirty seconds late. He sat down and checked the monitors again. A man was standing at the other end of the platform. Jack paused to give him time to board the train, but he didn't move so Jack shut the doors. He pulled on the lever and eased the train forward. Heading for East Putney station, he forgot about the man.

Jack was covering for a colleague on the Wimbledon line who did day shifts. Used to doing the Dead Late shifts, he missed the darkness. Only in the brick-lined tunnels, amid the dust, lit by the headlamps, like motes of gold, did he feel truly alive.

He resumed singing under his breath so that the passengers beyond his cab door wouldn't hear:

'Eating a Christmas pie;
He put in his thumb...'

His engine had been heavy, a grand thing to hold. The word 'Triang' was emblazoned on its boiler with the name, 'Puff-Puff'. Jack had taken it to the river, although his mummy had asked him not to.

'And pulled out a plum,
And said, "What a good boy am I!"'

Jack believed that what is lost will one day return. A circularity with no beginning or end. Even so, he was doubtful that the toy engine he had just seen was the same as the one he had lost in the water thirty years ago.

Distracted, Jack was midway through the West Hill tunnel before he recalled his self-imposed task. The tunnel ran beneath West Hill between East Putney and Southfields stations. Dictated by whimsy and coincidence – 'signs' – Jack was ever in search of hidden facts that would reveal profound truths. The length of the tunnel was one such fact. His colleagues didn't know and he hadn't found the answer on the internet.

Each time he entered the tunnel, something made him forget to collect the 'data': the time it took to travel from one end to the other. He only had a few more chances: his colleague would be back soon.

'And said, "What a good boy am I, am I
And said—"'

He stopped singing. The steam engine was a sign.

Jack stood in the dark hall and absorbed the silence of spectres. He went to the foot of the staircase and peered up. The banister wound into darkness and shadows of the spindles striped across the wall – like in a Hollywood film, someone had once said, perhaps his mother.

Every object, every shadow and splash of light had meaning or intent. When Jack was in his dead parents' house, he too was a ghost. Once, looking in the hall mirror to see his reflection and reassure himself he was alive, he had seen his mother's face through the blossoms of silver, a trickle of blood on her forehead. He had removed the mirror. An oval stain marked where it had been.

Tonight the house was not his friend. The owl knocker, as cold as brass, hadn't greeted him. He considered going to Rose Gardens North to see Stella, but remembered she was at Jackie's and then off to Heathrow to fetch her mother. Stella had rung him that morning, but not left a message. He wouldn't interrupt her at Jackie's.

In the dining room, printed music, discoloured to parchment yellow, lay open on the piano, the pages wrinkled with damp. Jack couldn't play the piano, it had been his mother's, but he knew the music by heart. The house was a tomb in which he glided wraith-like, catching snatches of conversation and glimpses of action in the low-wattage gloom. The threads of people's lives and deaths, the hidden facts. In the past he had craved their company. Tonight he wanted peace from his ghosts.

Another flier lay on the doormat. It would be an estate agent telling him someone wanted to buy his house, or maybe a pizza-delivery service.

It was none of these. One of his Tarot cards had blown off the hall table. Jack bent down and picked it up. He turned it over and stared at the image. A tower stood on the edge of a roiling sea, waves smashed against the sheer walls, the sky was dark and riven with a jagged thunderbolt. Out of the waves rose Poseidon clasping a trident, the representation of the crescent moon that connected the God to the night and to the instincts. In Tarot, the Tower augured the breaking down of old structures, the stripping away of the false self to reveal truth and integrity. Jack had turned up the card in the spread he laid out for himself on his birthday earlier in the year. He had not had it in a spread since.

His book of tides lay on the hall table. His mother had hit her head on the corner of the marble, a sharp corner, it had broken the skin. Jack shut his mind to the memory and snatching up the tide tables book, he flipped through the pages. He had promised Stella not to go on journeys in London at night, the time he liked best. The promise didn't include the eyot. The tide turned at two sixteen. If he got there in twenty minutes, he had hours before the river filled.

This time the owl fluffed her feathers. He assured her he wasn't breaking his promise to Stella – the owl was big on loyalty. Like the lions perched on plinths around the Square and the eagle preparing for take-off from the pediment above his head, the owl watched over Jack. Stella would despair if she knew that symbols on cards, creatures on door knockers, weather-worn gargoyles, even garden ornaments gave him direction and protection. He lifted the owl's tail feathers and lowered her; she tapped the strike plate. Time to go.

Eighteen and a half minutes later Jack was hopping and jumping across the exposed causeway to Chiswick Eyot. Fog blotting out rooftops on Chiswick Mall thinned briefly to reveal the tower. Then it vanished. Jack did a final sweep of the mall, and decided he was alone. He reached the eyot and climbed the bank, tracing a faint track into the undergrowth.

When he stepped into the silence of his Garden of the Dead, it occurred to Jack that it was strange that the Tarot card had fallen to the floor because he had secured the pack with an elastic band.

Had Jack waited, he might have seen that the pole by the embankment was not a pole. A man stood in the shadow of the moored barge. Jack's keen ear would have caught a sound and he would not have mistaken it for the rhythmic wash of the tide.

Across the mud flats he would have heard a lilting song:

'He put in his thumb,
And pulled out a plum,
And said, "What a good boy am I!"'

Six

Jackie was in the passage when Stella came out of the downstairs toilet. 'Stell, any chance you could drop William at the station? He'd like a private word.'

'I'm going to the airport,' Stella objected.

'Gunnersbury station is pretty much on your way,' Jackie cajoled. 'I said you might be able to help him.'

'Is it cleaning?'

'Not exactly. Best he explains.'

'OK.' She would say no if he asked her out. Simple.

All evening the man had seemed more interested in Stanley the dog. For some women, his tactic would have worked, but the way to Stella's heart was not through her dog. Mr Right had got it wrong and she would tell him so. It was better to be straight with people.

'Does the name Dale Heffernan mean anything to you?' she asked Jackie.

'No, should it?'

Stella shook her head. Her mother often confided in Jackie; if she didn't know the name, there was nothing to know. Meanwhile she had another man to deal with.

'Can I drop you at the station?' she asked from the doorway.

'Great!' He jumped up and his paper napkin floated to the floor. He was too pleased.

She waited in the van while Mr Right – she had forgotten his actual name – was no doubt thanking Jackie for setting up the evening. The dog was perched in Jackie's arms. Stella glared at him as if he too was in on the scheme.

When she came to collect him tomorrow she would insist that these blind dates stopped. She preferred being single.

Idly she watched a dark shape flit between the graves, the shadow of a branch moving in the wind. She looked back at the house. Now Mr Right – or whoever – was petting Stanley. She tapped her foot, although she had plenty of time. The shape in the cemetery was not a shadow. It was a man in a long black coat.

Only one person looked like that. Stella craned over the passenger seat and looked out of the side window. Jack. He must have seen she had called, but he hadn't rung her to see why. He would say he assumed her initial call was a mistake if she asked him. Giving a huff – Jack had a reason for all his seemingly unreasonable behaviour – Stella climbed out of the van. She was about to cross the road – somehow she couldn't bring herself to shout over to him – but he had gone.

Stella got back in the van in time to see a fox lope along the verge inside the cemetery and vanish among the graves.

It wasn't the dead she minded, decay disposed of bodies, but at night the sprawling space offered opportunity for anyone to spy on the houses on Corney Road. What better place to bury a body than in a graveyard? Stella frowned. Her mum had said she was like Terry, seeing crime around every corner. The blue Toyota had gone.

The man couldn't have been Jack, she concluded; he had promised her not to go walking late at night.

By the time Mr Right joined her, she was grateful for the company.

'Gunnersbury station.' She started the engine.

The journey would take five minutes, but a lot could happen in five minutes. It took two minutes to get out of Jackie's street, Burlington Lane was busy with late commuting traffic heading west. Another minute to Chiswick Roundabout.

'I've not been up front,' Mr Right blurted out. 'I wanted to meet you.'

Stella knew London like a cabbie. Mentally she mapped out a short cut, but all the streets led back to the Great West Road.

'Jackie has got the wrong end—' A horn blared as a car cut up a van.

Mr Right was speaking, his words lost in the sound. On Chiswick High Road, she braked at red traffic lights. She could smell his aftershave; she traced the woody scent to Burberry.

The lights went green, thirty seconds to go. Bolstered by this, Stella asked, 'Sorry, what did you say?' She made herself concentrate.

'I wanted to see you because Jackie told me that, apart from cleaning, you solve murders.'

Involuntarily Stella lifted her foot off the clutch and, with a judder, the van stalled.

Seven

May 1985

Justin was taking ages to lace up his shoes. Twice he got it wrong and undid them. Simon suppressed anxiety; they would be late.

'Shall I do it for you?' he asked politely.

'I can do it on my own.' Justin pulled at the lace and snapped it.

This was the first time they had been alone since Simon had found Justin's secret place in the kitchen garden. He had been told off for leaving the library by the librarian, whom some boys called 'the Oyster'; his jumper over the chair hadn't fooled her. But the Oyster hadn't noticed Justin was missing.

'Would you like my lace?' Simon offered, already loosening it.

Justin made a knot with the short length. Without looking at Simon, he stood up and jogged out of the room.

Simon folded Justin's clothes into a proper pile, as neat as his own. Everyone had to be kind to Justin because his mother had died. Simon sometimes wished his dad was dead. That would mean two good things: he could share being half an orphan with Justin and wouldn't have to see his father in the holidays. If his own mother died, he'd want to die too. Justin's mother couldn't have been as nice as Simon's mummy or Justin might have tried to die when she did. Baffled by the complexity of this, Simon raced after Justin on to the field.

'You're late. Next time it's detention!' Mr Lambert the games master roared at him. He shoved him to the other end of the line of boys to Justin. The last time they had done cross-country, Justin had got lost and come in late. Mr Lambert had been nice to him, but in case it happened again, Simon resolved to stick close to him. Running was the one sport that Simon was good at. He anticipated obstacles: protruding roots, puddles, dips and jutting stones; he conserved energy, paced himself. He kept a steady speed regardless of gradient.

Today it was like in his dreams: Justin was shadowing him. Simon felt a burst of joy; they would represent the school, get in the Olympics, go for gold. He ran blindly on, tactics abandoned; he had boundless energy. Bramble branches ripped his shirt; drops of water from overhanging trees wet his cheeks. Justin was his friend; he would ask him to be his blood brother. On they ran, heel for heel.

Ahead of them was the line of trees; they were coming to the woods with minutes on anyone else. Simon must warn him to increase speed before the woods because the level ground allowed even weaker boys to gain. With a tip of the hand he signalled for Justin to pick up pace.

Justin wasn't there. Simon faltered and, stopping, he turned right around. There was no one there. Fifty metres back came a straggling line of boys. They were gaining on him. The bright red of their shirts stood out against the browns and greens, the sweep of the Downs. Justin couldn't have overtaken him. Ahead, the woods were a fringe of dark green and, skirting them, Simon saw Justin. He had cut up around the base of the hill. He had left the designated track. He was entering the woods by the pheasant run.

Plunging after him, Simon smashed through bracken, crushing saplings, slipping and sliding, all tactics abandoned. He ran between the tree trunks, fast and nimble; he couldn't call out, he would give them both away. At last he stumbled out of the canopy of trees on to a track rutted with tyre tracks and hoof prints.

Two metres away, in sunlight, Justin was sitting on a steep grassy bank. Simon staggered towards him, his lungs bursting. Justin was sucking on an orange quarter and chatting with Mr Lambert. Simon saw he had emerged beyond the finishing line. It was too late to hide: Mr Lambert had seen him.

The sports master handed Simon two hours' detention for cutting out some of the route, which was cheating. The boy didn't say that he had been trying to help his friend. Busy with his orange, Justin couldn't have seen him.

Eight

Saturday, 19 October 2013

'Who's been murdered?' Stella stopped outside Gunnersbury station.

'My brother.' Frost unclipped his seat belt and turned in his seat to face her. His bulk seemed to shrink the van's interior.

'Thing is, I run a cleaning agency.' Stella wouldn't be rude, but it didn't do to lead people on.

'Jackie said you are a detective.' Frost gripped the dashboard with his left hand, his other hand around the back of the seat. 'She said you were good.'

Stella was on the brink of explaining that her previous cases had been her father's unfinished business, they didn't count, but then she heard her mum advising that she scope a job before refusing it. A real live murder case, unconnected with Terry, was as good as deep cleaning.

'How did your brother die? And when?'

'A month ago. He supposedly jumped in front of an Underground train, near here at Stamford Brook.'

'Supposedly?' Stella felt a stirring of anticipation. Stella hadn't expected to miss her mum, but had found that her absence revealed how integral to her routine Suzie had become. Stella missed the advice on potential new business and new cleaning operatives. No one else shared Stella's excitement about the latest equipment to further increase standards of hygiene. With Suzie gone, Stella needed something else to challenge her. Now she saw that what she needed was a case. Jackie, as ever second-guessing Stella, had sent her one.

'I want you to find his killer.' He kept glancing out of the

42

window as if the killer might be out there.

'Murder is a job for the police.' A year ago, the police had been her enemy. Her mum said that being a detective had taken her father away from his family. Stella hadn't thought of it like that, but fell in with her mum's take on it. By the time she was grown up, she saw her dad a handful of times a year and found little to say to him. After his death two years ago, memories of their time together from her childhood had returned so that she no longer felt antagonistic to the police – in particular Martin Cashman, a man a little older than her who had worked with her dad.

'They're not interested. Superintendent Cashman said there was no one else on the station platform and the only two witnesses, both drivers, confirmed Rick ran in front of the train. He was "satisfied" with the suicide verdict.'

'You don't agree?' Stella didn't want to go up against Cashman. He would suggest she stuck to cleaning and he would be right. 'Your brother's death sounds straightforward.' Wrong word. Jack was better at this stuff. She cast about for the name Jackie had said when she introduced him.

'Jackie warned me you'd be circumspect. All I ask is you hear me out.'

'Why do you think it wasn't suicide?'

'Killing himself isn't Rick's style. He sticks at things.' He looked away as if overwhelmed by his grief.

'Did he leave a note?' He spoke of his brother in the present tense. Perhaps he couldn't accept the man's death; in any case, she found his way of putting it unsettling. Odd to be in denial. Jumping in front of a train left little room for doubt that it was suicide. If Jackie hadn't referred him to her, Stella would give him no time.

'In the unlikely event that it was suicide, Rick would leave a note. He's hot on admin.'

'Was he— Had he had a drink?' Stella was careful. Not a good start to suggest the man's brother was a drinker.

'The post-mortem found whisky in his stomach.' He raked a hand through his hair. 'I know how it sounds.'

It sounded like the man had drunk enough to muster up courage to step in front of a train. She would let him down lightly.

'I have to go.' If her dad had died under a train she too would have doubted it: he wasn't that sort. Terry's post-mortem had been irrefutable. Yet he hadn't had a day off sick in his life, so his being dead had made no sense. It still didn't.

'Do you have siblings?' he asked.

'No.' She hoped he wasn't about to go down the 'you can't possibly understand' route.

'I hardly knew my brother. I'd say the guy was a fantasist. When we were boys, he was always playing soldiers. Not with me, I'm three years older. He had a gang, a couple of kids in his thrall. But he rang me an hour before he died. I had no signal so didn't hear the voicemail until after the police knocked on the door. I failed him once. I won't fail him again.'

'It's not failing.' Stella saw the time; she had to leave. 'What do you think happened?' Terry would have asked this first.

'Something – or someone – had frightened him. He sounded strange in the message. I hardly recognized him. I think he was murdered.'

Jack teased convoluted meaning from obscure signs; it frustrated her, but he did get results. Terry had followed hunches. Stella preferred the tangible.

'Can I hear his message please?'

'No. I deleted it after I heard it. Stupid, I know. The police clearly thought so.'

Stella's cleaning process was methodical. Stain by stain. She used the same process for detection. Clue by clue. However, this only worked if there was a stain – a clue – to start with. The only clue was the evidence. The man had jumped off a platform: end of, in all senses.

'I'm sorry Mr Righ— um, I don't see that we can help.' She turned on the engine. 'I have to get to the airport.'

'I'll come with you.' He clipped in his seat belt.

Nine

May 1985

He executed the plan perfectly. Every strut, every load-bearing beam, every cross fitted. He picked up the last girder – iron slats from a bench he had found behind the greenhouse – and, holding his breath, slotted it in. It held. Balanced on his haunches, he patted down the soil at the base of the stanchions.

Simon was in the kitchen garden. He had found a book on Isambard Kingdom Brunel in the library and he had made copious notes from engineering textbooks: a legacy of the owner of the house before it was a school. At first Simon borrowed books he'd seen Justin read, but soon he was on a path of his own. This afternoon he was constructing a box girder bridge. A present for Justin.

'It's the longest bridge in the country,' he would tell him. 'I made the arches and the central spans off-site, and erected the segments with a gantry crane.' He particularly liked the word 'gantry'. 'A gantry is a framework of bars, usually steel. It rests on two supports and is used for holding up road signs over motorways or for carrying electrical cables,' he told the garden. The bit about using a gantry crane wasn't true, but Justin wouldn't mind.

Mr Wilson had been thrilled to get a post at a boy's boarding school in the UK. It would go down well on his CV back home. Full of ambition and passion, he was determined to be the teacher the boys remembered when they were men playing their part in the world. He would be cited in articles, eulogized in biographies; through teaching he would be immortal.

It hadn't worked out that way. The boys mocked his accent. He had come into the classroom one morning to find 'Convict' daubed on the blackboard. It seemed that the English assumed every Australian had been deported from the UK. The fact that his great-great-grandfather *had* set off a spark of fury. Intent on flushing out the little tyke that had written it, he chose Simon as the 'fall guy' and accused him of the crime. He'd been sure that this would prompt the actual culprit to confess. He had been wrong. It seemed the boys were happy that Simon take the rap. He couldn't withdraw the accusation or he would look weak. The thing was a bloody mess.

Simon was the one boy who did what he was told. Out of all of them, in later life, he was most likely to cite Wilson as a key influence. The kid pored over leather-bound tomes; he wanted to be an engineer, not a boring banker or a Board Director or, buoyed by a trust fund, nothing at all.

While most of the boys mindlessly parroted answers learnt by rote or, like the kid whose mother had died, daydreamed, Simon was his star pupil. He read around subjects, told Wilson stuff he didn't know and made oblique connections. But soon the boy's adherence to rules got under Wilson's skin and bit by bit the man's objective shifted. A mild-mannered man, Wilson had become infuriated by Simon. He saw himself in the seven-year-old, a meek snap of a thing with no friends. Instead of encouraging Simon to find joy in new knowledge, he started to try to catch him out. He vented his annoyance at Simon's obsequious manner by gratuitously punishing him. He found justification in making an example of an innocent boy: it would bring the others into line.

The afternoon Wilson saw Simon leave the playground and sneak around the back of the kitchens was a gift. He went after him.

Simon walked his fingers over the boarding – he had taken the balsa wood from the workshop – and pressed hard. It creaked, but didn't break; the pressure was the equivalent of a ton. The spans had give and would withstand strong winds. Justin had explained that to him; he would remind him of that.

The boy was astonished at his achievement. Now he knew how to do it, they could build another bridge, or a tunnel – whatever Justin liked. Ideas raced fast and furious; hands together as if praying, Simon contemplated the breadth of possibility. It would be their secret.

He smiled at the distant thud of the garden door closing. Justin hadn't learnt his skill of stealthy tracking. Simon would teach him this. He scrambled to his feet, imagining Justin's face when he saw the bridge. Justin never smiled. Simon supposed it was because his mother was dead. He wanted to make him smile.

'You shouldn't be here.' Justin did a high singing voice. 'It's out of bounds.'

'I made it.' Simon realized Justin was imitating him. Unaccountably he felt afraid and fluffed his speech. 'I did the spans like Hammersmith Bridge.'

Hands on hips, Justin surveyed the bridge. 'The stresses are in the wrong places, it won't take a significant load.'

'I tested it,' Simon protested, his eyes swimming with sudden tears. 'It does.' Mentally he scanned his drawing for possible error. An engineer's mistake couldn't be hidden. Sir Stephen Lockett, the sanitary-ware millionaire who had wanted to be an engineer, whose house they lived in, had trusted the Tay bridge. It had collapsed. Sir Stephen's body was never recovered from the river Tay beneath. Forever restless, his ghost was said to roam the library at night.

Simon had imagined Hammersmith Bridge, the looping spans mirrored in the Thames. All he had achieved was a cluster of wood, stuck with glue. He saw it as Justin saw it and pulled on his bad finger. 'I did it for you.'

Justin's shoe caught a strip of wood. It broke off and fell into the 'river'.

'That's OK,' Simon said as if Justin had apologized.

Justin stepped on the bridge and crushed it.

47

'See? It can't take a decent load.' Justin kicked up a shower of gravel and, turning on his heel, strolled away up the path between the tall weeds.

Simon couldn't comprehend the devastation. He rubbed his palms on the back of his trousers.

'What are you playing at?'

Simon wheeled around. Mr Wilson was standing with his hands on his hips as Justin had.

'I built him a bridge,' Simon said and then corrected himself. 'I built a bridge.'

'You did, did you?!' Wilson folded his arms, wondering if the boy had whacked his head. He couldn't see a bridge in the mess of sticks and mud at his feet. 'Look at the state of you.'

'I tested it. My sums were right.'

He was dishevelled and pathetic. Wilson's triumph ebbed; he felt sorry for him and sick with himself.

'Simon, mate, you shouldn't be here,' he said gently. The kid was doing the thing with his finger, twisting and tugging it as if the injury was recent. No one knew how he came to lose his finger. Wilson would have a chat with Madeleine next time she visited the school. It would do him no harm for her to see him showing concern for her son. So many of the teachers here actually disliked children. If the boys knew why, they might stop teasing him. He'd even had it in mind to come up with a hero story in which the kid had saved lives and lost his finger in the process, but couldn't see how that would work, so had given it up.

'Come with me.' He ushered him up the path.

Intent on getting Simon away before another master saw him and insisted he get detention, Nathan Wilson didn't see the other boy crouched in the greenhouse.

Ten

Christmas Eve 1986

At the junction of Goldhawk Road and Chiswick High Road, traffic was nose to tail. Christmas Eve shoppers, weighed down with bags and packages, wove between the stationary vehicles. When the door of the off-licence on the corner opened, a burst of John Lennon's 'Happy Xmas (War is Over)' swelled above the idling engines.

None of this last-minute bustle reached St Peter's Square where tall Georgian houses, stucco dappled with lamplight, formed a stately contrast to the seasonal mayhem. The square, its park in darkness, was of the past more than the present. Frost sparkling between shadows of branches might be the footprints of ghosts.

Anyone watching from a window of a house on the west side, indulging in this fancy, might decide that the boy hopscotch jumping between the cracks in between the flags by the park railings was one such phantom. Nothing betrayed him as a child of the 1980s, when loads of money didn't so much talk as shout. He had stepped out of a Narnian wardrobe in polished brogues, his gabardine mac collar down despite the biting wind, hair in a precise side parting.

Many downstairs windows were a showcase for Christmas. Splendid trees were festooned with lights and quaint decorations in reds, gold and silver. Lanterns burned on sills; candles flickered on mantelpieces; darts of light bounced off glasses of red wine and port. Indeed, quintessentially Dickensian, the boy, suitably diminutive and pale, observed the tableaux through misted glass, quaking in the icy cold.

He arrived at a house on the south side. The curtains were closed. Perhaps the residents were away or perhaps they eschewed the festivities; the unruly box hedge and fractured plaster on Doric columns supporting the porch hinted at indifference.

An eagle was poised on the porch, wings spread. Timidly, his shoulders hunched, Simon regarded it as if it might devour him as easy prey. He scurried up the steps to the front door.

Simon had had no doubt that Justin would be pleased to see him. He would tell him he had left his boarding school too, that he lived near to him. They could see each other every day. He bent down and raised the letterbox flap. Inside was a fusty smell like the room under the school library. A black cloth had been pinned to the door, blocking his view.

'It's me,' he whispered. 'Your friend.'

Eleven

'Thank you.' Stella took the ticket from the machine and stuck it between her teeth. Talking to machines was more Jack's thing. Luckily William Frost – as she had finally remembered he was called – hadn't heard.

She found a space on the car park's third level. In the lift to the Arrivals hall, she questioned her wisdom in letting Frost come with her. Suzie wouldn't approve; she was unhappy about Stella 'playing detective', like her father. Nothing William had said on the journey to the airport – or his long brooding silences – gave her confidence that he would win Suzie over with charm as Jack had.

'What do you think we could find that the police haven't?' They were alone in the lift.

'The truth. You finding the killer will be worth the money.'

Stella hadn't considered charging a fee. Their last two investigations – the Rokesmith and Blue Folder cases (not counting a missing cat Jack found in an empty house he was cleaning) – had been Terry's cold cases. No money had changed hands.

Frost was expecting to pay for a service Stella probably couldn't fulfil. She had built a successful business by avoiding risks, expanding only when there was the capital and demand. She had not taken on bigger offices or rewarded herself with a higher wage. She paid her operatives properly and invested in the best equipment. She had stuck to what she knew. She was not a detective.

'If the police couldn't find proof that your brother was murdered, I can't see how we can.'

'You clean for Hammersmith Police Station, don't you?'

Jackie would not have told him.

'I saw you in the compound.' He stopped beneath the Arrivals board. 'You wouldn't have that job if your firm wasn't thorough. Jackie assured me you leave no corner unclean. My brother was murdered. I know you will prove it and solve the case.'

'Perhaps it was a cry for help that went wrong,' Stella persisted, feeling every inch the pretend detective.

'A cry for help is taking tablets then texting someone. It's not jumping off a platform in front of a fast train.'

'He did call you.' She had to say it.

'He asked to see me, if he meant to kill himself, why do that?' Frost was adamant. Jackie had given him airtime, Stella reminded herself. She refrained from saying it was possible to survive a fall on to the rails: a client of hers had slipped off a platform when he was drunk and got away with a gash in his arm. Still, she supposed living to tell the tale – he told it whenever she cleaned for him – was unusual.

'You didn't get the call. Maybe that tipped him—' Stella stopped herself crashing into the unfortunate pun and, turning away, scanned the Arrival's indicator. 'The question surely is, did your brother have a reason to kill himself?'

'Baggage hall' was listed beside her mother's plane. She took up position at the mouth of the gate.

The first passengers – identifiable by suntans and summer clothes – straggled out, battling with trolleys bulky with cases, bags, surf boards, giant stuffed kangaroos. Many were hailed – cries and whoops – by people waiting by the ribbon. Stella edged around a man with a square of cardboard against his chest for a clear view of the exit.

'He did.'

'Who did what?' She kept her eyes on the passengers.

'About a month before he died, Rick remarked that long ago he made a mistake that had come back to haunt him.'

'Doesn't that make suicide more likely?'

'He isn't the type.' Frost was a stuck record. 'He said it in passing, I ignored him, felt like saying his whole life was a mistake, now I see he was trying to tell me something.'

Stella risked a glance at the man. In the stark airport light, his complexion was grey, eyes red-rimmed. She felt rather sorry for him.

Passengers were streaming by, jostling with trolleys, heaving bags, rolling cases into each other's paths. Jack wouldn't need proof: he would follow instinct, pay attention to his precious signs; he got results. She should have called him when she saw him in the cemetery. What was he doing there?

'Could someone have pushed him? Did they see anyone on the CCTV?' Her mum would be last off the plane; unused to travel, she would have mislaid her passport or got stuck in her seat belt.

'They saw no one on the film, but not all the station is covered. Whoever did this would know that.' Frost was animated. 'He has a car. I found it parked a couple of streets from his house. Why didn't he drive to see me? Obvious, because he didn't want to be seen leaving.'

'Who might have been watching?' Stella wondered why taking the Underground made it less likely he would be seen leaving, but felt it rude to pick Frost up on every point. She would never question a client's cleaning requirements.

'Is that your mother waving?'

A woman in a wide-brimmed straw hat that hid her face was sailing along wearing one of those billowing coats with bat-wing shoulders Stella associated with Australia. Suzie. Her trolley was heaped with makeshift bags. She was going so quickly other passengers had to veer out of her path. Stella couldn't see the suitcase Suzie had taken with her, and she had three times the luggage she'd set out with. She was waving, not just at Stella, but at everyone waiting. Stella leant out to get her attention. Her mother snatched off her hat and flung it on to her tower of bags.

The woman's face was scored by lines; her tan suggested she never saw the inside of a house. She wasn't her mother. Stella's relief was brief, for behind the woman was an expanse of floor.

There were no more passengers. Her phone buzzed. Distracted by Frost, she had missed Suzie. Stella read the text.

Staying in Sydney for two weeks. Feed plants. Mum x.

'She's not coming.' When she finally spoke, Stella's voice was gruff. 'I should have seen this coming.' She turned on her heel. 'She's had an accident – or worse.' What was worse? Her thoughts were racing.

'People often act out of character and surprise us,' William Frost said.

'Like killing themselves.' She stopped. 'Sorry, I didn't mean that.'

'Fair point. Rick took the train when he had a car and he shouldn't have been at Stamford Brook. I live on the Goldhawk Road, near Shepherd's Bush Green – he was out of his way. He asked to see me, then he went in front of a train. It doesn't add up.'

'Went out of his way?' Illogical behaviour generally had an explanation. They took the lift back to the car park. Stella forced herself to concentrate. Despite her text, she was on the lookout for her mother.

'His nearest Tube was Hammersmith, he should have got a train to Goldhawk Road station. I'm three minutes from there.'

'We need to pay.' Stella nodded at a bank of ticket machines.

'Let me.' Frost began feeding coins into the slot in the nearest machine.

'You needn't.' Everything was slipping away from her.

'I've taken your time, let me recompense you.'

Jackie had 'sent' William Frost to her. Stella trusted her judgement; Jackie wouldn't set Stella up for a fall. Watching him pick out the right change from a pile of coins in his palm, she deemed the man calm and practical, perhaps not the sort to get stuff out of proportion.

'I'll talk to Jack, my partner, and let you know our decision,' Stella said.

'Do you want a deposit now, and an advance on expenses?'

'That's not a "yes". If we do agree, it's "no win no fee".' Jackie wouldn't like that, but Stella would explain it was a trial. She wouldn't say that she balked at charging anything for detection.

'Who is this Jack? Are you together?' Frost startled her. 'Sorry, that's not my business.'

'Jack's a colleague,' Stella said sharply. 'He has a lot of experience.' She didn't say that he had been lurking in the cemetery earlier; there was much Frost didn't need to know about Jack. There was much she didn't know about Jack. Her mood dropped further. Jack had broken his promise.

'Will he agree?' William sounded anxious. 'I'd be happy with you if he doesn't.'

'We are a team.' Technically, Jack being in the cemetery wasn't breaking his promise. A graveyard wasn't a street.

On the roundabout Stella came up with a horrible idea. Dale Heffernan, the man who liked Bruce Springsteen, was Suzie's Mr Right. That was why she had flown to Sydney at the drop of a hat. Stella overshot the London exit and, circling it again, she told herself this could not be. Mr Right did not exist.

Twelve

September 1987

On a chill Saturday afternoon in London, an insidious fog made wraiths of the lamp-posts and telephone poles in Corney Road, a suburban street near Chiswick House grounds. It wiped out wires slung between the poles and lent the gates into the grounds a ghostly aspect. Emerging out of the grey, traffic on Burlington Lane was a procession of indistinct smudges of yellow.

Built in the 1930s, Corney Road was one line of terraced houses. Even with the tiled roofs and gables wreathed in fog, the houses retained the comforting appearance of a hot-chocolate advert. Threads of smoke wending from chimneys hinted at a crackling grate and leaping flames. Clipped hedges and shingled paths suggested domestic stability. Twenty minutes' walk from the nearest Underground station, the houses fell within the buying reach of lower-grade professionals: teachers, middle-ranking police officers and council workers such as planning officers and auditors.

The homely atmosphere didn't extend to the other side of the street where wrought-iron railings bounded Chiswick Cemetery. Angels with broken fingers and chipped wings gazed heavenwards; sublime Madonnas overlooked headstones. A breeze pushed at yew trees and set a chain looped around the gate into a Newton's cradle motion. Rhythmically it chinked against the post, the lightly pitched sound spelling doom in the quiet.

From Burlington Lane two black shapes clarified to a woman with a pushchair and a boy, belted into a gabardine mac, hurrying along. The boy had one hand on the bar of the pushchair, revealing that much of his middle finger on his left hand was missing. They were talking and joking, lending cheer to the damp and gloomy afternoon. The child in the pushchair, a girl of about two, was asleep, her head lolled to one side, her thumb slipping from her mouth.

They stopped at a house outside which was parked a lemon-yellow Triumph sports car. The front door opened and a man in a black wool suit hugging a battered leather briefcase came out. Strands of over-combed hair were lifted by the breeze. His sallow, gaunt features and stooping posture might look more at home processing coffins into open graves across the road than behind the wheel of a shiny TR7.

'Off to the funny farm for me!' The joke was perfunctory. He loaded his briefcase into the boot.

'Drive safely, doctor,' his wife replied without humour.

Blowing her a kiss and nodding to his son, the man folded himself into the front seat and drove off towards Corney Reach. When the throaty exhaust faded to nothing, she hugged her son to her.

'Just you and me, darling, let's have a cosy "lap" supper!'

'What larks!' Simon gave a skip.

'Ever the best of friends; ain't us, Pip!' She completed the ritual exchange and, stroking back his hair from his face, handed him the key to the front door.

Simon's throat was constricted with joy. His father was away; his sister didn't count. It was a year since he had left his boarding school and was living at home all the time. Since his first visit on Christmas Eve last year, he had knocked on Justin's door in the tall house with dark windows every week, but got no answer. He refused to give up hope. Justin had to answer one day.

Tonight his mum had talked to him in their special secret way. It was a sign. For the rest of the evening Simon didn't let her out of his sight.

Thirteen

Monday, 21 October 2013

'Dale Heffernan, 38 Fisher Ave, Vaucluse. Likes sailing and B. Springsteen. Dislikes having time on his hands!'

Stella reread her mum's scrawled note for the umpteenth time while she waited for Mrs Carr to answer the door. This was her second visit. She could hear footsteps scurrying about inside and guessed her client was tidying up, as some of Stella's clients did when she was expected. But given the mess on Saturday, she was surely not bothered what Stella thought.

She was no nearer to discovering who Dale Heffernan was. Her mum had replied to her text asking if she was 'OK' with 'yes'. The name made her think of Engelbert Humperdinck. Her mum often said 'Please Release Me' might have been written for her. Maybe Heffernan was a pop singer from the sixties that her mum had Googled. Unlikely.

Vaucluse sounded French. She had put Heffernan into Google and got a restaurant. She had tried Vaucluse. Unsurprisingly there was one in France. Scrolling down, she had found one in Sydney, Australia, and her dread crystallized into pricking dismay. Her fear escalated. Dale Heffernan would empty her mum's bank account and there was nothing Stella could do to stop him.

'I'm on to him!' Mrs Carr flung open the door. Stella pushed the paper back into her pocket, picked up her equipment bag and struggled inside. Her client was perkier than on Saturday. She seemed to have forgotten her displeasure with Stella for not following her instructions. Stella had long ago decided that some clients were enlivened by disaster. Their homes were a battlefield; it was her job to clean up for the next skirmish.

'Where should I start?' Stella laid her bag at the foot of the stairs. Last time Mrs Carr had taken up half the shift complaining about the unfaithful husband.

'I've found out where he was when he texted he was working late and couldn't see me.'

Stella gave in. 'How?' Why did working late mean her husband couldn't see her? Best not to ask that.

'It's clever. You can see where someone is by their texts. Don't switch your location on if you're leading a double life, I will find you!' Mrs Carr breezed into the sitting room.

Reluctantly Stella followed. With an imperious motion of her hand, Mrs Carr indicated for her to join her on the sofa where, with the clothes and clutter gone, there was now room.

'Look.' Mrs Carr was waving a phone. 'You press this key symbol and up comes a map with a blue dot pinpointing his exact location.' She jabbed at the screen. '*Voilà!*'

Stella knew it was possible to track a user's whereabouts; she had done it during the Blue Folder case.

'He was here, look.' Mrs Carr enlarged the map.

'On Chiswick Eyot?' Stella knew the scrub of land. She had ridden her bike there as a child.

'Of course not! Chiswick Mall. It isn't far from here and, I tell you, it's not for the faint-walleted. Whoever she is, she's got money. I can't match that.' Mrs Carr slumped back, apparently deflated.

'He could have been walking along it.'

'You don't pass through Chiswick Mall, it's out of your way unless that's where you're going.' She glared at Stella, seeming a hair's breadth from blaming her for her husband's betrayal.

'He told me he didn't see her anymore.'

Stella tried deflection. 'Where does he work?'

This seemed to perplex Mrs Carr. She hesitated and then, as if repeating something by rote, said, 'Wherever people want CCTV fitted and all the other surveillance paraphernalia.' She shook her head as if the question was superfluous.

'He could have been visiting a client then.' Stella wondered at herself for finding innocent explanations for Mr Carr, who had undeniably left his wife. She had cleaned in houses on Chiswick Mall; Mrs Carr was right, no houses there would give change from a million pounds. Odd, since he was in security, that Carr had gone to so much trouble to hide from his wife and made such a basic mistake.

'So you'll help.' Mrs Carr placed her hands on her knees as if a deal had been struck.

'With what?' Distracted, Stella hadn't heard her.

'You'll find out the truth.'

'We don't...' Finding estranged spouses might be the bread and butter of most private detectives, but it would not be the route for Clean Slate. Stella must leave; Jackie could parry any fallout.

'You will sort it, you're a cleaner!'

Stella was as certain as she could be that Mrs Carr was mad.

'I have more of these, so don't run away.' Stella undid the dog's lead, holding his collar, and gave him a biscuit from the pouch dangling from her belt. 'Re-lease!'

The poodle sped away over the grass and just as she thought he wouldn't stop he tumbled to a halt and faced her.

A gust of wind smacked her fringe across her face. She dragged her hood up and another blast smacked it down again. She had no hat. Stanley had upset her routine; she had to take him out come rain or shine. Jackie had suggested she employ a dog walker, but Stella had promised to mind Stanley; she had to do it herself.

'Stanley, come.' She spread her arms. The dog raced back and, full tilt, crashed against her leg, finishing in a sketch of a sitting position. Stella gave him a biscuit.

The afternoon was gloomy, strata of greys in the sky; there were darker clouds over the turrets of Wormwood Scrubs prison. Stella had wandered far on to the common; Braybrook Street was in the distance. She knew the area. Jack and she had interviewed a suspect in the Rokesmith case who lived in the street. Her dad had grown up around the corner in Primula Street and been a policeman in Hammersmith most of his life. She had seen a newspaper photo of Terry with other officers on his hands and knees doing a finger search on the grass where she stood.

Another gust of wind. Jack would say Terry was giving her a sign. She zipped her anorak up to her chin.

She remembered the buzz of that interview, the thrill of a solid lead. They had planned the questions and their approach. Good guy – her; bad guy – Jack. Like a real detective, she had written up the details afterwards and filed them. It seemed easy, looking back: they had boxes of paperwork to go on, salient information to pull out. With William Frost's case, all they had to go on was his conviction that his brother had been murdered. Suzie would say they shouldn't touch it and she'd be right. Or she would if she were here. Stella frowned. In reply to her message to him the day before, Jack had texted saying he was driving all day. She didn't want to talk to Jackie while she was in the office, or indeed when she was at home, as she would be telling Jackie there was nothing she could do for Frost.

Stanley had met another dog. Stella headed towards them. She had learnt that dog owners' etiquette required humans as well as their dogs to interact.

'How old is he?' An elderly man in a baggy rainproof jacket, a hand-knitted scarf knotted around his neck, was regarding the dogs as they sniffed each other's behinds. In the dog world, this was apparently polite.

'About two.' Stella wanted to explain that he wasn't her dog and that she wouldn't have him much longer, but that was giving too much away.

'Molly's submitting for a change! What's his name?'

Stella blinked, resisting the temptation to say she didn't know, which would appear ridiculous. 'Stanley.'

The man exclaimed: 'Same as me!'

'Ah.' For a wild moment, Stella wondered if he was David's father, Stanley's namesake. 'What's – um – what's yours called?'

'Molly.'

'That's nice.' He had already said. Stella scuffed her boots on the grass.

'Good to have met you, lad.' The man addressed Stanley; another thing dog owners did was channel conversation through their animals. Stella approved of this. She preferred being at one remove. The man melted into the shadows, his dog with him.

Her phone buzzed.

Can we speak?

Stella deleted the text, the second in a week. No need to speak; David wanted the dog back. Fine. She would ask Jackie to sort it. A drop of water stung her cheek. The dark clouds were now overhead; she heard a rumble of thunder. She whipped Stanley's lead from around her neck and cast about for him.

He was cavorting towards her with the skittish leaps that she had understood meant he was up to something. Front legs up then hind legs, like a rocking horse. What might look enchanting to others filled Stella with foreboding. She spied two dainty paws poking out of one side of his whiskery mouth, a long rubbery tail dangling from the other.

A Londoner, Stella had grown up with the adage that she was never more than six feet from a rat. Right now it was a lot closer than that.

While Stella was becoming accustomed to the dog's unquestioning presence, regarding hygiene they were poles apart.

'Drop!' she hissed, although there was no one to see. His capering accelerated into joyous leaps. The rat was hardly smaller than the dog. It must have been dead when he got hold of it.

She headed off towards Braybrook Street without a backward glance, a newly acquired ruse which worked. Frustrated by the loss of her attention, he abandoned the rat and, tail down, disconsolate, fell in by her side. Inwardly congratulating herself, Stella clipped on the lead and joined the pavement by the memorial to the three murdered policemen.

'Here fell...'

She could recite the names and date carved in the marble. The date the police officers were killed in Braybrook Street – 12 August 1966 – was the day she was born.

When she was eight, Terry had brought her to the remembrance ceremony held by the Metropolitan Police on each anniversary of the shooting. Her mum said it was typical he should think it a treat. In fact Stella had appreciated listening to the speeches and being solemn. Someone had said she was lucky to have a daddy, not like the children of the three policemen whose lives they were commemorating. The voice, Stella didn't remember now who had said it, had also said that 'life had better mean life.' Stella had liked Terry holding her hand as if, like Stanley, she might scamper off. For no obvious reason, Stanley barked sharply. Jack believed dogs could detect ghosts. If Terry were to haunt anywhere, this was a likely spot.

Another buzz of a text.

Where shall we meet? Jack.

Ram. 7.30? New case. That should whet his appetite. Seconds later she was proved right.

I'll be there! Jx

Perhaps thinking of Mrs Carr's check on her husband, Stella pressed the symbol beside Jack's text. She was taken aback. Jack was in the same place as the elusive Mr Carr, on Chiswick Mall near the eyot. Jack said there was no such thing as coincidence. She shut her phone, vaguely ashamed to have looked.

The dog was sitting at her feet. She rewarded him, thinking absently how she would be handing back a well-trained animal.

'Heel.' Stella and Stanley headed along Braybrook Street to the van, away from the memorial and its ghosts.

Fourteen

September 1987

'Ready for hunting and gathering!'

'Ready and willing!' Simon stood to attention. It was his job to forage for items on his mother's shopping list. They were in Marks and Spencer's on Chiswick High Road.

'We leave the trolley here and bring stuff to it.' His reiteration of the instructions was part of their ritual; his method was quicker than pushing the trolley through the shop. He had parked it in a recess beside the dairy cabinet and the back entrance.

'I'll be back in record time.' Everything was back to normal. Last week his mum had gone shopping without telling him. She had said she would take less time on her own, and he had been dismayed. Today was about proving her wrong. He peered at the list she was holding and memorized the first three items. 'A packet of water biscuits and eight ounces of brie. Daddy's off cheese.'

'It's not for Daddy,' she snapped.

'You don't eat cheese.'

'It's for guests.' She ruffled his hair and the boy allowed himself to breathe.

'Are there going to be guests?' Simon hung over the trolley handle. He hoped it was the woman who had just moved in next door.

'See how many you can get in, say, ten minutes.' His mother gave him the entire list.

'I shan't need that long,' Simon asserted. Although he relished the challenge, the change in operation worried him.

'Do it properly.'

64

'Synchronize watches.' He consulted his watch with luminous hands and markings for seeing on night expeditions, or in bed. Mr Wilson and Justin both had Timex watches.

She was looking over at the door to the car park and not listening. The boy sped off to the frozen section where, rootling around for crinkle-cut chips, it struck him that without the list she couldn't hunt for anything.

Simon minimized journeys to the trolley by collecting armfuls of food. He dropped a bag of lentils reaching up for cornflakes. This was awkward, but lots of short trips took longer. He would explain this; she loved his theories.

With four minutes to go, she still wasn't by the trolley. Simon unburdened himself, mindful not to crush the lettuce, tomatoes, eggs and butter with cans and bags of vegetables as instructed.

The automatic doors to the car park swooshed aside and Simon was hit by a draught of cold air. A woman with a girl about the same age as his sister perched at the front of her trolley entered. His mother was in the car park. The door shut and he saw sense. It wasn't her. He fetched six cartons of milk from the cabinet, the last items, and trotted along each aisle in search of her.

The list finished in twelve minutes and thirty-five seconds, he returned to base camp. It wouldn't have occurred to Simon to pretend he had done it in the allotted time. He and his mother told each other the truth; they had no secrets. Justin would be impressed because the ten minutes was meant to include his mum doing some too. Simon recorded each feat so that when he met him again, he could tell Justin.

Gingerly Simon went over to the back exit. The door opened when he stood too close to it. He looked out. The woman was his mother and she wasn't alone.

'Could you either go out or come away from the door? You're letting in all the cold,' an old man clutching a wire basket rasped at him.

Taken by surprise, Simon went outside.

His mother had parked their car by the entrance; there was no need for her to be by the pavement. Simon inched around the car, reassured by its solid familiarity, and crept along the gap between the cars and the wall. He got as close as he dared, but couldn't hear what she was saying. Blindly he turned and ran back into the shop.

He drifted mechanically along an aisle, supported by the trolley. He joined a queue, imagining he could pay, pack the shopping in the boot and drive away. He bottled sudden rage that being nine he could do none of these things. Simon felt as he had when Justin had left the school and Simon was no one.

'I've been looking everywhere for you!' She wrapped her arms around him, cutting out the light. He inhaled her perfume and another smell – smoke. She didn't smoke.

'I was here,' he replied numbly.

'You were meant to stay by the trolley.'

'Ten minutes is over.' He was by the trolley, but he didn't say that.

'Not by my watch.' She briskly rearranged cartons and tins, although she didn't need to.

'I got everything in twelve minutes and thirty-five seconds. That was without you helping.'

'Did you get grapes?' She was consulting the list.

'No.' He scrutinized the trolley. Grapes should be on top with the eggs. He looked at the list. Grapes were not there.

'I'll get them.' He worried that if she went, she would vanish again. The store whizzed by, shoppers pushed him, trolleys dug into his legs, he was jabbed in the ribs with a wire basket. Red or white grapes? They never ate grapes. Red.

'Come on.' She was about to pay for the shopping. 'Didn't they have white?'

'No.' The cashier raised one eyebrow; he knew he was lying. Simon felt himself grow hot.

She took the bags off him without saying, *You're my rock, I can't do without you.*

'You'll never guess who I met!' They were driving into their street.

'Who?'

'Mr Wilson, your religious education teacher from Marchant Manor. He left soon after you did, he's been living in London all this time!'

Simon pulled on his half-finger, the habit formed when he was a much littler boy and had still harboured hope it would grow back.

'Did he come to see me?'

'Of course not!' She laughed. 'He said "Hello".'

'Is he coming to teach at my new school?' Mr Wilson had said he was his friend.

'Stop being silly, Simon.' She never called him silly.

Simon sank into the seat and decided not to ask why Mr Wilson had been holding his mummy's hand.

Fifteen

Monday, 21 October 2013

Jack knew the sounds in the house. The owl's thud resonated up to the top floor and, regardless of who was knocking, she lightened his spirit. This sound was sharper. It was the letterbox flap. He glanced at his watch: ten to seven.

He peered out of the sitting-room window. He was meeting Stella, he couldn't be delayed. It would be a charity or Jehovah's Witnesses. It wouldn't be Stella, she always texted first.

A man in a black coat, a baseball cap pulled low, was going down the path. He didn't look up at the house as Jack would have done, certain that someone would be there. He was walking past Isabel Ramsay's house without dropping in a leaflet. Stella had advised Jack to put up a 'No Junk Mail' notice, but he liked to know what people were up to. He couldn't say this, nor could he point out that Clean Slate did leaflet drops. Stella wouldn't consider them junk.

When his father was alive – his mother too, he supposed – post was left on the hall table. Nothing there now. Nor was there post on the doormat. Downstairs Jack did up his coat, pleased to be seeing Stella and excited by a new case. He considered following the man, but it would contravene his promise to Stella and he'd be late. Something was under the marble table. There was a leaflet after all.

To Let. A5 and pink: another leaflet about the tower. The owners obviously hadn't found a tenant.

Rereading it, Jack considered that the word 'cosy' wasn't usual estate agent vocabulary. Stella would have no truck with 'craving silence'.

... crave silence and a bird's eye view, then Palmyra Tower is your home. Guardian wanted for Grade 1 listed Water Tower. You will sign a year-long contract with no breaks and be available to take up residence as soon as your application is accepted.

The phrase 'detailed views' was peculiar. From high up, the view couldn't be detailed; it would be better to emphasize the breadth of the panorama. Whatever, by now the owners would have found a tenant.

You will.

His eye lit upon the pack of Tarot cards on the hall table. Since finding the card on the mat he hadn't looked at them. At some point, though, he must have replaced the Tower card, it was face up on the top of the pile, tightly bound by the elastic band. A sign.

Jack smoothed out the flier on the marble top and scanned the text. At the bottom of the flier he found an email address. *info@ palmyra-tower.co.uk.* He opened his phone and tapped out a message: *To whom it concerns, if it's vacant, please may I rent the flat in Palmyra Tower? Yours, J Harmon.*

On the doorstep he stroked the owl's tucked-in wing with a finger. 'You don't need a tower to see the world,' he whispered to her.

In the subway, Jack's voice was insistent and sibilant.

'Oh that I were where I would be,
Then would I be where I am not;'

He left the tunnel and hurried up the ramp on to Black Lion Lane.

Another voice completed the verse in the bleakly tiled tunnel long after Jack had gone.

'But where I am there I must be,
And where I would be I can not.'

Sixteen

September 1987

After dark, the gate to the cemetery on Corney Road was closed, so Simon used a hole beside a side entrance in the church passage. Inside, he scampered along between the mounds, alert for intruders. The good thing about living full-time in London was that he could go to his den more often. Another good thing was that no one at the Chiswick school called him 'Stumpy'.

It was two years since he had seen Justin, but he could picture him and hear his voice. Sometimes, in front of the bathroom mirror, Simon imitated his sniff and the jerk of his head. In two years, Simon's sister had learnt to jump and could manage a few words. Time and wishful thinking had rendered Justin a loyal confidant; he was Simon's best friend.

The boy cut along the boundary wall, out of sight of the houses that had replaced wharfs and factories by the Thames. The stench of the river deadened the air. His belted mac was damp from the pall of mist that was suspended above the squat stone tombs and mausoleums. Flaking and worn, the headstones had been erected in the early nineteenth century and their graves were sunken and smothered with browning weeds.

Simon looked across the cemetery and saw, far off, that the lit upstairs windows in his street were just a string of lights. He couldn't see his house. His dad wouldn't know he was out because Simon had pushed a pillow under his duvet. His mum said she was seeing a friend and Simon preferred to believe her.

The ground was crisp with fallen leaves etched with frost; his footsteps crunched in the chill quiet. Once he missed his footing and stubbed his shoe on broken masonry.

Simon reached a brick hut under spreading conifer branches. Originally used for storing tools which the maintenance crew had transferred to an aluminium shed by the Corney Road gate, one wall was lined with ancient plaques, scrolls and shields of blackened granite or slate, many stained the lurid green of carbonized brass. Traces of inscription – 'left us', 'dead', 'fell asleep' – were ghost messages.

Simon had noted all this on his first visit; they were signs to tell Justin about. That Justin lived so close to him in London was another sign.

He had stumbled upon the building two weeks earlier when he had rushed out after his mother, who had gone shopping without him. He had cut across the cemetery, intending to catch her at the Hogarth roundabout lights, but he was too late. Giving up, he had found the hut on his way back and made it his den.

A pile of leaves and branches was heaped by the side of the hut. He approached the door gingerly and, reaching up, tapped on the hut door. The rotting wood was spongy and crumbling and his knocking made little sound.

All clear. Inside it was pitch black. Simon's nostrils pricked with the smell of damp earth. He switched on his torch and found a broken flower pot by his granddad's old deckchair. First the mound of leaves, now this. He had an intruder.

He held the torch low to avoid light escaping out of the half-moon window. The table wasn't where he had put it; the wooden crates and the deckchair were set around it. Simon shone the torch into the supplies cupboard and saw his bottles of Coca-Cola were still there. He was pleased with himself for remembering the opener, although now that he was here, he wasn't thirsty.

He put his torch on end on the table and lowered himself into the deckchair. Now it faced the door, which was better. Who had been here? Practised at surveillance, Simon made sure no one followed him.

It was colder inside the hut than out and Simon wished he'd brought a jumper, but he was an explorer, so he mustn't mind.

The door burst open.

'Get out!' The command sliced the air. Hands pulled him out of the chair and pushed him across the table, pressing his face to the splintered wood.

'We've got a fugitive,' the voice shouted.

'Stop it!' Another voice – a girl, Simon thought. He couldn't move.

'I think you mean trespasser.' He mumbled politely, and decided not to say he couldn't leave because he was being pinned down.

'Name and rank?' The hand yanked his hair, forcing him up.

'Don't do that,' the girl said.

The hand let go. Simon fell to the ground and scooted over the damp earth to the wall. Peering up from behind a packing case, he saw a skeleton by the table. It had dark sockets for eyes. He melted with fear and the room dipped.

'Who are you?' The skeleton had a gun.

The room was dipping because the skeleton had picked up his torch and was waving it at him.

'Don't do that, you're blinding him.' The girl directed her own torch at the skeleton and Simon saw he was actually a boy with short hair and jutting cheekbones. Perhaps hearing the girl, he lowered the torch.

'I know him!' the girl said suddenly. 'He's at our school.'

'Shut up, Nicky, don't give away our identity.' As the spots of light cleared, Simon saw that the boy was dressed in army clothes, a jacket with epaulettes and lots of pockets that was too big for him.

'What regiment are you?' he rapped at Simon.

Simon knew the boy. He had seen him in a corner of the play-ground where no one went. He had been crawling along the grass below a wall, so at first Simon hadn't noticed him. He had stayed watching him; then, sensing danger, he had retreated before the boy realized he was there. No way out now: the boy was barring the exit and he had a gun.

'Answer!'

'Sorry, I—'

'What regiment?'

'I don't— There isn't a name.' Simon had no idea what he was talking about, but did know his life depended on giving the right answer.

'Who are you spying for?'

'No one.' If Justin were here he would kill the boy, Simon thought. 'I'm by myself.' He was lying, because in his mind Justin was with him.

'How do we know that? What are you doing here?'

'I was checking everything was in order. I was keeping watch.' Simon got to his feet, his mind busy. The girl placed her torch on the table and took Simon's torch off the boy in the army jacket. She laid it on its side. The beam bounced off the bricks and sent a dim glow around the hut. To Simon it looked like a cave.

The girl wore a duffel coat and her hair was pushed back with an Alice band, which made her look fierce. Simon knew her too. She had sat with him at lunch on his first day and asked about his last school. She hadn't been fierce then. She had got him seconds of sponge with hundreds and thousands and custard that he hadn't wanted because he was homesick, but made himself eat to please her. Best of all, she hadn't asked about his finger. He had since seen her in the playground and she had waved. Apart from his little sister, Simon didn't know any girls personally.

'You will follow my orders.' The boy's voice made him start.

'Yes.' Simon stood up straight and involuntarily clicked his heels together.

'Yes what?'

'I don't know what you mean,' Simon admitted.

'Yes, *sir*, I'm the Captain!' the Captain said. 'You are our prisoner. A trespasser,' he added.

Simon panicked. If they locked him in the hut, he would never be found. 'I have to get back or my—'

'He could join the unit. You keep saying we need to train up new recruits,' Nicky said.

There was silence while the Captain appeared to be giving this some thought.

'This is my lieutenant. She's our Official Codebreaker. Every undercover unit has one. If I were to let you in, you'd be a private and do as we say.' The Captain went to Simon's supplies cupboard. The torchlight glinted on Simon's bottles of Coke. The Captain took one out.

A flash of silver. Nicky raised her hand; she had a knife. Quaking, Simon flattened himself against the wall.

'You do it,' the Captain said to the girl and Simon saw it wasn't a knife, it was a bottle opener. He felt no relief.

The Captain sat down in the deckchair. This meant he had his back to Simon, but Simon knew there was no point in attacking him – he would get shot before he reached the door. Wrenching off the cap, the Captain stretched out long legs.

'You may not be fit for this unit.' He frowned at the bottle.

'Give me a chance,' Simon pleaded. If he were in a unit, Justin would be his friend. A unit changed everything. He could break codes too.

'Before you can join, you must prove yourself worthy.' The Captain tipped the bottle to his lips.

'How?' Simon felt despair. With his bad finger he would never be able to prove himself.

'Nothing and no one comes before the unit.' The Captain was rubbing at some mark on his trousered knee. 'You are trespassing in our headquarters, that's a capital crime.'

'He was here first,' Nicky said. From that moment Simon loved her. 'He must be brave. It's nearly eight o'clock now and he's out here on his own in the dark.' She added: 'We never come here by ourselves.'

'I do.' The Captain took a swig of Simon's Coke.

The girl looked at him and shook her head the way Simon's mum did at Simon's dad. 'I vote we set him free and recruit him. He could be useful,' she said.

Simon had never thought of having a friend who was a girl, although she had a boy's name.

'We have a Code of Honour. In this unit we look after each other. You have to swear allegiance and do your duty to me.'

'To the God and to Queen,' Nicky the Codebreaker said.

'To *me*,' the Captain repeated. 'Standing orders, you have to address me and the Lieutenant correctly and wear your uniform unless instructed by your commanding officer. That's me. You have to do as I say all the time or you will be court-martialled and shot.'

'*We look after each other.*' Simon had said that to Justin when he came to the school. He had found a unit that would look after him. Privately he swore allegiance there and then. Emboldened he said, 'I was thinking that your headquarters have been penetrated. It's contaminated.' He was pleased with 'contaminated'.

'What?'

The boy got out of the deckchair and leant over the table, knocking over the other torch. The shadows of the three children leapt and vanished as the torch rolled to a stop.

'There's leaves and stuff outside. They weren't there before.'

'It doesn't mean anything.'

'It means someone has been here. This flower pot wasn't here either.' Simon guessed that the Captain mustn't be contradicted.

The Captain snapped into action. 'The enemy is on the move.' He slammed the bottle on to the table.

'You're always saying that,' Nicky remarked wearily.

With a stab of perception that would get sharper as he grew older, Simon saw that the Captain was making it all up and that the girl had had enough of his stories. He saw a chink in the armour. Simon also saw that this didn't make the boy less dangerous.

Simon saw his chance. 'I saw someone so I came to investigate.' White lies were OK.

'I said he was courageous,' Nicky murmured, which seemed to anger the Captain. He chucked his empty bottle on to the ground, hitting soft earth. It didn't break. He faced Simon.

'Private, two tasks for you. In the next twenty-four hours you will find a new HQ and you will steal something valuable from your mother to prove your loyalty. If you fail, we will shoot you.'

'That's not fair,' Nicky protested. 'We didn't have to do anything to join.'

'We knew we could trust each other! He might have put those leaves there himself. Come on!' The Captain stomped out of the hut.

The mist had lifted; the headstones were luminescent in the pallid moonlight. A keen breeze sent leaves and twigs through the open door into the hut. Simon started to clear them, but as they were decamping, there was no point.

He was slotting the key into the lock of his parents' house when it hit him. The Captain had given him impossible tasks so that he would fail. Simon believed that if he stole from his mother he would die.

The boy looked back at the cemetery. Chiswick Tower loomed behind the yew trees. From high up there he could spy on the enemy.

Simon let himself breathe. He had found their new HQ.

Seventeen

Monday, 21 October 2013

St Peter's Church clock struck seven as Stella came out of the subway. She was deliberately early. The Ram had been her dad's local and she had suggested they meet there because it was close to Terry's. Since texting Jack, she had decided to refuse to take on William Frost's case. It was of the open and firmly shut variety. They wouldn't linger; she would return to Terry's and do a survey of industrial carpet cleaners, a task Stella viewed as a treat.

In the nineteenth century Black Lion Lane South had been a rural lane of workers' cottages fronted by hedgerows and surrounded by fields and orchards. The lane survived the urban creep of London until the 1950s when the extension of the Great West Road spliced it in two. Pedestrians reached the river from St Peter's church by a tiled tunnel. On the south side, a row of cottages opposite the Ram maintained a hint of country. The pub, once frequented by ostlers, street sellers and the coster-mongers and those who made a living from the reeds growing along the bank and on Chiswick Eyot, was now the hostelry of choice for professionals, bankers, actors and retired police detectives.

Stella pushed through the crowd and found Jack at a table out of the way, but with a view of the door. Still in his coat, reading glasses resting on the tip of his nose, he was deep in his *A–Z* guide to London. He jumped when her dog snuffled at his leg and pushed a glass of orange juice across to her. He wasn't drinking, not even his usual hot milk. To Stella's surprise, he had got a bowl of water for the dog.

'Did Suzie enjoy her trip *down under*?' He put on an Australian accent.

'I've no idea.' Stella hung her anorak over her chair and showed the dog the bowl, who bypassed it for a stray crisp. Tilting her glass at Jack in a vague toast, she sipped the orange juice.

'What do you mean?'

'I haven't seen her.' Stella got her Filofax out of her rucksack.

'Oh, I see.' Jack pursed his lips.

He would be thinking she'd not checked on Suzie since her return. For a man without a mother, he had plenty of advice on the subject.

'You *don't* see.' Stella flicked to the notes she had taken after talking to William Frost. 'She's staying in Sydney.'

'Forever?' Jack exclaimed. He looked stricken. Taken up with her own worry about it, Stella had forgotten how close he was to her mum.

'I'm to go on watering her plants. A clue that she plans to return. Or maybe not. Would you keep cleaning her flat, please.'

'Has she fallen in love?' Jack's eyes were brown liquid pools. Stella thought he looked upset.

'No!' she snapped because Jack had hit the nail right on the head. 'Mum says Terry was her wrong turning and that she's done with relationships.' Stella tried to remember when Suzie had last said that.

'Look, Stell, chill! Suzie is too astute to be fooled.' Jack fanned the pages of his *A–Z*, looking far from chilled himself.

Stella considered that she had taken more wrong turnings than her mum – some in this very pub. She should have suggested meeting Jack somewhere else.

'About this case, I have pretty much refused it. But Jackie suggested us to him and so I said I'd talk to you, not that there's much to say.'

'Talk to me.' Jack folded his arms and leant forward.

'In a nutshell, a man died and the verdict was suicide. His brother says he was murdered.' With repetition it sounded even more flimsy.

'What do the police say?'

'He spoke to Martin Cashman at Hammersmith. Reading between the lines, Cashman sent him packing.'

'What did he do? Hang himself, jump off Beachy Head?'

'Actually it was in your territory.' Stella realized she had been putting off saying how the man died. Jack was sensitive. When she first knew him, the colour green made him feel ill. She had cured him of that, but with Jack you still had to tread carefully. There was no way round this one. 'He was waiting for a District line—'

'Which station?' Jack interrupted.

'Stamford Brook.'

'When?'

'About a month ago.'

Stella got it. 'Was it your train?'

'No.' He shook his head. 'It was on the Piccadilly line.'

'But you know about it?' When Jack was upset he went a whiter shade of his usual pale. He looked like a ghost.

'I was there. His name was Frost – like the poet.'

'What poet?'

'Robert Frost.'

Stella consulted her notes. 'Frost wasn't a poet, he was in surveillance.'

'No, I meant— Never mind. I saw Frost go off the platform. Stamford Brook is one of the stations the Piccadilly line trains pass through at high speed. It's a good place for suicide, not that "good" is the right word.'

'So, it's cut and dried.' Jack's having been there gave them honourable grounds for turning down the case. It would be doing William a favour; he could let go and mourn his brother. Jackie was always saying you shouldn't bottle up grief. But Stella was disappointed. She wanted to work on another case with Jack.

'Why does the brother think it was murder?' Jack asked.

'Rick Frost, as he was called, told William he was being threatened and was on his way to tell him more when he died.'

'Feeling threatened sounds a good reason to kill himself.'

'You could say, but he's adamant Rick wasn't the sort. It's like Mum going to Sydney.'

'Delicious food, rich culture, sunshine and sea – how is that like jumping in front of a train?'

'It's out of character.' Stella checked her phone. It was breakfast time in Sydney.

'I'm telling him it's "no",' she decided.

'He'll be extremely upset.' Jack erred on the side of catastrophe. 'If Frost *was* murdered, it was a "perfect murder".' Jack opened his A–Z at the first page, as if preparing to read and said, 'the police checked the CCTV footage. He wasn't pushed – there was no one on the platform to push him.'

The dog growled. Stella was about to 'ssh' him when the growling erupted into a shrill cry, making heads turn. Jack was waving at the door.

'I remember him from the inquest.'

The dog was on his hind legs boxing the air, apparently full of joy at William Frost's arrival. Busy reining him in, Stella was too late to stop Jack agreeing to Frost's offer of drinks.

'Here's how!' William raised his glass and clinked theirs. Jack had asked for tap water.

Frost was dressed in the same preppy gear as when she'd first met him. Chinos, a lambswool jumper with a windcheater. When he took the jacket off, Stella saw one wing of his shirt collar was caught inside the jumper. This irritated her. If it had been Jack, she might have corrected it; as it was, she tried not to look.

'Jackie said I was in good hands.'

For a man who had lost his brother recently, Stella thought him too cheerful. 'I'm afraid we—' she began.

'Tell us about your brother.' Jack settled in to listen. Stella tried to catch his eye.

'I'm three years older than Rick, but it felt like a lifetime. We disliked each other from the off.'

'The spirit of the dead grows alongside the living. When you think of him in twenty years' time, he'll still be three years younger,' Jack opined.

Stella groaned inwardly. 'I should stop you, because the thing is—' she tried again.

'They live on through us,' Jack finished.

William Frost spread his hands on the table. Stella got the frightful notion he was going to suggest a séance. Jack would be keen on it.

'Rick was a fantasist. He tried to join the army, but he got turned down. He was prone to indigestion. He was rejected by the reserves too.'

'Makes sense. Soldiers have to be fit to fight.' Stella had intended to say nothing, keep it short.

'Rick should not have been in charge of a gun.'

'Why not?' Jack asked.

'He would have been trigger-happy, shoot you as soon as look at you. When he was a kid, he went around in full army gear, camouflage, the lot. Harmless stuff, but when most boys get interested in music or sport, Rick was still dressing up. I seriously thought he might blow us all up or become one of those weirdos who shoot their classmates.'

'Weird how?' Jack was leafing through the pages of his *A–Z*. He treated it like a bible, saying it helped him make decisions. Stella guessed that Jack had been fairly weird himself as a boy.

'As I told Stella, Rick was a surveillance consultant. Not MI5, more intruder alarms, CCTV. Suited his fantasy of pitting himself against the world. I pitied his wife. When he told me about the threat, frankly I ignored him.' He finished his beer and pushed the glass away.

'Was he in debt?' Stella asked.

'He was tight with money, but it's worth checking out his business. I know he hasn't left his wife sitting on a gold mine. Worth talking to her too. It wasn't all hunky dory in that particular garden.'

William hadn't told her this on the airport run. Jack had a knack of getting clients to open up.

'What about friends?' Jack was asking the right questions.

'None. At the funeral, it was just me and his wife.'

'What's her name?'

Any minute surely Jack would say he had seen Rick Frost jump off the platform. All these questions was him letting Frost down gently.

'Tallulah.' Frost frowned. Stella nearly pointed out that he would have to accept personal questions if they agreed to take the case. She avoided commenting on the name, partly suspecting him of making it up.

'You don't know what or who was threatening him?' Jack finished his water.

'No, but as I say, it's worth checking out his clients.' He wiped a hand down his face. 'I hardly ever saw Rick. I meant to say last time that it's my fault I didn't get that last call from him. If I had, think I would have put him off. I was on an all-nighter to finish a job – I'm a graphic designer, we have tight deadlines. If I'd not had my phone on silent maybe he'd be alive.'

'If he was murdered, it didn't matter,' Stella said, less to reassure than to be precise.

'Then I had a couple of constables at my door asking me to come and see Tallulah. I did try ringing him, even though they told me they believed it was his body at the station. Idiotic. Got his voicemail and assumed the police had his phone – in those situations they don't answer – but later I found out it was missing. Another reason why I think he was murdered. He was dead, how could he get rid of his phone?'

'What did the police say?' Stella asked.

'They thought it had been stolen by kids. Then when it hit the news that it had belonged to a dead man, they dumped it. Station staff found it a couple of weeks later, under the platform at Ealing Broadway.'

'Sounds likely.' Stella felt bound to defend Cashman and his team, who seemed in fact to have it sewn up. 'Who has it now?'

'Me. The police kept it, but it's been wiped so they found nothing on it so gave it to me. Odd, don't you think?' He laid a black iPhone down on the table. Its silver case looked to Stella as if it was bullet-proof.

Stella was grateful that Frost had brought them something tangible.

'Odd and not odd,' Jack murmured serenely. He was looking at his street atlas.

Stella was impatient. Jack didn't need the *A–Z* to tell Frost that he had been at the station, that he had seen his brother die and knew it was suicide. It was time to end this charade. She caught the words Chiswick Mall on the page; Chiswick Mall was the street where Mrs Carr's husband had texted her from.

'I'm guessing you've decided against taking this case?' Frost folded his arms. 'Jackie said you'd hear me out, so thanks.' He nodded to Stella.

'We'll take it,' Jack said. He reached out and, picking up Rick Frost's phone, put it in his coat pocket.

'Will we?' Stella was aghast. She was tempted to snatch back the phone and slam it down on the table.

'We will need to talk to his friends and relations, starting with his wife.' Jack jumped up, indicating the meeting over. Stella got up too.

'I can give you my sister-in-law's details, but she won't meet you. She's refusing to see me. Guess I remind her of Rick.'

Jack beamed at him. 'We can find ways in.'

Stella didn't think she would like Jack's 'ways'.

William Frost pulled on his jacket. 'I have an idea for getting into her house. Go undercover as a cleaning company and ask questions incognito. Clean Slate *is* a cleaning company so you have carte blanche to do a search and gather clues.' He was animated.

'Not a bad idea.' Jack was watching the dog nosing at his feet. 'However, we don't just turn up on doorsteps with our brooms, we have to be invited.'

'Cold call her.'

'For domestic jobs we post leaflets. We only call businesses after we've sent an email,' Stella intervened. They hadn't made cold calls since her mum had gone to Australia.

'Post her a leaflet.' Frost had an answer for everything.

The atmosphere had cooled.

'It's unethical,' Stella insisted. 'We don't clean under false pretences. As Jack said, we'll find another way to speak to Mrs Frost.'

'You're making it harder for yourselves. What if she's my brother's killer?'

'You are welcome to find another investigation agency.'

'I admire your approach.' Frost's face was stiff as a mask. He made a show of getting out his own phone and consulting it as if about to call a competitor in front of them.

'Do you think she is?' Jack looked away from the dog.

'Sorry?' Frost put away his phone.

'Mrs Frost – Tallulah – do you think she murdered your brother? It would save time if you told us your suspicions,' Jack said.

'She's not the killer.' He folded his arms. Jack said it was a sign of defensiveness, but, big and broad, William Frost would win any fight.

'Is she a beneficiary of his estate, life insurance, the house, death-in-service pension?'

'Yes, but why make a murder look like suicide? She won't get his life insurance.' Frost shrugged his shoulders. 'You have to fight fire with fire. You need to get into his house and knocking on the door all nice and polite won't do it.'

'It's possible she would get his life insurance.' Stella dredged up an unasked-for lecture from a client who was a lawyer, while cleaning his bathroom grout. 'Providing the policy was taken out a significant period before death and your brother disclosed any mental health issues.'

'Exactly!' Frost exclaimed, as if Stella were corroborating his point.

'Did he have enemies?' Jack wasn't giving up. Although the question cropped up in crime dramas, Stella found it unconvincing. She could number her friends on one hand – two fingers – but she didn't think in terms of how many enemies she had. Clean Slate's operatives, including Stella herself, had upset clients – cobwebs missed, bleach used instead of tea tree oil, rival companies hunting for tips that mystery-shopped their service – yet they couldn't be described as enemies. Or could they?

'Rick installed recording devices in air-freshener dispensers and alarm clock radios. He fitted those intruder alarms that collect stats on staff entry and exit. They lead to sackings, divorce, shattered reputations. Lots of reasons for revenge.'

'Would that be aimed at your brother's clients rather than him?' Jack queried.

'Who do you suspect?' Stella was pleased by the question. It would tell them as much about Frost as who might have killed his brother.

He pursed his lips. 'I don't point fingers.'

'It would help if you did?' Jack said. They were being a team.

'Look into his business. As I say, I bet he had a lot of enemies. He certainly had no friends. I'm sure the reason the army refused him was he had "psycho" stamped on his forehead.' He hadn't answered the question.

'Who do you—'

'If anything occurs to you let us know.' To Stella's surprise Jack got a Clean Slate card from his coat and scribbled a number on the back with the stub of a pencil.

When Stella shook William's hand, she was surprised that it was without grip.

After he had gone, she asked Jack, 'Why did you say we'd take it?'

'If it's not suicide, like I said, it's the perfect murder. His idea about going in undercover was good. Please tell me you were pretending when you said we wouldn't do it?'

'We're not compromising Clean Slate. People need to trust their cleaners.'

'Still, I'd like to know why Mrs F. isn't speaking to William. That stuff about looking like his brother is nonsense. I saw the picture at the inquest, I thought then how they didn't look like they were brothers,' Jack mused. 'We only have his word that he was at home all night.'

'The police went round.'

'Hours after his brother died.'

'Why would William ask us to solve a murder he had committed himself?'

'A clever murderer flirts with capture. He or she can't help themselves; they want to test their brilliance and stave off boredom. Behind his charm, Frost is ruthless. He didn't like your refusing his idea one bit.'

'And who is called *Tallulah*?' Stella groaned.

'Tallulah Bankhead, the actress,' Jack replied promptly. 'She laid a foundation stone in St Peter's Square when they built the Commodore Concert Hall. You must have seen it.'

Stella despaired of having an ordinary conversation with Jack. Although the name was familiar, so perhaps she had seen it. Terry had taken a photograph of the Commodore on fire when it was being demolished: she did remember that.

Stella reproached herself for her impatience. Jack had seen a man die; she should cut him some slack. If he believed this was a case, she would go along with it. But despite William Frost coming via Jackie, Stella did not trust him.

'If Tallulah was alive she'd be a hundred now.' Jack glanced at his watch. 'Goodness, I'm on the Underground in one hour, forty-three minutes and fifty seconds. Come on!' He stuffed the street atlas in his coat and jumped up.

'Where to?'

'Stamford Brook station. I'll show you where Rick Frost died.'

Eighteen

October 1987

The quarry moved along Burlington Lane. He kept a distance of ten metres, already composing his report for the unit. *A woman in a black coat and high-heeled boots and a black handbag is walking fast along...*

Simon's mother was visiting Mrs Henderson, the lady with the fishpond and a hundred knitted animals. She always gave him cake when he went too, but his mum said he was to stay at home with his sister because when he was working, his father forgot she was there.

'She usually comes with us.'

'No she doesn't.' She squirted perfume on her wrists. This lie had made it easy to steal her wedding ring from the lacquered box with the tiger's face. As soon as she had gone, Simon grabbed his mac from the rack and rushed after her.

She was crossing at the lights, the wrong way for Mrs Henderson's.

He could catch up and demand to know where she was going, but she would lie. Simon admitted to himself that she had been lying to him since he left Marchant Manor and was back living at home.

Traffic on the Great West Road slowed to a stop; a girl was staring at him from the back seat of a car. Simon smiled at her. She poked out her tongue and ducked out of sight. Simon stopped. Then the lights changed and the car moved off. When he looked again, the pavement was empty. He had lost his mother.

The tide was out. Disconsolate and unwilling to go home,

Simon crossed the causeway to the eyot and, scrambling up the bank, slumped against the trunk of a weeping willow. He looked back at Chiswick Mall through the reeds. There was no one about. Stuffing his hands in his mac pockets to keep warm, Simon felt something. Her ring. Since stealing it, guilty and ashamed, Simon had put it out of his mind. He held it to the sky: there were letters engraved on the inside, 'Vita Nuova'. This didn't make sense. His mother was called Madeleine not Vita.

Obscurely, this unfamiliar name convinced Simon that he had been tracking the wrong woman. His real mother would be eating cake with Mrs Henderson. If the ring belonged to someone called Vita, why was it in her drawer?

At his feet was a white stone, smooth as if polished by water. Inchoate with emotion, the boy snatched it up and, stepping across the clearing to a gap in the reeds, he hurled it as hard as he could into the river.

The front door was opened as he scratched his key at the lock.

'Where have you been?' She was wearing the National Trust apron he had bought her for her birthday.

'I went to see Mrs Henderson.' A master stroke. He stared at her, unblinking.

A clock ticked in the living room; somewhere his sister was laughing.

'What do you mean?' She wasn't looking at him.

'I had banana cake.' *Tell me I can't have. You were there, you didn't see me. Say it!*

'Simon, we agreed you'd stay here. I left Mrs Henderson early and went shopping.' She was walking away from him. 'Sweet of you to go, but tell me next time. I do love her banana cake!'

'Actually it wasn't banana, it was a Victoria sponge.' Demons urged him on.

'We're eating in five minutes,' she said as if to no one.

In the bathroom, Simon ran the gold ring over the fingers of his bad hand, his special trick. It was lighter than a coin. He told himself that his mum had been at Mrs Henderson's and then gone shopping. Next time he would give her ring to the Captain and say his mother's name was Vita. Next time he would lead the unit to the tower.

Nineteen

'There was a man of double deed,
Who sowed his garden full of seed;
When the seed began to grow,
'Twas like a garden full of snow.'

Jack's voice was amplified under the railway bridge. The wind had got up since they'd been in the Ram; it funnelled under the bridge, smacking Stella's hair across her face and flattening the dog's ears to his head. A train clattered above, wheels clunking on the tracks. Stella tugged the dog's lead to chivvy him, for the grey-encrusted pavements implied that, prompted by the racket, pigeons roosting on the girders might shit on them. It would not be a sign of luck.

Jack skipped out of the way as a straggle of late commuters came out of Stamford Brook station. Stella's acute sense of smell identified a mixture of scents and body odours and she hurried after Jack into the ticket hall.

'Single to Barons Court. Please.'

Stella was nine when she had made her first solo journey on the Underground. Terry had been called to a job, so she had to return by herself to the flat her mum had rented since their separation. Terry had folded a ten-shilling note into her purse with the lion motif and, crouching, patted her down and stroked her cheek with his thumb as if she was crying. She must *not* talk to strangers, she must be polite to anyone in uniform, even if they were strangers, and she must keep away from the edge of the platform.

'*It will be an adventure!*' He had tucked a strand of hair behind her ear.

'*I wish you were coming.*'

'*Next time, Stell. We'll go to Upminster and back!*'

Perhaps to sweeten the dull misery of access weekends, Terry told his daughter he would grant her three wishes – proper wishes, not things like wanting to fly or live with him and her mum like 'before'. Since these were her greatest wishes, Stella generally plumped for an ice-cream sundae at the Wimpy Bar or feeding ducks in the park, which was really for babies. The last time she had seen Terry alive, he asked if she remembered the wishes. She hadn't. The station brought them back. Too late. Terry was dead. No amount of wishes changed that.

Art deco glass lampshades hanging from the ceiling cast a washed-out light over the ticket hall. In 1975 it had been dingy and grim, and bristled with the possibility of bad people that her dad worked long hours to put away.

She heard a popping; Stanley jerked the lead. It came from a photo booth by the entrance. The curtains were shut; she couldn't see legs beneath. It was an odd time to get your photo taken, she thought. Stanley growled.

'Ssssh!' In here a bark would be deafening. She snatched him up and stroked him to distract him. Jack had started his chanting again:

'*When the snow began to melt,*
'*Twas like a ship without a belt;*
When the ship began to sail,
'*Twas like a bird without a tail.*'

He flourished his pass and swiped them through the barriers. 'This way!'

'I must pay,' Stella protested.

'We're not going anywhere.' Jack was running up a wide staircase. 'It happened at six minutes past twelve, later than tonight,'

Jack said when she joined him on the platform. 'There're three more trains after that. He used his Oyster card, he didn't buy a ticket.'

'Why bother, if he wasn't going anywhere.' Stella frowned at her quip. If an inspector asked to see her ticket, she didn't want to explain she was looking at where a man had killed himself.

Jack broke into her thoughts. 'A single or return ticket might have indicated his state of mind.'

Suicide wasn't an option, but if it were, Stella would approach it like cleaning. Clear the decks, identify materials and equipment, allow for the unexpected – damp, cockroaches or cancelled trains. An Oyster card saved money; even if there was to be no future to save it for, she would factor it in.

'An Oyster card says business as usual. It might mean he didn't expect to die.' Stella looked across to the eastbound platform where that afternoon she had waited as a child, avoiding the gaze of strangers. It was deserted now. Then she had been fearful of forgetting to get off at the right station or sitting next to a stranger. Most of all she had fretted that her mum would be cross that Terry had let her travel alone. That came true; Suzie still referred to how he had 'abandoned his daughter'.

The announcement board above their heads was blank and dark as Jack said it had been the night Frost died. It was a risk to let a child travel alone on the Underground. Terry had trusted her and she had justified that trust.

Trains still went from Stamford Brook to Barons Court, but her mum was on the other side of the world and Terry was dead. Stella pulled herself together.

'You said Frost was standing still, then he ran. Sounds like a snap decision. Sit!' Stanley was straining towards the end of the station, an area of darkness beyond the staircase balustrade. Dogs weren't like children, she couldn't warn Stanley about live rails or strangers.

'He's sensed Frost's ghost,' Jack observed.

'Or he's smelled a food wrapper.' The case was thin enough

without Jack introducing the supernatural. She could smell after-shave, no doubt lingering in the air from a passenger; there was no one but themselves on the platform. 'Besides, didn't you say he died up there?' She pointed in the opposite direction.

'He broke into a run, then swerved off.' Jack walked along the platform. 'Right here.' He crossed to the outer side, perilously close to the edge.

'Jack!' The dog was still pulling on the lead. Dogs were meant to make the owner feel protected. His behaviour was freaking her out.

'Before he jumped, he looked at me.' Jack was on his haunches. He continued to recite:

'When the bird began to fly,
'Twas like an eagle in the sky;
When the sky began to roar,
'Twas like a lion at the door.'

In the empty station his voice was different. Stella wished he wouldn't do this.

'A person about to jump looks at the train. Frost looked at me.'

'Perhaps he changed his mind.'

At last Jack moved away from the track. 'I heard a man on the radio who survived jumping off a bridge and straight away regretted it. Water is like concrete if you hit it at speed, and the impact sucks you under. Water is incredible,' he marvelled. 'It comes from the river and it returns to the river.'

'Did you tell the coroner?' Stella pulled him back to the present.

'They want facts, not impressions.'

Stella was tempted to suggest impressions weren't useful at any time, but Jack's impressions had played a role in solving their last two cases. He seemed able to place himself in the mind of a murderer.

'Why did he run along the District line side then cross to the Piccadilly?' Jack pushed his fringe off his forehead and scanned the deserted platform. In the dim light Stella couldn't see his face; his eyes were lost in their sockets. She looked down the platform; the wooden seating booths were empty, the announcement boards remained dark and the tracks were silent. She felt uneasy. It wasn't just that a man had died here. She zipped her anorak up to her chin.

'We should go,' she said.

'Plenty of time,' Jack replied. 'It was as if he changed his mind.'

'Frost was out of sight of the driver? Had he seen Frost, he would have braked,' Stella hazarded.

'Good point. At the inquest the driver's statement said Frost came out of nowhere and he had no time to brake. On the other hand he didn't need to run, why not simply step off?'

Jack's reflection in the partition glass of the nearest booth was warped and strange. Stella thought again how, if she didn't know him, she would be unnerved by meeting him at night. She *was* unnerved anyway.

As if to underline her thought, Jack walked on and resumed his rhyme:

'When the door began to crack,
'Twas like a stick across my back.'

Like this he was impossible. Stella let him go. She watched him until he stepped out of the last pool of light into the shadows and, giving into the dog's straining, she walked back up the platform towards the stairs.

'They never do what they're told, do they!'

Stella stifled a shout.

'Sorry. I didn't mean to surprise you.' A man was by the wall. She couldn't see his face, although he reminded her of someone – she couldn't think who.

'You didn't.' She kept her voice level, although surely he must hear her heart smashing against her ribcage. Besides, he would know he had surprised her.

'They have finely tuned senses,' he remarked. 'Lovely dog.'

Stella was impressed that he put the back of his hand towards Stanley rather than tried to pat his head. He must know about dogs. Stanley licked his fingers. So much for protection. Jack was at the other end of the station; he could do nothing.

She looked up the line. Behind the brick building, they were only visible to the driver of a westbound train, but there was no train at Ravenscourt Park station, a dot in the distance. Any driver would see two people chatting. Which was all it was. *Come on, Jack!*

'He's not mine,' she said. 'I'm giving him back soon.' The man would be surveying the track. Better to do it at night with fewer trains, she supposed.

'He's pretty.' The man took his hand away and surreptitiously wiped it on his coat.

'Thank you,' she said, as if the compliment were for her. 'I'd better go, my friend's waiting.' *Be polite to strangers.* She let him know she wasn't alone.

The Piccadilly tracks were humming. Whoosh! Lights strobed, making her blink; doors and windows flashed a hair's breadth from her. The clunkety-clunk then faded to nothing. Stella swept Stanley into her arms and ran down the platform looking for Jack.

'I thought I'd lost you!' He was in the last shelter, legs crossed, tucked into the corner as if resting after a Sunday-afternoon stroll. He was facing the Piccadilly line track. She collapsed next to him, too agitated to care when he continued to recite his rhyme. Jackie believed that reciting rhymes helped Jack to think.

'When my back began to smart,
'Twas like a penknife in my heart;
And when my heart began to bleed,
'Twas death, and death, and death indeed.'

'He wasn't running towards the track.' Jack linked his arm through hers and drew her closer.

'What?' She would put up with this from no one else. It was freezing, although the glass gave shelter from the wind.

'What's the matter with him?' Jack was looking at the dog. Stanley had begun straining on the lead again.

'He must want to go back up there. Sit!' Stella rewarded the dog's obedience with a fishy treat from the pouch strapped to her waist.

With Jack sitting so close, Stella began to warm up. There was a flicker and she saw that a Richmond train had been flashed up on the board.

'Fear. It wasn't the calm expression of a man acting on a decision. The look on his face was fear.' Jack let go of her arm and set off back up the platform. He continued talking. 'William Frost said his brother was frightened of someone.'

Stella caught up with Jack at the top of the staircase. 'Suppose he was where that inspector is? You wouldn't have seen him, after all. If not for the dog, I could have missed him there. It is probably out of the CCTV's line of sight.'

'What inspector?'

'A man surveying the line.' The dog wasn't pulling any more, so she let the lead slacken. 'Except Frost wouldn't have seen him either.'

'Where is he?' Jack demanded, seeming suddenly alert.

'Who?'

'The inspector.'

Stella lowered her voice. 'Behind that building at the end of the platform.'

Jack strode along the platform and around the brick building at the end of the station.

Stella started after him but, contrary to his behaviour since they had arrived at the station, Stanley now refused to move. She was still urging him to 'heel' when Jack returned.

'No one there. What did the man say he was doing?'

'He didn't say. I presumed he was inspecting the line.' Now that she thought about it, the man had no torch, no notebook and was all in black, unwise for working on the track. 'I suppose he was waiting for a train. Odd to leave when it's due.'

'Oh no!' Jack exclaimed.

'What?'

'Frost wanted me to see who was behind him. It was a sign. But of course I kept watching him.'

'Meaning?' Stella started walking down the stairs.

'Meaning you were right – there *was* another person on the platform that night.' Jack took her arm again, feet in step they returned to the ticket hall. 'I need to go or I'll be late for my pick-up at Earl's Court.' He let go of her arm and made for the eastbound platform staircase.

'I could give you a lift.' Stella was unwilling suddenly to let him go.

'Thanks, but there's a train in three minutes and thirty seconds. Are you OK going to the van by yourself?' Jack hesitated as if he'd picked up on her unease.

'Of course!' Stella shook her head at the idea she would not be.

'Oh, here, I almost forgot. take this.'

Stella saw a flash of silver. It was Rick Frost's phone.

'What can I do with it? You're the techno whizz.'

'It's been wiped, remember? You may as well have it for safe-keeping. For your files.' He nodded as if to emphasize his words. They were detectives, they would have case files.

Stella watched Jack until he vanished at the turn of the stairs. She was standing where Terry had that afternoon; she had turned at the top of the stairs and looked back to see him still there watching her. Jack didn't look back.

A square of white lay inside the photo booth: a set of rejects carelessly dropped. Stella batted aside the curtain and retrieved it; flipping it over she stared unbelieving. In each of the four shots was a man. He was facing the wrong way; the photographs were all of the back of his head. No one did that by accident. Not seeing a bin, Stella slipped the sheet into her anorak pocket.

Goldhawk Road was quiet – no traffic, no sign of the inspector or of the man who had used the photograph booth. On the bridge, the Richmond train slid to a stop, the windows yellow squares against the sky.

Hurrying Stanley beneath the bridge before the train moved off, Stella got an incoming text. It was Jack.

Frost wasn't running towards the train, he was running away from someone.

Twenty

October 1987

By half past four the last of the light gave way to dusk. A pewter-grey sky dulled the waters of the Thames, and conflicting currents between Chiswick Mall and the eyot, fast flowing and dangerous, plaited the surface.

The scrawl of traffic on the Great West Road was muffled by the brewery, a bulwark for the gale that smacked against the embankment wall and harassed mooring chains. On the far bank, spindly larches along the towpath bent against the force. An undulating moan resembled a wail of regret, ever more insistent. A storm was brewing; some talked of a hurricane.

On Chiswick Eyot, beneath the hiss of the wind, the river rose with the wash and hush of the turning tide and a constant trickling. Where once the Thames had dredged up oyster shells and fragments of clay beer mugs, now it offered up more vivid London detritus to the ragged shoreline. Plastic bottles, rubber gloves – blue, yellow, red – tangles of nylon rope, a fractured storage crate.

Three children scampered out from the church porch and, battling against the gale, made it to railings overlooking the beach. Abruptly one broke away and pointed with a half-finger. 'Follow me,' he cried.

Simon sounded more confident than he felt. Aided by the wind, he marched along the pavement, careful not to check that the others were behind him, for fear of betraying doubt that they would be.

He ducked down a cobbled passageway, the stones slick and black. Someone stepped on his heel. Simon switched on his torch. It was Nicky. The Captain was there too. They had obeyed him.

'Where are we going?' the Captain demanded.

'Can't you guess?' Simon shone the torch into his face. He ran along the alley and halted by the cage door. He shone the torch upwards. In open-mouthed awe, as if watching a spaceship land, the children gazed up at the tower.

'What is that?' The Captain's voice quavered. He rattled the cage. The hum of vibrating metal rang in their ears after he let go. 'We shouldn't be here,' he said to Nicky.

Simon pulled on his half-finger. If the Captain ordered her to leave, Nicky would go and it would be over. In the last hours Simon had formed two ambitions: one, he would impress Nicky so much she would be his friend; two, he would become the Captain. Lying in bed late the previous night, the boy had worked out that either of these ambitions would lead to the other. Somehow this would lead him to Justin.

'We shouldn't be *anywhere*,' Simon said. 'The unit works under-cover. We "slide under the wire of rules and regulations".' He had mugged up on spies. He saw Nicky smile and turn her head away to avoid the Captain seeing. It was going well.

Simon turned the handle in the grille. The door opened with a terrible groan.

'Anyone could get in. It's not secure,' the Captain objected. 'Let's go.'

Simon was thunderstruck. In a flash of a second he under-stood the situation. The Captain was scared. In all his planning and imaginings, Simon had supposed the Captain invincible, a formidable opponent. But he had an Achilles heel. With a steady hand, Simon shone the torch into the other boy's face and, deathly calm, said, 'We could get a padlock, but it would give us away.'

'How did you know about this place?' the Captain whispered.

'I found it on reconnaissance.' Simon was airy. 'It's the ideal HQ. It's fortified with full sight of the surrounding territory.'

'It must belong to someone,' the Captain persisted.

'It belongs to me.' In the dark Simon smiled. The future was unfolding: the water tower *was* his; he was the host and they would be his guests. He would be the Captain.

'We should come in the day,' Nicky said.

'It is the day,' the Captain snapped at her.

'I meant with more light,' Nicky said. She darted a look at Simon and he felt his nerve falter. As if it had been orchestrated, they were hit by a gust of wind. The metal vibrated and jangled.

'I'm Captain, I'm going first.' The Captain fell into Simon's trap.

'This is illegal. We can't go in, it's not ours,' Nicky said.

'We can if we want, we're allowed,' the Captain replied coldly.

Simon jammed his hands in his mac pockets. Used to exclusion, he was at home with the 'divide and rule' tactic.

'Don't be stupid, your mum would—'

'Shut up, Nicky.' The Captain rounded on her, yelling above the rising howl as the gusts became more frequent.

Simon took a risk. 'Perhaps we should wait for the light.' He addressed the Captain, careful not to look at Nicky, but hoping to indicate that he was with her. Living with warring parents, Simon had learnt how to be on two sides at once.

'Nicky is scared.' The Captain peered up through the criss-cross of silver lines.

'*You* hate heights and this is high!' Intending kindness, the girl unknowingly sealed both her own and the Captain's fate. The Captain was afraid of heights. That was his Achilles heel. Simon saw that Nicky was trying to protect him. That the Captain should need protection implied he was weak.

The Captain pushed past them into the cage and began to climb. The grille shook as he ascended, the high-pitched thrum mingled with the wind.

'You're mean.' Nicky's breath was hot on Simon's ear.

Simon felt that the giant columns stretching high above might crumble and crush him. He turned in time to see a shadow on the glistening brickwork in the passage. Nicky had gone.

The wind intensified to a howl. Stung by her accusation, he set off up the staircase.

A curving walkway was fixed to the base of the tank with rivets and protected by a thin metal rail. Simon tried to grab it, missed and fell on to his knees. The pain winded him. Grasping the rail, he shuffled forward. The Captain stood with his back to the tower wall as if at gunpoint.

'*You're mean!*'

Long ago Justin had said the same words. Simon flushed with shame. What had happened with Justin's tunnel in the kitchen garden wasn't mean. Justin was his friend; he'd tried to save him. He wouldn't save the Captain. He let go of the rail and, avoiding looking down, he strolled along the walkway towards him.

The Captain didn't move, obviously fearful that even a twitch would send him plummeting down.

Simon found a handle set into the steel; he pulled it and the door opened with a shriek.

'What is this place?' The Captain spoke like a ventriloquist, head stiff, mouth like a letterbox.

'It's a water tower, it stores water and redistributes it.' Justin had told him the basic principle; since then Simon had looked them up.

'If it's full of water, it's impractical.'

'It's empty, it was "mothballed".' If only Justin could hear him. 'This is a panopticon! We will spy on the enemy; they won't know we are here. If there's hundreds of enemies, they won't know there's only the three of us. Wherever they go we will track them. We have three-hundred-and-sixty-degree vision. The tower gives us supremacy!' Abandoning grammar Simon spread his arms like Tutankhamen, the Boy King.

'We can't spy all the time, there's school.' The Captain began a slow sideways shuffle towards the door. Once inside the tower he leant over, hands on knees, panting as if he had run a marathon.

'The enemy won't know when we're not here.' Simon cast back to his notes taken in Chiswick library. 'They won't know when to attack, so they won't attack.' Belatedly, he properly grasped the brilliance of the idea.

Before Simon could stop him, the Captain shut the tower door. The clang ricocheted around the walls like a series of explosions. His mum told him never to shut doors in unfamiliar places, like the chest freezer in the basement. Simon tried the handle and hid his relief that the door opened. He pushed it to, carefully. Justin said you had to respect buildings.

Light drifted in from a porthole high above. When Simon turned on his torch he saw they were standing by a twisting spiral staircase. Up and up it went.

There was a door to the left. The Captain kicked it open and went inside. They were in a huge circular room with rough cement walls. Simon kept the door ajar. With no windows there was no sense of how high up they were: this seemed to make the Captain braver. Simon's authority depended on the Captain's fear. He fiddled with his half-finger.

'There's loads of space for when we – *you* – recruit. And it's dry.' Simon didn't know why he was whispering.

'We can't see out? How do we see the enemy?' The Captain paced the perimeter.

'We go on to the roof. And there are those slits in the walls. They don't know we can't see through them. Anyway it's not what we see, it's what the enemy *thinks* we can see.'

'How do we get upstairs?'

Simon was saved from admitting he didn't know by a dreadful screech. Then an insidious hum like singing, accompanied by metallic tapping. The boys froze. Someone was coming down the corkscrew staircase.

'You idiot! The enemy are in occupation.' The Captain pushed Simon against the wall. 'Lure them off,' he hissed. 'When it's all clear I'll go for reinforcements.'

'He might be armed.' Simon realized that 'lure them off' meant 'let them kill you'. This was what the Captain meant by loyalty.

Simon was furious with himself for leaving the door ajar. His adherence to safety might now cost him his life. At least the Captain had shut the big entrance door, so the enemy wouldn't immediately suspect an intruder. As he thought this, a howling gale rushed into the lobby and he realized the entrance door had been opened. The powerful draught pushed their door open further. Simon tried to back away from the gap, but the Captain stopped him.

'Go out there,' he hissed.

Simon shook his head vehemently. 'I won't until they know we are here.'

The staircase was humming again. There was someone else there.

'Promise me you'll—' a man said.

Simon shuddered. The man was so close, that if Simon reached out he would be able to touch him, but the wind and his own terror stopped him hearing all the words.

He couldn't hear the other person.

' —next Saturday at Stam—. You won't regret—'

A mumbled reply. Simon shut his eyes, but could only hear the first man.

'You owe it to yourself. We only have— life— make— of it. When we're settled we— the kid. One step— time— like living in a coffin, you said so—!'

Simon crept to the opening and, peeping out, saw two people. In the thin light from the porthole they looked like Hosts. Simon's word for murderers, he had told Justin.

One was the man. His head was bald on top like a monk and he was bent over the other person. He was kissing them. Simon was repulsed and wished he was at home with his mum, but she was out with a friend. He didn't care about being captain, he just wanted to be on the sofa watching a film with her – the best of friends – the two of them.

The man moved towards the gap. Simon retreated, but again the Captain stopped him. The other person was a woman. Dark hair, blue coat. His mother's hands. There was the big red stone on her wedding ring. Her real wedding ring; it wasn't the one in his pocket. He could make no sense of what he was seeing. *It was his mother*. Instinctively he moved towards her and then was jerked backwards and manhandled to the floor. The Captain was on top of him, his hand clamped over his mouth.

The clanging began again. Then silence.

The Captain was by the door.

'She's gone.' He clasped his hands, bending forward as if in agony. 'That was a real live prostitute!' He snuffled with stifled giggles. 'Did you see?' He dipped about the tank, clutching his stomach.

A prostitute.

Simon kicked out at the Captain, but he was on the other side of the concrete room and out of his reach. He scrambled to his feet and launched at him.

'She is not a pros—' he spluttered.

'What else would she be?' The Captain grabbed him and spun him around. His height and age played against Simon; in seconds the Captain had him in a tight grip like a straitjacket. He shoved him up against the wall and hissed, 'Shut up! The man is still up there.'

Gradually it dawned on Simon that the Captain had never seen his mother.

It was not his mother. By now she would be making the tea at home, giving his sister a bath; he must leave.

'You're scared of her,' the Captain jeered.

'I'm not.' Simon edged towards the door, but the Captain was blocking him.

'Prove it.'

'How?' Now the Captain was being mean, but Nicky wasn't there to hear.

'Go up that staircase and come down again. Only after I've counted to twenty. Then you can be in the unit!'

'What if he comes out while I'm there?'

'That's how you prove your loyalty. If you don't do that, I'll have you court-martialled and shot.'

'I stole my mum's wedding ring, like you said.' Simon fumbled for the ring, but couldn't find it.

'You what?' The Captain grabbed Simon by the shoulders again and shook him, making his teeth clack together.

'Like you wanted, I stole it off my mother.'

'I didn't say steal her wedding ring! She'll call the police and expose us!'

'She won't.' Simon was suddenly sure. The ring had been in a box hidden at the back of her dressing table; his mother didn't want anyone to know it was there. She wouldn't call the police when she saw it was missing.

'You failed one mission, you'd better succeed at this one.' The Captain's voice was kind. He might simply be concerned.

'To twenty?' Simon confirmed.

The Captain gave a terse nod. 'Twenty seconds.'

Simon crept out into the little space at the foot of the stairs. He put his bad hand on the rail and stared up at the twisting staircase. The tower door was beside him; if he made a dash for it, the Captain would be too frightened to chase him. But he would never see Nicky again, he would never be captain and he could never recruit Justin to the unit. He would be a *no one*.

He climbed very slowly to avoid making a noise, but even so the staircase began to hum. The constant turns disorientated him. Halfway up there was another door, made of metal and very thick. It was open a few centimetres.

'Hon, you came back. I knew you would!' The man was inside. *One. Two. Three.*

Simon looked over the platform rail. The Captain was a few steps below. Simon hadn't heard him climb the staircase.

Seven. Eight. Nine.

The Captain was on the platform, behind the open door, his eyes blazing. Hazel flecked with green, they didn't blink. He was smiling as if he liked Simon.

A resounding crash echoed around the tower. Heedless of falling, Simon hurtled down the staircase and plunged out of the main door.

On the narrow walkway a violent gust flung him against the

guard rail. He teetered over the edge of the yawning darkness and dropped to the floor, his knees grazed by the cold metal. Fingers groping for the holes in the grille surface, he crawled along it to the staircase and flew down the stairs, his feet hardly touching the metal.

On Chiswick Mall, he stopped and looked up. The massive tank housing loomed above him, a crouching demon against the darkening sky. There was no sign of the Captain, but through the vents in the tank Simon believed the man with the bald patch was watching.

Simon cut through the churchyard; tripping and stumbling between the graves, he aimed for the string of pinprick lights of his street.

On Corney Road, a stitch in his side and with bloodied grazes on his knees, Simon slowed to a walk and limped along to his gate. His home was the only house with the curtains open, the lights blazing. His mum was sitting on the sofa. She glanced out of the window. Simon told himself that she had been there all the time. That it was him she was looking out for.

Twenty-One

Tuesday, 22 October 2013

> *'Mary, Mary, quite contrary*
> *How does your garden grow?'*

A scream. Balanced on his haunches, Jack grabbed at a willow frond. A gull was perched on the tide marker. As he watched, it opened its beak and let out another anguished cry.

The sun had gone behind a cloud; soon it would be dark. Absorbed in weeding his Garden of the Dead, Jack had not considered he could be stranded on the eyot. Usually alive to alteration in the rippling water, this evening, mulling on Rick Frost's mysterious death, he had lost sense of time.

> *'With silver bells and cockle shells*
> *And pretty maids all in a row.'*

Jack snipped the last of the reeds and grasses in the bed. The wild flowers – London rocket, wild garlic, poppies and flixweed – that, over the last year, he had planted in honour of the dead attracted bees and butterflies in the spring and died back in the winter. They surrounded a circle of white stones that represented the souls of his dead. At the centre was his mother.

He fetched his coat from beneath the willow and a paper flew out of the pocket. Jack snatched it up. Besides his planting and the stones, he left no trace of his visits to the eyot. Only once, when he was young, had he met others in his garden.

It was the flier for the tower. He thought he had filed it with the scant paperwork involved for his moving. It must be the first one he had received. Through the curtain of willow fronds Jack saw the water was rising. He stuffed the leaflet back in his pocket and wended his way beneath a canopy of brambles and briar to the western end of the island. His direction was counter-intuitive: the shortest route to Chiswick Mall was the other way, but the river had already submerged the end of the causeway by the eyot. Jack knew it was easy to slip off the causeway and be pulled under by the Thames's unforgiving currents.

The scene altered with every turn of the tide, but blocks of stone and brick remained embedded in the mud. He knew which would sink under his weight and to side-step slicks of slime that hid mud as deep as quicksand.

Two people were on the beach by Chiswick Mall, a woman and a boy of about three. The child ran about, his legs kicking. Arms flailing, he lacked economy of movement. At the edge of the spreading pool, he hurled a stone into the water, which plopped into the shallows. Jack would throw like that, letting go too late, curtailing momentum. When Stella threw a ball for Stanley, it could pierce the sky.

Jack paused when he reached the steps below Chiswick Mall. In the diminishing light the tower was menacing. According to the flier, it was no longer called Chiswick Tower, but had been renamed Palmyra Tower. He recalled that his father had been commissioned to build a bridge in Palmyra, a suburb of Perth in Western Australia. Seemingly insensitive to the fact that the boy had lost his mother, he had sent him a postcard of Fremantle Cemetery and told him about an unmarked grave for Martha Rendell who was hanged in 1909 for murdering her stepchildren. Jack kept it in his box of treasures. Substituting the name of the tower for one of a foreign city 'dis-located' it from its history and surroundings. It was, Jack felt, a betrayal.

None of the windows in the tower were lit, but still Jack had the crazy notion someone was up there watching him.

'Let's get home, have tea and then bath and bed.' The woman's voice carried across the beach. 'Leave those stones, you've got enough.'

The boy had gathered a bundle of rope, stones and wood. 'Can I have it like soldiers?' he piped.

'They're not soldiers, they're fingers. Yes, if we go now.'

Jack caught a reflection in the water of wings outspread. The gull he had seen earlier was floating on a thermal. Jack had once had a 'cosy home'.

They're not soldiers, they're fingers.

He leant on the railing overlooking the river. The road would flood in twenty-three minutes. The woman and her little boy hadn't passed him; he would have seen them. They must have seen the tide coming in, but even so he should have warned them. There was no one on the pavements; no car was driving away. Even the gull had flown away.

The boy and his mummy were the streaks of grey in the darkening sky, the snatches of light on the water. Jack understood why they left no footprints in the mud.

A glow lit up the wool weave of his coat.

'Hey!' He was hearty: Stella didn't believe in ghosts.

'My mum has faxed Jackie, she'll be back tomorrow evening. I'm to clean the spare bedroom and change the sheets. We know what that means.'

'Do we?'

'She's met a man!' Stella's cry was like the gull's.

'What did the fax say?'

'What I said about the sheets.'

'So she mightn't have met a man. If she has, is that such a—'

'My mum is a bad judge of men,' Stella huffed down the line.

'Not so bad. She chose Terry.'

'She walked out on him!'

'It could be the friend she's been staying with.' He wouldn't mention Stella's own shaky judgement of men. She didn't rush headlong into relationships, she made her mistakes after much consideration.

'It's not.' Stella was trenchant.

'She's asked you to make up the bed in your room, not her own bed. That sounds like a friend.'

'Mum would never share her bedroom.' Stella was arch. 'I'm to collect her – *them* – from the airport. I can't meet you, I have to get over to her flat now.'

'That's a good sign.'

'What is?'

'She wants you to meet this person, instead of springing him or her on you.'

'She *is* springing him on me.'

Above the brewery, the tower was a palpable presence.

'Shall I go with you?' Stella kept his ghosts at bay.

'Thanks, but no need. I've started putting together a plan of action. We need to know Frost's friends, his likes and dislikes, his routines. I'll send it. I've tried to describe the man I saw at the station. Meanwhile Frost's wife is our prime suspect and no, I haven't changed my mind, we'll find another way to talk to her.' She rang off.

Jack knew that Stella's objection to the man – if the mystery guest was a man – would be out of concern for Suzie. He suspected that were he in Stella's shoes, he would be concerned at having a stranger taking over his bedroom. He would mind his mother calling his bedroom 'spare'; it would make him feel as though he didn't exist. He hoped that if Suzie Darnell had met a man, he would like him.

Ghosts. Spare bedrooms. Hot toast and honey. The falling away of old structures. The revelation of the true self. *A cosy home.* His home. Jack recognized the signs. In the light of the lamp-post he saw he had an email. It was from– *info@palmyra-tower.co.uk* and headed without apparent irony: –

Your tower awaits you.

Twenty-Two

October 1987

The carriage clock in the sitting room struck two.

'I have to go out.' His mother was rinsing a mug under the tap.

'Where?' He had begun to hope she was staying in the house with him. He could tell her what she planned to do, but that would make it true and it wasn't true.

'Shopping.' She put the mug on the draining rack. It fell on to its side, but she didn't notice. 'For apple crumble, your favourite!'

He wanted to say he hated apples, but he couldn't lie to her. Her wedding ring – her real ring – was on the shelf behind the taps.

'You'll lose your ring if you leave it there,' he said instead.

'If I leave it there, it won't get lost.' She tipped water out of the washing-up bowl.

'I'll "forage" for apples.' He was suddenly happy. She really was going shopping.

'You've got homework.'

'I haven't got homework, I just have to write what I did at the weekend.'

'That's homework.' She still had her back to him. 'Simon, if you want to be helpful, go and get your sister.' She snapped off her rubber gloves.

'Is she going too?' That made no sense: his sister was too little. 'She can't "hunt and gather".' He had a thought. 'The weekend hasn't happened yet.' Justin would like that argument.

'Now!'

His sister was sitting on the sitting-room floor, walled in by big coloured bricks.

'You're going shopping, Beeswax!' His name for her because with her blonde pigtails and stripy jumper she resembled a bumblebee. It didn't occur to Simon to take out on her his resentment that she was going when he wasn't allowed. He made the expedition to Marks and Spencer's sound as exciting as he actually thought it was.

One by one he lifted away the bricks, sorry to dismantle her construction, then reached down and hauled her up. Staggering, he nearly dropped her. This highly entertained her and she let out a raucous chortle.

In the hall he cajoled her into her anorak and then fixed her into her buggy. He fetched plastic bags from the cupboard with the vacuum cleaner and jammed them into the buggy's carrier. When she craned around to watch him, he did a monster face and made a scary noise. She chortled again.

'Sah. Sah!' Her attempt at his name. She could say words like Mama, mat, bottle.

Heartened by her delight in him, Simon kissed her on the forehead. She smelled of talc and shampoo.

'Bees, your job is to spy and report back to me, OK?' he whispered.

If his mother thought she could keep secrets, she was wrong. When his sister said 'mat', she didn't mean the thing you wipe your feet on. She hadn't got to grips with 'n', she was trying to pronounce 'Nat'. Mr Wilson's name was Nat. The boys at Marchant Manor spelled it 'Gnat' and called him a stick insect behind his back. Simon didn't call him this because he had thought Mr Wilson was his friend. His mother wasn't going shopping, she was meeting Mr Wilson.

'I'm off, Simmy.' She used her name for him and fluffed his hair and, pleased, he considered he might be wrong about Mr Wilson and it was shopping after all. She took her coat from the hooks and opened the front door.

He scrunched up his nose. 'You smell funny.'

'Don't be horrid, darling, it's perfume as you well know. Start your diary. We've had most of today, haven't we, and when you've written it, read it to Dad.'

Today my mummy went away with Mr Gnat Wilson the Stick Insect. The Captain said she was a prosit… a pros—

His sister was tootling like a train, their sign; he shot her a smile and choo-choo sounds of an engine.

'I could write about the shopping.' Simon looked down. Her shoes were pointy and shiny with spiky heels. He had never seen them before.

'Sah. Sah!'

The buggy clunked over the brass threshold and the front door shut. His mother had left the scarf he had bought her with his pocket money on the hook. *Pocket money.*

Simon rushed upstairs and into his bedroom. He wrenched off the lid of his money tin. Inside were seven fifty-pence pieces. He dropped them into a pocket in his trousers.

He pulled on his mac and ran out of the house. Outside he saw her green Citroën 2CV. His mother had abandoned her pretence of shopping at the gate.

The water tower blocked out the sun. Simon waited until his mother appeared on the other side of the subway and then ran down the ramp, through the tunnel and up the other side. Chiswick Lane was a problem, a straight road with the park on one side and houses on the other so that there was nowhere to hide. Luckily she never looked behind.

By the time he got to the radio repair shop at the top of Chiswick Lane, she was metres from him on Chiswick High Road, walking fast.

He fell into pace with a woman holding hands with two girls, younger than him. If she glanced back, she would assume he belonged in their family.

The family peeled away, leaving him exposed. His surveillance skills were unnecessary: she didn't look anywhere but where she was going. He could have walked alongside her and she wouldn't have seen him.

They were nearing Marks and Spencer's – she might after all be shopping; she didn't need much so that was why she didn't want him to come. It was why she had left the car.

He dashed across the zebra crossing without waiting for the traffic to stop. A blaring horn, a slant of red as a bus missed him by centimetres. Someone shouted.

He hurried after her under the bridge, now so close he could hear the rattle of the buggy wheels. Outside Turnham Green station, he used a newspaper vendor as a shield. She was at the gateway to the platform when he entered the station. He asked for a return to Upminster, the end of the line; he could go either way with it if she was going to Richmond or Ealing Broadway. He had no idea of the cost of a train fare, so he pushed all of his fifty pences under the glass.

He shovelled up change into his bad hand and went up the stairs. There was a train in the station; he got on as the doors were closing.

Simon grabbed a central pole and looked up the carriage. She might not be on the train. He tried to see if she was on the platform, but the train was already out on the open tracks. She might have gone the other way. He was sick with himself for his stupidity.

He made his way up the aisle to the end, grabbing at poles, and peered through the glass doors. She was standing up, wheeling the buggy back and forth as if to lull his sister to sleep, but she was carrying her – the buggy was empty. As Simon noticed this, his sister looked at him and put out a hand, fingers splayed as if to catch him. He retreated and trod on something.

'Watch it!' A man in jeans, his woolly jumper tucked in, legs sticking out in the gangway, glared at him.

'Sorry.'

The jumper was striped, but red and gold, not yellow and black like his sister's.

'What you staring at?' the man said.

'Sorry.' Simon hugged a pole and risked another look through the carriages. His sister was chattering to his mother, she would be telling her she had seen him. 'Sah, Sah!' He hoped his mum wouldn't believe her.

At Stamford Brook station, his mother turned the buggy around and backed off the train. A man helped her lift the buggy out on to the platform. Simon jumped down and saw instantly that his sister was looking for him. His mother glanced in Simon's direction. He didn't have time to move, but she was looking right through him as if he was invisible.

He waited until she disappeared down the staircase, then chased after her, holding his trouser pocket to stop the change jangling. Outside the entrance on Goldhawk Road, she pushed the buggy over to one side and stopped. It was precisely three o'clock. All of sudden he understood what was happening. He had caught only a fragment of their conversation at the tower, but he knew his mother did things by the clock – in that she was like his father. She was leaving home with Mr Wilson. Properly leaving, not going shopping or going to the tower. She lived in a coffin and now she was escaping. Why hadn't she asked him to come with her? Simon pulled on his half-finger. Why was she taking his sister? She was meeting Mr Wilson on the dot of three. She was on time.

His head filled with questions, the boy drifted out of the ticket hall into plain sight of his mother. She had her back to him and was looking up and down Goldhawk Road, her handbag hanging from her shoulder, the flap open.

Simon realized he was exposed and shrank back behind a closed newspaper stand. The headline on the vendor's box read *Lester Piggott Jailed*. He didn't know what to do. Justin would know. He saw that one of his sister's arms had flopped over the side of the buggy. She had fallen asleep. He wanted to lift it up and lay it on her lap. *There, there, Beeswax, sleep tight and make lots of honey*. Their private joke.

The minute hand on his watch went around five times. He risked leaving his post and wandered back into the station. One strategy was to tell his dad everything and let him deal with it. He dealt with disturbed people all the time. He could 'section' Gnat Wilson, a thing his father did that Simon assumed meant cutting people up into pieces.

Simon looked at the station clock. It was a quarter past three. Mr Wilson was fifteen minutes late.

The man with the jeans and the stripy jumper from his train was running towards him from the road. Fleetingly Simon supposed he had got off at the wrong station. He tried to move out of the man's way, but was stopped by the photo booth. Stepping away from it, he lost his balance and his leg slid out from under him; he tried to get his balance and felt a boot catch his calf. There was a thump. Mr Wilson! He grabbed at the man and kicked at his leg.

It wasn't Mr Wilson. It was the man from the train. Simon was shoved aside by a man in station uniform who grabbed the man and pushed one of his arms behind his back.

Something flew across the ground. Instinctively Simon caught it. Black leather with a flap that was open. It was his mum's handbag.

'Police!'

'Thief!'

'Get him.'

Stamford Brook station teemed with people: passers-by, station staff, passengers from an Upminster train pulling out of the station. There was the whoop-whoop of a siren and a Ford Focus with chequered strips and flashing lights tore up to the zebra crossing. Two police officers pushed through the gathering crowd. It took a few moments for someone to see a small boy in grey school trousers and a jumper with a tear in the sleeve, sitting slumped against the photo booth clutching a woman's handbag. A few more moments for the people who dragged him to his feet to understand that he wasn't the accomplice of the culprit but the son of the woman whose bag had been snatched.

Simon was taken outside to where his mother was talking to a woman police officer. His sister reached up a hand and he squeezed it.

'You and me against the world, Beewax,' he whispered to her. 'I'll protect you. Always.'

'Bzzzzz!' she replied confidentially.

'Kid's a hero,' a man in London Transport uniform told the police officer. 'Tackled the guy – piled in there. Fearless. That boy loves his mum!'

Simon didn't take his eyes off his mother. Unblinking he stared, and when she looked away he spoke quietly so that no one else would hear: 'Since he's not come, we can go hunting and gathering.'

Twenty-Three

Wednesday, 23 October 2013

Stella waited while Stanley sniffed at a lamp-post. She swapped hands on the lead as he pottered around the post to prevent him becoming wrapped around it. They were outside the house on Primula Street in Hammersmith where her dad had been born and lived until he moved with Suzie to Rose Gardens North. Terry had swapped the hum of the A40 for the Great West Road. Stella had a photograph, presumably taken by Suzie, of Terry leaning in the doorway, with her nana and herself, aged four, on the doorstep of the house she was outside now.

Terry's father had died of a heart attack when he was fifteen.

'I was at school, I rushed out of the biology lab, dodged across roads, I didn't care. I stood on the path outside our house and yelled, "Not my dad! Not my dad!"'

When Terry himself had died of a heart attack, Stella had resented the disruption to her work.

Not my dad!

The semi-detached red-brick house looked smaller than she remembered. A wheelchair ramp had replaced the step. Her nana would disapprove of the double mattress slumped against the wall and the television dumped on balding turf. Gone were the marigold borders and window boxes in the photograph. A plastic urn, faded and cracked, flourished with dandelions by the ramp.

Her nana's ashes were scattered at Golders Green Crematorium. Terry used to visit the memorial book on the anniversary of her death. Terry was cremated at Mortlake. It hadn't occurred to Stella to put an entry in the memorial book for him. Suzie hadn't let

Terry's death get in the way of expressing her dissatisfactions about him. Recently, Stella realized, her mum had been quieter on the subject. She had someone else on her mind. *Dale Heffernan.*

Her phone was ringing. Jackie.

'William Frost wants to get hold of Jack.'

'Did he say why?'

'No. You OK with working with him?' They hadn't yet spoken about Jackie referring the case.

'Yes, although I'm not sure we can help,' Stella said. She saw a face at the upstairs window and for a second assumed it was her nana. 'He said he knew you when he was a boy.'

'Hardly. William's brother Rick used to play with our neighbours' kids. We'd just moved in, all our cash was soaked up by the mortgage, we were on rations, no sofa or table. There were two children next door, a sweet boy as thin as a rail and his cute sister, think her name was Lulu, something like that. Their parents' marriage was on the rocks, the dad was a psychiatrist with a fancy car, chap never passed up a chance to be sarcastic about his wife – talk about airing dirty linen! The boy was playing substitute husband, protective little mite. I made Graham promise that those parents wouldn't be us one day. I think we've succeeded! The boy – or man – moved out years ago, he rented the house out and is only selling it now. We're holding our breath as to who buys it. Good neighbours are gold.'

Stella drifted along the street, content to listen to Jackie's chat about her home life.

'Anyway, William got Jack's answer machine. I said to call you. I'm guessing that with Jack's new venture, he can't spare the time.'

'He's not driving every day.' Stella assumed Jackie meant the day shifts Jack was doing for a colleague whose partner was unwell.

'I'm thinking of his move. It's today, isn't it? He's already in a state about that owl! I told him, "Take it with you." He won't, he said it's like taking the fireplace or half the garden. She – he says it's a "she" – belongs with the house. Jack gets attached to things. I said to Graham, "That owl is a constant in his life. The lad's not got many, poor lamb!"'

'Not many owls?'

'Things, people, places. A legacy of losing his mother young means that he's slow to trust others, you know that. I do hope this is a good decision. He could get lonely up there.'

Jack hadn't said he was moving. His working for Stella wasn't a pass to his private life, but Stella had supposed they were friends. Jack didn't have a pet, certainly not an owl. He wasn't interested in her dog, not that Stanley was her dog.

Jack was leaving Clean Slate.

A man was walking towards her. Stella moved to let him pass. He moved too.

'There you are!' William Frost was barring her way.

'Jackie, I'll have to go.' She rounded on him. 'How come you knew I was here?'

'My brother designed this app, it shows me where any of my contacts are at any time. I'm testing it for him.' He shrugged. 'I *was* testing it. I found you in minutes.'

'What do you want?' Stella did not like being 'found'.

'I tried Jack. What a dark horse he is!' He seemed oblivious to her annoyance.

'He's moving house,' Stella retorted. She didn't have Jack's new address. Unwilling to admit that he hadn't told her what it was, she hadn't asked Jackie for it.

'You and me then!' Frost said. 'Let me buy you lunch.'

The pub was crammed with sleekly dressed lunchtime office workers. Bulky in her wellingtons and anorak with a small poodle on her shoulder – in case he trod mud into the carpet – and wind-tossed hair, Stella felt out of kilter. She went for cheesy chips and a ginger beer and, while William threaded his way through the crowd to order food and drink from the bar, she retreated to a table at the back. It was next to a cleaning cupboard and immediately the whiff of polish calmed her. She gave the dog water in his collapsible bowl. He drank greedily and then flopped against her leg, his sodden muzzle soaking her trousers. Once this would have horrified her, now she barely noticed. She flipped to a clean page in her Filofax, clicked on her Clean Slate ballpoint and wrote today's date at the top, underscoring it for good measure. Glancing up, she caught sight of Jack by the door. Dropping her pen, she half rose.

'Food's on its way.' William slid into the seat opposite and handed her a frosted tumbler of ginger beer. 'This is nice!' He clinked a large glass of red wine against hers. 'Here's how!'

'Cheers.' Stella sat down and drank her ginger beer. She gave a spluttering cough – she had forgotten she hated fizzy drinks. Bubbles bursting in her gullet, she looked for Jack, but couldn't see him.

'Two seconds.' She got up and, unleashing the dog from the table leg, pushed through the throng to the door. The pub faced Wormwood Scrubs common, an expanse of green. There was no one there. No sign of Jack. She was about to text him, but saw she had no signal. Reluctantly – she could do with Jack with her – Stella returned to the table.

'Let's start with your brother.' She spoke with a confidence she didn't feel. Jack was moving; perhaps he'd come into the pub to get a sandwich.

'As I said, it's his wife you should be talking to.' William raised his glass as if in another toast. 'Being his brother didn't mean we were close.'

'It's a start.' Not having a brother, Stella couldn't argue, but she found his unwillingness odd. Why had he gone to such trouble to find her? 'Let's start with his likes and dislikes.'

'How will this help find his killer?'

Stella tapped her pen on her lips. She didn't know how it would help or why she'd asked. She glanced at her phone, hoping, despite the lack of signal, that Jack had texted. 'If this is a pre-meditated murder, his personality and his routines might have contributed to his death. Obviously if it was a random killing, it won't help at all.' Faintly pleased with herself, Stella wrote 'Likes' and 'Dislikes' divided by a line.

'Liked the army, disliked me, liked spying on people, disliked heights.' William gave a satisfied huff as if giving the correct answer in a pub quiz and sat back for a young man to put a plate heaped with a slab of steak and a mountain of chips in front of him.

Stella's chips came on a large platter nestling beside a jungle of salad that was way beyond a garnish.

'What was he like as a boy?' Stella untangled a chip from threads of molten cheese.

'I was three years older, a big age gap when you're small.' William drained his glass. 'We didn't share friends.' He was devouring his steak with the urgency of someone refuelling before whizzing off to do something dangerous and pointless, a quality Stella grudgingly admired.

'Who were his friends?' she asked.

'That's overstating it. He didn't have friends as such; he had a gang who did what he told them. They had a hideout in a grave-yard near our house.' Frost looked around him as if expecting to see Tallulah Frost in the pub. Stella looked too, still hoping to see Jack. It couldn't have been Jack, she decided.

'Rick was the sort of boy who pulls legs off spiders. One of them ended up marrying him.' William dropped his voice as if they might be overheard.

'One of the children in his gang?' He couldn't mean spiders.

'Total surprise. Rick wasn't interested in relationships, gay or straight, he was in love with the army. Can't say there was much love lost between them.' He frowned. 'And hey, the army don't want soldiers chewing on Gaviscon double action before going into battle!' He tossed his balled napkin on to his empty plate, the edges soaked red with bloodied juices. 'Me, they'd have had like a shot, as it were!'

Stella could imagine William Frost leading a platoon in the army, striding forth without hesitation. She doubted he suffered from indigestion.

'He designed that tracking app. If he didn't know anyone, why did he care where anyone was?'

'I didn't say he knew no one, just that he didn't have friends. No point in tracking someone you trust.'

'Can anyone use that app?' Stella examined her fingers, an idea forming.

'Give me a name and bingo!' He snatched up his phone. 'The one drawback is that the person can tell you're "watching". A pair of eyes pops up at the top of their screen. You have to hope they don't notice – and few people would. Rick would have sorted that if he'd not—'

'In general' – Stella waved her hand – 'does it keep a history of people you've followed? If we knew your brother's movements, we might find out who he thought was a threat.'

'The software must be at his house.' His reply was pointed.

Stella got the hint. She was not dressing up as a cleaner. Their plates had been taken away without her noticing. She berated herself; she was too easily distracted to be a detective.

Jack had been doing day shifts on the Underground – for a friend, he'd said. She had thought that, apart from herself and Jackie, he had no friends. She didn't count Lucille May, the flighty journalist they had consulted for the Blue Folder case who, like lots of older women, had a soft spot for Jack.

'Do you want a coffee?' William was on his feet. Again he glanced about him.

'White no sugar, thanks.' So far in this interview she had netted nothing. They had said their prime suspect was Rick Frost's wife. Perhaps Jack's idea that William Frost had executed the perfect murder and couldn't resist boasting was correct. He seemed intent on saying how he was better than his brother and something was making him jumpy. She felt a wave of unease and was grateful to be in a packed pub and, although he was fast asleep at her feet, to have the dog with her.

While he was at the bar Stella scribbled down a list of questions. Jack would angle them to encourage William to talk laterally, to ramble on and give himself away. Stella wanted to cut to the chase and instil shock value. *Did you murder your brother?* If Frost could commit a perfect murder, he would lie as convincingly. She needed Jack to scrutinize body language while she asked the questions. Jack was on her mind; that was why she thought she had seen him. Where was he moving to?

William had left his phone on the table. Stella could see him at the bar giving their order to a woman. She snatched up his phone and brought it to life. Nearly passing out that he hadn't protected it with a password, she tossed the handset back on to the table.

The woman was pouring coffee into cups on the counter. Stanley must have sensed something was wrong because he was on his hind legs, front paws on her thigh. 'Ssshh!' she admonished him, although he had made no sound.

William was leaning on the counter in conversation. The woman had stopped what she was doing. Ignoring Stanley, Stella retrieved Frost's phone.

She had no idea what the app was called and swiped screens back and forth looking for it. She found an icon of a magnifying glass. *Stalker Boy*. She shivered and glanced up; the woman was putting saucers under the cups. The dawdling would be annoying in another circumstance, but now every second counted. Stella willed Frost to keep up the banter as her fingers, damp with perspiration, dabbed on the icon and opened the software.

It worked intuitively, like Google Maps. She keyed in Jack's number and pressed a button unreassuringly labelled *Seek and destroy*. An explosion motif spread across the picture to the sound of glass shattering. It must have reverberated around the pub and she looked to see if William had heard, but he was still chatting. The phone emitted the sound of footsteps, slow and measured, then louder and faster. *Come on!* She cursed Rick Frost's sense of humour – or drama. William was holding the cups; he was moving away from the bar, still talking.

A crosshair symbol targeted *Chiswick Lane South*. Stella grabbed the handset and guided the cursor to it. The *Seek and destroy* legend changed to *Shoot*. She 'fired'; the image did a kaleidoscope swirl and up came a shot of a concrete cooling tower. So much for the accuracy of the app. She had no time to check that she had put in the right telephone number because William was coming across the carpet towards her. She dropped the phone; it slid over the table and landed on William's chair.

'Sorry about that, the barmaid was telling me her life story.' William put the cups down and noticed his phone. The backlight was on. Stella nearly fainted as he handed her a coffee. Stella took it, her hand trembling.

'My mother's arriving home tonight.' She dared not look at him. Taking a sugar sachet from a bowl on the table, she ripped it open with her teeth.

'My app will tell you if she's in flight this time!' William picked up his phone, seemingly unsurprised that it was open, the icons ready. Stella went ice cold. 'What's her flight number?'

Her mouth dry, Stella read it from her diary, the numbers and letters swimming before her eyes. Frost was playing her; he was letting her know he had seen her with his phone.

He had said it stored previous searches. Stella hadn't erased her search. She went into a flop sweat and it was all she could do not to fling her coffee at the phone.

Seek and destroy!

'Last sighting was at Sydney Airport. She'll have turned her phone off. I think you can be confident she's coming this time!' He laid the phone down in front of her as if it were a gun.

'Thanks.' Something was escaping from the folder in her Filofax. It was the sheet of pictures from the photo booth at Stamford Brook station. On an impulse she pulled it out and laid it on the table.

'Do you recognize the person in this picture? I realize it may be difficult.'

She had forgotten to tell Jack about the pictures. Looking at them now, even upside down, Stella was surprised to see the back of the man's head bore a resemblance to Jack. Was that what he was doing when she was talking to the man on the platform? It was horribly likely.

'Is this a joke?' Frost's friendly manner had evaporated.

'It's a bit of a punt. I found it where your brother died.' She didn't say where. Terry would say, 'Keep something back.'

'He's facing the wrong way. How could I?' William pushed the sheet back to Stella and pocketed his phone.

'Did you enjoy your brother's company?' *What did you enjoy about your brother's company?* might elicit more. She was sickened. By searching for Jack on *Stalker Boy* she had revealed to William – and to herself – that she didn't trust Jack. She had exposed them.

'Not one bit.' William's eyes were like pebbles.

Twenty-Four

Wednesday, 23 October 2013

Jack closed the door and the quiet was instant and profound.

His desk and chair were bathed in sharp sunshine; a rectangle of light shone on his bed. Through the north-facing window he could see only sky. It was so high up, nothing interrupted the view. The kelim from his parents' hall lay beside the bed. He had never noticed that it matched the bedspread; his parents had probably bought them at the same time. There was so much he didn't know. His cupboard was set between the flat door and the north window.

The removers not only worked to a short lead time – it was a mere two days since he had answered the advert – they had had an acute sense of space – it was a prerequisite for transporting furniture in confined areas – but this was different, they had put everything where he would have put it himself. Someone had a mind like his own.

He crossed to the south-west window. From there he could see all of Chiswick Eyot. He could also just see his meandering path into the centre of the eyot, but was relieved that his garden was hidden. He could follow the Thames in both directions: towards Barnes and past Hammersmith Bridge.

The window sill was the thickness of the tower wall, over a foot in depth. Jack settled into the alcove. As the leaflet said, the views were detailed.

He hadn't visited the tower before signing a six-month lease with Palmyra Associates. As well as being able to move in so quickly, Jack had been astonished to get a reply within the hour accepting his request. He had offered references, Stella as his employer and Lucie May, his journalist friend, for character. The second was foolhardy; Lucie wouldn't know if he was trustworthy and nor would she care. Isabel Ramsay had known him from when he was a baby, but she had been dead two years. The email said references were not necessary. Jack had never rented a property. After his parents died, he inherited their house and when he stayed with Hosts he did so in secret.

The lease had arrived that morning. When he posted back the signed copy to Palmyra Associates, he'd noticed that the PO Box on the 'return' envelope had a West London postcode. Their website was a holding page which, considering Palmyra Associates only operated online, was surprising. But then, he had found the tower through a flier so maybe they didn't need one.

They had forgotten his stuff. Jack leapt off the sill. The removers had not brought his photograph albums, newspaper cuttings, Host notebooks, journals mapping his train journeys: the record of his life. At some stage he would have to put his mother's clothes, paintings and papers into storage. Jackie had sourced him a self-storage unit on the Great West Road. Time enough for that. Stella – who was being tardy in selling her dad's house – would at least understand that.

Stella didn't understand that he believed inanimate objects – like clothes, books, furniture, even his owl door knocker – had feelings. He was in no hurry to pack up his house. He couldn't bear to think of the suitcases, his mother's clothes and pictures locked in a cell with no light or sound, abandoned. Jackie said he would have a key and could visit any time. She had assured him he could rent a unit with an ambient atmosphere, free of damp and insects. It might be rather better than everything remaining in his unlived-in and unheated house, she had carefully suggested. Jackie was the Queen of Tact. If she was here now, she would retrieve all his things with no fuss or bother.

Jack ran around the partition. The table from his playroom and two of the kitchen chairs were under the south-east window. The logical place for these was against the partition, leaving a route to the bathroom. Jack would also have put them by the window so that he could watch. He looked out through the reinforced glass. He could see the detail on the turrets of Hammersmith Bridge; over in Kensington, a cluster of green would be the trees in Holland Park. Far off, the North Downs morphed into a bank of pink-grey clouds like a snowy mountain range. It would be too late to fetch his things tonight.

Jack slid aside a panel and revealed a large space, the quarter of the circle. Were he not upset, he'd be excited by the shower. Tiny nozzles in the ceiling would send out powerful jets of water. In an old water tower, there would be ample pressure.

Jack had chosen the removers recommended by Palmyra Associates because they knew the tower. Few firms would be willing to negotiate the stairways outside, even less the spiral stairs to the flat. Clean Slate offered attic clearance and Stella wouldn't balk at a tower, but he had been keen to do the move alone. Although Stella would have arranged the furniture according to logic rather than spirit, at least his stuff would be here.

Jack plodded back to the main living area and sat on the end of the bed, nursing an ache in his chest. It was a kind of homesickness, although he had only briefly known a home to be sick for when he was very little. The door to his cupboard was ajar so he got up to shut it.

Every shelf was full. Cardboard wallets, file boxes, bundles of letters, notebooks in a row, spine out. At the top, exactly where he would have stowed it, was his biscuit tin of particular treasures. Beside the cupboard by the north window to the right of the door was the clay bust of his mother set on its square plinth. How had he missed it?

So quick to panic, he had missed his laptop, his street atlas, his green-glass lawyer's lamp. The removers had stocked the kitchen cupboards with his pans and the hot milk mug Stella had given him. In a drawer they had stowed his parents' cutlery. On a shelf above they had arranged the blue enamel tins labelled 'Tea', 'Coffee' and 'Sugar' that Isabel Ramsay's daughter had given him after the house clearance. They had left a litre of fresh milk in the fridge, semi-skimmed as he liked it, and thought to leave out his pot of organic runny honey beside the cooking knives.

Jack stifled any disquiet that strangers had handled his personal things and read his mind and set about heating some milk. After years of searching he had found a home.

He sat in the kitchen, sipped his milk and watched a man walking his dog along the towpath on the south side of the river. On Hammersmith Broadway, cars moved with more order than was perceptible at ground level. Before him was the city in miniature; he was floating above London as if on a magic carpet.

His elbow jogged a leather case tucked into the corner of the sill. It wasn't his. He prised open the lid and inside found the most beautiful, elegant pair of binoculars he had ever seen. Chrome and black, substantial but not heavy, with a soft leather strap. He had planned to buy a pair, but it seemed that they came with the tower. Palmyra Associates had thought of everything. He put the strap around his neck and raised the binoculars.

Jack trained the glasses on the river, inching it over the eyot, along the mall to the Ram pub. Tilting the sights a fraction to the right, he hovered at the bottom of the Bell Steps. In the dwindling light, Hammersmith Bridge was a watercolour sketch, lights reflected in the water. Rush hour had started: headlights and brake lights on the Great West Road, the Hogarth roundabout and the flyover were broad sweeps of a paintbrush, red and white streaks. Holding the binoculars steady, Jack surveyed London. He saw without being seen. He had found his panopticon.

He swung back to the bridge and focused on a double-decker bus creeping south. On the top deck, two women sat on the front seat. One was laughing as she glanced at her reflection in the window and adjusted her hair. Her companion faced ahead. Behind them, a lad in his teens was wearing the neutral stare of disinterest typical of passengers travelling alone. Headphones on, he chewed gum mechanically. Jack felt the engine's vibration and heard the laughter and the tinkly chatter of music escaping from the headphones as if he were there too.

Jack's scrutiny was diverted to the footpath on the bridge. There was someone leaning on the railing. He craned forward, thinking that if it was someone contemplating suicide, there was nothing that he could do to prevent them. He could call the police, but they wouldn't get there in time.

The man was wearing a baseball cap pulled low over his brow. Abruptly the man stepped back from the balustrade and, looking towards the tower, he shifted his cap as if in greeting. Jack was in an unlit room a quarter of a mile from him, yet the man was looking at him.

The binoculars hit the table with a crash. Jack tried to apply Stella's logic. Without binoculars he couldn't see the bus, so the man couldn't see him. Stella would say guilt that he was spying had convinced him that the man was looking at him. She wouldn't like him secretly watching people. This was the second time a man had been drawn to his gaze. There had been the man on the bus outside Stamford Brook station the night Rick Frost had died. He too had worn a baseball cap. Plenty of people did.

The binoculars were undamaged, but had dented his table. He looked again at the bridge and adjusted the focus. It was hard to keep a steady sight on a target or track a moving one because with the slightest twitch of the wrist he travelled hundreds of metres. The bus had gone. Jack felt no guilt that he was watching unseen. The tower gave him 360-degree surveillance.

Jack returned the binoculars to their case, relishing the musky scent of the leather. It was dark, so he felt his way around the partition to the main room and found the light switch. A gentle glow revealed dips and grooves in the concrete wall.

Under his desk he spotted four blue lights: a Wi-Fi router. There had been no mention of Wi-Fi connection in the leaflet or the contract, and Jack had been content to do without it.

He fired up his laptop and was presented with a choice of two routers. This high he hadn't expected to pick up other connections. 'CBruno'. Unwise of the owner to use their name; it gave easy advantage to True Hosts, murderers or would-be murderers who stopped at nothing to catch their prey. His own router identifier was a mix of letters and numerals. Jack typed in his password and seconds later saw he had an email.

It welcomed him to the tower. They had sent a workaday list of instructions: where to find the fuse box, spare light bulbs and window locks, how to work the boiler and the thermostat and when it was bin day. It wished him well in his new home and was signed 'on behalf of Palmyra Associates'. The company might be large, or perhaps, given the lack of website, was small posing as large. Jack didn't care. Typing a 'thank you', he reflected that the tower was perfect and he had the perfect landlord.

He was preparing for bed when he heard a glug from the sink in the kitchen as if liquid was being poured down it. He tiptoed to the doorway. Of course there was no one there: it was one of the sounds of his new home.

His phone was glowing.

Need to see you. Where are you? Stella D.

Unlike Stella to write so late and to put the 'D'. There was only one Stella.

He texted the address of his tower and went to the kitchen. Palmyra Associates had left him a packet of Brooke Bond tea, Stella's favourite.

Twenty-Five

Stella found a space in the short-stay car park by a column marked '3D'. Jack would like that. She regretted refusing his offer to come with her to the airport; why had she thought she should meet Suzie's new man on her own? She told herself that Stanley, a good judge of character, would sniff out this Dale bloke. With the dog trotting at her heel, she crossed to the lift lobby.

'Excuse me.' A stocky man in a hi-vis jacket cut her off at the lift. 'No dogs allowed in the airport.'

'I wasn't thinking.' Rattled by William Frost, Stella had completely forgotten to leave Stanley with Jackie. She gave a tight smile and, 'tssking' at Stanley as if he was there without permission, she returned to the van and, with the dog on her lap, paws resting on the steering wheel, texted Suzie: *In car park with Stanley. 3D.*

The airport's website told her the plane had landed half an hour ago. Stella told herself that Jackie had a point; it would be good for Suzie to have someone special. Maybe she'd stop complaining about Terry as if he were still alive.

She turned her attention to the case. They had three suspects, not counting anyone Rick Frost may have exposed through his surveillance techniques. Tallulah Frost, William Frost himself and thirdly whoever had been at the station when Frost died. Being stringent she should include the man she had met when she and Jack were there. Although there was no reason to suspect him. He might have been doing exactly what she had assumed he was doing, inspecting the line. She dubbed him the inspector. Finally William himself. He had been strangely unwilling to help since bringing them the case and at lunch had seemed oddly nervy. He wasn't all he seemed. Stella put aside her antipathy towards him for using his brother's app to find her and returned to the question about Frost. Why commit murder, disguise it as suicide – and then persuade them it *was* murder? Jack thought it was warped vanity, Frost wanting credit for his cleverness. It was less gratifying to clean houses for sale after a death with no client to appreciate dazzling surfaces and germ-free crevices. The wife stood to gain the most by Rick Frost's death even if his specific policy didn't pay up for a suicide. They needed to meet Mrs Frost and see the house she had shared with her husband. Try as she might, Stella could think of no honest way to do this.

Stanley scrambled off her lap on to the steering wheel. He stood on the horn; his furious barking was drowned out by its deafening blare.

Stella saw Suzie weaving between the vehicles towards her, gesticulating with great sweeps of her arm. She wore her old macintosh, with the red scarf Jackie had given her for Christmas wound around her neck. Nothing indicated she had returned from an Australian summer – she didn't even have a sun tan. Stella got out of the van. Stanley was straining towards her mum, choking with the effort.

Her mum wasn't beckoning to her. At the end of a line of concrete supports (3A, 3B, 3C), a man was wrestling with a wayward trolley, mountainous with luggage. As if tacking a sailing boat, he leant out and slewed the trolley full circle. He pushed it into a pool of bleak lamplight.

It was Terry.

Suzanne Darnell took the man's hand and, grabbing Stella's, she pushed them together. 'Stella, Dale. Dale, Stella!'

Twenty-Six

October 1987

Before he went into the cage, Simon checked the alley behind him. There was no one. On his way through the cemetery he had hatched a plan. He would form his own unit, and the tower would be HQ. He wasn't scared. He would recruit Justin and Nicky. His little sister could be the mascot. He would let Justin be captain. The old Captain would be the enemy. After what happened the last time they were in the tower, Simon considered the Captain as good as dead.

It was a week since Simon's picture had been in the newspaper, together with an article about the brave little boy who had saved his mother from a mugger. Nicky had been impressed, although she hadn't said anything at their last meeting back in the old HQ. The Captain hadn't said anything either.

Simon forced himself on to the semi-circular walkway at the top of the staircase. He had forgotten how high it was; the ground far below tugged at him, urging him to leap – it was like walking the plank. The wind was much stronger up here; it, too, goaded him. He held on to the guard rail tightly, his woolly gloves slipping on the metal. Justin warned against leaving fingerprints. Not true – Justin had said, leave no trace. With no suspicion, there would be no reason to look for fingerprints. Simon heard the other boy's voice as if he was beside him now. Simon didn't trust himself to leave no trace. He let go of the guard rail and, hands and back flat to the concrete, shuffled to the door and crept inside the tower.

He swept his torch beam around. Its light bounced off the tri-angular metal stairs. This time, regardless of safety, Simon shut the tower door. He listened: Justin advised entrance to a property only after all sounds had been identified. The rumble of traffic and the harsh wind couldn't penetrate the thick walls. Simon believed he was alone. The door to the chamber where he had hidden with the Captain was set into a recess behind the staircase. It was closed.

His torch picked out something on the floor. Two black leather gloves. Simon's gloves had been knitted by Mrs Henderson to match his sister's mittens, but these gloves were for grown-ups. He didn't need to read the name in the lining. He guessed that the Captain had dropped his gloves when he'd run away and left Simon to die. He had complained they had been stolen; he would be too scared to come back for them.

Simon put them into his coat. When he placed a foot on the spiral staircase, he wanted to poo and had to clench his bottom until the cramps subsided. His heart smashing against his ribs, he began to climb.

This time the door was shut. He crept over the landing and put his ear to the metal. His bowels stirred again. Silence wasn't good, Justin said, better to hear the enemy and locate them. He craned over the rail; the steps wound off into the dark. No one knew he was in the tower. He could go. He went down four steps, spiralling this way meant he was facing the door, his nose at floor level. He ran up the stairs again and before he could change his mind, twisted on the ring handle. The door opened with a groan.

The boy was hit by a terrible stench of lavatories, potties and nappies, and thought that after all he had messed his pants. He felt himself. No, his trousers were dry. He took a step inside.

Dark streaks, dried and crusted, were smeared on the concrete floor. Simon went further into the room and saw that, after all, he wasn't alone.

Twenty-Seven

A figure was on the metal walkway, tall against the London skyline. Fleetingly it occurred to Jack that, with no security camera, he could have no idea who was outside until he opened the door.

'He's my brother!' The voice was muffled within her hood; but for the dog glaring malevolently at him from her shoulder, Jack wouldn't have known it was Stella.

'Who is?'

'Dale Heffernan is not my Mum's new man, he's my brother.'

'Sugar?' He pulled forward one of Mrs Ramsay's blue enamel tins and lifted the lid. It was empty. They were in the kitchen. Stella sat with her back to the south-east window. The binoculars were behind her on the window ledge. Jack didn't know why he'd rather she didn't notice them.

'I don't take sugar.' He knew that.

He sloshed milk into his mug. The carton was light; he would need to buy more. Shopping involved a long descent, then a climb back up – a tiny price for living in a panopticon.

'Are you sure?' He handed Stella a mug of milky tea. 'Suzie had two relationships with Terry? Like Elizabeth Taylor and Richard Burton.'

'Yes.' Stella smiled wryly as she took the tea. At her feet Stanley emitted a guttural growl. Jack had forgotten about the protective force field the dog erected around his mistress. Stella didn't need protecting, and if she did, an animal the size of a tea towel couldn't do it. He led her through to the main room. Indicating she have the chair by his desk, he retreated to his bed a distance from the dog.

'They went out with each other for six months and split up. Eighteen months later Mum went back to him. She calls Terry her "wrong turning". Seems she took it twice.'

'That would put her back where she started.' Jack traced the journey in the air with a finger. 'Actually, no, if you turn right instead of left, then you would—'

'Jack! It's complicated enough.' Stella was still in her anorak, despite the effective heating. Jack hadn't worked out how to turn it off. 'Her parents didn't want her to marry a police constable. I never knew my grandparents, but she says they were snobby and interfering. When she found she was having Terry's baby, they made her give him up for adoption. She's regretted it ever since. The way Mum told it tonight, you'd think Terry was the love of her life.' Stella sipped her tea and shot him a look of gratitude: he'd got it right. 'They met the first time when Terry pulled her over one night for speeding in her Mini Traveller on Holland Park Avenue. He said he wouldn't charge her if she went out on a date with him.'

'I told you that.' Jack had found that out during the Blue Folder case. Stella hadn't believed him. Now he felt petty and was relieved that she hadn't heard. She had insisted that her mother had met Terry Darnell, then a spruced-up Mod in two-tone suit and winklepickers, at the Hammersmith Palais. Jack couldn't help himself, 'So they didn't meet while dancing?'

'Yes, the second time around. Terry taught her to do the bossa nova and she claims she never looked back.'

Stanley was sniffing along the wall by the door, pattering back and forth across the floor, his claws tapping on the wooden boards. Jack wished Stella would stick him back on his lead, he didn't trust him.

'Are you sure this Dale is Terry's son?' Nor did he trust Dale Heffernan. He recognized he was disappointed that Suzie hadn't confided in him. Had he known, he could have warned Stella. Except Suzie would have told him in confidence so it would have been another secret to keep from Stella. Better she had not told him.

'Are you listening?' Stella seemed jumpy. She clasped her mug of tea as if to warm herself, although she must be sweltering. 'Yes, I *am* sure!'

'I was thinking, Suzie can be impressionable. You hear stories of parents reunited with lost children and it turns out it's not them. People believe what they want to.'

'He's the spitting image of Terry, he must be his son,' Stella mused into her mug.

Jack didn't know how to help her. 'Shall we ring Jackie?'

'What for? Dale's not a client and it's past midnight.' Stella looked up abruptly. 'How come you've moved?' she asked. The words 'without telling me' hung there.

'It was a snap decision.' Stella didn't take action without meticulous planning, backed up by contingency plans. 'It was time for a change.' He couldn't say he was escaping his ghosts or that the tower was perfect for finding True Hosts.

'Are you leaving Clean Slate?' Stella addressed the question to the dog, who was still sniffing about by the door.

Lucie May would call her question self-serving, Jack knew it was as close as Stella could get to asking if they would no longer be friends. He sought to reassure her. 'A change of where I live, not of whom I know.'

Stanley began to bark, the volume increasing with each one.

'Sssh!' Stella put a finger to her lips. 'Good guard dog.'

The barking subsided to rumbling. Jack followed the animal's steely gaze to the door. There could be no one outside; he had made sure he'd shut the door downstairs.

'He doesn't need to guard. We're at the top of a tower.'

'He hears stuff we can't.' Stella looked about her. 'Who owns this place?'

'A company.' Jack didn't know anything about the owners. 'Their email said I am their first tenant. It used to be a water tower. We're in the tank.' He jumped up. 'Would you like a tour?'

Stella signalled for Stanley to 'heel'. Jack didn't want the dog prowling about his new home. The dog was recriminatory: his bark told Jack he should have asked Stella to help him move in; she was at her best when being practical. Yet she wouldn't have arranged everything as perfectly as Palmyra Associates. Stella cleaned houses; she didn't create homes.

The kitchen sink made the glugging noise of earlier. He leapt on an opportunity to get Stella's advice. 'It keeps doing this. Should I call the landlord?'

Stella turned on the tap. With the rush of water, the glugging stopped. Stanley tottered on his hind legs, reaching up, front paws skittering along the edge of the cutlery drawer trying to see. He was like a toddler, constantly wanting to be involved, grouchy if attention wasn't on him. Jack just prevented himself from saying, 'Shoo!'

'It's an air lock. Happens when water is drained from two sinks, or a bath and sink, at the same time. It's caught in the reservoir of one sink and when you drain one, air gets pushed up the pipe of the other one.' Stella visibly cheered up.

'I see.' Jack clasped his hands together. The world was uncertain and mostly he dealt with it – he was unafraid of darkness, literal or in the soul of a True Host – but sometimes nothing but the warm bright glare of Stella's practical attitude would do.

The tour took less than five minutes. Stanley barked when Jack slid aside the partition between the kitchen and the shower room. He was a nervy creature, more like himself than Stella, Jack observed. Stella noted the lack of frosted glass in the window and the toilet right beside it. He reminded her that no one could see in. She appeared to approve of the functional chrome lavatory with water-saving cistern on the criss-cross metal flooring, commenting only, 'You prefer baths.' She was still tetchy. He did like a soak in a bath, to the light of one candle, where he floated free and unfettered. Lucie May said he was trying to return to the womb and she was right. He couldn't explain that to live in a panopticon, he could forgo a bath.

'They can't risk flooding from this height,' he said.

'It's a water tower, a bath is a fraction of what this structure must have supported.' Stella wandered back to the main room, the dog at her heel.

The contract said no dogs or cats; Jack hoped this excluded visiting animals. Stella was inseparable from the dog. He wondered what she would do when she had to hand him back.

As if illustrating this attachment, Stella tipped out her rucksack on to his desk. A collection of dogs' toys and poo bags landed by his laptop. Out of this she extracted a stuffed meerkat in a Father Christmas robe and waved it at the dog, who, back snuffling by the skirting, ignored her.

'Did Terry know about his— this Dale?' Jack wouldn't grant him the status of 'son'. It must be hard for Stella.

'No.' Stella took her empty mug through to the kitchen. He heard the tap run, no glugging sound this time. When she returned, she was carrying the binoculars. She went to the north window and, lifting them, peered out into the blackness. 'If Dad had known, he would have included Dale in his will.' She adjusted the focus like a pro. 'He would have told me.'

Jack knew that Stella's father hadn't made a will, another of Suzie's complaints. *'He thought he was immortal.'* Stella had inherited all of Terry Darnell's estate – a house, no savings – because she was his sole surviving child. Or so Terry had thought.

'This One Under case is tough.' Stella held the binoculars steady.

'I've had an idea about how we might meet his wife.' Jack went with the change of subject. Stella didn't dwell on personal stuff.

'I can see the house of one of my clients from here,' Stella exclaimed. 'These are so powerful I can make out cracks on the pavement outside the door.'

This was the reason Jack was living in the tower, but Stella wouldn't be pleased to hear that.

'Someone's coming out. Well, that's odd. If I wasn't here, I'd think—' She darted forward and the instrument banged against the glass. 'Ouch!' She rubbed the bridge of her nose. 'I should go. Mum's bringing Dale to the office tomorrow – today, rather.'

Stella kept calling him Dale as if they were already best buddies.

She turned to him, still looking through the glasses. Jack wanted to shield his face as if she could see right into his head. She wouldn't like what she saw there. Often he didn't either.

'By the way, I bumped into William Frost today. We had a bit of lunch. I went through our questions with him.'

'We were going to do that together,' Jack protested. First Dale Heffernan, now William Frost. 'I was going to watch to see if he lied.'

'What with moving, I guessed you'd be tied up.' She lowered the binoculars, looking at Stanley.

Stalemate.

Yesterday Jackie had suggested he tell Stella about his move. He should have done. Stella hated surprises, so why had he given her one? He nearly told her about the steam engine on the monitor at the station, how finding the toy placed on top had stirred up disturbing memories long buried. But Stella would guess he was doing it to appease her and she wouldn't welcome hearing about it with her own past having come back to haunt her. Besides, it was probably not important.

'Why is your mum taking him to Clean Slate?' Suzie and Jackie would fuss over this Terry lookalike.

'Dale wanted to see where I work. He wants to watch me clean.'

'That's nice.' Surely the man had seen a woman use a vacuum before. Jack tried to believe it was straightforward: Heffernan had found a younger sister, he was keen to get to know her. He was not a bounty hunter intending to fleece his new family of their money. Stella lived frugally, but Clean Slate was doing well, and with Terry's legacy she was not on the breadline.

'He wrote to Mum via the adoption agency. He's upset he didn't pluck up the courage to do it while Terry was alive. He had assumed we'd resent him turning up. I told him Dad didn't like surprises, maybe this was for the best.'

So Stella had confirmed to Dale that Terry would not have welcomed him. Full of the best intentions, she could be clumsy around feelings.

'Why's he here now?' Jack had realized that Terry Darnell had doted on his daughter. Not something he understood: his own father Hugh had found having a son a challenge, as if he were a rival. Jack had never tried to rival anyone. *Not true.* Long ago there had been someone. He dismissed this thought.

'Mum is overjoyed to be reunited with her "long-lost boy"!' Stella rolled her eyes.

'So she lied about staying with a friend.' Jack was chastened by his barb.

Stella frowned, the idea clearly new. 'Not exactly.'

Stanley erupted into shouty barks and crouched low, facing the door, legs braced, tail flailing. Each bark jerked him off his feet. He began to dig, front paws blurred with the effort.

'What's the matter with him?' Jack didn't want the dog to scratch the wood – Stanley was demented. *No animals or children.*

'He's picked up a scent, a dead mouse or food dropped by the people here before.'

'No one was here before me.' Despite the busy rate of his paws, Jack saw he was doing no damage.

'Stanley!' Stella had an instant effect. She whisked over and, clipping on the lead, brought the dog to the desk and commanded he sit. He stared at the door, pupils dilated, eyes a smouldering brown.

'He's seen a ghost.' Jack went to where the dog had been digging. Of course it was colder on this side of the room, which was closer to the staircase.

'I'm guessing he doesn't like heights.' Stella shook Stanley's flapping paw as she gave him a morsel of chicken. 'What ghosts? You just said you're the first person to live here.'

Jack felt dread. The dog had come into the flat, tail up, full of curiosity. If he didn't like heights he would have objected on the way up. He touched the bars of a tubular radiator by the door. It had cooled; his indiscriminate twiddling of knobs earlier had worked. It must explain the drop in temperature. The dog continued to stare at the floor where he was standing. He looked down. There was nothing there.

'I'll take him away or the neighbours will object.'

'We're in a tower, there are no neighbours.' Jack should have been pleased by this. He suddenly missed the short-eared owl. Perhaps he should have brought her.

'Better go anyway, I'm seeing Dale in a few hours.'

'I'll see you out.' Jack quelled peevishness that she was leaving him to see 'Dale'.

'"Seeing me out" is not a simple matter.' Stella opened the flat door. 'Will you be OK with all these stairs? What about when you need to buy milk?'

'I'll stock up.'

When he opened the door, Jack expected it to be colder, but the landing was warm.

Stella craned up the spiral staircase. 'Have you been on the roof?' Her voice rang in the metallic vault.

'I don't have a key.' He must take this up with Palmyra Associates. It was autumn; they probably thought he wouldn't want access. Stella followed him down the stairs, the dog lolling on her shoulder, now calm. Above them the stairs wended out of sight. Jack opened the tower door and was hit by a blast of cold air. He reeled back and trod on Stella's boot. Steel-capped, she wouldn't have felt it, but he saw his clumsiness as a sign of how badly her visit had gone, as if they were strangers. As Stella said to him, they were supposed to be a team.

When she put him down, the dog pulled his lead free and shot off along the walkway, too close to the edge. Jack dived after him and stamped on the flailing lead.

'You saved him!' Stella shouted into the wind.

Jack watched in horror as the dog lifted its leg against a metal strut and peed over the side into mid-air. Stella brightened.

'*That* was why he was barking. He's really pretty easy to read. So, what was your idea about us meeting Rick Frost's wife?'

'Do a stakeout, park near her house in the back of the van. It's legal, it's what detectives do,' he added for good measure.

'We've got nothing to lose, I suppose.' Stella spoke over her shoulder as she went down the outer staircases, boots clattering, the grille humming with her tread.

Jack stayed on the narrow metal walkway after Stella had gone as the humming died to nothing. London was a cluster of lights like a circuit board. He went back into the tower and shut the door.

He was outside his flat when he remembered what Stella had asked about the roof. He didn't actually know if he could get up there – he hadn't tried. He crossed the little metal platform and continued up the spiral stairs. At the top he found a large roof light, showing only the night sky. It was a black rectangle. He shot aside two bolts and pushed it upwards. It was stuck fast. He took off his coat and, rolling up his sleeves, wiped his palms on his trousers and tried again. This time he lifted it a few centimetres. He climbed to the top step and, using his body as a lever, succeeded in opening it. Lacking a hydraulic hinge, it had nothing to keep it open beyond gravity. He would find some kind of prop.

He was at the edge of a vast circular area of decking surrounded by a wall. Pushing back the roof cover – he hadn't brought his phone, and did not want to be stuck up here – he clambered out and went over to the wall. It reached to his waist. Not high enough; again he was filled with the temptation he always had with heights, to chuck everything he was holding off and then to follow. He retreated from the wall and took in the vast panorama before him. The river was a stretch of darkness flecked with minute lights. He smelled the air: a mix of sulphur, mud, exhaust fumes and wood smoke. He raised his arms towards the sky and felt the wind blow his hair from his face. At last he had his very own tower. He was truly alive.

Bizarrely, right in the centre of the decking, was a garden shed. Jack supposed that was there to save him lugging tools up for tending plants. There were no plants, however; the space was bare. The shed doors were fixed with a padlock. He would ask the landlords for the key. It would be nice to have some pots up here; he could grow tough hardy grasses able to withstand cold air and the wind. A Garden in the Sky. It would be the antithesis to his Garden of the Dead.

He went back down the staircase to his flat. The heating had gone off, and the spot on the floor where Stanley had been digging was no colder than the rest of the room. Perhaps the fluctuation in temperature was to do with circular walls. His father would have known.

Stella had been his first visitor. That was a good sign. Jack looked across at his chair, which faced outwards as Stella had left it. He had suggested the stakeout to appease her. It wasn't sufficient. He should have said that the reason they worked well together was because she stuck to the rules and he worked in between the lines and beneath the surface.

Despite Stella's visit, he couldn't shake off the homesick ache. Before his promise to Stella not to walk the streets late at night, Jack would have taken a journey across the city to assuage the dull pain. He fetched the field glasses from the window sill, relieved that Stella hadn't asked about them. If she had, he would have had to tell the truth. He disliked lying to Stella.

He went to the window Stella had been watching from and trained the glasses on the Hogarth roundabout. He was rewarded by the sight of a white van, ghostly in the sodium lighting, waiting to join the Great West Road. Stella drove a van without the Clean Slate livery – Jack guessed it was because she preferred anonymity – nevertheless he was sure it was her white van he was watching. Moments later his conviction was proved right. He could see her clearly as she accelerated, keeping within the speed limit, towards the rise of Hammersmith flyover. She wasn't going to her flat. His heart sank. She had said she was seeing Dale in the morning, but it seemed she was going to Suzie's flat now. Without telling him.

One by one he studied the little streets that lay between the A40 and Chiswick High Road. Stella had seen a client's house from this window. He was looking from this window because in an oblique way it made him feel closer to Stella.

After a night journey, Jack used to 'retrace' his steps on Google Street View and take screenshots of houses, doors, windows and the blurred pedestrians and then store them in a file. Now, as he travelled along the streets, magnified through his lenses, he had to rely on his photographic mind to log the detailed views.

Jack rolled on to his back. He couldn't work out where he was. Gradually shapes resolved into his cupboard, the bust of his mother, the two rectangles of mauve-blue light were the south-west and north windows. He listened for what had woken him.

Tap. Tap. Tap.

He flew out of bed and around the partition into the kitchen. The mixer tap was dripping; water was collecting in the spout and dripping into the sink.

He turned on the tap, grabbed a beaker from the little draining board and filled it. He drank thirstily, refilled it and, tightening the handle, wiped his palm under the spout and cleared it of excess water.

Two thoughts bothered him. The dog didn't like him. That didn't matter, but it was affecting his relationship with Stella. She would have stayed longer if he hadn't been barking. What had bothered him was the look in the dog's eyes. Stanley had detected something he and Stella couldn't see, something Jack wasn't sure he wanted to see.

The other thing was Stella's brand-new Australian brother. Heffernan had dropped everything to return with Suzie to England. Why?

Jack knew he was apt to imagine the worst at three in the morning. He was at the mercy of treacly dark narratives that ended with him alone or being harried by strangers with no reason to care about him. If he made progress with the case, Stella would be pleased.

He reached for his phone. One person was awake at this hour.

'How're you fadging, poppet?' The corncrake laugh. 'Why aren't you here!'

'Are you free tomorrow, after my shift? I could be with you by ten to midnight. I'm driving a dead late.'

'Don't you mean thirteen and a half minutes to?' Lucie's idea of a joke. London Underground trains operated in split minutes; every second was counted. May descended into starter-motor mirth. 'Better than driving the Late Dead.' She began to cough violently. 'For you, sweetie, I'll cancel the moon! Although not tomorrow, I'm in Lincoln, meeting a ninety-nine-year-old twin who left Hammersmith at birth. The day after?'

After he had put the phone down, Jack settled under the covers. The tapping had stopped. He would become used to the tower.

His mind was caring for him: it conjured up music. From somewhere in his mind he conjured up the moody strains of the Smiths' 'How Soon Is Now?', his favourite. It mingled with Lucie May's clattering laughter. Jack fell into a deep sleep.

Twenty-Eight

The three children walked in strict single file down to Chiswick Mall, the Captain in front. It was Sunday afternoon and Simon had reluctantly 'come out to play' as the Captain had put it to his mother in a smiley voice that Simon hadn't heard him use before. She had agreed on his behalf. 'Nicky is such a sensible girl.' Simon was dismayed; since last going to the tower, he had avoided the unit. The Captain had brought Nicky to convince his mum to let him out.

He had just persuaded his mum to go on a 'jaunt', her private name for their walks. They would stroll arm in arm around Chiswick House grounds – like an old married couple, she would say. She had told Simon she wished she'd married a lovely young man like him. One day he would make a girl very happy.

'*I will marry you!*' he had insisted.

'*Darling, you can't, boys don't marry their mummies. But you are my favourite.*'

'*More than him?*'

A shadow had passed across her face. '*More than Daddy.*'

'*Not Daddy.*' Before he could stop himself, but she hadn't heard.

They hadn't gone to the park for a long time, not since he had been to the tower and found— Simon had hoped after that everything would be normal again, but it wasn't. His mother behaved as if Simon were a ghost and, hardly eating, she looked like one herself.

'Left right, left right!'

Last in the line, Simon fell back into step with the other two. 'Where are we going?' he called out.

The Captain didn't reply.

Simon took consolation from the fact that Nicky had been invited, so he'd have a chance to show her he wasn't mean, to make her his friend again. On Chiswick Mall, the tower bore down on them, dark and menacing. Simon shuddered at what was up there.

The Captain pushed Simon against the railings on Chiswick Mall. He looked out over the beach to the eyot; it was shrouded in a bank of mist, losing definition. Water, slick as oil, was creeping across the stretch of mud. Simon was cross with his mother for agreeing when the Captain had asked her if 'Simon could come out to play?' He had stared and stared at her to make her say no, because they were going out to the park. But she had said yes straight away, without looking at him once. Then she had made it worse by kissing him goodbye, which ordinarily would have been nice.

'You murdered a man,' Simon said.

'No, I didn't,' the Captain fluted. Simon thought he looked guilty.

'He's dead up there.' The tower was above them. 'I saw him.'

'I left before you,' the Captain said, but with his cracked voice it sounded like a lie.

'You left me to die.' Simon believed this.

'You didn't die.'

'I saw you go up the corkscrew stairs into that room and I heard a fight.' Simon spoke clearly so that Nicky would hear every word.

'How do you know there is a room?' The Captain had him there.

'I went back and saw it.' Simon was quick. 'You dropped your glove on him. You told me you had defeated the enemy. The police will know it's your glove on the man's body. It has your name inside.'

The Captain was crying. Simon was amazed by the potency of his words. A plan took shape.

Nicky turned to him. 'Stop making up stories, Simon. If we're going to the island, we should go. It's getting dark and I have to get home.'

151

'He's a murderer,' Simon asserted. The lure of his own home and the tea on the kitchen table was lessening as he drove home an unforeseen advantage.

'No one's murdered anyone. Both of you, stop it!' Nicky sounded like his mother, Simon thought.

'I have my gloves.' The Captain bashed at his jacket, tugging out a handkerchief, a spray of bus tickets and sweet wrappers.

'Let me make this easier.' Simon was his dad talking to his mum, chatty and reasonable while Simon held his breath because his father made his mother cry and that always made his sister cry. He folded his arms and spoke reasonably: 'This unit works for the good of the country. We don't break the law. Murder is illegal. I am afraid to say that you'll be flung in jail and killed.' Simon's breath was like smoke in the chill evening. The Captain had snot coming out of his nose.

Simon took a black leather glove out of his pocket and dangled it at the Captain.

The boy lunged towards him. Simon skipped out of the way.

'The other glove is up there in the tower. It links directly to you. If you throw this one away, I shall say I saw you do it.' He took the plunge. 'And so will Nicky because she is here too.'

After the man in the tower was dead, Simon had thought it would go back to the way it was before, but it had not. His mother kept looking out of the window as if waiting for someone to come. *Him.*

'What do you want?' The Captain had meted out enough coercion himself to recognize it when it was applied to him.

'I shall be captain.' Simon folded the glove back into his mac pocket. 'You and Nicky are privates. You follow my orders. If you stage a coup, I'll tell the police you are a murderer.' Simon had rehearsed this bit. 'I shall recruit my deputy. He's called Justin and he is my friend.'

'Yes.' The Captain agreed readily.

Had Simon been less intoxicated by the success of his cobbled-together ruse, he might have found this suspicious.

'Yes what?'

'Yes, Captain.'

It took him a second to realize the Captain was walking away. He stalked down the exposed slipway to the beach and was heading for the raised path that led to the eyot.

Nicky's voice startled Simon. 'I'm not going to be your "private", or his. This is a stupid game and it's gone far enough,' she told him. 'Give him his glove back and start being nice.'

'I am nice,' Simon said.

'You *were* nice.' Nicky went after the Captain; Simon had no choice but to follow. Stinking mud was all around him. Simon grimaced; his trousers had been clean on today. He slithered after the Captain and Nicky, hopping over jagged glass and jutting blocks of concrete.

Simon clutched the glove in his pocket and the leather, cool and limp, gave him faint hope. Gaining courage, he strode along the causeway to Chiswick Eyot. The glove was his talisman. He would win in the end.

He clambered up a fortification of concrete moulded as sand-bags. Sprigs of groundsel and thistle thrusting between the gaps offered tenuous handholds. He plunged down a path that was covered by overarching branches that formed a dark tunnel. He caught a bramble; thorns scored a cut across the palm of his bad hand.

Super-sensitive – perhaps as a result of surviving in an unhappy household – Simon was alert to shifts in atmosphere. He had a sixth sense. As he made his way through, he felt a tingling at the back of his neck. Hardly daring to hope what it meant, he increased his pace.

Twenty-Nine

Thursday, 24 October 2013

'I know you say he didn't like surprises, but I wish I'd found my dad while he was alive.' Dale was helping Stella slide the bed in Mrs Carr's spare room back against the wall. 'I envy that you got to spend time with him, to grow up with him. I have a great adoptive dad, but once they told me, I was always wondering what my real parents were like. I wondered what I had missed.'

'Why didn't you contact them when you were younger?'

'Ah, you know, loads of reasons. I didn't want to hurt my parents' feelings, I was busy building the business, cowardice too maybe. What if they had told me to stuff it?'

Downstairs, the front door banged. Mrs Carr hadn't been there when they'd arrived. Stella had found a note pinned to the front door saying that the key was under the recycling bin and to put it back when she left. Horrified, Stella had done as instructed. Being dumped by her husband had made Mrs Carr careless.

Ultimately Stella had been relieved to find she wasn't there. It avoided the palaver of introducing Dale to her. This wasn't the ideal job for him to accompany her to, but when Suzie had suggested Hammersmith Police Station, Stella, keen to avoid the even greater complications of Dale asking questions about Terry's work that she couldn't answer, had suggested they come to Mrs Carr's. At least here he could be helpful.

That morning Stella had introduced Dale Heffernan to Jackie and Beverly and shown him around her office, which, being two rooms, was a quick affair. Now, kitted out in Clean Slate's uniform of a green polo shirt and blue trousers, he had already vacuumed the stairs and landing and shifted furniture in the spare room.

'He was by the river – Chiswick Mall again – where I saw him walking with *her*. I tried to follow him, but my car was on yellow lines. By the time I'd reparked, I'd lost him. No point in texting him, he would be furious if he knew I'd tracked him.' Mrs Carr stood at the end of the bed. 'Hello, who's this?' She stopped in her tracks.

'I hope you don't mind. This is my bro—' Stella corrected herself. 'This is my colleague. He's assisting me. I left you a message?'

'You did, but somehow I was expecting a girl!'

'I'm sorry to disappoint!' Dale was reattaching the headboard that had come loose when they moved the bed.

'Hardly!' She gave a laugh. 'Are you an Australian?'

'Got it! Dale. Good to meet you.' He arched his back and let out a sigh as if exhausted. Stella supposed there was no point in explaining he must always look 'ready and willing'.

'Are you sure it was your husband?' she said to distract Mrs Carr from asking Dale about himself and discovering who he was. That was a step too far.

'Of course I'm sure.' The animation that had made Stella suspect Mrs Carr wasn't entirely sane returned. 'Lulu to you.' She leant over and shook Dale's hand.

'Did you speak to him?' Stella asked. *'Lulu to you.'* Suzie had said Dale was a charmer. 'Mrs Carr?'

'And say what? He lied to me. What's to say? I'm tempted to tell my brother that I saw him.' She was batting the open door back and forth between her palms. 'Should I?' She was looking at Dale as if she had guessed his relationship to Stella and wanted his 'brother-take' on it.

'Ah, look, don't sweat it, that's what brothers are for!' Dale trod on the vacuum lever and the flex whizzed back into the cylinder, the plug flying about dangerously as in her staff manual Stella had warned it would.

Stella had texted Jack to join them and meet Dale; he had replied, saying he was doing a day shift. She was sure he hadn't mentioned this last night and caught herself wondering if it was true.

'My brother believes in loyalty.' Lulu Carr was talking to the door.

'Brothers are there through thick and thin, longer than husbands!' Dale offered.

Stella steered Lulu Carr back to the practical. 'Mrs Carr, your note said where to find the key. Anyone could have got in.'

'How else would you both have got in?' Lulu wandered out on to the landing. She nodded at Stella, 'And call me Lulu.'

'I could have come another day.' Stella had expected Mrs Carr – Lulu – to see her mistake.

Out on the landing she remembered they needed to empty the landing cupboard, and then she noticed Dale had missed patches on the stairs; she would have to do them again.

'You said you had the locks changed to prevent your husband returning. If he had come round, your effort and expense would have been wasted.' Stella hit on a key argument.

'If he was following me, he wouldn't have been here.' Lulu Carr went ahead down the stairs, leaning heavily on the banisters like a child trying to slide down them.

'Got you there, Stell!' Dale laughed. 'Mind you, that note would render your insurance void – it was clear instructions for the robbers.'

'You are right!' Lulu Carr reached the hall and stood watching Dale descend, clearly impressed with him.

Stella drove off along Perrers Road and paused at the end to join Dalling Road. In the off-side mirror, Stella saw that Lulu Carr was waving; she waved back. Dale had pushed the seat back and lay half prone, legs stretched out, eyes shut as if exhausted. He was only a couple of years older than she was, about to be fifty apparently. Surely a bit of vacuuming hadn't finished him. Stella, not one for going abroad – or taking holidays of any kind – did not factor in jet lag.

What she had said to Jack last night was true. Dale Heffernan was unquestionably her father's son. He had the same brown hair, although a trendier style, sticking up at the back and no doubt thickened with product; the parting was in the same place. On his forehead between the eyes was Terry's deep crease, deeper still as he got older and had carried some weight. With a shock, Stella saw that Dale had the same shaped hands as Terry, large with stubby fingers.

'We get clients like that, living a fantasy.' Dale settled further into the seat and, opening his eyes, folded his arms across his chest. 'Last summer one guy booked a table for two. No one else turned up. We were feeling sorry for him, guessed he'd been jilted. We see that a lot. Then he called over my old maître d', Barry, and complained at how long he'd been waiting to give his order. Barry was about to say that we were waiting for his friend when he realized the man had started talking to the chair opposite and he'd filled two wine glasses. He consulted with the chair, then ordered food for two. The whole evening he kept up a conversation with the chair. The food got eaten, but Barry and the waiting staff that night swore they never saw him touch the other plate. He'd created a *real* imaginary friend!'

'How is Lulu Carr like him?' Stella felt protective of her client. She shouldn't have confessed to Dale Heffernan her doubts about her sanity. It was a breach of confidentiality. She also thought that she didn't know her parents any better than Dale did, even though she'd grown up with them.

'The cheating husband? I'd bet my life that's total fiction. She strikes me as inauthentic.'

'What do you mean?' She felt unaccountably riled.

'Something about her doesn't add up. Mr Husband toddles off leaving a pile of clothes behind and lots of clobber. What man does that? He'll have to go shopping for a load more! It's like that English MP who faked his suicide. He left his clothes on the beach. My guess is our Lulu's made it all up, but why?'

'Whatever, it's not our business.' Stella was firm.

'You're right. Our job is to keep the lie intact. When the man left, Barry held the door open long enough for two people to walk out and he said goodnight twice. If any of my front-of-house staff had cracked a smile, they'd have been washing up for a week.'

Thrown by Dale's suggestion that Lulu Carr might not have told her the truth, Stella took a wrong turning at Hammersmith Broadway and drove on to the Great West Road. Ahead of her was Jack's tower. She had seen it many times, but, never having been asked to clean it, hadn't given it a thought.

Someone was on the roof. Jack had told her he didn't have access. Had he lied?

A car cut into her lane; she braked and flashed her lights. When she looked again, Jack wasn't there.

Thirty

January 1988

Chiswick Eyot was cut off from the mainland when the tide was in, but, Simon conceded to himself as he scurried along the path, the tingling sensation mounting, it would make a good HQ. At low tide, protected by thick, oozing mud, the advancing enemy would sink and die. It wasn't as good as the tower. But the tower was out of bounds now.

He arrived in a patch of scrub. At his feet was a circle of white stones with a patch of sunlight. They looked luminous. A small trowel and a fork lay in the soil beside the stones. Simon assumed they were the Captain's. The soil had been dug recently; lumps of fresh earth lay beside the stones.

Simon indicated the stones. 'This is brilliant.' His mouth was dry with mounting dread – the Captain must have a plan. He backed away.

'Stay where you are!' The Captain stood with his back to a screen of reeds.

'Don't speak to him like that,' Nicky said. Simon wanted to sing with joy: she still liked him. Despite Nicky being nice, Simon wished he were at the lake with his mum.

His mum had only agreed for him to come out with the unit because she wanted him out of the house. *She was going to look for the Stick Insect.* It gave him no satisfaction to know she wouldn't find him. Justin had told him that in America stick insects were called 'ghost insects'. A sign, but of what Simon had no idea.

'These mark where bodies are buried.' The Captain pointed at the stones.

The sun had gone in. The stones were still there, but now looked randomly scattered.

'You don't know that.' Nicky shook her head. '*Captain!*'

The reeds rattled in the wind, so tall they reached above the children's heads.

No one could see them from the shore. Simon's foreboding escalated to terror. The Captain hadn't brought him here to show him a new HQ. So taken up with his glove, Simon had been ambushed. He drifted closer to Nicky. She wouldn't let anything happen to him.

'My mum's expecting me. We're going out,' he blurted.

'*Mummy* said you could come out and play!' The Captain gave a short laugh. 'She likes me.'

'I should be getting—'

'I think they mark where there's buried treasure,' Nicky said brightly. 'The way they're arranged, it's like a clock.'

She was deciphering a code. Simon was impressed. When he was captain, he would keep her as Official Codebreaker.

'Anyway, Mummy's not there.' The Captain didn't seem to have heard.

'What do you mean?' Simon knew what he meant.

'Your *Mummy* left after us. Let's guess where she was going!'

'She's going to the park. I'm meant to be there too.' Simon pulled on his half-finger as if it might magic him away.

'Oh, I don't think so. Try again. It begins with a "T". Where do *prostitutes* go?' His tone could be mistaken for kind, but Simon, used to his dad talking to his mum, knew better. 'We understand why you knew all about the tower.'

'And we know what you did there!' Simon heard himself retort. The sound of the river rushing through the reeds hurt his ears.

'Stop it!' Nicky was looking at the Captain.

She didn't know what the Captain meant. Simon moved even closer to her, thinking to suggest they left. Before he could speak, he felt a thump on the back and was pushed to the ground. He was on his hands and knees, flailing at the reeds for purchase. The reeds cracked and snapped like gunshots.

The Captain had Simon by the collar of his mac and was dragging him over the earth. He shoved him through the gap in the reeds. Below was the river, fast flowing, grey and green. Simon heard the fabric of his mac tear; it was giving under his weight. Then everything went quiet and he clearly comprehended – a thought devoid of emotion – that he was going to die.

Flecks of foam were spinning on the water. He saw his own face, white and impassive, before it vanished in cloud of scum. Heat ripped across his scalp as the Captain yanked his head back by the hair.

'Leave him.'

Simon fell on to the ground and, gathering himself, looked across the clearing.

A boy stood in a ragged shape of light inside the ring of white stones. 'You are trespassing,' he said to the Captain.

For a split second Simon thought he was dreaming. So entrenched were his fantasies about his friendship with Justin that he had eliminated the two years in which he had not seen him. He discounted the numerous times he had called at the big house with the owl knocker and got no answer. In his mind the friendship had begun in the Pullman carriage of a train. He and Justin were like Guy and Charles in *Strangers on a Train*, his mother's favourite story. Justin was his friend.

'This is my land.' The Captain didn't sound very sure. 'We've occupied it.'

'You are trespassing.' Justin had grown taller since Simon had last seen him. He was taller than the Captain. He wore a black coat which reached to his ankles, the sleeves folded back. His hair was longer, long like a girl's.

'I knew you'd be here!' Simon exclaimed. 'This is who I meant!' he shouted to the Captain and gave an involuntary tug on his bad finger.

Justin didn't reply or look at him.

'Do you know him?' the Captain said to Simon.

'Yes.' Simon adjusted his belt and smoothed down his hair. 'He's my friend.'

'You are trespassing.' Justin addressed the Captain as if he hadn't noticed Simon or heard him.

'So you're friends with "Mummy's Boy"?' The Captain clearly hoped he had pounced on a weak link.

'I don't know him,' Justin replied calmly.

Above their heads a seagull screeched, long and drawn-out like a baby's cry.

'Justin, it's me, Simon, from that school with the garden. We made the tunnel there, remember? We, we had lunch in the Pullman carriage, steak and chips with ketchup.' Simon dashed at his eyes with the heels of his palms. 'Now I'm in a unit. You can be in it too. You can be captain – it will be brilliant!'

'He doesn't know you.' The Captain edged closer to the boy in the coat as if by diminishing the spatial distance between them he might forge an alliance.

'You are all trespassing!' Justin didn't raise his voice. 'The tide is turning. If you don't go now, you will be cut off from the mainland and drown.'

'You're lying,' the Captain said. But Simon saw that he believed Justin.

All the children heard a steady trickling and, through the reeds, Simon watched the river rise.

'Quick march!' the Captain shouted, and pushing Simon ahead of him, directed him back along the path. Away from Justin.

Simon looked out across the river. Properly dark now, he could just tell that the tide was coming in as Justin had said it would. The river lapped at the bottom of the slipway; the island was cut off. Justin could still be out there.

Simon had given the Captain the slip in the cemetery and had doubled back. He was by the railings on Chiswick Mall. The eyot was a dark crouching hulk, the trees and the land one black mass merging with the night sky.

'Justin,' he yelled across the water.

He flung off his mac and hung it on the railings; then he

struggled down the ramp and set off across the vanishing cause-way of silted gravel to the eyot.

'Justin!' His cry, hollow like a seagull's and lost in gathering wind, went nowhere.

Simon was up to his knees in freezing water. From deep in the river, invisible hands tugged at his legs, trying to drag him off the causeway. There was no causeway: the finger of land was submerged.

The bells of St Nicholas' church struck five. When the wind blew from the east, the chimes could be heard in Corney Road. Simon's mother was assuring her husband she had been out for a walk by herself around the lake in Chiswick House grounds with their daughter.

'Why the fuck does she keep saying "mat"?' Simon's father demanded, infuriated by the little girl's insistently repeated sound.

His wife suddenly understood what the toddler was trying to say. Panicked, she explained how she was leaving the upstairs cur-tains open for Simon, who was still out with his nice friends, to see the sitting-room lights. But her frequently snatched glances out of the bay window were not for her son.

Thirty-One

Friday, 25 October 2013

Jack watched Tallulah Frost's house. He preferred to visit Hosts at night, but he was on another day shift and later was meeting Stella. She had been busy with Dale yesterday. Stella and Suzie had invited him for a late afternoon tea to Richmond Park, but he had said he was busy sorting out his new home, although the flat in the tower, being small, needed little sorting. Jack was in no hurry to meet the Brand-new Brother.

He had cased her house with his binoculars from the north window of the tower and confirmed the topography on Street View. He had logged 'alerts': a repair to asphalt on the camber, cracks in the pavement – stepping on cracks was very bad luck.

That morning Jack had chased up William Frost for his sister-in-law's address. Frost was still keen they go in as cleaners. Although he privately agreed, something in the man's tone had made Jack uneasy. He had refrained from telling Frost that his method of entering people's houses required no disguise.

Leaning on the trunk of a plane tree in the sunlit street, rolling a cigarette, Jack told himself he was reconnoitring for his stakeout with Stella.

Clicking the cursor on Street View, he had swooped and darted around the street with the aerodynamic ease of a bird noting all points of vulnerability, street lamps, sightlines from upstairs windows, frequency of vehicles and pedestrians. There were points of advantage too: trees, parked cars and a wall all offered hiding places from which he could observe unobserved. Jack had established dimension and distance between kerbs, gates and trees. Like any good intruder, he had identified the means of egress. On Google Street View's fabulous new feature – a timeline bar – he compared the image of the road in 2008 to 2012 when the last shots were taken. In four years the front door had changed from racing green to royal blue. Not keen on green, Jack approved. The bush in the front area had grown; straggling branches poked through the railings, obscuring the downstairs window. A point of advantage – he would not be seen.

The door was opening. Jack sidled back behind the trunk, snapping his newly made cigarette into his case along with the rest. Mrs Frost might only be putting something in the bin. People popped out of their houses with rubbish, leaving their doors open, allowing Jack to slip inside. In Perrers Road the bins were in view of the street, and in broad daylight, it wouldn't work.

A woman shrouded in a quilted jacket, hood up, was wrestling with an umbrella. It wasn't raining, but she didn't seem to have noticed. She pointed it directly at Jack's tree, opened it and, ducking beneath, stooped to the doormat. Jack nearly shouted with triumph – it could not be. She was leaving a key beneath it. He had been tempted to follow her, but she stopped by a car parked ten or so metres up the street and unlocked it. He moved around the trunk as her car, a blue Renault Clio, swept past him.

Jack nonchanlantly strolled across the road, noting a Neighbourhood Watch sign fixed to the telegraph pole. He opened the gate without hesitation, intending that a neighbour would assume him a friend, and with a carefree spin on his heel confirmed that no one was on the street. He latched the gate after himself – a watching neighbour would disregard a man who took trouble. Jack pressed the bell.

Thirty more seconds went by. Jack noted that weeds thrusting up through the brick path in 2008 and in 2012 had gone. Somewhere a car door slammed. A blackbird chirruped. A dog gave an urgent bark, answered by another further away. Reminded of Stanley, Jack felt a twinge of guilt; Stella wouldn't approve of what he was doing.

Thirty seconds, then he rang the bell again. After another thirty seconds, he lifted the mat and retrieved the key. This wasn't breaking and entering, he imagined telling Stella, this was visiting.

He opened the door and replaced the key under the mat. Without looking behind him for fear of rousing suspicion, he stepped inside.

Had Jack looked at the plane tree where he had been standing moments earlier, he would have seen he was wrong in thinking that no one was watching him. Nor did he see a figure stroll across the street, with the same nonchalance as he had exhibited moments earlier and, lifting up the door mat, take the key from underneath it.

Thirty-Two

Friday, 25 October 2013

'Have a scone, Stell. See how an Aussie does them!'

Stella had agreed to morning coffee round at her mum's. Dale slid a plate heaped with bite-size scones dotted with plump sultanas across the coffee table to her. Stella wasn't hungry, but refusal wasn't an option. She smelled the warm aroma of cheese.

Dale settled beside her on the sofa and popped a scone in his mouth. He was wearing a chef's outfit: white shirt, chequered trousers. He had been happy to wear Clean Slate clothes when he cleaned yesterday. She hoped he wasn't going to get her cooking and expect her to dress up.

'Not as good as our mum's, you're thinking!' He was calling Suzie 'Mum'. His adoptive mum was dead. Dale had said he was sure that from above she approved.

Stella didn't say that Suzie hadn't baked after she left Terry. She moved the plate away from the edge of the table in case the dog was tempted to take one. With an explosion of crumbs, she tasted butter, fruit and cheese. It was, she had to admit, delicious. She took another and was contemplating a third when Suzie breezed in carrying a tray with three mugs of tea. Stella noticed how well her mother looked. Even without the expected suntan, Suzie glowed with health. She had put her hair up in a bun, which gave her an air of authority. Sydney – or maybe Dale – had transformed her.

'Dale wants to open another restaurant. We've got a proposal.' Suzie clapped her hands upwards as if releasing doves. Stella couldn't help glancing at the ceiling.

'No, he has *not*!' Dale shook his head, a hand in front of his mouth to catch crumbs. 'This is Mum's idea. Sure, expansion is on the cards, but not until I've accumulated capital. I will *not* borrow.'

'I'm not suggesting borrowing, or not like *that*,' Suzie continued undaunted. 'Not from a bank. Stell, if you sell Terry's house, you could invest in Dale's restaurant business.' Her hand hovered over the plate, then quickly, as if stealing, she took a scone from the furthest side and appeared to swallow it without chewing.

'What did I say this morning? Stella's known me for five minutes. Days ago she didn't know she had a brother. It's "no go", OK? I'm good as things are.' Dale reached for another scone.

Stella felt the usual mix of annoyance and respect for Suzie. She never let the grass grow under her feet. Although once unwilling to venture further west than Richmond Park or, until relatively recently, from her armchair, her mum dreamt up expansion plans for Clean Slate and a job for herself and her dreams came true. Not this dream. Dale Heffernan was right, she hardly knew him. Besides, she rarely ate out, knew nothing about the catering industry or his cooking. A few scones wouldn't have her putting the house on the market. Jack thought she was holding on to it for her dad, which was obviously nonsense since he was dead. She wasn't ready to sell the house. It needed cleaning.

'Show Stella your book.' Suzie lit upon another scone and tossed it into her mouth like a seal receiving a fish. 'You have a magic touch, Dale-kins,' she mumbled into her hand, hunching her shoulders in delight. Stella had only ever seen Suzie like this with Jack.

Dale-kins.

'What book?' Stella managed to ask. Recipes, she supposed. Suzie must know she wouldn't be interested. Stella didn't cook, she microwaved a variety of ready meals, among which shepherd's pies predominated. She took another scone. Stanley was dozing, his chin on her boot. She kept still so as not to disturb him.

'Stella's a busy woman.' Dale flapped a hand and flashed Stella what she had come to think of as one of his smiles.

'No, I'd like to see it.' Stella inhaled a cloud of crumbs and coughed. She slurped some tea and washed them down. The tea was hot. She had expected it to be tepid. Few people made it as she liked it. One of these was Jack. Again she found herself musing on how odd this was when he only drank hot milk.

'Consider it, Stella, it's a sound investment,' Suzie hissed in a stage whisper when Dale was out of the room. He was sleeping in Stella's bedroom. She had peeped in on her way down the passage. Apart from a sleek black suitcase, tucked under the desk, it looked no different. 'Keep it in the family!'

'*Enough.*' Dale was back, a fancy-looking photograph album under his arm. Patterned with silver and gold flowers, it put Stella in mind of a memorial book. A black ribbon tied in a bow reinforced this impression. 'The restaurant business is volatile, customers are fickle, food prices erratic. Barry left last month to work for a vine-yard out in W. A. I put my sous-chef out front and a customer complained he had the eyes of a serial killer! Lost a lot of covers! I took out a loan so I could come back with Mum. If you get a kick out of pumping ten-dollar bills down a plughole, I'm your man!'

Suzie pulled faces at Stanley, still dozing at Stella's feet, imply-ing this was nonsense. Stella steeled herself; her mother on a mission was unstoppable.

'Hey, if Clean Slate was up the road, I'd hire you! We need excel-lent cleaners, and you treat hygiene as top priority. Now *that* is a sound investment!' Dale pushed the empty scone plate aside and laid the album down. It took up most of the table. Stella's mind raced with excuses to get out of ploughing through Dale Heffernan's family snaps.

Stella stared at a logo on the inside cover. 'That's the same as—'

'Isn't it remarkable!' Suzie clapped her hands again, sending a spray of crumbs over the carpet Jack had cleaned. Stanley pounced on them and moments later they were gone. One good thing about a dog, Stella had noticed.

'Sixty-Four' was the street number of Dale's first restaurant in Sydney and was apparently the year he was born. Set within an oval, the logo was made up of a six and a four back to front – like on a police car, Stella thought vaguely. Stella wasn't great on design, what had got her attention was the colours. The light blue six was Pantone 277 and the four was a vivid green – Jack used to hate it – Pantone 375. Dale's logo exactly matched the colours of Clean Slate's branding.

'Weird, isn't it?' Dale murmured.

For a fleeting moment Stella wondered if it wasn't weird and he had deliberately chosen them. But then he said he had only just found out who his biological parents were. The logo was over thirty years old.

She was relieved that Dale didn't fawn over each picture. Not of his family – it was a compendium of reviews and photos of his cafés and restaurants, from the catering service he had operated out of a clapped-out combi in the 1980s to '64', now a restaurant frequented by celebrities and the wealthy in Rose Bay. Ignoring Suzie's cries to linger, Dale whizzed past five-star reviews, profiles cut from newspapers and glossy magazines, and the sumptuous illustrations of 'sensational' dishes. Stella found she was interested and wished he would slow down, but she was due at Lulu Carr's in half an hour.

'So, that's my "brilliant career"!' Dale shut the book and returned to his corner of the sofa. Suzie put out a fluttering hand and brushed his arm.

'It's great.' Dale had kept a record of every year of his business. It hadn't occurred to Stella to chart Clean Slate's history. There had been reviews in trade magazines, a few awards along the way; she cleaned for celebrities, but wouldn't dream of naming them. Stella hadn't considered her working life as a career – brilliant or otherwise – it was just a job.

Dale and Suzie went into the kitchen to prepare lunch. Listening to her mum's laughter, Stella was sure that Jack suspected that Dale had come to London with the intention of worming his way into Suzie's affections and claiming his share of the inheritance. Jack would never have actually come out and said this, but it wasn't like him to turn down tea with her mum in Richmond Park. If this was Dale's plan, he was on the way: Suzie was hooked. Yet he had been quick to slough off Suzie's idea. Jack must be wrong. The man had asked sensible questions about Clean Slate, he was a sharp businessman. He didn't want shareholders; like Stella he kept control of the reins. But what if it was an act? More than once Stella had paid the price for being fooled. Perhaps the album had been cobbled together for Suzie's benefit – a soft sell. If it was, she had bought it.

Stella glanced at the kitchen hatch. Unusually it was closed. Dale must have shut it – Suzie liked it open. She pulled the album towards her. On the first page was an article from a newspaper called the *Sydney Morning Herald* about Dale opening a café on 8 August 1988 in a suburb of Sydney called Redfern. He had chosen that day, he was quoted, '...*because the date, 8888, is auspicious. I hope it will bring me good luck.*' Just like Jack.

She had been operating Clean Slate from her bedroom that year, resisting Suzie's demands to lease an office and 'put a stake in the ground'. Stella felt the prickling of goose bumps. But for the Simon Le Bon hair, the twenty-something Dale, lounging against the door of the café, the proud owner, might be Terry. In the photograph of Terry outside her nana's house, he had leant on the door in just the same pose.

Dale wore an apron with the legend 'Dale's Place'. Her dad had hated fancy restaurants as much as she did. He would have been unnerved by a son who cooked food with French names. Stella rubbed her face. Terry would have been astonished to discover he had a son. He wouldn't have cared what he did.

People, probably friends rather than real punters, could be seen waving through the café window. Stella had had no official opening for Clean Slate. As she had later told Jackie, people don't fuss about cleaners. Some even give the impression they do the job themselves and for those Stella used her plain white van. Dale's Place had served hot food all day. Terry would have liked it there.

Her eye skimmed a shot of a young man and a woman below

Dale's picture. The woman looked vaguely familiar, but she had one of those finely boned faces to be found in every generation. Stella's attention drifted to the article above the image.

FEARS MOUNT FOR MISSING TEACHER

Five years to the day since English teacher Nathan Wilson vanished, police say they have no clue to his whereabouts. The forty-year-old bachelor, on a sabbatical from Menzies High in exclusive Vaucluse, set off last October on a three-month walking tour of New Zealand to 'feed his soul' and never…

'You'll stay for lunch.' Suzie swept into the room, bearing a bundle of cutlery and a clutch of wine glasses.

'It's nearly eleven.' Stella shut the album. She would be late for Lulu Carr.

'Not now. It's moules marinières with lemongrass. There's fresh parsley!' As if parsley was a rarity. 'Dale's making fresh crusty bread for it and at the same time he's preparing sea bream with milk-braised leeks for tonight, with saffron and vanilla cream sauce.' Suzie picked up the album and held it with the tips of her fingers.

Stella was on the verge of retorting that it must be usual for Dale to cook several meals at once, but Suzie had decided he was extraordinary, so no point. She was secretly impressed. She could be floored by the calculation of timings for microwaving two shepherd's pies for her and Jack.

'I've too much on.' She wouldn't mention the case. 'Say goodbye to Dale.'

Suzie lifted the album. 'We'll do a copy for you.'

Stella snatched up Stanley and pecked Suzie on the cheek. She hesitated in the doorway. The smell from the kitchen was appetizing; she was hungry. Suzie was cradling Dale Heffernan's life-story album as if it were a baby.

Thirty-Three

'Mrs Frost?'

The fridge hummed; the boiler fired up. Silence. Checking the time out of habit – it was ten forty-five; he would stay no longer than an hour on this first visit – Jack glided along the passage on his rubber-soled shoes. He pushed at a door on his right with a finger, the way people do in public toilets to check if they're free. It swung open. He bent down and looked around the door. People look for intruders at eye level, and don't see a person crouching ready to pounce. He was the intruder. Jack didn't want to frighten anyone, not even a True Host who made it their business to frighten others before they snuffed them out. Senses acute, he could pick up a shift in the air, a change in atmosphere. He called out again.

'Yoo hoo? Mrs Frost? I'm a friend of William. He suggested I drop by.'

In the sitting room, a sofa, an armchair and a coffee table faced a fireplace inlaid with Delft tiles. Jack's eye was drawn to a flat-screen television on the wall above the mantelpiece. Rick Frost had been in security, he would have rated gadgets and electronic equipment higher than a Rothko or Matisse. The Frosts obviously didn't go in for fuss or sentimentality. Stella would like the stream-lined look: nothing to collect dust.

Stella was all set to do a meticulous internet search into the deceased's character, but they needed to know the stuff people kept to themselves. Interviews weren't enough and anyway Stella had gone ahead and interviewed William Frost without him.

Jack must work undercover, which was appropriate, since Rick Frost had made his business from selling surveillance equipment. Stella would be pleased with the results. No need to say how he came by them.

On the mantelpiece was a silver framed photograph of a man and a woman. The man wasn't Frost, Jack had seen him both dead and in a picture released for the press. The haircuts were 1980s, big shoulder pads, bouncy hair. They must be Tallulah Frost's parents; she'd be unlikely to keep up a picture of her in-laws after her husband's death. He thought them both faintly familiar, but as a train driver, he saw a lot of faces; it made everyone look like someone he had seen before.

Along from the picture was a silver Wee Willie Winkie candlestick holder with snuffer. A ball bearing lay in the base. Jack sent it rolling around the candle. His skin pricked with horror; he shouldn't touch or move anything. *Leave no fingerprints, no trace.*

In the kitchen he found the back-door key hanging by the back door. An odd breach of security for a surveillance expert. Jack opened the door and stepped out on to a gravelled patio of about three metres square. The gravel would warn of the enemy's approach. A log bin under the wall provided escape: one hop and he would be over. A way out and a way in. Jack returned to the kitchen, locked the door and, hesitating, replaced the key. There was plaster dust on the top of the light-switch plate suggesting that the hook had been fixed recently, no doubt since Frost's death. That explained it. Frost would have known how easy it was for an intruder to smash a pane in the door and reach in. Jack doubted that Rick Frost used to leave the front-door key under the mat. Perhaps, shattered by his death, his wife had grown careless. Generally, the bereaved were keen to keep up the deceased's routines. Stella cleaned Terry's house and maintained everything as it had been in his life. Tallulah Frost had transgressed, which made it easy for him. Jack was disappointed to have no tax on his skill or experience. It had been too easy – a bad sign.

On the staircase Jack saw what had been troubling him. The

Frost home was clean. Not a speck of dust. Everywhere sparkled. In the sitting room someone had smoothed the carpet pile after vacuuming, leaving no tracks. Tallulah Frost didn't need a cleaner.

Cleaning could be an antidote to grief; although she'd never admit it, Stella's shifts had increased when her dad died. Jack relished cleaning, ever hoping to recreate the home he had lost long ago. If Mrs Frost did her own cleaning, she must be very upset indeed. Either that or she had found a cleaner on a par with Clean Slate. Stella had competition.

Singing softly under his breath, he mounted the stairs. If anyone walked in now, he had nowhere to hide. Jack's fingertips tingled. This was how he liked it.

'Old Mother Goose,
When she wanted to wander...'

Invisibility wasn't all about keeping to the sides of stairs or to the ends of floorboards where there was least give. Jack dipped into rooms unseen and crouched in a strip of shadow when the Host was near. He wasn't like the enemy Rick Frost had sought to ward off with alarms and sensors, he joined the household and learnt its darkest secrets.

'... Would ride through air
On a very fine gander.'

On the landing he listened for breathing or for the silence of held breath. All clear.

No dirty grouting in the bathroom or limescale on the bath. The chrome plugholes shone. On the landing Jack opened a built-in cupboard. It contained Mrs Frost's summer clothes and, judging by a gap on the left-hand side, had once held her husband's too.

At the back of the house Jack opened a door by the bathroom.

'Hello, Rick.' This was Rick Frost's sanctum. He lingered in the doorway, picturing the man who had lain broken and bleeding on the sharp stones. Jack felt profound sadness. Death was expressed by the gaps in wardrobes and the silence of overly cleaned rooms.

'Please give up your secret,' he breathed but detected no ghost.

Rick Frost had run his business from this room. The walls were taken up with shelves crammed with books on coding and intruder monitoring. Jazzy-coloured boxes of security software were emblazoned with exclamatory titles: 'Duress!' 'Panic Stations!' 'Dispatcher!'

Three filing cabinets left space for the arm of an L-shaped desk with a *Mastermind* chair in the corner. The other arm of the 'L' would have had a view of the back patio, but for the frosted window. Dedicated to combating human transgressions, mostly inspired by the darkness of the soul, Frost hadn't required daylight. To beat the enemy, it was necessary to have the mind of the enemy.

Beside the desk was a dustbin-sized shredder where Jack guessed Frost destroyed every scrap of rubbish.

Jack fitted his Clean Slate pen through the desk-drawer handle and was surprised when it slid open. Inside was typical desk stuff: a stapler, staples and a staple remover, a cloth tape measure, a roll of sticky tape and some AA batteries. Shutting the drawer he heard a clunk as something rolled to the front. He opened it again and found a bullet. Not so typical. When William had said his brother took part in battle re-enactments, Jack had supposed this was jousting with shields, not using modern weaponry. At the back of the drawer he found a rolled-up canvas belt bristling with more bullets. He shivered. Although no ghosts, he felt a nasty energy in the room.

On the desk was a thin silver laptop with a printer. Jack sat down in the spacious chair, appreciating how comfortable it was. He turned on the laptop. The machine sprang to life and demanded a password.

He'd expected this; Frost was in security. Most people were unimaginative about passwords, choosing pets' names or whatever they saw when they glanced up from the monitor: Webster, Shakespeare. Stella had used 'hygiene' until he made her change it. Frost would have a strong password, alpha-numeric for starters.

A wireless mouse lay on a blank mouse mat. No company logo. Frost's was a clandestine business: he would rely on word of mouth for customers. They must find out who they were and what he had done for them. There was a shiny dip on the right of the space bar; otherwise there was an equal amount of wear on the keys. No way to establish the letters in the password, which, infrequently typed, wouldn't be evident.

The mouse was on the left of the laptop. At the inquest the pathologist had said Frost's left wrist was broken, as if, going under the wheels, he had instinctively tried to protect himself. Jack had forgotten. Frost *had* raised his hand, not to stop the train, but to Jack. He had been trying to point something out to him. Not something. *Someone.*

The prime suspect was Stella's 'inspector'. Was he returning to the scene of his crime? Or had he followed William Frost to the pub and overheard Jack suggest to Stella that they go to Stamford Brook station? Suddenly Jack was sure the man was not there simply waiting for a train.

Jack peered closer at the desk. There were scratches on the laminated top, so faint that, but for the strip of sunshine on the desk, he would have missed them. Someone had written something on paper with ballpoint, leaving the indentation on the desk. A single moment of carelessness, for there were no other marks on the laminate. The error suggested the action was untypical, perhaps in a moment of stress.

Jack patted the breast pocket in his coat for his notebook and pencil. Laying a sheet of paper over the scratches, he shaded it with the pencil, keeping his pressure consistent. Gradually he revealed a series of marks, white against the pencilled background. He held it up to make sense of them and saw the camera.

Fitted above the door, it was white like the walls. It moved fractionally and a red light blinked. It had been filming him since he entered the room.

Numb with horror at his stupidity, Jack didn't hear the diesel engine until it stopped. He strode out to the landing and opened the door of the room at the top of the stairs: Mrs Frost's bedroom. It was probably a delivery van. The driver would go away when he or she got no answer – or it might not be for this house. He tiptoed to the window and peeped out through slatted blinds.

Outside was a van, back doors open. Beneath it Jack could see legs encased in trousers and sturdy boots. He knew them instantly.

Jack Harmon could break into and live in a stranger's home with a steady pulse and cool nerve, but as Stella heaved her equipment bag on to her shoulder and headed to the front door, the dog at her heels, he nearly fainted.

He ran to the landing and blundered into the bathroom, then back to the landing. Stella had agreed to William Frost's plan, she was working undercover as a cleaner. It explained the hyper-clean rooms, the lack of vacuum tracks on the carpet, the precise positioning of ornaments and the ball bearing at 'six o'clock' in the well of the candle holder until, like a game of Russian roulette, he sent it spinning. It wasn't the work of a rival cleaning company or of a widow assuaging grief, it was Stella Darnell at her best.

Jack must help her in with her bag. He froze. Stella hadn't told him she had changed her mind. She didn't want him, or William Frost, to know. A detective's daughter, she would be uncomfortable about her decision. If Jack greeted her in the hall, aside from frightening her, he would cause her deep shame.

He spun around, hands wringing. It was worse. Stella would realize he had broken his promise. He had betrayed her.

Thirty-Four

Friday, 25 October 2013

With green lights all the way from her mum's flat, Stella made it to Lulu Carr's on time, but she hadn't been able to drop Stanley off at the office. She could have left him at Suzie's. Dale said he loved dogs, but he seemed to 'love' everything so she took that with a pinch of salt. She would explain to Lulu Carr that Stanley, being made of wool, wouldn't moult. If she had allergies – and Stella suspected she did – the dog would not set them off. She rehearsed her speech in her mind as she reversed into a space outside the house. If there were any accidents – there won't be, he's toilet-trained – or if he caused any damage – he knows not to touch anything – she would reimburse her. Stella pulled her equipment bag from the back of the van and slung it over her shoulder.

She was reaching for the doorbell when she heard a single chime from somewhere in her anorak. A text.

Had to see bro. Key under mat. Lulu. x.

Not again! If this cavalier attitude to security was Lulu Carr's revenge on her estranged husband, it was self-defeating. She wondered about the brother; if he was loyal, he was probably also protective. When a person slid into chaos, it was often the relatives who called in Clean Slate. Stella hoped he wasn't fuelling Lulu Carr's obsession with her husband. Having just acquired a brother herself, Stella had no idea what to expect. However, Lulu not being there did mean she needn't explain why she had Stanley in tow.

There was no key under the mat.

This hitch did at least give her a reason to leave and get on with the 'One Under' case. So far they had three suspects backed up by flimsy evidence. Her internet search on Rick Frost had resulted in one page of double-spaced text, including a photo that looked like a passport picture. The lack of available information on him might be apt for a surveillance expert – Frost had left the faintest of footprints – but it wasn't helpful for finding his killer. But 'stick to one job at a time' had been her motto since she started Clean Slate. Stella texted Lulu Carr, *No key. Will you be long?*

Lulu texted back immediately. *Another one above door. Don't be cross!*

Stella stepped back from the door and looked at the narrow lintel above the door. She caught a movement in one of the upstairs windows. She shaded her eyes against the morning sunshine and saw only a flash of light as the sun hit the glass. She wouldn't put it past Lulu to be in there, watching, testing her. Perhaps if she had left without texting, Lulu would have cancelled the contract. At this moment Stella doubted she would mind. She could see the key. Checking there was no one in the street, she took it down.

She unlocked the door, picked up the equipment bag and, with Stanley beside her, squeezed inside. Stella was pleased to see that Lulu was still keeping the house tidy; perhaps she was on the road to recovery. It was good too that she was seeing her brother and not scouring the streets for Mr Carr and his mistress.

Stella laid the towel she kept in the van to dry the dog off after walks down in the hallway and directed Stanley on to it. Obediently he flopped down and contemplated her with a doleful expression.

She lugged the bag into the living room and got out her 'light-clean kit'. The room was already spotless, but Stella was the first person to applaud the cleaning of a clean room.

Ten minutes later, as the clock on the mantelpiece struck eleven fifteen, Stella came out of the living room to fill a bucket with warm water from the kitchen and saw the towel on the hall floor. No Stanley.

She ran into the kitchen and tried the back door. Surprisingly, given Lulu's lax attitude to keys, it was locked. She knew he wasn't in the sitting room. She took the stairs three at a time to the landing.

Stanley was sitting on the crimson mat, bolt upright, staring at the cupboard built into the space behind the banister rail. He was making a hideous guttural growl. Stella realized she had heard the sound for some minutes but, engrossed in getting the windows spotless, hadn't taken it in.

When he saw her, Stanley began to bat at one of the doors. It was loosely fitting and made a resounding bang. The cupboard had stored many of the husband's clothes, jumpers and more combat gear, which Lulu had carted off to the dump. Stella had helped her put her own clothes in there. There was nothing that Stanley could want.

'Stanley!' David had told her that if Stanley was fixated with getting under a sofa or nosing behind a bookcase, there would be a good reason. Last week, giving in to his barking at a filing cabinet, Beverly and Jackie had eventually shifted it, a half-hour effort, to find his stuffed rat wedged behind it. There could be no toy in this cupboard.

'What are you doing up here?' She reached for a liver treat, but the pouch around her waist contained cleaning gear. She went closer and stopped.

Lulu's bedroom door was open. She *never* left it open.

There was one room in the house that Lulu didn't want her to clean: her bedroom. Stella had dreaded to think what state it was in, so, looking in, was surprised to find it immaculate. Dominating the room, beneath swathes of fabric suspended from the ceiling, was the biggest four-poster bed she had ever seen. More suited to a stately home than a modest house in Hammersmith. Soft linen and lace billowed from the ceiling, suspended there like clouds. Great dust collectors, she fleetingly thought.

Mirrors placed at strategic points reflected the bed into infinity. The bedspread twinkled with gold and silver threads; intertwining blossoms in blues, green and reds were lit by a sun motif in the centre. The sun was not as bright as the flowers. Floating on top of the silk was a pool of water, golden like the sun. The awful truth dawned.

Stanley had peed on the bed.

'No, no. *No!*' Stella scrubbed at her hair. She bundled up the counterpane. No point in reprimanding Stanley, the moment he had laid claim to Lulu Carr's territory would be lost in his past.

Something dropped to the floor. Stella reached down for it. It was Lulu's driving licence. There were bite marks in the plastic cover. Flushing with horror, Stella flipped it open, praying that Stanley hadn't rendered it invalid. The photograph wasn't Lulu; the face that stared out at her was the same as the one turned up in her internet research. It was Rick Frost.

'Stanley!' Stella closed the bedroom door. Holding the counterpane high to avoid tripping, she hurried down the stairs. She piled it into a large IKEA bag she kept in her equipment bag for emergencies such as this, got her phone from her anorak and called Jack.

Pick up!

Stanley cantered back up the stairs barking frantically. The phone clamped to her ear, Stella raced after him, worried she had forgotten to shut the bedroom door. He was back at the cupboard. She swished his lead from around her neck and clipped it on, but he wouldn't move.

She heard a buzzing. It sounded like a trapped insect. It must be what he could hear.

At that moment Jack's phone cut to answer machine.

Closing her phone, Stella went over to the cupboard. The buzzing had stopped. Holding on to Stanley's lead, she flung open one of the doors. A fragrant smell drifted out, aftershave mingled with fresh cotton. No trace of her beeswax polish, and there shouldn't be aftershave: she'd washed down the wood after removing the husband's clothes. Jilted clients hired her to eradicate all trace of their partners. She would have to clean the cupboard again.

'Nothing, see?'

Stanley backed away, tail down. There were smells he disliked: lavender oil, Jack's washing detergent. This reminded Stella that she needed to find Jack. She shut the cupboard door and carried the dog downstairs. Picking up the IKEA bag, she opened the front door, and formed the proper question: Why was Rick Frost's driving licence on Lulu Carr's bed?

Driving to her flat to wash the counterpane, more questions winged in. Was Lulu having an affair with Rick Frost? Had his wife found out and killed him? Was that why she wouldn't agree to meet? If Lulu was having an affair with Rick Frost, that might be why her husband had left, although it was blatantly unfair to blame him. Conversely, it made it likely that, torn in half by two women, Rick Frost had killed himself. Or had Frost refused to leave his wife? That gave Lulu Carr herself a motive for murder. Perhaps she had hired Stella to wipe away the evidence. But then, why leave her bedroom, where the most evidence might be, untouched?

Waiting at lights on the Hogarth roundabout, hunched over the wheel, Stella's head jangled with the chaos of possibilities and incongruities. She needed Jack to restore the order, even if it did involve signs and ghosts.

Checking on the dog, she saw something by his feet. She leant back to see properly. It was a glove. He must have taken it from Lulu Carr's bedroom. She started to reach behind to pick it up, but saw his eyes. He had taken possession of it. They would have to trade. She hoped he would resist destroying it before she got to the flat.

Stella saw Jack's tower. Yet again there was someone on the roof. She leant on the wheel and narrowed her eyes. Jack was holding something. Binoculars. He was looking at her.

She was brought to by a cacophony of sound. Furious faces in her rear mirror, fists and fingers raised, horns blaring: she had missed the lights. Stanley joined in, emitting short sharp barks. Miming apology, but unable to drive forward, Stella pressed 'dial' on her steering wheel.

'Name?'

'Jack Mob.' Stella was as monotone as the computer. The lights changed to green.

'This is Jack, who are you? Tell me after the beep.' She pulled away.

She wouldn't leave a message. Her 'Missed call' would be enough. On second thoughts: 'I just saw you. Please call!'

Thirty-Five

'I just saw you. Please call!'

Jack took his train out of Southfields station. As if to emphasize Stella's voicemail, there had been two little eyes at the top of the screen on his phone as if she were watching him. The flat light of a dull grey day filling the cab matched his low mood and reminded him why he liked the darkness of the Dead Late shift. Again, he had forgotten to measure the time it took to pass through the West Hill tunnel. He had been distracted. Last time it had been the red Triang engine on the monitor at Putney Bridge station, a sign he had yet to understand. Today, he had been shocked by how close he had been to Stella – or her dog – finding him in Tallulah Frost's cupboard.

He fretted about Stella's text. She had seen him. He went over the words in her text, analysing them like a political correspondent for meta-meaning. 'Just' – presently, in a minute, a minute ago, recently, how recently?

Stella had broken her code. She had gone into Tallulah Frost's house disguised as a cleaner. Jack felt cold fear at the prospect of seeing her; he dreaded her telling him she had done it. Or far worse, that she didn't tell him at all. She said she had seen him – maybe she would divert her guilt to him for trespassing? Jack toyed with pre-empting any of this by telling her himself. She might forgive him.

He acknowledged the driver of a train coming out of Wimbledon Park. The woman looked like Stella, shortish dark hair. He had Stella on his mind.

Stella didn't end relationships with grand announcements. There would be no special treatment for him as her friend. She would stop giving him cleaning shifts or inviting him to Terry's for shepherd's pie. No more detective cases. They would drift apart. From his tower, Jack would watch Stella leading her life and have no part in it.

Jack couldn't explain to Stella that what she liked in him – his knowledge of human nature, his interpretation of actions, above all his cleaning – depended on walking night-time streets and keeping vigil in the homes of True Hosts until they let their guard down. Telling Stella was not an option. She would never forgive him.

'I just saw you. Please call!'

At Wimbledon Park, he watched passengers get off and on. The red steam engine was there on the driver's monitor, exactly where it was last time. He stared at the number on the boiler: '26666'. It was the same number as the engine he had lost in the river when he was a child. Did they all have that number or was it the same engine?

Even as he reached for the engine, he expected it to disappear, a ghost engine, so was surprised by cold metal. Instantly he was taken back to being a tiny boy, crouched by the river's edge, pushing his engine down the slipway.

Jack got back into the cab and put the engine in his bag. He pressed a button and, with a collective swish, the carriage doors closed. He pulled the lever and eased the train forward.

As the monitor slid out of sight at the top right of its screen, Jack saw a figure at the far end of the station. The shape, the bearing, was familiar. He had seen the same figure in another monitor screen at another station. That man, like this one, Jack guessed, had made no attempt to get on the train.

On the return journey to Upminster, leaving Wimbledon, Jack made himself think of nothing but the West Hill tunnel. Leaving Southfields, he could see the mouth of the West Hill tunnel ahead. Jack checked his watch: thirteen thirty-three. He forced himself to concentrate.

The second hand hit the fourteenth minute past the twelve. He fixed on the tracks, his mind blank, and maintained forty miles per hour. The darkness enveloped him.

'*I just saw you. Please call!*'

Thirty-Six

Friday, 25 October 2013

A strong gust of wind buffeted her. A tower might sound exciting on paper, but in reality it was dangerous and scary. Especially in the middle of the night.

She should have rung before coming. Jack hadn't replied to her text and, unwilling to text him again, she decided to surprise him. He did it to her all the time.

There seemed more stairs than last time and they were steeper. She had left her gloves in the van, and her hands burned on the frozen metal rail. The wind was like in a horror film, a moan rising and subsiding. Stella told herself it was the sound of it blowing through the holes in the metal stairways, but couldn't shake the impression of a baby crying in the dead of night. It was late, past ten o'clock. She was letting her imagination get the better of her.

There was a click. Jack had come down to let her in. Stella called out, 'It's me.' Stanley tensed. Probably because he wasn't keen on Jack.

She stepped on to the walkway, which was narrower than she remembered. No sign of Jack. A flurry of wind slapped her against the tower wall. She held the dog tight, mindful of breaking his ribs. They would both break everything if they fell off the walkway.

There was no bell. Stella huddled in the door recess and, sheltering Stanley in the folds of her anorak, rang Jack again.

'This is Jack, who are you? Tell me after the beep.'

Jack was always advocating spontaneity, yet here was proof it didn't pay off. Stella dared not look down. She might be on the ledge of a cliff face, darkness all around. She had never felt more alone. There was one place she could go.

Stella parked up opposite the mansion block in Barons Court. Ahead was the station, its lit fascia like a beacon. She thought of the fish Suzie had said Dale was cooking for supper and wondered if there was any left over. Too late to visit: Suzie liked an early night and Dale, who her mum said had jet lag, would be asleep. Stella had never had jet lag. She wasn't sure how it worked. It didn't seem to affect her mum.

When Jack was driving, he turned off his mobile. That was it. The living-room lights were on in her mum's flat. She was still up. A shadow slanted across the ceiling – two shadows. Dale and Suzie came to the window and, like subjects in a framed photograph, looked out. Stella fumbled with her key and pulled away from the kerb.

She got through the lights at the Talgarth Road junction and was soon back on the flyover. What could Suzie and Dale find to talk about? Stella talked about work when she visited her mum. They couldn't be swapping recipes; Suzie would soon run out.

Stella slowed at the Hogarth roundabout lights, where that morning she had seen Jack on the roof of his tower. He wasn't there now.

Since Jack was doing day shifts for a driver friend, it must mean his nights were free.

A man was striding briskly along the pavement. He passed the pub, head down, walking with a bounce on the balls of his feet, like a teenager. He wore a long black coat and his hair hung in locks to his shoulders. He merged with the shadows, vanished and then reappeared. There was only one person it could be. Stella slowed as he reached the subway. She couldn't stop or turn around. She lowered the passenger window to shout, willing the lights to go red. They stayed green. She looked in her driver's mirror in time to see Jack go down into the subway. If she went around the round-about she could catch him on the other side. No, there were too many cars, even at this time of night; she couldn't swap lanes.

Jack had been coming from the direction of the tower. He had been there all along. He had broken his promise to her – he was walking at night. Stella minded less that Jack had lied; she was worried for him. One day he would get himself killed.

On Kew Bridge her phone rang.

'Number unknown'. Not Jack.

'I've found her!'

'Found who?' Stella tried to place the voice.

'My husband's mistress.'

Lulu Carr. Stella pictured the bedspread airing in her study. The stain had come out. She had forgotten about the glove.

'I'm on my way there!' Lulu's voice boomed in surround sound and Stella adjusted the volume.

'Stay where you are.'

Lulu opened the door before she could knock. She was waving a piece of paper like a flag of victory.

'I was right, I was bloody right!' she exclaimed in a hoarse whisper guaranteed to wake the street. Stella hurried her through the house to the kitchen.

'I found this in the cupboard on the landing.' She slapped the paper down on the table.

'What is it?' The paper was covered with pencil shading like a child's scribbled-out drawing.

'Secret writing. It's a number, look!'

Hardly secret then. Stella could see some random marks. She tilted the note to the light. The marks did look like numbers.

'I know where he is.' Lulu was looking out into the garden as if that was where her husband was. Stella had to end the charade.

'Lulu, when I was here earlier—'

'Nicola Barwick's been dying to get her hands on my husband.' Lulu slumped down on a chair. She spoke as if reciting from a script.

'Who is Nicola Barwick?' Stella remembered what Dale had said about the man in his restaurant with an imaginary friend.

'The spectre at our wedding. She was the bad fairy. My brother made me invite her – he has a soft spot for her. So did my husband. She twists men around her little finger. She's been waiting to twist the knife.'

'Lulu, I found—'

'They mucked around as kids, skulking in the cemetery over the road from us. My mother worried about my brother, he took it so seriously. I heard her suggesting to my dad they take him to a doctor, but my dad was a psychiatrist and it wouldn't have done to have a bonkers son, so he did nothing.' She spoke in a whisper and kept glancing at the back door as if afraid of being overheard, reminding Stella of William Frost's behaviour in the pub. She looked too, but saw only their reflections in the glass.

'What are you saying?' She closed her fingers around the driving licence in her pocket. Where was Jack?

Suddenly it struck Stella that Lulu might not know Rick Frost was dead. Years ago, one of her clients had been having an affair with a man who fell off a ladder at his home and died. He didn't turn up at the arranged place. Her client had seen a memorial notice in a newspaper six months later; by then she'd destroyed everything he had ever given her, assuming he had dumped her. Exactly as Lulu had been doing.

Lulu was still talking.

'This is written in invisible ink. He could never do anything normally. If we arranged to meet in a station or a café, he got there early to watch me waiting for him. Sometimes he wasn't there, but I felt I was being watched all the same.'

'Are you talking about your husband?' Stella might point out the marks weren't written with invisible ink since they could see them and she had a distant memory that invisible ink was made with lemon juice.

'What?' Lulu looked oddly guilty.

'I cleaned that cupboard, I didn't see this.' Why had Stanley been so interested in the cupboard?

'Exactly! Don't you see, someone's been here. No prizes for guessing who. I'm going to wipe away her crocodile tears!'

'Maybe wait until the morning.' Stella saw the time on her watch: ten past eleven; it nearly *was* the morning. 'Lulu, how do you know Rick Frost?' Gentle and friendly, she imitated Jack asking contentious questions.

'What do you mean?' Lulu stiffened and shut her eyes tight like a little kid hiding.

'I found this.' Stella laid the driving licence on the table beside the note. There would be time later to explain about her dog. The paper and the licence looked like exhibits from a crime scene. Perhaps they were. 'Were you having an affair with Rick Frost?'

Lulu opened her eyes. 'No, I bloody well was not!'

'Why have you got this?' Stella was morphing from cleaner to detective in one job.

'Why have I got any of his things?'

'You tell me.' Stella coaxed. *Take your time*, she nearly said.

Stella felt the sensation that Jack often claimed to feel, like an autocue: she saw Lulu's answer before she spoke.

'Rick Frost was my husband.'

Thirty-Seven

Friday, 25 October 2013

'How's Stella Darnell? Still cleaning for England or cleaning up England?' Cigarette smoke puffed from between Lucille May's lipsticked lips.

'She works hard,' Jack said levelly. At best Lucie and Stella were openly hostile towards each other.

'Sure I can't tempt you with a nippet? No milk, but a whole damn bottle of Tanqueray is cooling its heels!' Waving her glass of gin and tonic at him, Lucie shut an eye against the smoke and eyed him beadily with the other.

Jack shook his head. 'No, you're all right.' Lucie held a scary amount of drink without obvious impairment to her thinking or her memory. A 'nippet' – a triple gin with a splash of tonic – would fell him.

It was ten past ten. Jack had returned from his driving shift that day restless and dissatisfied. Shocked by Stella coming to Tallulah Frost's house that morning, he had failed – despite his determination to focus on it – to calculate the length of the West Hill tunnel. If he knew the mystery fact, it would unlock other hidden facts.

He hadn't yet faced examining the steam engine he had found on the monitor. It was a sign of something he had tried to forget.

Stella had texted, saying she had seen him. He was scared to see her and was appalled with himself. He had been called a coward in the past – it was true.

He was taking refuge with Lucie May. Unfettered by a moral code, Lucie pursued her stories with blind ambition. While this wasn't an attitude he admired, being with Lucie, her diminutive frame lost in a jumper – a relic of a husband divorced along the way – curled on her sofa, substituting smoke for air and consuming gin as if life, not death, depended on it, Jack felt a braver and better person. He nestled in his corner of the sofa. The coffee table was lost beneath piles of back copies of the *Chronicle*, on which Lucie May had been chief reporter for nearly forty years.

Lucie had just filed a story – 'Hush hush, Jackanory, it's embargoed until next week' – so was 'demob bloody jubilant!' She had once told him she never drank on the job, but he could see that alcohol was taking its toll. Her skilfully applied foundation didn't hide a pinkish complexion or the crazy bright of her eyes.

'You've decorated.' Stella would approve of the newly whitewashed walls. Although with Lucie's nicotine habit it would not be white for long.

Lucie had reinstated the numerous photos of herself with the great, the good and the royal (the Queen in 1970, Prince Edward in 1985).

'I've scared away the ghosts.' Lucie contemplated her glowing butt, fitted it between her lips and sucked on it before pinching it out in an ashtray shaped like a woman's upturned hand. Jack's own palms tingled.

Long ago, a woman had killed herself feet from where they sat. Lucie had bought the house intending to write a book about the case – her pension plan – but the ghosts had got to her first, so there would be no book. Jack doubted a lick of emulsion would scare them away.

'Certainly should,' he said nevertheless. Perhaps, after all, it was a good sign.

'So what can I do you for?' Lucie rasped. Swirling her glass, she sent ice whizzing around it, faster and faster. 'Or is this just a social call?'

He got to the point. 'What do you know about the Palmyra Tower?'

'Zilch. Should I?' Lucie drained her glass and mussed up her expensively dyed blonde hair. Her gestures and tics belonged to a long-ago younger self, but somehow she got away with it. She reached for her cigarette packet on the sofa arm, but then seemed to think better of it. 'Where is it, Italy? Going on holiday, darling? Can I come?' She gave a cackle and picked up the cigarette packet.

'Chiswick Mall.' Jack was disappointed; he had been relying on Lucie, a mine of information about West London, to shed light on his new home.

'Oh, you mean Chiswick Tower!' She flicked up a fresh cigarette, lit it, inhaled and puffed out a swirl of smoke. 'Talking of ghosts!' She shifted about happily. 'Dead Man's Tower! I knew it was finished. Luxury accommodation! They'll make a mint from some poor sod happy to climb that scaffold and live in a water tank!'

Jack's head jerked and he sniffed to cover the tic that rarely surfaced. 'That's me.'

'Say again?' Lucie's cigarette hand was above her shoulder, the smoke spiralling upwards.

'I'm living there.'

'Lordy-lou!' Lucie funnelled smoke up to her brilliant white ceiling. 'Even for you, that takes the biscuit!' she said eventually.

'Have you written something on it?'

'*Wind Drowns Out Terror Screams!*'

Like himself, Lucie had a photographic memory. She could recite from pieces she'd written decades ago, both the headlines and whole passages from the articles. She had facts at her fingertips that no amount of Tanqueray would blur or blot out. Jack felt a buzzing in his solar plexus: dread or excitement, he wasn't sure.

'Tell me.' Jack tucked his own feet up, shoes clear of the sofa – Lucie was house-proud – and prepared for a cracking story.

'Chiswick water tower was erected in 1940 to protect local industry, the brewery and a shipbuilder's on the wharf where Pages Yard is now. It was meant to put out fires caused by German bombing, but I don't think it ever did. Unlike the one on Ladbroke Grove – a bomb hit the cemetery nearby and sent a headstone smashing into the side of a gasometer. But for that tower, Shepherd's Bush would be a memory!'

Gone were Lucie's corncrake tones and her brash flirty style. The reporter was cool and authoritative, her mind a fount of fact and folklore. Jack got a glimpse of the professional, brimful of hope and principle, that Lucie had once been.

'It was decommissioned in the sixties and became a white elephant. One resident campaigned to have it demolished in the late seventies, but the whole community rose up and objected. It might be a concrete monstrosity, but it was their concrete – you get it!'

She went to the cabinet on the other side of the room and, with Faustian precision, put together another nippet.

'It was listed and in the eighties a company bought it to turn it into luxury apartments. But it was a bridge – or a tower – too far and they went bankrupt. It stayed empty for another couple of years, Chiswick's own Centre Point. A consortium bought it about five years ago and began redeveloping it. They wouldn't do interviews – the project was cloaked in secrecy. Even I couldn't get a sniff. If you ask me, that was the point, talk it up – or not talk – so I gave up. I won't play that game.' She dropped a lemon slice into her drink and sucked on another. 'I didn't think the place would ever get a tenant. Trust it to be you!'

'Why? It's got amazingly detailed views.' Jack accidentally echoed the leaflet. The sensation in his solar plexus clarified into dread.

Wandering to her French doors, Lucie sniffed her drink with anticipatory delight. 'Because a man had lain dead there for nearly a year. Sorry, darling.' She turned around and grimaced at him.

'There's no sign of him now.' Thinking of Stanley's furious digging and sniffing, Jack wasn't sure this was true.

'The police couldn't identify him. He had perfect teeth, no fillings, nothing, but no dentist had him on their books. Teeth was pretty much all that was left – the corpse was skeletal after all that time. He was discovered by a representative of the consortium. You sure about it? I sure as hell wouldn't like to live in a place where a person had died.'

Jack refrained from pointing out that Lucie was doing exactly this, or that most flats and houses over thirty years old had witnessed a death.

'Who was the man?'

'They never found out. I dubbed him "Glove Man" since that was pretty much all there was of him. The nationals ran with that, not that I got any credit.' She opened the French windows and seemed to Jack to float on to the patio into the darkness beyond. He got up and followed her.

'I'm sorting this too,' she was muttering, glass in hand, as she leant down desultorily and wrenched up a weed, tossing it into next door's garden.

'Why did you call him Glove Man?' In the slant of light from the sitting room, Jack noticed that at long last Lucie had got rid of the rusted swing that had stood for decades in the middle of the lawn. He felt a twinge of regret. He fancied flying up into the night, but on a swing he would have to come down.

'They found a glove on the corpse's back. There was some argy-bargy at the inquest about whether he could have placed it there himself. Terry demonstrated it was just about possible, but the question remained, why would he? If he was going to kill himself and make it look like murder, then he should have framed someone. Obvious candidate was the owner of the glove, but that was never established. His fingernails showed signs that he had gone for the door and the walls, but being metal and concrete he had no purchase, nothing to grip, poor bloke. So he wasn't in a "framing frame of mind"!' Jack suspected she had made the pun more than once before.

'What was the verdict?' Was this another case of Terry's that had got away? That was the reality of being a detective. If you wanted to truly restore order, you should be a cleaner. He might say that to Stella. *Stella*.

'Open. The police thought he was homeless. He thinks: set up shop in the tower, but the door shuts. Effectively he's trapped in a giant toilet cistern! In the old days he'd have got out through the roof, but the builders had stripped out the pipework by then.'

'Why didn't you think he was homeless?'

'Apart from a sleeping bag, there was a champagne bottle in there, a high-class choice of tipple for a guy living on the street – or *above* the street. A used condom suggested he wasn't alone. They found more than one set of fingerprints, but nothing that figured on police records. Over the years enough people had been up there. I suggested to Terry it might have been a paedophile and his family were keeping *shtum*. What better way to disown him than his being locked in a tower? They might even have locked him in there!'

'Why did you think he was a paedophile?'

'The glove was too small for an adult. It wasn't his.'

'Could have been dropped by kids afterwards.'

'That was the official police line. But, as I said to Terry, even a kid knows better than to incriminate himself. Terry agreed, but without cogent evidence he couldn't raise a budget to take it further. Another mystery that haunted the poor guy.' She sipped at her drink. Despite her threadbare jumper, she didn't seem to feel the cold.

'Sounds like you had the answer. He drank too much, shut the door and was unable to escape.'

'There was no reason for the door to shut, it was at the top of a spiral staircase, as you know, so could only shut if someone deliberately pushed it. Ergo, someone who intended to lock him in. After so long the pathologist couldn't pinpoint time and date of death, but they narrowed it to late 1987. As I said, October was the month of the Great Storm, that hurricane that famously wasn't forecast. The wind was like a tempest – the lead flashings on our house rolled up like foil and we lost a load of roof tiles. It was deafening. No one would have heard Glove Man yelling for help. Even on a quiet night, I doubt the sound would have carried.'

She ground out her cigarette into the grass with the toe of her boot.

Jack was about nine in 1987; he had a hazy recollection of streets blocked by fallen tree trunks, pavements strewn with branches and smashed glass, cars abandoned. It gave him a bad feeling, the same feeling he got when he thought about the steam engine.

'Hundreds of feet up in a concrete vault, the man must have been stark staring petrified. It was likely he had heart disease, probably undiagnosed. Being a bag of bones they couldn't verify that. But it's likely the terror of being locked in a tank miles in the sky did it for him. Bam! His ticker packed up. Terry's lot did call-outs to surgeries, but drew a blank; no doctor had a missing patient with a dicky ticker. Poor Terry. A literal skeleton in the cupboard!' Lucie was gazing at the sky; she seemed to have forgotten Jack was there.

'I swapped notes with Terry. I had a bulging file because of the demolition protests. We kept each other's secrets.' She pinched up the lemon from her drink and threw it into the bushes. 'Stupid bugger, I said he needed exercise.'

'Who?'

'Terry.' She produced her cigarettes from the waistband of her trousers and stuck one between her lips. 'Stella see much of her mum?'

'Yes.' Jack knew the tactic. Lucie would appear to be asking after someone, but everything led somewhere. He wouldn't let his guard down.

'Mobile phones were a rarity then and they were the size of houses. So, end of Glove Man.' Lucie was with the story again.

The door in the tower was original. A man had battered on the galvanized metal before he collapsed with a coronary. The dog had tuned into the frequency of the man's terror and anguish; Jack, usually so alive to the presence of the dead, had sensed nothing. He had abandoned one set of ghosts – of his parents, of the self he preferred to forget – for a more potent phantom.

'How old was he?'

'Between twenty and forty, which gives lots to play with. One clue, he had a receipt in his trousers from the Fullers wine shop, as it was in 1987. That one on the corner of Goldhawk Road and King Street – your old neck of the woods, darling. No CCTV then and no one in the shop recalled the purchase. In that area, getting a bottle of bubbly is probably not a rare occurrence!' Lucie paused and contemplated the sky, where Jack could just make out faint stars.

'Stella's mum back from Oz yet?' she asked airily.

'Yes.' She was homing in. He steeled himself and tried to deflect her. 'I got a leaflet through the door about the tower.' If he was honest, Jack was thrilled to be living on a murder site. Another of Terry's unsolved cases: it was a sign. He would offer it to Stella as a recompense for his being in Tallulah Frost's landing cupboard. Except if he said Lucie had told him, it would make things worse. Stella wouldn't want to hear that Lucille May and her father had worked on a case together. It would be no recompense at all.

Stella and Lucie, chalk and cheese. Chalk and chalk as they weren't so different. Both of them had loved Terry Darnell. Jack wished they could get on.

'What's this Palmyra shit? What's wrong with plain old Chiswick Tower? Is that your name for it?'

'No, it was on the leaflet.' Jack pictured the pink sheet. Apart from Palmyra being an ancient Syrian city and a suburb in Western Australia, he had no idea what connection it had with the tower. With little sleep, his mind was a fog. He wondered again at his luck in getting the flat – not luck in Lucie's view. It had taken two mail-shots, so maybe she was right, potential tenants had found Lucie's articles about the dead man online and been put off.

He and Lucie were mavericks. Few would relish knowing someone had died a horrible death a couple of metres from the bottom of their bed.

'Palmyra rings a bell with me, but the older one gets, the more bells ring. Stay, young Jack, stay as you are!' Lucie touched his cheek with the back of her hand and meandered back to the sitting room. 'You should check out what your mystery guest looks like.' She pulled shut the French windows.

'Sorry?' Jack sat in his corner.

'Mispers!'

'Bless you.' It wasn't a sneeze, he realized.

'The Missing Persons' website. It lists the lost and unclaimed of Britain. Bodies found on commons, in alleyways, drowned in the Thames or hit by trains on railway lines. Glove Man hasn't got a photo, unfortunately, so nothing to see. They've done a sketch, so maybe one day someone might recognize him. I hope it's me.'

'I'll take a look.' Jack frowned to hide his excitement.

'Course you will, Rapunzel!' Lucie punched his arm. 'As soon as you're back in your tower!'

Jack drew his coat around him to hide that she was right.

Lucie May lit her cigarette and said in her Lucille Ball accent: 'Has Mrs Darnell brought a present back for her "one and only" offspring?' She smiled sweetly through a pall of smoke.

Ground Zero.

As if he hadn't heard, Jack asked, 'Does the name Rick Frost ring any of your bells?'

Thirty-Eight

Friday, 25 October 2013

Stella lived in a gated complex in Brentford, bought off-plan. She had opted for a corner flat on the fifth floor in the block – high enough for privacy (she was indifferent to the 'stunning views of the River Thames and across London'), but accessible should the lift break down. Had Stella been given to mulling on such matters, she might have thought it not dissimilar to Jack's tower. Silent and secure, with 'detailed views'.

For the first couple of years the building had been 80 per cent unoccupied. This had suited Stella; she didn't move to find a community in which to play an active part. She signed up to Neighbourhood Watch because keeping an eye out for intruders was what she did anyway. When the economy improved – for the income bracket that could afford Thames Heights – there had been an influx of new residents. Now only a handful of properties were empty. Despite this, Stella rarely met anyone going in or out.

Taught by Terry to be security-conscious, Stella appreciated the automatic gates that juddered open on to a drive winding between undulating lawns to garages and numbered bays. CCTV monitored the door of a fully glazed marble-clad foyer more in keeping with a multinational corporation HQ than a block of flats in Greater London.

With Stanley at her heels, Stella punched in the key code and slipped into the lobby. The door shut swiftly with a sigh, narrowly avoiding Stanley's back legs. Stella was gratified: her complaint about how long it took to close had been heeded. Most of her complaints – sporadic cleaning of the common parts and security lights that worked in the day but not at night – were ignored.

She was keen to get to bed: it had been a long and unsatisfactory day, culminating in the discovery that Lulu Carr was Tallulah Frost and her husband hadn't left her for another woman, he was dead.

At the end of the cavernous lobby – housing two lifts – a line of ceiling bulbs had blown, throwing it into gloom. Stella made for the lifts and was brought up short by the sudden hush of the lift doors opening in unison, a rare thing.

Two paths of bright light flooded the marble. Stella hung back to make way for passengers in both lifts. No one came out. She might have taken it in her stride, but Stanley began to quake, his tail between his legs. Tired and troubled about Jack's recent appearances in odd places – the roof of his tower, a cemetery and the pub – Stella was assailed by panic. To reach the staircase or the main door, she would have to cross the slants of light.

It was inconceivable that both lifts had descended empty at the same time. Someone had to have activated them. Stanley began to growl, giving her away. She snatched him up and, rushing across the marble floor, shouldered her way through to the stairwell. Behind her she heard the same hush. The lift doors were closing.

Up or down? Stella made a snap decision and ran up the stairs to her flat rather than down to the basement. Fifty steps versus ten. After twenty, her legs became leaden as if she were wading through water. Stanley had gone quiet, but with every step he got heavier. Her rucksack, weighed down with her laptop, bumped against her spine and her boots scraped on the concrete stairs, giving her away. All the time the lift must be travelling upwards, faster than she could run. Or it had gone down. She had no way of knowing.

Each floor was numbered, which was lucky because Stella soon lost count. She couldn't keep up her pace. Her lungs bursting, she had to stop. She stood for a moment, trying to get her breath, her chest heaving with hot pain. Hearing nothing, she edged to the banister. She looked up and then down, scared of seeing someone patiently waiting, looking out for her.

No one need do that. They would know exactly where she was.

Stella powered up the last flight and flung herself through the door at level five. She raced along the carpeted corridor, feeling for her key with her free hand. She hit the lock, missing it. She inserted it at the same moment as the lift doors were opening.

Stella tumbled into her hall and kicked shut the door behind her. Terry hadn't trusted CCTV or electronic locking devices; all you need is a power cut, he had said. As she turned the keys in the two extra five-lever mortice locks, she silently thanked him for advising she fit them, along with the London bar that made jemmying the door impossible.

Stanley leapt down and trundled off down the hall and into the living room, tail twirling like a flag. Slumped against the front door, her heart still pounding, Stella heard sloshing from the kitchen as he guzzled from his water bowl. Business as usual. She stumbled into her study, the 'second bedroom' opposite the living room, and took out her laptop. The lifts must both be faulty, she assured herself.

She began to close the blind and stopped, her hand on the cord.

A man stood on the path leading up from the gates. Only because she hadn't yet switched on the study light could she see him, because with no security lights it was dark outside. Tall in a long black coat, hands in his pockets. Jack. Full of relief, Stella reached for the window lock; she wouldn't bang on the glass and disturb the neighbours. The key was in the living room.

She waved. Jack didn't respond, although she was sure he could see her. He hadn't been there when she arrived – she would have seen him and he would have called to her. He had a key to the basement, so he could get inside. She got out her phone and texted him. Her fingers trembled and she made several mistakes before managing: *Are you ok?*

Nothing in his body language intimated he had received the text. No light glowing in his pocket. She dialled his number.

'This is Jack, who are you? Tell me after the beep.'

She would have to go down to get him.

Stella was about to open the front door when her phone lit up.

Fine. You? Jack didn't waste words.

Why are you here?

She froze. There were two watching eyes at the top of the phone screen. It must be William – he *was* stalking her. She was startled by the ping of a text.

Why are any of us here? Jx.

Stella went back to the study and, neighbours or not, raised her hand to bang on the glass.

Jack had gone.

Thirty-Nine

Saturday, 26 October 2013

Gender	Male
Age range	20 to 40
Ethnicity	White European
Height (cm)	172
Build	Medium
Date found	30/9/1988
Estimated date of death	Late 1987 (possibly October)
Body or remains	Body – skeletal
Circumstances	A male body was found in Chiswick Tower in Chiswick Lane South
Possessions	Empty bottle of Veuve Clicquot champagne
Hair	Medium-length brown
Facial hair	N/A
Eye colour	Unknown
Distinguishing features	No tattoos
Clothing	Casual Millets anorak, zip-up front, size 44; beige cotton trousers size 32 (brand name Racing Green); braces – blue; kipper tie – blue; leather brogues, leather uppers, plastic soles – black (brand name Clarks); crew-neck jumper – turquoise (brand name Reiss)
Hose	Calvin Klein blue Y-fronts with red piping and waistband. White socks
Jewellery	Gold metal ring engraved with 'x' in centre of which tiny diamond. Gents Timex wind-up watch, no numerals, markings dabbed with luminous paint. Black leather strap with lighter stitching

On a trawl of the Missing Persons' Bureau website, Jack examined pictures of dead faces – reachable by surmounting several warnings to stop the unwitting stumbling upon one. 'Glove Man' had been submitted by the Metropolitan Police on 30 September 1988. No picture, as Lucie had said. Jack thought the pencil sketch familiar, it could have been any one of his male passengers – that parade of faces on platforms when he pulled into stations.

After a year in the empty water tank, the man was beyond recognition. Jack could imagine the skeleton, wrist bones poking from the 'casual Millets anorak', the fabric fusty and faded, nibbled by mites. Grey bones mapped with scraps of brown leathery skin, a skull tufted with 'medium-length brown hair' the consistency of dried grasses. A skull's bared-teeth grin, which always struck Jack as gleeful rather than sinister. The empty eye sockets would have gazed back sightless. The man had died alone and unheard, perhaps unloved. After decades it was unlikely he would be matched with a missing person. Missing, but not missed. Once upon a time, over fifty years ago, Jack hoped there had been a celebration of Glove Man's birth. His individuality, the man he had been in life, was distilled on a website database to his taste in champagne.

Jack leafed through Lucie's file. 'If you find out who he is, he's mine, darling.' Side-stepping credit suited Jack. Stella had been uncomfortable when he'd asked her to take the kudos for their work on the Rokesmith and Blue Folder cases. *The Detective's Daughter Does Dad Proud* had been one of Lucie's headlines. Stella had only agreed when he pointed out the merits of anonymity: he could work incognito.

An hour ago Stella had texted enquiring if he was *OK*. She might be feeling guilty at going behind his back and – a classic tactic – projecting her guilt on to him. Jack had hoped she would suggest he came over to see her; although it was the middle of the night he could do with one of her shepherd's pies. They had much to debrief. But she must be avoiding him.

The first article Lucie had written on the case was printed in the *Chronicle* the week after the corpse was found and was headed 'Who Is the Man in the Tower?' Jack sang under his breath:

> *The man in the moon*
> *Came down too soon...*

The man in the tower hadn't come down sooner or later. The file included torn leaves from Lucie's notebook. He read that 'the corpse's jumper was knotted around his neck, although anorak zipped up'. This wasn't on the website, probably because it wasn't relevant to identification. Lucie had got it from Terry. She had said that the knotted jumper suggested a jaunty, laconic mood far removed from screaming in a concrete chamber until the heart gave out. Jack agreed that it belonged with quaffing champagne, if it had been drunk and had not evaporated over the months. The man had put on his anorak without unknotting his jumper and putting it on first. Lucie said this showed he must have died soon after he knew he was imprisoned. The night of the hurricane would have been cold; crazy to have a sweater, she had said, and not wear it.

Jack had momentarily forgotten he was in the room where the man had died. Not a room then, a concrete tank that for a year had served as a tomb. The place on the floor where the body had been was in shadow. The glow from his laptop drew the curving walls closer. He thought of a cardboard tube rolled tighter and tighter until there was no room to breathe.

He went to the door and, getting down on his hands and knees, shuffled across the floor. Oak boards laid over the concrete base were warm. A heat-exchange system took water from the Thames to cool and heat the tower.

In 1987, little had been done to the 5,000-gallon tank. According to Lucie's notebook, slats beneath the ceiling, glazed with red-and-yellow-coloured panes of glass, were part of that first tranche of development and not in the original tank.

The tower's designer – given its function Jack presumed it was an engineer rather than an architect – would have dispensed with conceits like a cupola on the roof. Access to clean the tank would be through a hatch in its ceiling; there was no sign of it now. The ceiling was over a metre above Jack. He was tall and could easily get to a hatch using a stepladder, even a chair. In 1987 the man had only a champagne bottle. If there had been a hatch it would have been out of his reach.

Why was he there? In the second article covering the inquest, Lucie – keeping within legal bounds – speculated on suicide. As she had told him, the man had no identification, a typical suicide trait. He had bought the champagne either with the right money, or returned to his home after buying it and left his wallet there before going to the tower. Every so often there were stories of people lying dead in their homes for months, even years. Neighbours would claim that the person had kept themselves to themselves. The inoffensive, it seemed, were less missed than the argumentative, boundary-disputing ones. Neighbours had assumed they were on holiday or had moved without saying goodbye. Glove Man must own his home or the police were right and he had no home. Otherwise someone was chasing some serious rent arrears.

If he had been murdered, a careful killer would remove anything incriminating or that would hasten the identification of the victim. The body was the biggest clue in a murder. Lucie believed it was murder and eventually Terry had agreed.

Jack rubbed his eyes. It was ten past three and he was driving in a few hours. He reflected that cases were like number-nine buses, not like trains: you waited for hours, then two came along at once. A man in a tower and a man under a train.

Lucie was convinced that the killer was a woman, whoever had shared the champagne with the victim. She had conceded that the man might be gay, but attributed the tidy scene to the feminine touch. Terry had agreed. A tidy man himself, Jack didn't share this logic.

Why not take everything with her? Terry had countered. Lucie had thought of that. She said the imagination behind the killing was a woman's. Carefully, she had constructed a suicide scene for the police. The man climbed the tower once. At the top, he had opened the bottle and toasted himself and his shit life. He had swallowed a handful of tablets and drunk the contents of the bottle until he lost consciousness. But his attire suggested panache, respect for style and ritual, 'strolling out' rather than going out with a bang. The killer hadn't legislated for a heart attack brought on by terror or the grazed and bloodied fingers. Lucie's notes reached a definite conclusion: Glove Man was having an affair and was murdered by his lover. One day Lucie would write the book, she said.

Jack saw there might be something raw and romantic about drinking champagne and making love in an abandoned water tower high above the city. The lack of windows would put him off, but there would be no need to give false names at a hotel or make up some story that the staff clearly did not believe. It was also possible that their relationship was legitimate: sex in a tower to spice up a stale marriage.

For the past few hours he had been dwelling on a case that wasn't just cold, it was cryogenically so. Apart from hiding in a cupboard from his co-detective in the house of a possible suspect, he hadn't progressed the Frost case for which they would be paid. All he had done was to betray the person he cared for most in the world. He could at least look at what he had found there.

He grabbed his coat from the bed and went through the pockets. The piece of paper with the marks on the desk was not in any of them. He flopped on to the bed, head in hands.

The sink's glugging brought him back to the present. He went into the kitchen. The tap wasn't dripping, although the bottom of the sink was wet. He hadn't run the tap since he came home. The last time was when he washed his Shreddies' bowl at 5 a.m. yesterday morning; it couldn't be damp from then. There must be a problem. He would have to contact the consortium about getting in a plumber. He hadn't the spirit to appreciate the humour of there being a leak in a water tower. To stop the glugging, he did as

Stella had and turned the tap on full and then turned it off. The pipes made a dull clunk. Stella had explained it was an airlock caused by two taps in a building being turned on at different times. At the time he had accepted her explanation about two sinks, but it didn't make sense: there was only him. His father would have understood how the tower worked. They had never had to call in a plumber or electrician when he was alive.

Jack returned to his laptop. He opened Outlook and addressed an email to Stella. Too late to text: she would be in bed.

Let's meet to take stock of what we have so far, he pecked at speed with two fingers, using one of Stella's phrases to reassure her. *Tomorrow. I'm on the Wimbledon line, finish late afternoon.* He was about to say he hoped the cleaning was going well, but she would think that odd. She cleaned somewhere most days.

I'm upset you didn't tell me you had changed your mind about pretending to be a cleaner— Jack stopped. He was about to say Stella was his lodestar and she had let him down. He pressed 'delete' and the cursor chewed up the last sentence. Better to say it in person. He sent it off and, returning to the Missing Persons' site, picked up Lucie's file.

There was nothing in any of her pieces or on the website about a used condom. 'On the right as you go in,' Lucie had told him, keen for Jack to match up his new home with the 'murder' scene. Terry's theory, she said, was that the man and his companion arrived and left separately, her first, leaving him to clear up. It explained the bottle and condom (only once, poor chap, Lucie had crowed): he had been about to stuff everything into the bag when the door shut. Later someone had taken the bag away. It had never been found. It would be at the bottom of the Thames, Lucie said.

She had said the door couldn't have blown shut in the hurricane and, looking at it now, Jack could verify that. It was at the top of the spiral staircase, out of the draught.

The prime suspect was an absence. Another kind of missing person. In the intervening decades no one had come forward to rule themselves out or hand themselves in. Perhaps the person had not intended to kill the man – he or she had expected him to get out. Or had planned to return but the hurricane had stopped them. People had died that night – perhaps the phantom companion had been one of them? Terry had conjectured that it might have been kids messing about and, finding the man dead, they had fled in panic, one of them dropping a glove. Lucie had decided that the glove was a 'red herring' left by kids who had nothing to do with the man being trapped. They had never claimed it for fear of being accused of murder.

The police had appealed to local sex workers, asking if anyone had had a client who had taken them to the tower. All had said no and that if asked they would refuse the job however high the pay. This made it unlikely that a woman had murdered her client.

The glove, black leather with a popper fastener and a crown motif indented on the cuff, came from Marks and Spencer and according to the label fitted boys aged between ten and fourteen. Terry had told Lucie it had lain along the man's spine, fingers pointing towards his head. The police withheld this information, as possible leverage with a suspect. Jack was surprised he had told Lucie. Being a journalist, she couldn't boast trustworthiness among her good points.

The police traced all the customers who had bought gloves in this range from the Marks and Spencer on Chiswick High Road with cheques, Access, Visa or American Express, but it yielded no leads. With such a wide time frame for culpability, alibis were meaningless. Nine of the 121 children for whom the gloves had been bought had lost one or both since purchase. Of these, three boys and a girl lived near the tower and of them, three – not the girl, Jack was gratified to read – were frightened of heights so incapable of making the precarious climb. The girl had lost her glove on a trip to the science museum. Lucie had added in the margin of her notes that Terry said her glove was later found.

Nearly thirty years later, he imagined Mr Glove Man still filed unidentified in a drawer at Hammersmith Mortuary.

Jack scribbled 'glove owners' list' on his pad to follow up. The man had been wearing a ring but no spouse had reported him missing. Perhaps they were separated or the woman had already died and he was a widower. Too many possibilities.

The website had a picture of the Timex watch and, as soon as he saw the simple dial, Jack recognized it. He shut his eyes and saw the 'TIMEX' written under the twelve. Like Glove Man's, this one had only a six and twelve with no date.

Jack's first watch had been a wind-up Timex. His father had had a Timex given to him by a German client, but it had a chequered band across the face. The trouble with having a photographic memory was that his mind was full of images most of which were of no consequence. In the eighties, there must have been lots of men, apart from himself, his father and the dead man, who wore Timex watches.

Jack gave a long-drawn-out yawn and his eyes watered. He looked again at the details on the database entry. No tattoos. For an organization seeking to identify corpses, the more marks or scars on a body the better. Tattoos, a moderately contentious form of expression in life, were a welcome clue in death. He had a scar on his thumb – so deep it must have scored the bone, Lucie said.

Jack looked to see if Stella had replied to his email, knowing she would not have. Although she frequently worked late, this was so late it was early. A thought occurred. She hadn't invited him over because she was with her Brand-new Brother. He would be making himself at home in his father's old house. Stella's house. He would be sizing up its worth.

His email to her was still in the Outbox. Jack was sure he had pressed 'Send'. He did so now. He received an email about money-saving tips, but the email to Stella remained unsent.

He confirmed there was a blue light on the router before remembering he had had incoming mail. There were five bars at the bottom of the screen depicting an 'excellent' signal.

His laptop wasn't connected to his router. It had jumped on to the one called CBruno that he had been offered when he first connected to the internet. The owner – C. Bruno presumably – was clearly not savvy about security. While he was using this connection, Jack's own account was not secure. He clicked to the dropdown list of routers – his and C. Bruno's – and as he did so, noticed the CBruno router script. WPA2-PSK. The code indicated a secure router, which meant he shouldn't have been able to access it without a password. Yet he had. Given this, why hadn't his email to Stella gone? He sent it now.

Jack heard a sound. If he hadn't worked it out from the silence, Lucie's information about the Glove Man told him that in the conversion the tower had been soundproofed. He could hear a buzzing, intermittent and insistent.

It was his phone. His imagining the Glove Man dying in panic and distress centimetres from his bed had upset him, his nerves were on edge. A blue subterranean light from his phone sent an insidious glow across the curving walls. He saw the room as the concrete tank it had been that night.

Open the door.

Jack dropped the phone before he had seen whom the message was from. He heard a distant boom: someone was banging on the flat door. He caught himself in the wardrobe mirror, a poster boy for a horror film, mouth and eyes wide open, hands clasping the sides of his face.

Far off, through the thick cladding, he heard his name being called. Without pausing to consider if it was safe, he flung the door open.

Stella was on the spiral staircase with Stanley in her arms. Never had Jack felt so warmly towards the dog, although from the fathomless brown eyes, it was unclear if the feeling was mutual.

'Lulu Carr is his wife!' Stella marched past him into the flat.

Forty

Saturday, 26 October 2013

'Stella I need to tell you—' Jack started as he shut the door.

'We've made a breakthrough!' Stella had intended to confront Jack about coming to her flat, but, reassured by his email saying that he wanted to 'take stock' – they were a team – she let it go. Jack would have had his reasons; best not to probe.

She dropped on to the chair by his desk and swivelled to face the room. Stanley sat at her feet, eyes on Jack. She didn't trust his mood and fished a liver treat from her anorak, popping it in his mouth. Jackie said Stanley got jealous of her giving Jack attention. Stella had disagreed. She and Jack were ships in the night – or day; she saw more of the dog so no problem. Besides, he was just a dog.

Jack went to the window, arms folded, his hands under his armpits. 'I wanted to explain why I was—'

'I'm cleaning Rick Frost's house. Lulu Carr is his widow!'

'We already know his wife is called Tallulah Frost.' Jack pushed off the window sill. Stanley got up, tail whirling.

'She's using her maiden name and a diminutive of her real name. Lulu is short for Tallulah. Tallulah Frost says she wants a fresh start, like we offer at Clean Slate,' Stella ploughed on.

'Is this your client whose husband left her?'

'He didn't leave. He's dead.'

'She lives in Perrers Road?'

'Yes!' It was late; Stella forgave Jack being slow to grasp the immensity of her discovery.

'So you were cleaning there already?' Jack asked. 'Before we got this case?'

'Yes! I've spent hours listening to Lulu – or Tallulah. I know more than I might if we'd interviewed her, except now I don't know what's true and what's made up. I told her we were working for her brother-in-law. She said he should mind his own business. He was right, no love lost there.'

'Stella, you are the best of Wonderhorses!' Jack spread his arms.

Stanley gave a shrill bark. Stella decided that Jackie was right about him getting possessive.

'It's a sign! Amongst the fabrication will be a kernel of truth. Her husband may have been having an affair. Strip away the narrative and we've got betrayal at the core of this case.'

Stella didn't quite see how Jack had arrived at this conclusion.

'Dying is like leaving. Suppose he was having an affair with this Nicola and then he died. Tallulah Frost or Lulu would feel rejected. OK, so now we have a suspect with a motive.' He put his phone and a plastic box of dental floss on the bedspread in front of him, presumably to represent suspect and motive. 'Lulu/Tallulah Frost finds out and chases him off the platform. She can't accept she's killed him so reframes it as being jilted which, as I said, is also true. I guess she's more comfortable being the victim than the persecutor.'

'She told her brother about the affair.' Stella felt exhausted. There were too many facts that might be fiction. Now she understood why Lulu's husband had left so much stuff. Where Lulu's husband had gone, he couldn't use an iPad.

'Speaking of Rick Frost, I had a word with—' Jack began.

'But she told me and Dale she saw him in the street the other day. Which obviously she couldn't have.' Stella felt a tightening under her ribs. She had been lied to. Lying was betrayal. She had been fooled.

'Probably believes she did. You often see a person you're grieving for out and about, on buses or waiting on the platform for a train. That sense that they've just left the room.' Jack was rolling a ball of rose quartz between his palms as if kneading dough. A birthday present from Jackie, it apparently signified love. Jack held store by lucky stones. Stella couldn't see how a lump of mineral signified anything. She had given Jack aftershave and had yet to smell it on him.

'So Dale was spot on!' Stella exclaimed.

'How come?'

'He said she was lying about something. He said she was "inauthentic". He got it straight away.'

Jack shook his head. 'Yes, well, it's easy to see stuff if you're not involved.'

'Lulu's not a murderer.' Stella didn't know why she had said that.

'Because?'

'She's not organized; her place was a mess. You've described this as a perfect murder. If Lulu planned to push her husband off a platform, we'd know exactly what happened.'

'It is possible to achieve perfection by accident. Like the beauty of light falling on the river because clouds part while you are standing there.'

Jack spoke to the rose quartz as if it were a crystal ball. Stella scanned the room for the aftershave. She had given him Armani Code Ice, not for the smell but the word 'code'. Maybe he kept it in the bathroom. She zipped up her anorak; right now Code Ice fitted the temperature of the tower.

'Let's do an audit of the suspects.' She brought Jack back to the matter in hand.

'William Frost.' Jack was prompt; he manoeuvred the dental floss to the centre of the bed. 'As we said, him having brought us the case doesn't absolve him of guilt. If he's so keen to solve this, why choose a cleaning company and not an established private detective? Or go back to the police.'

'He did go to the police and Martin Cashman wouldn't touch it. We came recommended by Jackie.' Stella would accept cleaning from a detective agency if Jackie vouched for them, but decided not to say this. She wanted Jack on point.

'Do we *know* the police aren't interested?' Jack narrowed his eyes. 'We only have his word he spoke to them.'

'You were at the inquest and you saw Rick Frost die. The verdict was suicide.'

'Nevertheless, it might be worth giving your mate Martin a call. Check out his thoughts, they might not tally with the official view.'

Stella was reluctant to waste Cashman's time. As her dad's old friend and colleague, he would give her plenty of it, but he would be humouring her. However, after her lunch with William she did wonder if he had been straight with her. He had definitely seemed nervous and wasn't happy when she made it clear she was going to investigate the case her way. Putting aside her growing guilt that she had used his app – with his permission and without – she didn't like that he had used it to find her. What else did he use it for?

'Lulu-Tallulah Carr-Frost is an obvious suspect and now we have a motive. She has the most to gain, as we've already said. Her lying to you puts her up at the top. I asked Lucille May about Rick Frost.' Jack slipped that in, knowing she wouldn't like it. 'She had already gone into his business. It seems that Frost only had one client, an engineering company. She couldn't remember the name: she's getting back to me. She thinks we're wasting our time and Frost's money.'

'Nice of her to worry.' Stella bridled, although she was beginning to think so too. She was peeved that Jack had gone to Lucille May without agreeing it with her. Some team. She hadn't meant to see William without him. She announced blithely, 'There's the mistress.'

'A mistress!' Jack had the right response this time.

'Lucille May didn't mention Nicola Barwick?' She felt bad for the smooth surprise. 'Well, according to Lulu, she was a wicked fairy and cast a bad spell at their wedding.'

'Did she?' Jack's natural belief in curses and bad fairies was greater than his capacity to be hurt. Stella was chagrined at her effort to put him on the back foot.

'Lulu was all for going to see her tonight. I had to stop her.'

'Why now?'

'As opposed to when?'

'Frost died six weeks ago – why is she tackling her now? What's changed?'

'She said she saw her in the street with her husband this week.'

'Which can't be true since he's dead.'

'Not if she's grieving.' Stella reminded Jack of his earlier point.

'That's different. Actually thinking you saw a dead person and acting on it by trying to see them is delusional.'

'So she's lying about that too?' Stella was losing patience with the woman who had called herself Lulu Carr.

'Maybe. Maybe not.' Jack tipped the rose quartz from one palm to the other. 'Something's nagging at me,' he said after a moment.

'What?'

'It's gone – probably means it's important. Go with her to see Nicola Barwick. Whether she's a mistress or not, she'll give us insight into Rick Frost's character.'

'It could be messy. What if Lulu attacks her?'

'Do you think she will?' Jack raised his eyebrows. 'You don't think Lulu capable of murder.'

'No, but—'

'Mess is what we need. Detectives stir the rubbish around and up comes an oyster!'

'Pearl.' Stella knew about searching through the rubbish: Suzie had gone through a phase of losing things in the pedal bin.

'What about the inspector?' Stella had the self-conscious impression she was playing at being a detective, deliberately calling innocent passers-by suspects to make it feel like a real case. She was no better than Lulu Carr. The man had been waiting for a train, he had been nice to her and to her dog, then he'd got on the Richmond train and gone on with his life. Were they twisting facts calling him a suspect?

'Describe him again?'

'It was dark. He was my height, so tall. I think he had brown hair, but there was no light so it might have been black. He was wearing a coat, I think. I didn't see his face.' Stella saw the hopelessness of the situation. They had no means of finding the inspector. He might as well have been one of Jack's ghosts.

Jack grinned. 'Sounds like me.'

'Not at all!' As soon as he said it, Stella realized that the reason why the man had seemed familiar was because he had reminded her of the side of Jack she preferred not to dwell on.

'Could it have been William Frost putting on a different voice?'

Stella was about to say no, but realized she couldn't. The man was tall, and so was Frost; his hair was dark, as was Frost's. Frost had a deep voice, but it would be easy to lighten it and the man at the station had said little.

'I don't know,' she said finally.

'William Frost, Lulu Carr, Nicola Barwick and the station inspector who may be Frost. Unless they all have alibis, that's three if not four suspects! Lovely!'

'How is that lovely?' It complicated an already complicated problem.

'The more suspects we have, the greater the chance we'll keep an open mind and ward off prejudices and preconceptions. Lulu and William will have alibis – the police no doubt checked them out, although, unless they're watertight, it doesn't rule them out. The other two are problematic. Pass me my phone – it's on the desk. I'll take minutes on the notebook app.'

Stella stopped herself rolling her eyes. Jack never took notes and certainly not minutes. Swivelling the chair around, she rootled amongst a sheaf of papers by Jack's laptop. Wistfully she recalled the wealth of material they had gathered for the Blue Folder case.

Dead Man in Tower, Screams Unheard.

'What is this?' She waved a photocopied sheet at Jack.

'Ah-hmm.' Jack cleared his throat. 'I was going to mention that.'

If Jack had been nervous about Stanley, it was nothing to how he looked now. His usual pallor was sheet-white.

'What dead man?' She read the byline: Lucille May. The journalist would be behind why Jack had moved to a desolate tower reachable only by a dangerous girder-type thing hardly wider than a pipe. She counted to five before she trusted herself to speak.

'*A man died after being trapped in a tower during the 1987 storm.* It was in *this* tower, over *there!*' Stella pointed to the floor by the door and uttered in a whisper. 'He literally died of fright all alone—'

'What is he doing?' Jack followed her finger.

Neither Jack nor Stella had noticed that Stanley had woken up. He was crawling very slowly along the floor, his stomach sliding over the boards, sniffing at the skirting by Jack's bed.

'That's why I went to see Lucie,' Jack whispered. 'The dog is never wrong, you told me that. He's sensed the ghost.'

'I meant about biscuits under the sofa, not a dead man in the living room!' She looked closer. 'What's he got in his mouth?'

Jack moved down the bed.

'Careful, he gets fierce when he's stolen something.'

'I can see fingers!' Jack breathed.

'Damn, it's Lulu's glove.'

It was the one that Stanley had been guarding on the seat in the van after leaving Lulu Carr. Preoccupied with the wet bedding and the driving licence, Stella had forgotten about it.

'Ignore him and he'll drop it. What ghost?' She heaved a sigh. This case and everything to do with it was out of control.

'Little happens in this part of London that Lucie hasn't delved into. She was working on a story about this tower until—' Jack stopped.

'Until what?'

'Until she stopped.' Jack kneaded the rose quartz between his palms.

'Why did she stop?' As she had with Lulu Carr, Stella knew what Jack was going to say.

'Terry died,' Jack finished.

'It was Dad's case? But this tower isn't in Hammersmith.'

'Terry wasn't working for Hammersmith. She said he was doing a stint in Chiswick.'

'How did he think the man died?' Terry would have got the

measure of Lucille May; he would know that any attention she paid him was for the sake of a story.

'He suspected murder, but had no evidence. He worked on it with Lucie in his spare time. The set of prints on the champagne bottle was most likely the dead man's, but being a skeleton they couldn't prove it. Terry's theory was that the murderer removed everything incriminating.'

'So you moved here to solve it?' Jack hadn't asked for her help.

'No. I've always wanted to live in a tower. I rang Lucie when Stanley alerted me to the ghost, and there've been noises.' He twirled a lock of his fringe around. Stella thought he was on edge.

'How did you know about it?' Stanley was back, his head resting on her foot.

'I got a leaflet through the door.'

'Who put it through?'

'A man. I didn't see his face. The consortium – my landlords – did a leaflet-drop.'

'What is this consortium?' Suzie had used the word when she suggested she buy Dale Heffernan's restaurant business. It was a posh term for too many cooks – or chefs.

'I don't know.' Jack shrugged. 'Not a consortium. I might be muddling it with the previous owners of the tower.'

Stella was exasperated. How could Jack rent a property without looking into who owned it? Anything could happen. Anything *had* happened.

The dog had dropped the glove. She got up and retrieved it from the floor by Jack's cupboard and returned to the desk. It was damp from Stanley's mauling, but undamaged. She turned it part inside out.

'It's got what looks like an "R" inside.' She laid the glove on the desk. 'Perhaps it's not Lulu's after all. Certainly not Rick Frost's, unless he had small hands.'

'He didn't. I saw them,' Jack replied.

'I can't see your phone.' Stella remembered her reason for looking amongst Jack's things. She needed to get to bed.

'It must be there.'

'It's not. Oh, but I almost forgot!' Stella spun the chair around and plunged her hand into her rucksack. 'Lulu found this in her landing cupboard. I'd already cleaned there, somehow I missed it.'

She showed Jack the scrap of paper, grubby with the shading of soft pencil. When Jack took it, she noticed his hand was shaking. She wasn't at all sure he'd done the right thing moving to a tower where a man had been murdered.

'Stella, I was—'

'It might be a phone number or a password, although it's too long for a phone number even with the country codes. Then I wondered if it was an IP address, but that's too long too.'

'I should have seen.' Jack knelt on the bed, the paper before him. 'These gaps are deliberate!'

'What gaps?' Jack made life decisions based on the set number allocated to his trains: all numbers were signs. However, like Stanley and his missing biscuits, Stella was learning to trust that he seldom got it wrong.

'These ones between the numbers. Frost must have been off guard because I got that almost immediately. Or he made it deliberately easy.

Jack scrambled over the bed and held the paper so Stella could see it.

'19 9 13 15 14   19 8 21 20   20 15 23 5 18   4 15 15 18.'

'It could be the serial number of the computer in his study,' Jack mused.

'Stupid if it's meant to be secret. You're always telling me to memorize passwords, not to write them down. He not only scratches it into his desk, but he takes a rubbing from the scratches and then drops it in a cupboard. So much for security!'

'The thing is, Stella, he didn't actually—'

'His wife has no sense of security. She left two keys outside the door.'

'If he did it in a hurry on the only available surface...'

It was nearly four o'clock. Far across the river, she saw faint lighter streaks of dawn. Jack seemed to have woken up while she was becoming as befuddled as the case – two cases now.

'I need to grab some sleep.' She got to her feet, rousing Stanley. At the door she stopped. 'I nearly forgot.' She told Jack about her mother's idea that she should invest in Dale Heffernan's business. She was quite aware that by telling him as she was leaving, she was making it seem unimportant because he would be bound to object. Jack was careful with money. So she was surprised when he merely nodded, but made no comment. She wondered suddenly if he was afraid. The place was very quiet. Creepy really.

'You OK staying here? You could come back with me.' Jack must have come to her flat earlier because he was afraid, and then, unable to admit it, had left. She would not embarrass him by bringing it up.

'I'm fine.' He pulled on his shoes, leaving the laces trailing. 'I'm doing a day shift tomorrow, it's easier to set off from here.'

Stella opened the door, noting the handle on the inside. At least Jack wouldn't be trapped in the tower.

'Yuk!' She clamped her hand over her nose. The smell on the landing was greasy and cloying. Like a decomposing body, but that was long ago.

'It's an olfactory hallucination.' Jack was behind her. 'A ghost smell.'

Setting off down the stairs, she heard the ping of a text and saw a series of numbers, no name.

Please can we meet? We need to talk.

'No we do not!' she retorted out loud.

'You all right?' Jack was behind her. Stella breathed in detergent, fresh cotton and clean wool. The smell in the cupboard at Lulu Carr's. Jack used the same detergent as Rick Frost.

'Yes.' She felt far from all right.

On the metal walkway, the wind was stronger. Reaching the staircase cage, she struggled down the first flight; then, looking up, she yelled over the howl of the wind, 'Lulu obviously hasn't told

William I am cleaning for her. Let's say nothing to him while he's a suspect. Agreed?'

'Yes.' Jack waved at her. 'Brilliant work, Stell!'

He craned over the gantry, hair streaming like a young king in a fairy tale. She was getting as fanciful as Jack.

'It was a coincidence. I had no idea it was Frost's house.' Stella made laborious progress down the vibrating metal stairs, eyes ahead because to look down would be fatal.

'No such thing as a coincidence!' came Jack's vanishing cry.

Stella had forgotten to show him the photographs from the station booth. It was too late to go back now, she felt dead on her feet.

Had Stella gone back when she thought about it, she would have seen that she wasn't Jack's only visitor that night.

Forty-One

Jack didn't think he had slept, but the blue lit numbers on his alarm said four fifty and he couldn't account for his thoughts since he had gone to bed after Stella left. He had been hugely relieved that she hadn't lied. But he hadn't confessed to hiding in the cupboard, nor had he admitted that he had rubbed the numbers on to the paper. That he had confessed to visiting Lucie May netted him nothing; Stella wouldn't consider dishonesty up for barter.

Stella didn't claim to be flawless. She had transgressed in the past, but he had never thought she had lied to him. Why had he thought it this time? The answer was Dale Heffernan.

Four fifty-one. The digits on the clock floated on the inside of his eyes. He feared Stella would be influenced by the Brand-new Brother. Jack was certain the man had come for her money. He had passed up the chance to meet Heffernan, knowing that in a week he would be gone. A mistake: Stella never saw the enemy coming; Jack should judge Dale for her.

He rolled on to his back. He heard birdsong far below in the gardens of Chiswick Mall. He lay listening to it, and then was puzzled. He had shut the windows before he went to bed, wanting absolute silence. The tower was high above the trees, too high up for birdsong. It was another auditory hallucination. His mind was busy compensating for what he had lost.

The pale blue light of dawn outlined his binoculars on the north window sill. When Stella had looked through them on her first visit, she had said she could see one of her client's houses. Although she had many clients all over West London, he was sure the house she meant was Lulu Carr's. If Stella had pointed out the house to him, he would have recognized the address when William Frost gave it to him and the whole cupboard thing needn't have happened. If—

He shut his eyes. This case was different to the others because a client was paying them to solve it. It mustn't make them change how they operated. Jack met subterfuge with subterfuge; he looked for minds like his own and inhabited them. He read the signs. His eyes snapped open. He had a sign.

He reached over the side of the bed and pulled the steam engine from his bag. He switched on the bedside lamp. Post-office red with 'Golden Arrow' painted in yellow on the boiler. Below this were the emblems of the Union Jack and the French Tricolour. The engine was the same model as the one he had lost in the Thames as a boy.

Jack got out of bed and padded into the kitchenette. He placed the toy on the south-east window sill overlooking Hammersmith Bridge.

He returned to the main room and, opening his cupboard, fished out the biscuit tin in which he kept his treasures. He laid them out on the bed. Tokens from True Hosts; a teaspoon; a chip of green glass; three milk teeth (not his own); two postcards; a pure white butterfly pinned in a box; postcards from his dad's work trips abroad, including the one of Fremantle cemetery. He put aside the pack of passport photos held with an elastic band, faces he carried in his mind. Lastly, he found the lock of his mother's hair. A musty smell of damp dust, stale perfume and of all the homes he had stayed in drifted up from the open box.

The newspaper cutting lined the bottom of the tin. It was dated Thursday, 22 October 1998.

STUDENT MUGGED IN GRAVEYARD

By Lucille May

A woman walking her dog found what she thought at first was the body of a young man lying across a fallen headstone in Chiswick Cemetery just before 07.00 a.m. yesterday morning. However, when the police arrived at the scene, they detected a pulse and the man was rushed to Charing Cross Hospital.

The man, identified by a cheque book and later confirmed by his distraught father as Simon Carrington, aged 20, of Corney Road, Chiswick, is in a critical condition at Charing Cross Hospital with his family keeping vigil by his bedside.

Detective Inspector Terry Darnell of the Metropolitan Police is appealing for witnesses.

There it was in a small square of black and white. Leaving the cutting on his desk, Jack shut his box of treasures and returned it to the cupboard. Unbidden the words came into his mind. Dead people can't kill.

You are safe.

It was not what he thought, Jack told himself.

Returning to bed, he found he had a text. Lucie May.

Ring re RF inquest. LM.

In the dead of night, Lucie was on the job. As she had been when she worked with Terry. The police detective and the hard-nosed reporter swapping notes and information, both of them restless and stubborn, unable to let the mysteries lie. Jack shuffled further under the duvet. He hadn't told Stella his suspicion that exchanging information about an unsolved case was not all Terry Darnell and Lucie May had done into the small hours.

The sink made its glugging sound. Living up here had blurred the line between reality and dreams. As if to illustrate this, the Smiths' song 'How Soon is Now' drifted back into his mind.

Jack dreamt that Stella was there at the foot of his bed, holding her dog. 'I wanted to be your friend.' She had the voice of a boy.

'We still can be.'

'You denied you knew me. Three times.'

'No, that was Peter, the disciple.'

'I know your name.' It wasn't Stella, it was—

Jack was dully aware that he was dreaming and tried to wake.

He forced open his eyes, the lids heavy with exhaustion. There *was* someone at the bottom of his bed.

'*Stella?*'

He tried to speak but sank back into sleep. This time he didn't dream.

Forty-Two

Saturday, 26 October 2013

It was ten o'clock and the streets were quiet. Stella had insisted on fetching Lulu Carr; she wouldn't put it past her to go earlier than an agreed time and tackle Nicola Barwick before she arrived.

Barwick turned out to live around the corner from Jackie in Corney Road in Chiswick. Although Jackie had brought her the case, Stella didn't want to bump into her on the job. Jackie belonged to the bright world of cleaning and tidying, not to the mess of an adulterous separation and a wife confronting a possible mistress.

They parked opposite a modern terrace house in Pumping Station Road, a quiet street parallel to the Thames. According to Lucille May's article, the development of detached and semis had replaced the light industry and wharfs that had occupied the stretch on the north side of the river for over a century. Stella knew the terrace; one of her first clients had lived here.

'She killed him to keep him.' Lulu had said this several times on the journey from Hammersmith. She was regarding the house opposite with malevolence.

'You don't know that.' If Lulu had killed her husband, it made sense to point the finger at someone else. Stella was trying to resist prejudice or preconception about the suspects, but she rather liked Lulu and didn't want her to be guilty. This was not thinking like a detective.

'I need to hear her say, "I was sleeping with your husband."' Lulu batted at the dashboard pettishly.

'She won't say it if she wasn't.' Stella looked over at the house. A light glowed through diamond-patterned glazed glass in the front door. It briefly dimmed; someone was in the hall.

Stella remembered the client because the woman had called the police to report that she had seen Stella going into the DHSS on Shepherd's Bush Road. She accused Stella of claiming benefit while earning. Unknown to Stella at the time, Suzie had gone to the woman's house and 'frogmarched' – Suzie's word – her to Shepherd's Bush Road. The woman had mistaken the police station for the benefits office; Stella had been visiting her dad. Terry confirmed this. The woman withdrew her complaint, but never apologized or paid her bill. The latter was the point of the exercise, Suzie believed; she had taught Stella to be circumspect about customers: they were not 'kings or queens', they were humans and didn't have to be obeyed. The episode had resulted in Terry and Suzanne Darnell meeting in the foyer of Hammersmith Police Station, united in their determination to clear their daughter's name. It was the last time they saw each other.

Stella reached behind, unclipped Stanley and plonked him on her lap. She shouldn't have brought him, but Jackie was vetting new office spaces and Beverly was at the dentist.

'How could you have seen him with Nicola Barwick the other day? You knew Rick was dead, you went to his inquest,' Stella asked.

'Yes, how could I?' Lulu perked up, apparently enlivened by a mystery she herself had invented.

Stella nearly shouted with exasperation. Was this what Terry's life had been like? She expected people to give straight answers. She yearned to be applying a cleaning agent to a cornice or wiping dust from the slats of a Venetian blind, tasks both fiddly and satisfying. Being a detective was like looking for hens' teeth.

'Look at this!' Lulu pulled a ball of paper out of her pocket and smoothed it out on the dashboard. 'One of Rick's "surveillance reports". He followed me around Marks and Spencer's on King Street, then met me for coffee at the Lyric Theatre as if he'd been there all along. Typical.'

'Did he give it to you?' Stella tried not to judge clients, but what with William's descriptions of his brother, and now Lulu's, she wasn't warming to the man.

'I found it in his jacket. He had the handwriting of a twelve-year-old. The mind of one too.'

'Maybe he told Barwick he wouldn't leave you,' Stella was mindful of keeping Lulu calm for the confrontation with Nicola Barwick. 'After all, he didn't.'

'So she killed him. Better he's dead than with me.' Lulu patted Stanley on the head – a dangerous move for he was head-shy. 'You know when a person has fallen out of love. That warmth you've taken for granted vanishes. You're feeling low and he chivvies you to buck up instead of kissing you better. He points out food on your lip and orders you to wipe it off instead of doing it for you. You ask if he's OK and he intimates you're mad. You believe you *are* mad. That's what you think, isn't it? That I'm mad! You must have felt that cold breeze of dying love, the gritty sick sensation of betrayal!' She bashed the dashboard again. Stanley tensed.

Stella didn't know about 'dying love'. Jackie said she did the leaving to avoid being left and suggested she give people more time.

Stella had put last night's text out of her mind, but sooner or later she would have to agree to speak to David. She shifted Stanley out of reach of Lulu.

Stella did know the gritty feeling of betrayal. It had kept her arms stiffly by her side when her dad waved at her before he drove away from her mum's flat the day they separated. She hadn't let either parent carry the little pink case her dad had given her for 'going away' to the new flat in Barons Court. He hadn't remembered she hated pink. Stolidly she had lugged it up the steps into the cold lobby of the mansion block, clacking across the tiles all by herself.

She was startled by a text. It was Jack.

Ask Lulu C about the glove. Why did that matter?

'Lulu, do you know—'

Lulu was already out of the van. By the time Stella had

untangled herself from her belt and the dog's lead, Lulu had knocked on Nicola Barwick's front door and was stamping her feet on the step, against the cold or perhaps with lack of patience.

'I know you're in there!' Lulu smacked the flat of her hand on the glass pane.

The door opened.

'Where is Nicky?' Lulu demanded.

'I'm afraid she's not here. Can I help?'

'This is her house,' Lulu insisted.

'Lulu, let's go,' Stella murmured.

'I know she's here. I have seen her.'

'She's moved.' The woman looked genuinely regretful.

'I'm her friend,' Lulu asserted.

'I'm sorry, but—'

Stella knew what the woman was thinking. If Nicola Barwick had wanted a friend to know where she was, she would have told her.

'It's a mistake. I'm sorry,' Stella said to the woman, who turned to her.

'Stella Darnell!' She put out her hands. 'You haven't changed a bit!'

Stella backed against a holly bush by the door, hardly aware of the prickles. It was the client who had reported her to the police.

'I know she's here.' Before Stella could stop her, Lulu had barged into the hall. 'Nicky?'

'Really, she's not—' the woman protested.

Stella gathered her wits. The woman was the same age as the client had been; she would be in her seventies now.

'You have been quick! I just rang the office. I didn't expect you so soon. And not *you* – I imagined you far too grand – one of your staff. I was going to send my regards but I got the answering machine.'

Stella had learnt to admit it when she didn't recognize people: ex-clients often hailed her in the street or in the bank. When she had improvised, waiting for a clue to identity to emerge, it had led to a minefield of misunderstanding.

'Do I know—' she began.

'Liz Hunter! You never were good with faces, but you had the nose of a bloodhound!'

Stella had first met Liz in primary school before she moved to Barons Court. They had gone on to the 'big' school together. When Terry was leading a major case and was plastered over the newspapers and TV, Liz Hunter was the only child at Stella's comprehensive who hadn't tried to worm information out of her, or ask her for his autograph. Had the term 'From Hero to Zero' been in use then, someone would have applied it to her dad. In the days after the Rokesmith murder, everyone wanted to be Stella's friend, but over time, as the case dragged on and Terry was on screens asking for the public's patience, the fifteen-year-old became the failed detective's daughter. No more invitations to parties and illicit trips to the pub. She wasn't asked to join the group going to the Duran Duran concert at the Hammersmith Odeon. Simon Le Bon's autograph beat Terry's by a mile. In the midst of this Liz Hunter invited her home for tea.

Liz would wait beside the bus stop on Kensington High Street where Stella alighted from the number 28 each morning and walk with her up to the school. She materialized by the gym block gate during lunch where Stella went to get away from questions about Terry and shared her sandwiches with Stella. Stella didn't have to pretend interest in the photographs of the Hunter family cat that Liz took for a project on feline genetics. Liz never asked her about Terry's case. Stella began to look out for her at the bus stop. She found a textbook on genetics in Hammersmith library and photocopied a paper on the domestic cat for Liz. When Liz was off school with a bug, Stella went round to see her. From then on she was a regular visitor. Stella thought it would be nice to have a brother who was good at maths. Liz had two such brothers.

After school, they went different ways. Stella started cleaning and Liz studied French at a northern university. Stella couldn't have said why she didn't reply to Liz's letters. After a while they stopped coming.

At the end of the Blue Folder case and of whatever she had had with David, Jackie had urged Stella to find friends outside the business. If she wouldn't join a book group or a knitting group, why not look up old friends? Stella said there were none. She had briefly thought of Liz Hunter, but doubted she would reply if she contacted her.

'I want a cleaner. I went online to find a reputable firm and found an article about you solving that case of your dad's that happened when we were at school.' Aside from lines bracketing her mouth and one or two grey hairs in an auburn bob, Liz was the same. 'Of course I rang Clean Slate!' She stood aside. 'Come in. Let's find your friend and have a coffee!'

'She's not my friend.' Glancing back at the van, Stella froze. Jack was standing beside it, his back to her. He had said he was driving today.

'I know him,' she exclaimed

'Know who?' Liz Hunter stepped out on to the pavement.

Jack had gone. In the distance Stella saw his tower, tall and menacing in the grey morning light.

'No one.' Stella went inside.

Stella was assailed by colours: green skirtings, yellow walls, a rug of red and orange stripes. A low table was crowded with vases of blues and greens. A nightmare to clean, but whatever the cost Stella would give Liz Hunter a large discount.

On a chair beside a door to a Juliet balcony sat Lulu Carr. Stella felt distinctly uncomfortable. Lulu was too calm. Legs crossed, her alabaster-pale complexion paler against the garish décor, she was smiling as if butter wouldn't melt. She was up to something.

Forty-Three

Saturday, 26 October 2013

Jack had one more chance to time the tunnel. It was his last shift on the Wimbledon line before he was back full-time on the Dead Late shift.

He placed his watch on the sill and, his hand steady, adjusted the lever to a speed of forty kilometres per hour. In the sun the tracks sparkled bright silver; up ahead was the West Hill tunnel. Jack cleared his mind. Stella would wonder why it mattered that he knew the length of the tunnel. He couldn't explain that it would lead him to discover who had left a toy train on the station monitors. Although Jack believed in ghosts, he didn't believe that a ghost had left it there. He could not tell Stella that the answer to the calculation about the tunnel would help him learn the identity of Glove Man and know who had caused Rick Frost to die under a train at Stamford Brook.

He braced himself. Second hand at the one-minute mark before ten: three, two, one! He plunged into darkness.

Bricks flowed up and over his cab, lit by the yellow of the train's headlamps. Six seconds, eight, twelve. At exactly twenty-four seconds Jack brought the train out of the tunnel into blazing sunshine.

Time and speed. The two numbers, 'forty' and 'twenty-four' were stepping stones; he was closer to the truth.

The platform at East Putney was crowded with morning commuters. Jack could see a station attendant talking into her loudspeaker pack, announcing his train. He slid his eye over the waiting faces, registering every one. He clipped his watch back on and opened the train doors.

He consulted the driver's monitor to the left of his cab and his good mood drained away. There was something there. He got off his stool. On the lower quadrant of the split screen he could see the attendant waving 'all clear' with her paddle.

The 'something' was a toy railway carriage. Jack whirled around and scoured the platform. It must have just been left or another driver would have seen it. The attendant would have seen it. She was now the only person on the platform. She did a shrugging motion: was he all right? Jack gave her a 'thumbs up' and got back into the cab. He shut the doors and eased the train forward. In his mind he trawled through the faces he had seen on the platform on the way in. One of them had been familiar but, as if in a dream, the image had faded.

You denied you knew me. Three times.

The sun shone through the windows. The cab was warm, but Jack felt cold.

Who could know that as a boy he had owned the same toys? He had been dismayed when his father replaced his steam engine with an inferior one of plastic. It pulled three carriages like the engine now on his window sill in the tower. Jack didn't suppose his dead father had placed the toys on the monitors. Nor had— He could not bear even to think his name. A name that belonged to a past that was better buried.

But someone had put the engine there. Someone who knew about the engine he had had when he was little. The back of his neck tingled. The connecting door between the cab and the passengers was shut. Even so, Jack was convinced he was being watched.

Jack stopped on the balcony overlooking the District line platforms at Earl's Court station and took the carriage from his bag. His carriages had been full of tiny figures, moulded in beige plastic. When his tunnel collapsed, the passengers were thrown from their seats and choked by mud. The tragedy wouldn't have happened if he had been driving. Until now Jack had succeeded in blotting out that afternoon in the kitchen garden of his school when his train had crashed in the tunnel.

The toy carriage wasn't empty. A man sat near the front. He was looking at him.

Jack shuddered as if the passenger could see into his mind. Pieces of a train set had been placed on top of the monitors. By a person who played with codes and signs. Someone with a mind like his own. Jack's own mind was being monitored. He had to keep it shut. He knew how to do that. Shoving the carriage into his shoulder bag, he began his calculation. He didn't need a notepad; his photographic mind held the numbers as if lit in neon.

Forty kilometres per hour was two-thirds of sixty kilometres per hour. Sixty kilometres per hour was one kilometre or one thousand metres per minute. Travelling at forty kilometres per hour he covered 666.66 metres (recurring) per minute. He had taken twenty-four seconds to go through the tunnel, 66.66 (recurring) metres every six seconds. Jack leant on the balustrade; below him a Wimbledon train arrived at the far westbound platform. Two drivers were swapping over. The new driver climbed into the cab; the other began to climb the central staircase.

There are four sixes in twenty-four. Jack multiplied 66 metres by four. A peace descended on him. The length of the West Hill tunnel was 266.66 (recurring) metres. He drew his coat around him as a dusty breeze swept out from the tunnel below. His mind was a vast plain on which images and ideas ranged far and wide. This hidden fact would lead him to more. This was being a detective.

Jack wouldn't be back on the trains for a week. He had time.

Into his opened mind came a glove. A black leather glove was found on the body in his tower.

Black leather gloves were two a penny, but it was less common to have a crown motif on the cuff and a popper fastener as Lucie had described in her notes. The glove Stanley had in his mouth in the tower had a crown indented in the leather. Focused on the dog's white teeth and mistrustful glare, Jack had seen the crown indentation by his upper incisor. Stella said the dog had stolen it from Lulu Carr's house.

There was no such thing as a coincidence.

Jack turned on his phone. Stella would be at Nicola Barwick's house. He hoped she was all right. He shouldn't have let her go off with a suspect on her own. His thumbs flew over the keyboard: *Ask Lulu C about the glove.*

He continued along the footbridge towards the Exhibition Centre. The tunnel was 266.66 metres in length; the fact had opened his mind and given him the glove. One fact led to another.

There is madness in your method.

Jack pummelled at his forehead. The thought – although a fact – had come unbidden into his mind; it was not his own. He had the notion he was being watched and, turning around, heard someone speak:

'It's Jack Harmon, isn't it?'

Jack looked at a stocky man with backcombed thinning hair. He had rheumy eyes as if in the grip of an allergy. He recognized the driver who had got off the Wimbledon train a few minutes ago, but he didn't know him. Another face he couldn't place.

'Yes.'

'Darryl Clark. We met at the— I was driving that train that—'

'Of course!' Jack saved him from finishing the sentence. Darryl Clark was the Piccadilly line driver who had the One Under at Stamford Brook. 'I saw you get off a District line train just then.'

'I got a transfer. I can't face that track. Still the same line, but it's not the same. You doing all right?'

'Oh yes, but then I wasn't driving the train.' It occurred to Jack that he wasn't doing all right. With all that had happened – the move to the tower, the toys on the monitor and Stella's brother – he had been distracted from the actuality of the death on the track. Darryl Clark brought it back. Rick Frost's expression: now he thought it was of fear and perhaps some vain effort to make Jack understand what he was trying to convey.

'Have you got time for a quick drink?' the man asked.

'It's a bit early for me.' Jack wanted to see Stella.

'Me too!' The man gave a sudden laugh, a shout, the sound pushed with effort from the depths of his chest. 'I meant a coffee.'

'Yes of course.'

The two men returned along the footbridge to the staff canteen.

'What was your set number?' Jack asked conversationally as they descended the staircase

'My set number?' Clark looked at him.

'For that train you just handed over.' Jack picked up his pace. Clark was shorter than him, but he was walking fast.

'Two six six.'

The length of the West Hill tunnel: 266.66 metres.

The signs were working.

Forty-Four

'Please could I use your loo?' Lulu Carr stood up when Liz Hunter returned with a tray of coffees.

'By the kitchen, door on the left.' Liz placed three white china mugs of coffee on the coffee table and pushed a plate of biscuits towards Stella. She sat in a chair matching Lulu's on the other side of the balcony door. 'Is your friend all right?'

'She's not my— She and Nicola Barwick have unfinished business.' Stella accepted a biscuit and nibbled at it, reminded of Dale's scones. The biscuits were not as nice. Aware of how odd Lulu's behaviour must appear, she was tempted to tell Liz Hunter everything, but however annoying Lulu was, she wouldn't betray her confidence.

'It's ridiculous that I can't give her Nicola's address. But she was adamant. I must tell *no one*!' Liz Hunter handed her a cup of coffee. 'I can pass on a message for her though.'

'I'm not sure that will—'

'But hey, it's so good that you turned up in person! Fancy you not realizing it was me when they told you at the office. Have to say, I've often wondered about you. I've missed you, Stella.'

Liz Hunter had always said what she felt. Stella hadn't missed her or she would have seen her. Stella thought that Jack would agree about it being more than a coincidence. Whatever it was, she felt distinctly uncomfortable. She would do Liz an estimate and leave. Lulu would have to make do with leaving her number for Nicola Barwick.

'I'm fine, thanks.' Although Liz hadn't asked how she was. 'What about you?' Stella enquired in a spray of crumbs.

'Life's been in turmoil. I'm coming out of a divorce.' Liz gave a laugh as if she had made a joke.

'So you haven't lived here long?' Stella took another nibble of the biscuit and bit the side of her cheek. She washed down the biscuit with lukewarm coffee. Where was Lulu?

'I came back from Paris when Dad died two years ago to be nearer Mum. My brothers are here, but they're worse than useless! Max never visits and although Rob manages the odd afternoon, he flops on the sofa and watches telly with her. At least he doesn't bring his washing any more. I was sorry to read about your dad – he was a kind man.'

Stella had never thought of Terry in those terms and was interested that Liz had noticed.

'Sorted!' Lulu Carr was in the doorway, beaming at them both. Stella would underplay a visit to the loo rather than treat it as an accomplishment.

'Tuck in.' Liz waved at the coffee and biscuits. Stella remembered that it was typical of Liz not to ask questions. Right from when she had rescued Stella from a cupboard in their infant school, Liz Hunter had taken any crisis or unusual situation in her stride.

'Actually I must dash,' Lulu said. 'I've had a text from my brother. He needs me!'

She blew them both kisses and was gone before Stella could gather herself and go with her. With growing unease she excused herself and went to the toilet.

Stella stood in the little cloakroom and considered the low-slung toilet. There was a tiny corner sink from which hung a diminutive towel. The cistern wasn't filling, but the tank was small; it had probably already done so.

The towel was soft and dry. A bar of lavender soap was wedged behind a squat mixer tap. Stella picked it up. It was tacky, not wet. Running water over her hands, she worked the soap to a lather. It slipped from her fingers and shot into the basin. She captured it and put it back behind the tap, then rinsed and dried her hands.

The soap was now flecked with suds, and the towel was damp. Lulu wouldn't go to the toilet without washing her hands. Whatever she was doing while she was out of the room, she hadn't been near the toilet.

Liz was in the kitchen, washing up the mugs. 'Another coffee? I'm having one.' She flicked the kettle switch.

'Yes, thanks.' Stella would do the estimate and allocate an operator for Liz. Wendy would be right for her. She settled into a chair at the end of a long wooden table that was large enough to sit ten.

A tall blue Smeg fridge matched eggshell-blue units. A set of shelves was stacked with assorted mugs and plates, many with chipped rims. A collection of glass Kilner jars was grouped together on the fridge. The vibration of the motor would shift them incrementally and eventually they would fall. Stella decided against pointing this out. The fridge door was papered with neat rows of notes, takeaway menus and cards for different trades clamped by large magnets in primary colours. Apart from the top one, they were arranged with five items per row; Stella liked this. During the estimate she would photograph their precise positions so that after cleaning they could be put back accurately. Her phone buzzed.

'Where are you?' Her mother's first question whenever she phoned Stella's mobile.

'At a friend's.' She doubted that her mother would remember Liz.

'A friend?' Her mother sounded disbelieving.

'A client,' Stella said to put Suzie off.

'I won't keep you. Dale and I are going to Richmond Park again, he's taking me in his lovely hire car.'

'That's nice.' A hired car would be more comfortable than her cleaning van, although Dale had said he thought it was 'cool'.

'Stella, just to say, make sure you're in tonight, he's got a surprise for you. Seven fifteen. I've left Terry's key with Jackie.'

'I'm not sure I can—' Suzie had gone. Her mum knew she didn't like surprises. Stella considered phoning back, but thought better of it; she would seem ungrateful and after all it could do no harm for Dale to go to Terry's house. Terry had been his dad too. Belatedly she wondered how Suzie knew Stella went there in the evening.

Liz interrupted this thought. 'How's your mum doing?

Stella had intended to say Suzie was fine, that working at Clean Slate got her out of the house. Instead she told Liz all about how Suzie still behaved as if Terry was alive and how she'd upped sticks and gone to Australia. That Stella had gone to the airport and her mother wasn't there, that she was still in Sydney. Finally Stella told her about Dale Heffernan. How he looked just liked Terry and that her mum hadn't complained about Terry being a 'wrong turning' since Dale had arrived. This bit hadn't occurred to Stella until she told Liz. She described how Dale had taken her mum on shopping trips to the West End, to posh restaurants and cooked for her. Suzie seemed to be having the time of her life. This too hadn't occurred to Stella before. Drawing breath, Stella realised she hadn't asked her mum where she was meant to be 'in tonight'. She spent her evenings at Terry's, but Suzie didn't know that. Liz was talking.

'Sounds like he's bonding with his biological mum – with you both – it doesn't always work out that way.' Liz was ripping up basil leaves and scattering them over fanned slices of avocado, tomato and mozzarella on a plate. She presented food on the plate with care like Dale did.

Stella had drunk the second cup of coffee and eaten all the biscuits without noticing.

'Rather strange for you, perhaps?' She looked at Stella with concern.

'I've hardly seen him. When he goes back to Australia, everything will get back to normal.' When Dale Heffernan had gone, her mum would return to her job at Clean Slate. They would resume their trips to Richmond Park every other Sunday with fish and chip suppers on Thursdays.

She heard a sploshing. Stanley was drinking out of a dog's bowl on a mat by the back door. Stella had forgotten about him. Liz had given him water. He caught her eye and, tail flapping, trotted over and put his paws on her knees. Stella stroked sodden fur back from his muzzle, drops of water dampening her trousers.

'He can lie on this while we eat.' Liz returned with a cushion from the front room and dropped it in the corner by the fridge. 'Lie down.' She invited him nicely.

Stanley approached the cushion, nosed it about, dragged it away from the fridge to the middle of the kitchen and climbed onto it. He flumped down and, heaving a sigh, went instantly to sleep.

Stella had assumed the food was for Liz and was about to say it was too early to eat, but her watch said it was five to one. They had been talking for three hours.

'You've trained him well!' Liz laid out tubs of olives and hummus, a plate of hot pitta bread and another of sliced meats. 'Stanley! Lovely name.'

'I'm minding him for a friend. Stanley was his father.' Liz had told her about her husband and his affairs, how she had had it with the 'sting of betrayal'. If she had stayed, Lulu could have joined in. Stella wasn't ready to swap stories about the Mr Rights who went wrong. David had not been Mr Right. That morning she had ignored another text. She wondered how she could give Stanley back without meeting him or involving a third party.

'Tuck in, Stell.' Liz took two bottles of mineral water from the fridge, one still and one sparkling. No one but Jack and Jackie called her 'Stell'. Liz had been the first to do so.

'Thanks.' Stella picked up her knife and fork and unfolded one of the triangles of kitchen towel that did for napkins, relieved there was no fuss and formality.

'He's going to miss you. Any chance your friend might let you keep him?'

'No chance. Stanley is attached to him.'

'He's attached to you, he's fixed on your every move!'

Stanley wasn't asleep. He was watching her. Without a dog to walk or think about, she would get more done, Stella reminded herself.

Stella scooted a helping of avocado salad onto her plate. She had first tasted avocado at the Hunter house. Liz's mother had coaxed her. *Just a smidgin, love, you can't dislike what you've never tried.*

Liz's family didn't call her dad a failed detective. Liz's dad had said he wished all the police were like Terry, a 'people-person'.

On the few occasions Stella had eaten avocado as an adult – generally at Jackie's – she would think of Liz and wonder where she was.

Liz poured mineral water from the still bottle into Stella's glass, a green tumbler dotted with air bubbles. Jack said imperfection was a sign of perfection. Liz hadn't offered the sparkling bottle. She must have remembered that Stella hated fizzy drinks.

'I'm sorry I wasn't able to help your friend.' Liz was tipping the leftovers into plastic boxes and stowed them in the fridge. Stella had completely forgotten about Lulu Carr, neither of them had referred to why Stella was there in the first place.

It was an hour and a half later and Stella was washing up the lunch things.

'I did try to tell her.' Stella didn't say again that Lulu wasn't a friend. She would have to explain about the case and Liz would think she was trying to be a detective like her dad and feel sorry for her.

'I'll drop Nicola a line and let you know what she says.'

'Thanks.'

'To be honest, Stell, I was cautious because, when she left Nicola made me swear to tell no one where she was staying. Very cloak and dagger.'

'What do you mean?' Stella rinsed the last bowl and fitted it into the draining rack. She knew why. She should level with Liz. Nicola Barwick had been involved with Rick Frost and, when he died, she had guessed Lulu had found out or that Frost had told her. She knew Lulu would want to see her. Stella saw suddenly that the floaty, feminine manner was a front. Lulu worked like a steel trap.

'I don't know Nicola well, we worked together. When I needed somewhere to rent, she offered here. A friend had died and she needed a change of scene.'

'What did you mean by "cloak and dagger?"' A detective, she probed deeper.

'At work she was as cool as a cucumber, ahead of the game, but nice with it. One of the few you could trust. When I came to see the house, she was quite different – nervy, talking fast, she seemed hardly aware of me. She hustled me inside as if someone was out there watching her. When she gave me her forwarding address, she confessed that she was being hassled by an ex. I had to promise not to give it to anyone. I presumed her friends and relations knew. But then this man turned up asking for her and now you've come. Nicola doesn't seem to have told anyone but me.'

'What friend?' Stella asked sharply. Stanley sat up.

'A guy she's known since they were kids – not the scary ex, I soon established that. He said they were only friends. He asked for Nicola's address – so difficult when you have to refuse someone nice. He told me she had asked him to check I was OK and that he would handle anything I needed. He was the only person in touch with her. I've found out since that he was testing me to make sure I didn't give away her address. I passed! To be honest I couldn't have given it to him because at that point I'd managed to lose it!' She dried the plates and put them back on the shelf. 'He warned me not to trust anyone – even murderers are charming!'

'He said that?' Stella pulled off the rubber gloves, finger by finger. She wondered at the comparison.

'He's rather put me on alert.' Liz laughed. 'Little traffic goes down this road and, except at weekends, hardly anyone walks by, so I catch every footstep. At night, it's as quiet as the graves over the road! My mum used to say I had a vivid imagination, you remember!'

'Has this man been back?' Mrs Hunter had told Stella she kept Liz's feet on the ground. Stanley's chest was pigeon-puffed, head back, ears pert as if he had heard something. The relaxed mood of lunch had gone.

'Yes! I was coming to that.' Liz rocked on her heels. 'We're seeing each other! Nothing serious. Justin – that's his name – understands that after Gary I can't rush into anything. Although between you and me, this time I don't mind if I do! I'd joined one of those dating websites and what happens? I meet a guy without leaving the house!'

'That's great. What does he do?' Stella's mind raced. Was Nicola Barwick frightened of the same person as Rick Frost?

'You sound like Dad, he used to quiz me about boyfriends!' Liz was girlish. Not the girl Stella remembered, who had been cool-headed about boys, but more like the sort of girl Liz had little time for at school, who lost interest in talking to other girls when a boy she liked came over.

'Justin's an engineer, he's passionate about his work. Gary was down on everything so it's refreshing.'

'How do you know he's a friend of Nicola Barwick's? Despite what he told you, he could be the ex.' Detectives had to take risks, even if it meant losing the friend she had only just found. If Lulu was right and Nicola Barwick had killed Frost, she had gone to some effort to cover her tracks.

'If you met him you'd understand. I trust Justin.' Liz filled the kettle and flicked down the lever; it began to hiss. 'He and Nicola were close, he says.'

Stella wasn't sure she trusted anyone. Not even Jack, it seemed.

'Were?' she echoed.

'*Are!*' A shadow passed across her face. 'Justin talks as if he'll never see her again.' Liz put the bottles of mineral water back in the fridge.

'I thought you said he did see her.'

'He says she's stopped answering his calls. He's upset she doesn't trust him – as I say, he thought they were close.'

'Is he sure she's OK? Suppose this man has found her?' Stella said.

'She told him not to contact her again. She says it's a risk.'

'What's the name of this ex?' Stella mentally put him at the top of their list of suspects.

'Nicola didn't say.'

'Doesn't your guy know? Justin.'

'He says she never introduced her men to him. I can imagine that; Nicola never talked about her private life to me either.'

'Do you have a number for her?'

'She only left a postal address. She told me to take any repair bills off the rent. I had a problem with the boiler, but Justin sorted that. He doesn't just build bridges and tunnels, he can turn his hand to anything!' Liz was fiddling with the fridge magnets. She straightened two and closed the gap in the top row that had irked Stella, who had forgotten that they had shared a liking for order.

'That's odd.' Liz held up a bright red magnet.

'What is?'

'Nicola's address isn't here.'

'Are you sure?' Stella might suggest that leaving the address on the fridge for all to see was unwise, but then Jack said that the best place to conceal something was in plain sight.

'Yes.' Liz got down on the floor. Sensing a game, Stanley beetled over and snuffled around her. 'It can only just have fallen off, I found it last week and finally posted off a letter that's been sitting here for weeks, making me feel guilty.'

'You said this man – Justin – has it. Couldn't you have asked him?'

'I couldn't admit I'd lost it; he's adamant that we must tell no one. Now I've lost it again!' she wailed.

'It must have fallen off.' Stella doubted this as soon as she said it.

'Maybe it's losing strength.' Liz examined the magnet as if she could tell by looking.

'Magnets last forever if you keep them away from power lines and don't expose them to high temperatures. It must be here.' Stella dragged the chairs away from the table. In the snugly fitted kitchen there were no crevices or cavities. The truth dawned.

Lulu had not received a text from her brother. She had gone looking for a clue to where Nicola Barwick might be and she had found it on the fridge. She knew where to look: she hid keys in plain sight. She hadn't been near the toilet. She had got Nicola Barwick's address and would be on her way there now.

'Liz, there's something I need to tell you.' Stella took the plunge and told Liz who Lulu was and how she suspected Nicola Barwick of having an affair with her husband. She left out the bit about Lulu accusing Nicola Barwick of murdering Frost – no need to make Liz feel worse than she did.

'Where did you forward the letter to?' she asked Liz.

'I can't remember.' Liz clamped the magnet back on the fridge.

'We need to warn her!'

'I've only sent on one letter.' She was staring at the magnets.

'Try to think, was it in this country?' Stella must not hurry her; Liz had always thought before she spoke, a trait Stella respected.

'It made me think of drawing,' Liz said eventually.

'What?' This was like being with Jack.

'The word was something you use for a... charcoal, that was it!'

'Is it a place?' Stella pulled out her phone; she would call Lulu Carr and hold her off.

'It's not the name, it's what I associated with it.'

Stella got Lulu's answer machine.

'I'm in mourning, I can't talk. Please don't leave a message after the beep, I shan't call back.'

Stella prevented herself letting out a wild scream.

'Charbury!'

Stella dabbed Charbury into Google Maps. There was one near Chipping Norton in Oxfordshire and one in East Sussex.

'What was the county?' She forced herself not to shout.

'East something.'

East Sussex then. Stella knew the name. Two years ago, Isabel Ramsay, her favourite client, had been buried in the churchyard at Charbury. The Ramsay family had invited Stella to the funeral but, unable to face another funeral so soon after her dad's, Stella had done a cleaning job instead. Jack had gone alone. For a mad second Stella believed that if she had gone, she wouldn't be facing this problem now. She should leave the magical thinking to Jack. The length of the journey to Charbury – one and a half hours each way – had been her excuse for not going. Lulu had been gone over five hours, ample time to find Nicola Barwick.

Forty-Five

Saturday, 26 October 2013

Jack laid the tray on the wood veneer table. Tea for Darryl Clark and hot milk for him. The canteen wasn't large, about twenty-six metres by ten, and today there was only one other person there, a middle-aged black man in a blue driver's polo shirt reading an *Evening Standard* by the serving hatch.

The staff canteen at Earl's Court was a bland combination of pinkish quartz screed flooring and salmon walls, with faux wood tables and red plastic chairs. Fluorescent lights chequered a tiled drop-ceiling, casting an even light and ensuring that drivers relaxed, yet remained alert.

A used tea bag lay soaking into a napkin on the table, a plastic stirrer placed beside it – like items of evidence in a crime, Jack found himself thinking. Pulling himself together, he gathered up the tea bag and tossed it into a flip bin by the food hatch. He caught an item on the noticeboard. Three flats for rent in West London, all apparently within easy distance of the District line. Nothing matched the Palmyra Tower; he had been lucky.

The driver by the servery lounged with his chair tipped back, arms folded, seemingly unaware of Jack. Nevertheless, to avoid their conversation being overheard, Jack moved closer to Darryl Clark.

Clark sat like an obedient child, hands on his lap, the shadow of a smile on his face as if determined to be cheerful. Jack recognized a man suffering from trauma. Clark unloaded the tray and propped it against the table leg, but made no move to drink his tea. Instead, he picked up his stirrer and with trembling hands swirled

252

it back and forth in his tea, although he hadn't sugared it. He stopped abruptly.

'How are you doing?' Jack asked softly.

'OK now.' Darryl lifted the mug with both hands and drank in gulps. 'I started back on the Piccadilly, but coming out of Hammersmith, I felt like shit. That was with a co-driver doing the driving. At Stamford Brook, I swear I felt the train go over a bump where he fell. I kept quiet about that, didn't want them thinking I'm mad. Bloody feels like it.' He blew too hard on his tea and, without noticing, slopped it over the side. 'They fast-tracked the transfer to the Wimbledon line.'

'You're not mad.' Jack swept away the spill with his napkin.

'You OK? Were you off work too?' Clark's eyes flicked from side to side.

'No, but it's different for the driver.'

The man cleared his throat. 'Have you had one before?'

Jack understood Clark's need to ask a question that only a driver who had had a One Under could ask another.

'No.'

'It's my second. About twenty years ago.' Clark snapped his stirrer in two. 'A young woman. Joanna Hayward, she lived in Barking. She "got off" at Earl's Court.' He had a stolid expression. 'Turned out it was her third attempt. She was alive when she went down. They often are. I shouted down to her to keep away from the rail, the juice was still on. She never took her eyes off me as she put out a hand and grabbed it. Just like that.' He snapped the stirrer into smaller pieces. 'In those days, as I remember, they had you back on the trains sharpish.'

'Tough,' Jack agreed.

'Yes and no. I was young, I was pissed off with her for choosing my train!' Clark shook his head. 'It's like cooking with a knife and then slitting your wrists with it. Or, well, maybe not—' He picked up Jack's stirrer and broke it in half.

Jack was reluctant to join in, unsure it would help Clark to discuss the pros and cons of suicide.

Shaking his head, Darryl picked up the remaining sachet of sugar and poured it into his tea. The man was on autopilot.

Jack remembered Clark had sought him out. 'How are you now?'

'It hits me at night, like a film going on in my head. You get that?'

Jack didn't say he had a song replaying every night when he went to sleep, or mention the hum on the spiral staircase, the mythical birdsong and the glugging sink. Clark wouldn't want to know about his ghosts. He looked over at the hatch: he might get an apple muffin to take to the tower. Two even.

'It was harder for you. You were with him,' Clark remarked.

'What do you mean?'

'All that time waiting for the train and then he jumps. Did you see anything odd about him? I had him for a split second, so in my statement for the inquest I couldn't even say what he looked like. You were waiting on the platform with him.' He looked hostile, as if Jack had been remiss.

Jack felt a change in the air. He glanced again at the hatch. It was shut. The other driver had gone. The only witnesses to the death had been himself and Darryl Clark. The novice driver in whose cab he had travelled hadn't seen a thing. Still, he had been affected; he had since handed in his resignation.

'I wasn't on the platform.' He was careful not to embarrass Clark by pointing out his mistake. 'I was in the District line train.'

'I saw you.' Darryl was implacable. He snapped Jack's stirrer into splinters.

'You saw me afterwards. I was in the office.'

'You were on the platform, at the Hammersmith end. I didn't know you were with the Underground until I saw you clearing the station.'

'I was on the other train,' Jack repeated gently. He put down his mug. 'Are you saying there was someone else on the platform other than Rick Frost?'

'Was that his name?' Darryl Clark's drink was midway to his mouth. 'I tried not to hear.'

'Yes.'

'He's nobody to me. I don't want to know why he did it, or anything about him.' Clark's voice grated.

'But are you saying you saw someone else on the platform with him?' Jack had seen this before: drivers who didn't want to know that the person who had been killed by their train was human, with a name, a home and a family.

'He was looking at the dead man, before he died, I mean.' Clark gave a mirthless laugh and rounded up the snaps of plastic.

'Did you tell the police or the station staff?' There had been nothing in Clark's statement about another man.

'I assumed you'd tell them it was you.'

'It wasn't me,' Jack said again, more to himself.

'Nowadays I'm checking every bloody passenger for a sign they might top themselves.' Clark wiped a hand down his face and took a shaky sip of tea.

Clark hadn't been at the inquest; his manager had read out his statement. He had described the 'deceased' as 'flying out of nowhere'. He had followed protocol to the letter. He had left his cab, turned off the electricity and escorted his passengers off his train.

In the deserted canteen, Jack heard again the squeal of brakes and the piercing whistle Clark had sounded to alert station staff. Since moving to the tower, his mind was full of new, unfamiliar sounds. Maybe the recurring Smiths' 'How Soon Is Now?' was his brain's way of blotting out the soundscape of Frost jumping in front of a train.

'Another drink? A muffin maybe?' He had forgotten the server was shut.

'Food sticks in the craw. My wife's got me on Complan! The counsellor says it's a long haul.' He flashed Jack a smile.

A bad death would be hard: ghosts were the restless dead unable to make peace with themselves. Jack wondered if, like many drivers, Clark believed in ghosts. He saw all sorts of phantoms, wraith-like figures flitting about the platforms of the ghost stations.

'I keep thinking, could I have dropped the handle sooner, hit the brake quicker?' Darryl Clark leant over the table and Jack caught a tang of hair product; Stella would identify it instantly, he thought irrelevantly.

'I've killed a man. My kids' dad is a murderer. I repeat that every morning in the mirror.'

'You didn't kill him.' Every time they climbed into the cab of a train they risked a One Under. The incidents were rare, but it could always happen and they knew it. In that sense Darryl *had* killed Rick Frost.

'It's on the cards every time I'm in that cab.' Darryl had read his mind. Jack felt queasy; since living in the tower his mind wasn't his own.

'It was suicide, not your fault,' Jack insisted. No need to muddy matters with his suspicions of murder. 'What did this other man look like?'

'Like you, since I thought he was you.' Clark's patience was clearly wearing thin.

This had to be Stella's inspector, the man dressed in black she had met at the end of the platform. Jack wanted to text Stella, but with Clark there, it would seem insensitive.

'That bit of track after Hammersmith used to be my best bit of the journey,' Clark said ruefully.

Drivers didn't usually refer to their shift as a 'journey', that was Jack's word. Jack warmed to him.

'You were at the inquest.' Clark sat back in his chair. 'What did he say?'

'He wasn't there.' Whoever was on the platform hadn't come forward. He and Stella had established that the area where she had met the man was a blind spot, out of camera range. Jack tried to recapture the faces of the passengers he had ushered out of the station. None fitted Stella's description; no one had looked like himself.

There had been a man on the top deck of the bus that stopped at the zebra crossing on Goldhawk Road that night. Jack had been unable to see his face; he had a cap pulled low over his eyes. With no evidence, no proof or reason, Jack was quite sure that it was the man he called Stella's 'inspector'.

The Piccadilly train had come down the line from Hammersmith. Clark had seen a man step out from behind the staircase housing. Looking behind him, Rick Frost had seen him too and had started to run. The last person he had looked at, with his hazel eyes flecked with green, was Jack.

'You didn't murder him,' Jack said again to Darryl Clark. He wished he knew who had.

Forty-Six

Saturday, 26 October 2013

Stella drove around the corner into Corney Road and pulled in by the cemetery when she remembered it was a one-way street and she was going the wrong way. She was about to turn the van around when she saw she was outside Jackie's house. She had a sudden longing to knock on the door and invite herself in. But it was nearly four o'clock and Jackie would be at the office. Instead, she must drive to a village fifty miles away in pursuit of a woman who misguidedly wanted vengeance on her husband's mistress. Liz had urged her to call the police, but Stella wanted to hold off. She didn't think Lulu capable of violence: she was all theatre and bluster.

She had turned down Liz's offer that she come too; she had also refused to leave Stanley behind. Hazily she supposed that having a dog with her would be a good thing in a remote village in the countryside. Her recollection of Mrs Ramsay's description of Charbury was that it was in the middle of nowhere.

She did want Jack. If Lulu Carr had found Nicola Barwick, he'd know what to do. She tapped out his number on her phone on the dashboard. At the same moment a woman's voice reverberated around the van.

'It's me.'

There was a huff from the jump seat: Stanley was preparing to bark. 'Sssh.' Stella put a finger to her lips. She had answered an incoming call.

'What?' It was Lulu Carr.

'You took the address!' Stella snatched the phone from the cradle and clamped it to her ear.

'You would have done the same. She was being jobsworthy not giving to me.'

'That doesn't mean— Oh never mind.' Lulu was unrepentant, but Stella should have bargained for this. Lulu operated on a different plane, one where her own needs dominated all others. Perhaps a good detective couldn't afford to put honesty and respect for privacy before the case. Jack would agree.

'Did you find Nicola Barwick?' Stella pictured blood, mess, flashing blue lights. She should have called the police.

'Stella? I can't hear you! You've gone dead!'

The oldest trick in the book was to pretend the line was bad if asked an awkward question. Stella's mum did it all the time.

'Stella, hello?'

Stella took the phone from her ear to give Lulu a moment to decide to play it straight and saw she had pressed the phone too close to her ear and activated the mute button. She sighed and switched the call to the van's speaker system. 'Yes, I'm here.'

'Thank God. I thought you'd been attacked.' Lulu sounded as if she was inside a metal box.

'Did you find Nicola Barwick?'

'She escaped minutes before I arrived.'

'Escaped? You mean she had gone?' Stella tried to keep it real.

'Liz Thing tipped her off.'

Stanley made a stuttering noise in his throat. Stella looked around; he was staring at her, his pupils dilated. A spooked dog was all she needed. 'Good boy,' she mouthed.

'She wouldn't do that, and anyway, she didn't have her number.' Stella shook her head as if Lulu could see her. 'I was with her the whole time,' she added as a sliver of doubt inserted itself. Liz could have warned Nicola Barwick... but no, Liz wouldn't have lied to her.

There was a light on in Jackie's sitting room. Perhaps the dancing son was at home?

'Do you actually have a brother?' she heard herself say.

'Yes! I texted to say I had her address and he texted saying "You won't rest until you've been there." He watches out for me.'

'Would he have gone there?'

'I didn't exactly give him the address. I want to fight my own battles.' Lulu's voice quavered. Perhaps she recognized that texting her big brother didn't fit with her new-found independence from him.

'What does "exactly" mean?' Stella felt she was clutching at straws. Terry had said, pay attention to the words people use, just one word can give them away.

'I said it was Charbury. I said I'd used Google Street View, Rick was always on that. I said the house was next to the village stores. He wasn't interested. My brother's a busy man.'

Lulu Carr spoke as if Stella might dispute this. Stella had enough to deal with, with her own newly acquired brother, so she wasn't about to tackle someone else's.

Stanley began to sing, an insistent mewing that was almost human. He had been on a cushion in Liz Hunter's kitchen for hours. Stella was cross with herself; he needed to pee. She reached around and unfastened him. He plunged through the seats and landed on her lap.

'When did Nicola Barwick leave?'

'A neighbour said about an hour before I got there. Serves me right for stopping off for some lunch. I posted my number through the letterbox to ask the owner to ring me. Doubt they will. I said there'd been a death in the family, which is true!' Her voice was sibilant, and the consonants popped like small arms fire. Stella adjusted the volume on the dashboard. 'Nicola guessed I was on to her.'

Stella opened the door and Stanley scrambled on to the pavement. He pulled her across the road to the cemetery. With a balletic sweep of the back leg, he hopped along the verge, spraying the railings as he went. The droplets of pee glistened in the lamplight.

'Lulu, to stop you barking up the wrong tree, Nicola Barwick told Liz she was being stalked by a bloke who can't accept their relationship's over. Was Rick like that?' Not unless her stalker is a ghost, she nearly added.

'He was exactly like that. I told you. He had me on twenty-four-hour surveillance.'

'But he's dead. If it was him, it means that Nicola could come back to London,' Stella said. Not, however, if the man was someone else entirely. Or, indeed, with Lulu in her present mood. Up until now Stella had thought of Nicola Barwick only in relation to Frost's death. Liz had described her as nervy, and someone had driven her to leave her home and go into hiding. Now she had moved on. Liz was right; they should ring the police. Stanley was straining on his lead.

'I spend a fortune on a taxi haring down to some godforsaken place in Sussex on a wild-goose chase and you tease out the answer over a lunch. Stella, you are a great detective!' It was impossible to tell over the phone if Lulu was being ironic. Stella was inclined to think not – it wasn't her style. It was the second time in twenty-four hours she had been praised for doing pretty much nothing. Jack had been ridiculously happy that she had found out about Lulu being Mrs Frost. Then, as now, Stella didn't have the energy to disagree. She ended the call with a promise to see her on her next cleaning shift.

Stanley pulled her through the gates of the cemetery. Stella was surprised it was still open: it was hardly practical to tend the grave of a loved one in the dusk. Her mind on Nicola Barwick, she let Stanley lead her off the path towards a wall that she realized was the one opposite Liz's house. She would have been tempted to go back, but as she was leaving Liz had received a text from her new man so she wouldn't be there. Stanley lifted his leg by a danger sign that warned of open or sunken graves, unstable memorials and uneven ground.

In the distance was the church. High above the spire Stella made out Jack's tower. Splashes of sodium-orange light illuminated a track winding between the graves. It was not sensible to be alone in a cemetery after dark. Stella promised herself they would have a quick walk, then return to the van and she would ring Jack. She increased her pace.

Women were murdered by stalkers. Stella had heard of a case on the news recently. The police had ignored more minor bullying until the day the man had smashed his way into the woman's flat and strangled her. Nicola Barwick could be in danger. She stopped by a Madonna and got out her phone. The signal was down to one bar, but she got a connection.

'Cashman speaking.'

'Martin, it's me, Stella Darnell.'

'There's only one Stella! I hoped you'd ring, I just heard about your brother.' His voice reverberated: he was on speakerphone. 'About time he turned up! Be good to meet him.'

'My brother?' Stella was momentarily blank.

'Darren, David—?'

'Dale. How did—' No need to ask. Suzie, so hot on privacy she disliked coffee shops recalling she liked a double espresso, had been telling the world that her son made 'soufflé as light as gossamer'.

'Shot me back twenty years to when I first met Terry.' There was a click as he took the receiver off speakerphone. Sounding more intimate, he continued, 'Fancy a drink? I told Terry I'd be there for you if stuff ever came to light and Terry was... hmm... wasn't here.'

'Thanks, it's fine.' Stella was about to ask what Martin meant when Stanley tugged hard at his lead. Concerned that he might drag her into a sunken grave or an unstable monument, she unclipped him. Why did Martin think she needed to talk about it? Dale was here and then he would go.

Terry had been Martin Cashman's boss and his best friend. After Terry died, Martin had made it clear he was 'there' for Terry's daughter. At the time Stella had rebuffed his help; later she had asked him a favour and he had turned her down. Now she was circumspect: Martin had been Terry's friend; he owed her nothing. Since Terry hadn't known he had a son, by 'stuff' Terry couldn't have meant a situation like this.

'Brothers! Mine borrowed my Lexus last week, to impress some new woman he's conned into dating him, and he pranged it on a post box!'

Jackie had said it was a shame Cashman was married with kids – a chip off Terry's old block, he would be perfect for Stella. Solid and practical, he would take no nonsense. Stella didn't believe in 'perfect' and didn't ask what 'nonsense' from her it was that Cashman wouldn't take.

She was buffeted by a gust of wind.

'Blimey, where are you?' Cashman exclaimed.

'I'm by a grave – on a path – I'm outside,' Stella said. She told him about Nicola Barwick, leaving out that Lulu Carr suspected she had killed her husband. Terry's daughter or not, and despite her track record in solving cases, Martin wouldn't like her turning detective. 'Leave it to us,' he had said.

Tapping on his keyboard, he breathed loudly into the receiver, as loud as the wind. 'Nothing on the system – she hasn't put in a complaint. I can check with Sussex, though there's not much we can do if she hasn't come forward and with no hard facts...'

'She can't come forward if she's missing.' A patch of white that she had thought was Stanley was a headstone. Hearing herself, Stella added, 'But I see what you mean.' Were it not for Liz Hunter, Stella might doubt that Barwick even existed.

'The neighbour told your friend that Nicola Barwick said she was going away.'

'Something must have happened to make her leave,' Stella said.

'Trouble is, unless she tells us, or fails to turn up where she is expected, our hands are tied. My guess is that she'll ring your mate when she knows her new location. When she does, encourage her to give us a call. We can slap an order on this bloke – he may already have a record. Get me some information and I'll see what I can do.'

Stella thanked him. About to end the call, she was hit by another squall and staggered into a dip in the ground.

'Stella?'

'Yes.'

'Up for that drink anytime, OK?'

Right now she could do with sitting in a pub with Martin Cashman, swapping information about the latest cleaning products with 'stop and search' stats.

'OK,' she agreed. 'Martin, what do you know about that man, Rick—'

A busy man, Cashman had gone.

Stella wandered deeper into the cemetery, peering into the spangled darkness in search of Stanley. The street lamps on Corney Road were dots. The pale shapes of headstones mingled with shadows of trees, created Stanleys everywhere. She heard a scuffling and blundered off the track, furious with herself for letting the dog off his lead.

'Stanley!' She was loath to shout, though there was no one alive to mind.

She tripped on tussocks and clods of earth and, at last coming upon a path, found the source of the noise. A plastic bag caught on a bramble was not Stanley.

'Stanley!' Stella dared raise her voice. Wind smacked at the plastic bag and whooshed through the branches. No dog.

Flitting blobs of beige danced and goaded her amidst darker shapes. She was fooled by finger-pointing angels, more Madonnas, and laughing cupids with dimpled cheeks. Row upon row of headstones, half hidden by grass and brambles where light didn't penetrate: none were Stanley.

Stella fumbled inside her anorak for the whistle. Sickened, she pictured it in the glove box with the spare poo bags.

A stick cracked, a scurry of footsteps. Stella plunged on, keeping the wall on her right as rough navigation. Her ears attuned, she shouted 'Biscuit' and 'Chicken': anything to lure him to her. Twice she tripped on sunken masonry, heedless now of falling into a coffin-sized hole. The ground dipped and she fell on to one knee and made herself listen.

Nothing. Her mouth dry, she put her fingers to her mouth and gave a long low whistle. Her heart lurched when the sound was repeated. She did it again. Again there was a whistle, long and low, longer than hers had been. It wasn't an echo. Someone had whistled back. Stella fought the impulse to run. Jack said running gave the enemy your location. What enemy?

Trees outlined in the gloom swayed as one, leaning eastward as blusters ripped at the last of their leaves and tore at their branches. In gaps between gusts, Stella heard rustling. It came from the darkest section of the cemetery. She walked purposefully towards it, skidding on loose stones, her boots crunching on the hard, but even surface, giving away her location.

Stanley was running towards her. It really was him. His movements were jerky, back legs flinging up and then down. Stella remembered the dead rat; he had something forbidden – anything he found here was forbidden. Ecstatic at his transgression, he wouldn't let her put his lead on and would refuse treats and ignore commands. They would be here for hours.

Stanley cavorted away in the direction of Corney Road, pausing every so often to confirm she was coming. The trick was to go the other way. Stella had no choice but to go further into the cemetery because, lacking traffic sense, if she pursued him to the road, Stanley would see a car and give chase.

Stella walked towards the boundary wall, not looking to see if he was coming or he would race away. Poodles possessed a lethal combination of intelligence and tenacity; she must keep her wits about her.

In front of her was a brick building. In the light of street lamps beyond the wall, she made out graffiti tags sprayed on the brickwork. A silver stencil of a skull and crossbones gleamed in the thin light. A grille was fitted over the doorway, another covered a half-moon window.

Intent on ignoring Stanley, Stella pulled on the grille and it swung open. Something pushed against her calves and she nearly shouted with fright. Stanley dropped whatever was in his mouth and nosed through the gap.

Got you! Stella swiped up the discarded bunch of dead flowers and tossed them into the bushes. She remembered that Jackie had put a torch app on her phone. Switching it on, she went in after him.

The air was chill and dank. High up in the wall a semi-circular window let in pinkish light. Even without a door, the hut offered shelter from the wind, which was now a distant moan.

She clipped on Stanley's lead and shone the light about her. In one corner was a warped and dirt-encrusted cupboard. Through mesh doors she saw two cans of Coca-Cola and a bag of crisps. A flea-bitten deckchair and three broken packing cases were grouped around a table. There were no leaves or rubbish on the floor, no tell-tale cigarette butts: it was as if someone had swept it recently. Probably a kids' den – house-proud kids. Stella approved, although a cemetery wouldn't be her choice.

She heard the whistle again. Stanley growled.

'It's the wind.' Hearing her voice, feeble and hollow in the crypt-like hut, Stella was less sure. Surely it was late to be putting flowers on a grave. She scooped Stanley up and, tripping on the deckchair, hurried to the doorway.

Two things happened. Her torch went out and the grille shut with an ear-splitting clang.

Forty-Seven

Saturday, 26 October 2013

'Sorry, wrong house.'

It wasn't the wrong house, it was the wrong year. The man regarding Jack with an enquiring smile was Terry Darnell. Not the Terry Jack had met briefly, but a middle-aged Terry with life still to lead. A ghost.

'You all right? You look like the driven bloody snow!' The timbre of the voice was Terry with the West London accent swapped for North Shore Sydney. In a minute Jack would pinpoint the suburb. It wasn't Terry Darnell, it was the Brand-new Brother.

'You wanting Stella?' *Stellah*. The man lounged against the door jamb, a tea towel on one shoulder, as if he had all day. Jack, who did not have all day or night, considered barging past him.

'She's expecting me.' He was terse. 'I texted.'

'Sure. Come on in. I've just got the central heating working – place was cold as a tomb!' He stood aside to let Jack in.

'Crows' Nest, zip code NSW 2065,' Jack murmured, looking up the stairs and into the living room, expecting Stella.

'Bang on, Professor Higgins! Stella tell you?' Dale banged shut the front door. The man was noisy.

'I worked it out from your accent.' Jack frowned to hide his pride. No one had called him Professor Higgins before.

Dale continued, 'You know Sydney?' He whipped the tea towel off his shoulder and began flexing it between his hands as if exercising his pectorals. Jack guessed he was one of those men who need always to be testing themselves and, more annoyingly, testing others.

'Yes.' He stared into the sitting room. The table lamps and side lights were on. He caught lavender oil. Stella preferred plug-in deodorizers; essential oils were liable to stain. He went on down the passage to the kitchen where, it being exactly eight, Stella would be microwaving her shepherd's pie. A cloud of garlicky steam billowed out when he pushed open the door. It made him aware he was hungry. Stella would heat up a ready meal for him too, but it had never smelled so good as it did tonight.

'She's due any time now.' The Brand-new Brother trod on his heel. While aware it was an absurd notion, Jack had hoped he had gone. Why was he here?

'Is she expecting *you*?' Jack nearly voiced the question.

'The more the merrier, unless you're a veggie?' Dale was clattering at the stove. 'If so, I can rustle up the finest omelette this side of – where are we? – *Ham*-mer-*smith*!' He flapped his towel as if his pronunciation were a linguistic triumph. 'Place of my birth!'

'Sometimes I'm vegetarian,' Jack said haughtily, ignoring the last comment. Did Dale think being born in the same borough as Stella gave him carte blanche to her house?

A large pan was bubbling on the back ring of the stove. Light drifted through the glass panel in the oven door. Jack pinpointed background whirring to the oven fan. He perched on the edge of a chair and fished his phone from his coat. No text from Stella. Last night she hadn't said the Brand-new Brother would be here. No reason she should, yet he was put out. Stella couldn't have known.

'Is today a meat-eating day? We've got lamb stew with baked potatoes. Big surprise for my little sister. Her favourite, Suzanne says. It's my old man's recipe and goes down a bomb at our pop-up café on a winter's night! Too rough and ready for my restaurant crowd!' He let out a guffaw. He must have seen Jack's face because he said, 'The dad I knew as my dad, not my biological dad. The dad that dealt with the daily shit and footed the bill!' He gave another hooting laugh and, diving forward, sipped on a spoon of stew and smacked his lips. He picked up a clean spoon, dipped it in the mixture and passed it to Jack. 'Catch the cumin – hope you like raisins!'

Jack couldn't come up with an excuse to refuse. He took the spoon and blew on it, then put his lips to the bowl of the spoon. It was the most delicious food he had ever tasted. Garlic, cumin, lemon with coriander as an aftertaste. Each herb and spice had kept its separate taste while blending to create perfection.

''S nice,' he admitted.

'Oh, wait on, I never introduced myself! Guess you know all about me from Stell.' Dale thrust his hand out to Jack. 'Dale Bardia Heffernan. And you are the train driver?' He gave a toot-toot. Presumably this was a joke.

'Jack.' Jack shook the outstretched hand, mindful to clasp tight. For a moment the two men were in a contest, each gripping the other's hand as if their lives depended on it. Jack let go first because he felt silly.

'Bardia?' He arched his eyebrows, disliking himself for asking the question that had begged to be asked.

'Yeah, don't hold back, everyone has a view! Dad was a bit of a hero in the Second World War. The guy was forty-three when I was born – I've got three older sisters. Dale Senior was part of Operation Compass; he took part in the liberation of the port of Bardia in 1941. My sister has it as a middle name, but when the longed-for boy came along, they dusted it off and gave it to me too! My party quip is: Thank God he wasn't at Dunkirk!'

Jack refrained from asking why that name would be worse. He noticed it would be easy to miss that Heffernan had been adopted: he spoke of his Australian family as 'real'. Jack wondered if he spoke this way with Stella and her mother.

'Stella generally heats up a ready meal. She hates fuss,' Jack pronounced, arms folded.

'I'm on that. The coriander garnish is optional, but I recommend it. I had a tussle with the garlic, then went for it. D'you think she'll hack it?'

'I don't know.' Jack was honest. Stella liked honesty. Dale

appeared concerned to please Stella, but if he wanted a share of her legacy – the man was a bounty hunter – he was wrong to think cooking a slap-up meal and heating up the house was the way to her purse.

In the two years since she'd inherited the house, as far as Jack knew, Stella had never turned on the heating or the oven. She maintained Terry Darnell's synchronized lighting, on timers to fool burglars. She had changed nothing. For a time, at the end of the Blue Folder case, he had thought she would sell up, but then she slipped back to the old routine of being custodian, as if keeping it clean for the day when Terry returned. Or so Jack believed.

After Dale's cooking spree, Stella would have to air the house to chase out the stale stew odour or it would hang about for days. In Terry's house her adherence to rituals – cloths and sponges laid out in readiness for cleaning – was votive. All the signs of Terry that she had worked to preserve had been erased. His cereal bowl, spoon and coffee mug that she kept on the draining board had been tidied away. In one evening the Brand-new Brother had obliterated everything.

Jack felt grim satisfaction that Dale and his lamb stew would get short shrift from Stella. She would be stunned by the warmth, the mood lighting and the smell. Jack dreaded the hurt that would flit across her face and her stilted efforts to hide them. He couldn't bear to witness her struggle to make sense of the transformation. He considered leaving, but that would be the act of a coward.

Despite seeing Heffernan's true motive, Jack did feel rather sorry for the fellow. No one was going to enjoy the next few minutes.

'Fancy a drink while we wait?' Dale held up a bottle of De Bortoli, a New South Wales Merlot, and a glass. Jack's stomach did a flip; Heffernan's smile was Stella's when she was relaxed. He was about to refuse, he wanted to keep a clear head, but if he was to help Stella he must be more relaxed than he felt. He nodded.

'Jack, help me out here. I'm wondering…' Dale held the bottle at the base, a hand behind his back like a waiter.

'What?' Jack signalled for Dale to stop pouring.

'Stella is like me.'

Jack bristled. 'How?'

'Reliable, does what says she'll do. She was meant to be here at seven fifteen. What'd she tell you?'

Jack shrugged. Stella wasn't expecting him. Terry had kept the wall clock three minutes fast, but even so that made it ten past eight. She was late.

'Are you worried the food will spoil?' he sniped.

'Hell no! It's a stew, the longer it mulches the better. I'm bothered by Stella being late. Suza— my mother told her about tonight. She agreed to be here.'

'Here or at her flat?'

'Jackie said to come here; Suzanne asked her to give me a key. Stella's not the type of girl to bail out, is she? You know her well.'

'I don't.' But he did. Stella fulfilled agreements, she saw contracts through, however difficult. She never 'bailed out'. A trawling dread overtook Jack's trepidation about Stella's reaction to home cooking and a functioning central-heating system. He grabbed his phone.

'This is Stella Darnell, please leave me a—'

He felt a wash of shame that, overtaken by his own feelings, he hadn't considered Stella's safety. She was never late. Not unless something had happened—

'I don't want to ask Suzanne, that'll worry her. Jackie's not at the office any more,' Dale said as he turned off the heat on the hob and the oven.

Stella had gone to see Nicola Barwick that morning. Although it was hot and steamy in the kitchen, Jack shivered. Stella hadn't been in touch with him since – why had he only just noticed?

A loud rap on the door startled both men. A shadow filled the glass in the door, silhouetted in the porch light. Obliquely Jack observed there was a porch light. He had the crazy notion that this time it really was Terry's ghost.

Dale got there first. He flung open the front door. 'Hey, sis!' With a flourish of his tea towel he welcomed her inside.

Jack found he couldn't move.

'Sorry, I couldn't find my key. That lamb stew smells brilliant.' Stella stopped rummaging in her rucksack and came in, Stanley at her heels.

'It was meant to be a surprise!' Dale crowed with mock disappointment.

'Stella has an acute sense of smell. She could tell you all the ingredients,' Jack said, but no one heard.

Stella looped her rucksack over the newel post and nodded to Jack with an expression he couldn't fathom. With Stanley pattering at her heels, she went after Dale down the passage to the kitchen. Jack trailed after them.

'It's my favourite.' Stella was sluicing her hands under the tap. 'I'm very hungry.'

Stella was never hungry. She ate when she was empty or because it was on the schedule; she regarded food as a nuisance. Tonight Jack was inclined to agree that it was.

'Hey, little feller!' Dale swept the dog up and held him on the other shoulder to the tea towel. He fired up the ring on the hob.

'He will bite – he doesn't like being held. It's best to warn him…' Jack subsided into silence. The dog was systematically licking Heffernan's face.

He stood in the doorway. Brother and sister were chatting and joking, moving around the room, getting out plates, knives and forks, filling wine glasses as if they had known each other forever, rather than three days. Jack was the odd one out, the stranger.

He was opening the front door when Stella called to him. He would walk and walk and never stop. This was worse than if she had found him in Lulu Carr's cupboard.

He nearly didn't answer. 'What?'

'There's a litre of milk in my rucksack. Bring it through. We'll need it for your hot drink in our meeting after supper.'

Jack shut the door and, fending off an impulse to cry, lifted the bag off the post. He sat on the bottom step, the bag between his knees. The milk was cold; Stella must have just bought it. Was that why she was late? The bag tipped open; he clamped his legs together and caught something in his lap.

Even if Dale had not switched on all the lights, Jack would have recognized what he held in his hands. The Pullman carriage belonged to a train exactly like the one he had owned when he was little.

Forty-Eight

Saturday, 26 October 2013

'You never lose track of time.' Jack waited until Dale had shut the front door behind him and they were alone.

'I lost track of Stanley.' After her account of her visit to Nicola Barwick's house and the discovery of a long-lost school friend, Stella described an escalating ordeal in Chiswick Cemetery. It had finished with being stuck in a shed, the gate having jammed shut in the wind.

'Stanley dragged me in. On the way out, a noticeboard said they don't allow dogs in at any time!' She seemed rather excited by her inadvertent transgression, Jack thought.

Stella tossed a treat into the dog's basket – the only addition to the house since Terry's death. The dog caught it mid-air, snapped it in his jaws and curled into a ball. If she hadn't had the dog, Stella wouldn't have gone into the cemetery, Jack thought. Owning dogs was dangerous. Cemeteries and dark unpopulated stretches of ground in a city were short cuts or choices of murder sites for his True Hosts. Bodies were often found by dog walkers, he knew that.

'I saw that toy carriage in your bag.' He was stirring honey into his hot milk. He had briefly entertained the fancy that it was a present for him, but Stella wouldn't buy him a toy, she thought toys were for children. Jack shuddered. The carriage had given him a bad feeling.

'I found it in the shed when I was looking for another way out.' She placed the carriage on the table. 'I panicked and must have shoved it in my pocket. I'll take it back tomorrow.'

'Don't go back!' Jack said.

'It was a kids' den, it'll belong to them. I've stolen it.'

Stella rolled the carriage about on the table, stopping by the mugs as if they were stations. Jack was anxious to have a go.

'I'll do it for you.' He peered in through the carriage windows. Unlike the carriage he had found earlier that day, this one was full of passengers sitting at the tables on which were glued plates, cups and minute cutlery. Delicately, Jack prised open a door and revealed a steward balancing a tray with a glass of brandy and a cigar. A man sat alone; his table had no food on it – presumably the order was his. Although the dining car must be heated, the figure wore a coat and what looked like a baseball cap. Everyone else was eating or in conversation with fellow diners, while the man looked out of his window, but not with the ruminative expression of a lone traveller: he was looking at Jack. Although moulded in beige plastic, Jack was certain the figure was a model of the man standing in the middle of Hammersmith Bridge he had seen through the binoculars the night he moved into the tower. The same man had watched Jack from the bus on Goldhawk Road just after Rick Frost died.

'It's a sign,' he breathed.

'A sign?' Stella echoed. 'Of what?'

Jack was back in the school kitchen garden. He saw a flash of broken crockery, smashed glasses, stricken faces pressed against jammed windows, lobster thermidor, pâté de foie gras mixed with mud and spliced with the lolly sticks he had used for tunnel struts. The sound of the Smiths couldn't drown out the screams and cries for help that would never come. In the silence of the aftermath of the crash, he had heard a chinking, like a timorous call for attention and, finding himself alone, he had left the smashed-up tunnel and followed the sound. He had come across a gate leading out beyond the school kitchen garden. It was out of bounds. A dog lead dangled from a post. In the zephyr-like breeze the catch clinked against the wood. Even then he had known it was a sign.

Jack put his mug down. Fingers steepled, he whispered, 'There's stuff – I haven't said.'

He told Stella about the other carriage and the engine on the monitors in the stations. He told her about the length of the tunnel and that the answer, 266.66, was repeated on the engine. His finger trembling, he showed her that it was the same as the number on the side of the Pullman carriage: 26666. He got out the carriage he had found that morning. Another 26666. He coupled it to the Pullman and sent it around the table, stopping at Stella's mug stations. Stella didn't interrupt or tell him it was nonsense or that he was imagining things.

St Peter's church bells chimed midnight. Jack and Stella had been awake most of the last twenty-four hours.

Finally he told her about the boy called Simon who had wanted to be his friend at school. The boy was dead. Jack said he had made himself forget that time long ago. Until the toy train brought it back. Suffused with shame, he found the words to tell her that at his boarding school he was for a time a bully. He had been bullied too, he said, wondering suddenly if that bit was true. Was what Simon did to him actually bullying? Huddled in his coat, his milk gone cold, Jack told Stella all about Simon.

When he'd finished, she took the carriage on another round of the table, stopping at his mug, then at hers, berthing it at the honey pot. She said, 'School can be a tough place for kids. Jackie says it was hard on you being sent away after your mum—' She set the carriage off on another circuit of the condiments. 'Are you saying you think this boy – man – called Simon killed Frost and left you these bits of train? He'd surely have got over you having a go at him by now. Could he be the inspector I met on the station?'

'No, Simon's dead. He's been dead for years.' Jack put his hands to his ears. He heard the pounding of the sea crashing on some far-off shore. More and more he felt his mind wasn't his own.

'How did he die?' Stella was examining the wheels of the carriage; Jack could tell she was trying to be tactful.

'He was mugged. Actually in that cemetery you were in tonight.' He used 'actually' to imply it was a coincidence, so as not to worry her. 'He died later in hospital.'

'So these toys were left by a ghost?' She betrayed no sarcasm.

'No.' *Yes.* 'Simon was only trying to help me.' Simon had wanted to be his friend. Jack had never let himself think this before. He had punished him for liking him – perhaps because he didn't like himself.

'Anyone could have found the carriages or the engine. It wasn't your usual route, you drive the Richmond to Upminster line, and I certainly didn't plan on going into the cemetery.'

'Someone could have followed you and left the carriage where you'd find it.' Jack spoke as his thoughts unfolded. 'Did you hear anyone while you were there?'

He could see from Stella's expression that she had.

'I thought it was the wind,' she admitted. 'How would anyone know I would go in or that I'd find the hut?'

'He – or she – could have lured Stanley away from you. Did you happen upon the hut by accident or did Stanley lead you there? The most potent of plans are plotted in chunks and put into action as situations occur. This person didn't lure you to the cemetery, but if they were watching you, they'd have seen you go in. Cue to set the plan in motion. If you had gone after Lulu Carr to Charbury, they would have left the carriage on Isabel Ramsay's grave.'

'I was following Lulu, I mightn't have visited the grave. How would they even think I might?'

'Wouldn't you?' Jack said levelly. Mrs Ramsay had been Stella's favourite client.

Stella reddened. 'Yes, I would.'

'Such a person will do their homework. They enter someone's mind and alter the course of their actions. When the time comes, they end their life. We are dealing with a merciless professional.'

Stella grabbed a brush from the corner of the kitchen and began sweeping the floor. 'Have we now got three cases to solve?' She didn't sound fazed by the prospect.

Jack stroked his chin. 'Not necessarily.'

'Could this Simon from your school have a relative he told about you?' Stella scooted a minute scrap of onion skin and a stale dog biscuit into a dustpan, and banged it into the swing bin. She gripped the brush handle like a spear. 'Is someone out to get revenge?'

'There was a sister.' He was impressed at Stella's lateral thinking – detective thinking.

'What was her name?'

'No idea, although I'm sure he told me. I tried to block him out.' He had tried to disappear Simon. *Simple Simon*. 'He made us prick our thumbs and press them together so we'd be blood brothers.'

'That's silly nonsense – it didn't make you brothers. What did you do exactly? Why was it such a big deal?' Stella leant on the brush handle.

The distance that divided them was a metre of lino. It might be a yawning chasm.

'I said I didn't know him.'

'Was that all?'

He didn't want Stella to understand. He wanted to keep her opinion of him intact.

'If someone was out for revenge, and quite honestly I doubt they are, then this is a weird way to go about it. Anyone who knows you would see that a train is the perfect present.'

'True.' Pleased by Stella's observation – she knew him – Jack resumed his drink, although it had cooled. 'Their intention would be to unsettle me. In fact – well, I have to say it's working.' He didn't look at Stella.

'OK, so this is what we do. I'll return this carriage to the cemetery; you can hand in the ones you found to Lost Property. We'll show him or her that we don't care. We've got bigger fish to fry.'

Stella washed her mug, scrubbing vigorously inside it with a scouring pad. She put it on the draining board. The cereal bowl and spoon were back. She had cleaned and put away the empty stew pan after supper. Jack was faintly reassured: Terry's kitchen was restored; it was as if Dale had never been there.

'That wouldn't work.' Jack couldn't say that though Simon was dead, he lived on in his head. Getting rid of the train wouldn't expunge him. Stella's straightforward and honest solution belonged to a cleaner, sunlit world. 'You shouldn't go back to the cemetery on your own. I'll do that.'

'Why would that be better? At my primary school a girl stuffed me in the cleaning cupboard. I got Ajax powder in my hair. I haven't been minded to drop expensive toys around London for her nor can I see anyone doing it on my behalf.' She looked at Jack. 'She worked for Clean Slate a few years ago. I gave her the top clients; she got into corners and sanitized stainless steel sinks to a sparkle.' Stella seemed cheered by this recollection. 'My friend Liz rescued me from the cupboard.'

'Was that why you launched Clean Slate?' Jack wanted to steer Stella off cupboards.

'No.' Stella cast him a look. She flipped open her Filofax and wrote 'Rick Frost' on a blank page and put today's date. Subject closed. Case meeting open. 'That text you sent me about asking Lulu Carr about the glove Stanley took?' She clicked on her ballpoint. 'What with the drama of Barwick's disappearance, I forgot. What's the significance?'

Jack couldn't say his calculation of the West Hill tunnel had led him to make connections that were intuitive with no basis at all in everyday reality. Stella had been patient when he explained how working out the length had opened up his mind; he wouldn't tax her patience further.

'It's tenuous. Lucie May said that the dead man in my tower was found face down with a black glove placed on his back.'

'You think it's the same glove?' Stella was doing her very best to go with him.

'I know, it's tenuous, but because of the 26666...'

Stella would consider herself honour bound to contradict any information given by Lucie May. Now was not the time to say that Terry had told Lucie about the glove. As she so often did, Stella surprised him.

'Tenuous is us. Black gloves are common, but not ones with crowns on them.' She wrote 'black glove with crown motif' in her Filofax and looked at him. 'Are you thinking the cases are linked?'

'One connection is Terry, but since he was a police officer, no surprise there.' Jack silently blessed Stella for the open mind she must have resolved to keep.

'Jack, if you seriously think there is someone out there looking for you, come and stay in my flat, just till we gauge the lie of the land. There's CCTV, a London bar and three mortice locks.'

'I live in a tower, how much safer could I be!'

Jack squinted in through the Pullman carriage windows and gave a yelp.

The dog leapt from his basket and bounded about the kitchen barking, head thrown back. It was the same sound he had made in the tower, and it struck a note of dread in Jack's chest. Dogs sensed more than humans.

Stella had dropped her pen. 'What's the matter?'

'The man has gone.'

'What man?'

'The man who was waiting for his brandy, the one looking—' Jack gesticulated at the empty table in the carriage window.

'Oh for goodness— He – *it* – must have fallen out. Shake the carriage.' Stella puffed out her cheeks. She shooed the dog back to his basket and fed him another treat. She retrieved her pen from the floor.

'Found him.' She handed Jack the plastic man. 'That glove is for a child, but Lulu does have small hands. I'll confirm it with her. OK, so back to our suspects. Lulu, William Frost, the inspector, Nicola and Nicola's stalking ex. I really do think we can rule out Lulu Carr. The woman's impetuous, but I don't see her harming anyone.'

'What if she had found Nicola Barwick and is pretending she didn't?'

'She's not that wily. I'm not even sure she believes they were having an affair. I wonder if she's made it up. She strikes me as inauthentic.' Stella folded her arms as if pleased with her idea. 'Mind you, I do think she's hiding something. She did lie to me about her husband leaving her, but even so I don't think that makes her a murderer.'

'And William Frost?' Jack asked.

'I don't trust him. Ever since he brought the case to us, he's been evasive and unhelpful.' Stella added William Frost to her task list.

'What about this man your friend Liz is seeing? He claims to be a close friend of Nicola Barwick's, but she never told him about moving from Charbury. Nor did she give him her Charbury address in the first place. Now he's involved with her lodger. Fishy, don't you think?'

'People can't help who they like,' Stella said. 'Liz wouldn't do anything stupid.'

'Whom,' Jack said before he could stop himself.

'Sorry?'

'People who make mistakes rarely think they are making them.' Too late Jack realized that Stella would think he was referring to her past; in fact he was thinking of Dale. 'What's his name?' he asked hurriedly.

'I've forgotten.' Stella looked annoyed with herself. 'I'll ask her more about him.' She noted 'Liz Hunter's man' down on her list.

'What about this brother of Lulu Carr's? If Frost was cheating on her, the brother might be unhappy – that's a motive.'

'It's a big step from being unhappy to killing a man.'

'That's the kind of thing brothers do. Goodness knows what Dale Heffernan would do on your behalf.' Jack was being sarcastic. Immediately ashamed, he wished the words unsaid.

'Dale isn't my real brother,' Stella said in a small voice.

'Yes he is.'

'I know *you* better than I do him. Blood isn't everything.'

Jack hid his pleasure. He opened the carriage door and slotted the little figure through and tipped up the carriage until he was back at his table awaiting his drink. He took the carriages around the 'stations' again.

'Lulu Carr says he's protective,' she said. 'That means he might do anything.'

'What's his name?' Jack heard himself repeating the question. 'The inspector, the brother, the boyfriend: we need names and faces for these people.'

'Is he a suspect?' Stella was arch, although he hadn't meant it as a dig.

'Until we cross him off.'

'Lulu didn't say. I might ask William rather than make her curious.' Stella noted this down and sat back contemplating the growing list with evident satisfaction.

'After what Darryl Clark – the driver of the train that hit Frost – said, we need to focus attention on your inspector at the station,' Jack said.

'I keep forgetting to show you.' Stella fiddled in the pocket in her Filofax and brought out a square sheet. 'What do you make of this? I found it in the photo booth the night we went to Stamford Brook. Someone must just have left the booth before we came down from the platform. You'd gone to get your train.'

Jack stared at the four images. They were of the back of a man's head. His hair, thick and brown, fell just below his collar. He was wearing a white shirt. He looked at all four pictures although they were repeats of the same shot.

'His back is to the camera,' he said at last.

'Er, yes!' Stella was impatient. 'Who does that? I wondered if it was the inspector-man I met? I heard the machine going just as we were going up to the platform. I thought then it was an odd time to get your picture done. The timings would fit. He probably dived into the photo booth to avoid us seeing him.'

The corpse in the tower had been face down. When Simon had come to say sorry about the things he said in the room below the library, Jack had turned his face to the wall.

You denied you knew me. Three times.

Stella was still talking. '—I thought at the time it was a funny mistake to make. I've had duds in those machines when the flash goes before you're ready but I always face the right way! It does look a bit like him.' She held up the pictures.

'I thought you said you didn't see the man's face.'

'I didn't, but as we're keeping an open mind—'

'I didn't see him at all.' Jack pushed the pictures back. 'We need to see him from behind.' He was thinking out loud now. 'There's an Agatha Christie story in which the murderer is seen from the back, in fact it's on a train—'

'Jack.' Stella's patience had run out. 'Would you go back to Lucie May and ask her what else Terry told her?' She called Stanley out of his bed and fastened on his lead.

Another of Stella's surprises. While he'd been worried about upsetting her, she was concentrating on the case. He was sure she didn't know there had been anything serious between Lucie and her father. She was able to put aside personal feelings for the bigger picture. He could only dream of being like her. Inchoate with emotion, Jack could only nod.

'What shall we do about the toys, since you don't want to hand them into Lost Property?' Stella asked. 'You shouldn't go back to the cemetery on your own.'

'Let me check a few things.' Jack wasn't ready to share the idea he was forming. He wasn't ready to take it on himself. He jumped up and rattled at the handle of the back door. 'Where's the key?'

'Same place as usual, with the forks in the cutlery drawer.' Stella slung on her rucksack. She knew him well enough not to ask why he was going out the back way.

'Lock up after me.'

On the patio an icy blast stung his cheeks. Stella stood by the door, the dog at her side. Behind her the kitchen looked cosy; an aroma of stew lingered. Hauling himself up onto the wall at the back of the garden, Jack imagined going back with her to her flat and drinking hot milk on her spotless cream sofa.

'Be careful.' But his words were flung away by a powerful gust. Balanced on the garden wall, he turned to wave. The kitchen was dark.

He caught the distant slam of the van door, the engine firing, the sound drowned by the howling wind.

Forty-Nine

The south-east window in Palmyra Tower looked out on to the looping spans of Hammersmith Bridge. On the sill were sticks and coils of twine that Jack had collected from the riverbank as a child. These were shored up by flint and limestone washed smooth by the Thames. On top of the 'embankment', Jack had laid the steam engine.

He took out the two carriages from his workbag and coupled the new rolling stock to the engine. He repositioned everything on the ballast. He had a train. He contemplated his tableau.

He heard the sneeze of the funnel and shaded his eyes from the smoke. The hot furnace made his skin smart and his arms ached from heaving shovelfuls of coal. At full pelt, pistons racing, the engine could do fifty-four miles per hour.

The sink glugged. He went over, ran the hot tap and chased out the airlock. Yet again the water was cold – he must email the consortium – but then it went warm again, and the issue lost its urgency. He returned to his train and became aware of the buzzing he heard intermittently and had vaguely attributed to a trapped fly or wasp. A red light winked on the burglar alarm sensor above the window. The instrument should be pointing to the front door to catch an intruder at the only possible point of entry. It was pointing at him.

Jack was about to reposition it, but it was delicate, he could break it. It would be there for insurance purposes. As he had told Stella, the tower was safer than anywhere. Elbow resting on the table, chin on his cupped hand, he imagined tucking into Dale Heffernan's lamb stew in the Pullman car.

This fantasy was shattered by the memory of earth and stones raining down. The tunnel had caved in on the train. Jack had blamed himself for the miscalculation of width and roof strength. But he never made stupid errors.

He fetched his binoculars from the north window sill. He trained them on the beach by Black Lion Lane where he had gathered the flotsam and jetsam. No one there. He swung the glasses away and tracked the towpath along through Furnival Gardens to the bridge. A lone car was making its way across to the Barnes side.

Jack lowered the instrument. He picked out a cotton bud from a pot on the table and dipped it in a pot lid filled with steam oil. He loved the delicate smell of the oil. Holding the engine steady, he travelled the bud along the coupling rods and over the crosshead and sidebars. In a hoarse voice he spoke to Glove Man's ghost: 'Dust is the enemy of wind-up clocks and steam engines. It must be kept out of the mechanism. Oil enables smooth working, but the paradox is that it also attracts dust.'

His memory of that afternoon in the kitchen garden was visceral. He could see every step of his construction. The roof struts had been strong; he had designed the width of the tunnel to allow for wide rolling stock. He had made no error in tension or loading. Simon had hijacked the engine and driven it too fast into the tunnel.

Few had known Jack had lost his red steam engine. One of them was Simon. He had made the mistake of confiding in him: he had hoped that if he told Simon a secret it would get him off his back. But Simon was dead; he *was* off his back. Jack had tried not to be relieved when his father showed him the newspaper cutting, but he had hoped that his bad memories would die too.

As if to reassure himself, Jack went to his desk for the cutting. He shifted his laptop, moved aside his *A–Z* and the lamp. No cutting. He looked underneath the desk, widening his search to the floor and under the bed. No cutting. He emptied out his treasure box on to the bed, but the cutting wasn't there, nor had he expected it to be. He remembered leaving it on the desk. Stanley must have taken it. Jack tried to remember if Stella's dog had visited since he had taken the cutting from his box, but his sense of time since moving to the tower was unreliable. Yesterday seemed years ago. Years ago uncomfortably close.

Jack scratched day-old stubble on his cheek. He didn't need the cutting to know that Simon was dead. For a long time he had relegated him to a dark unvisited place in his mind. Someone else must know about his red steam engine.

You denied you knew me. Three times.

His mind was not his own.

The Smiths 'How Soon Is Now?' drifted into his head. Jack stuck his fingers in his ears, not expecting it to work since it was inside his head, but it did lessen the sound.

Jack found his phone. 'Lucie, it's me.'

'Of course it is,' Lucie May crooned. It might be three in the morning, but Lucie was, as he expected, wide awake.

'Please would you search your files for a mugging in 1998?'

'Honey, there's been a few of those!' She guffawed. 'Drill down for me, would you?'

'A teenager called Simon was found dying in Chiswick Cemetery that year.'

'Why didn't you say? "*Body Found in Graveyard!*" Come!'

The line went dead. Jack left the tower.

Fifty

Sunday, 27 October 2013

'It was mistaken identity.' Lucie May was eating a carrot, still with a flourish of leaves attached to the end, as she leafed through a bulging file.

A fire burned in the grate, drawn curtains shut out the damp gusty night. Jack sipped the mug of hot milk and honey she had presented him with on arrival and nestled into his corner of her sofa.

'Proof, if we need it, that life is stranger than fiction.' She handed Jack a photocopied sheet on which she had scrawled, '*The Sun*, Saturday 24th 1998.' She took a bite of the carrot. 'I played a blinder with that story, straight into Fleet Street, it paid for a new boiler. Called myself Lucille to please my mother! God rest her.'

DEAD MAN WALKING

By Lucille May

Two sons. Two futures. One life. Madeleine and Harry Carrington kept vigil for hours by the bedside of the young man they believed was their 20-year-old son Simon until he died.

Found badly beaten in Chiswick Cemetery on 20 October by a woman walking her dog, the man never regained consciousness. The dog owner, Joan Evans, told us she assumed he was a tramp until she saw his 'nice shoes'. Her neighbours' son wore an identical pair. His face hugely swollen, he was identified by Harry Carrington for his shoes and light blond hair. Blinded by tears, he signed permission for his only son to have emergency surgery on his internal organs.

The young man battled for his life. His 13-year-old sister read him messages from pals, family and our readers. His mum read articles about bridges and tunnels – Simon was to be a civil engineer after graduating from the University of Sussex. The family played his favourite song, the Smiths' 'How Soon Is Now?' and told Simon they loved him until his heart stopped.

When the pathologist, Dr Peter Singer, was preparing to conduct the post-mortem he noted the medical records. Simon Carrington's eyes were brown, and he was six feet one inch tall. The body on Singer's slab had blue eyes and was five foot ten. Simon was missing half a finger on his left hand. The dead man's fingers were intact.

That night 20-year-old Simon walked through the door, toting his dirty washing, asking, 'What time's supper, I'm famished!'

Detective Superintendent Terry Darnell told a crowded press conference, 'We are overjoyed that Simon is alive. However, someone's son has been murdered. We must establish his identity so his family can grieve. We will work to bring his killer to justice.' Asked if the police had any leads, he declined to comment. Darnell dismissed any connection between the man found dying in Chiswick Cemetery and the decomposing body of a man discovered a stone's throw away, locked in Chiswick Tower, ten years ago almost to the day, in October 1988. That man has never been identified.

'So how come you missed this?' Lucie sounded as if she was astounded Jack had not read all her articles.

'I wasn't living in the UK,' Jack said.

'Fancy.' Lucie May gave a shrug of mild disapproval.

In 1998, Jack, like Simon, had been twenty years old. Simon wasn't dead. Jack was supposed to feel relief. He did not. He had told himself that the idea of his mind being invaded was absurd. It was a symptom of tiredness or, as Stella might have said, 'his overworked imagination'. Simon wasn't dead. He had never been dead.

Jack marshalled himself. 'The attack was in Chiswick Cemetery, so why was Terry involved?' Chiswick Cemetery was opposite Jackie's house. Stella had been wandering around it a few hours ago. So had someone else.

'The young man died in Charing Cross Hospital, and the two police divisions cooperated on the case with Terry in charge.'

'Did they ever identify him or catch his attacker?' The print swam. Jack put down the article. *Simon was alive.*

'A damp squib of a story! The police had the dead kid's fingerprints on file. He was eighteen. They hadn't checked because of the kid's father identifying him as his son. Fancy not remembering your boy had lost a finger! None of the family spotted it. Sounds like my family. I could have sat down to supper with an arm missing and my dad wouldn't have batted an eye.' She nibbled the carrot down to the leaves and tossed the clumsy bouquet on to the table. She went on, 'Shock, he said. His wife looked embarrassed. Unhappy pair. Anyone could see she wished it was him on the slab instead. The dead boy was Ryan Morrison, unemployed, no qualifications, an incompetent petty thief. His prints were all over two houses in Corney Road. The owner of the other house had caught up with Morrison and chased him into the cemetery. He reclaimed his transistor radio and a toaster and smashed Morrison to a pulp. Job done, didn't think to let the police know!'

Lucie scrambled off the sofa, walked on tiptoe to her drinks cupboard, did a pirouette in her stockinged feet and returned. She was on another of her wagons, Jack concluded.

'He got a suspended sentence for a disproportionate response. We had sacks of letters in his defence, many saying "good riddance" to Morrison. There are some lovely people out there!' She gave a corncrake laugh.

Simon hadn't been interested in tunnels and bridges at school.

Jack remembered Simon rolling coins over his fingers, the stump moving like a lever. The coin flashed and danced before his eyes.

If Simon was alive in 1998, it didn't mean he was alive now. Jack banished the thought. You only got so many wishes that another person was dead before you had to die yourself.

'So, I hear Terry Darnell's boy's been found?' Lucie May switched on an e-cigarette and regarded it happily.

'Who told you?' Jack snapped.

'Who didn't! It's all over Hammersmith Police Station. The Dowager Darnell is swinging from the rooftops, crowing that she's got her baby back. I was thinking, maybe she'd do an exclusive for the paper. It's a great story!'

'It's private.' Stella would be horrified. Lucie gave short shrift to Suzie, the love of Terry Darnell's life, at least according to Jackie.

'If only Terry had lived to see him.' Lucie was fleetingly pensive. 'Anyway, darling, what's your interest in Carrington?' She puffed on her e-cigarette, eyes bright with news-hound fervour.

Jack told her about the steam engine and the carriages, and about the boy who had tried to be his friend when he was seven.

'You're saying this steam engine means that this bloke is telling you he *still* wants to be your friend twenty-eight years on?'

'He's the only one alive who knows what the engine means to me.' Lucie, like Stella, didn't have time for semiotics or portents; neither woman would change plans because of a squashed lump of chewing gum shaped like a shark on a pavement. 'I don't think he wants to be my friend any more.'

'Your steam engine was in the papers.' Lucie scowled as she vaped on the e-cigarette. 'You had a tantrum in the street cos your dad wouldn't buy you one. Hardly top secret.'

'Most people won't remember. But Simon won't have forgotten. You've put here that he was training to be an engineer: when we were at school he wanted to be an astronaut.'

'A typical little boy's ambition. Like wanting to be a train driver, it's not real. Or not usually.' She blew steam at him.

Jack didn't say that when they were boys Simon had shadowed

him, copied his gestures, taken out books when he returned them to the library. Had he copied his ambition and made it his own?

'How would he know where you are and why would he care enough about Stella Darnell to be creeping among graves after her? If the guy's an engineer, presumably he's got some engineering to do.' Lucie puffed out another cloud of steam.

'If he's following me, he would know Stella is my friend.' Jack went cold. Simon had been following Stella. Jack needn't wonder how he'd found her; the Simon he remembered would have found a way.

'Here's my take on this, Jackdaw. Some kid left the engine at the station. A bloke – any woman would have handed it in – is rushing for his train and he dumps it where a driver – you, honeykins – will see it. The parents will have reported it lost if it's worth a bob or two. Mystery solved!'

'Passengers aren't allowed beyond the gate where the monitors are.'

'Oh and this Simon character would let that bother him?' Lucie widened her eyes.

Despite him telling Stella they were dealing with the meticulous planning of a ruthless professional, Jack couldn't see how Simon could know about his shifts: he agreed them at short notice. Simon would have needed access to his rota. A shadow of unease passed over him; again he reassured himself that at least in the tower he was safe.

Lucie batted his arm. 'Listen up! After you left the other day, I dug out my file on your "One Under". I texted you, remember?'

'Oh yes.'

Ring re RF inquest. LM. Some detective, he had forgotten about it.

'After the inquest, the widow was at it hammer and tongs with Rick Frost's brother in a side street. You know me, never off the clock, I hid behind a van and watched it all.'

'They were having sex?'

'No! Arguing. I couldn't hear them, but they looked fit to kill. Suddenly they start kissing like two bloody turtle doves, not breaking, but making up. They saw me and sprang apart. I added in a para about them comforting each other and left the rest to the imaginations of our gifted readers. Even so, my soiled nappy of an editor said we couldn't use it.'

Which brother was Lulu Carr upset about? Another lie. Like Stella, Lucie liked hard evidence. He had hard evidence. Jack gave her the glove Stanley had stolen from Lulu Carr's house and left in his tower. Handing it to Lucie, his fingers tingled. His intuitions were never wrong.

'This glove was found in Rick Frost's house. Did Terry tell you the names of the children whom the police interviewed about their lost gloves? This one has the letter "F" inside the lining. That might be a "W" or maybe a "V", but it's smudged.'

'Now you're talking!' Lucie flung down her e-cigarette and, scrambling off the sofa, ran out of the room. He heard her taking the stairs at a faster pace than he imagined her capable of. She returned with another manila file and another carrot. He wouldn't dampen her resolution with a warning about excess consumption of beta-carotene.

Lucie licked a forefinger and, flicking through the file, drew out a page of lined foolscap covered with what looked like crazed hieroglyphics. Her shorthand was faster than most people's speech.

'Terry told me this in confidence – pillow talk! I keep a secret by forgetting I know. If I'm ever hypnotized, governments will fall. Luckily I wrote this down. This is just for you, Jack.'

Jack wasn't fooled. Lucie claimed to adore him, but she worked alone or, it seemed, with Terry. Anything she shared would be chalked up as a favour to him that one day she would call in. He felt a coil of unease, less about the prospective favour, than because he saw he was right about Lucie's relationship with Stella's father. Stella must never find out; it would break her heart.

'So here's the list. Alphabetical and look who's at the top!'

Jack tried to take the sheet of paper from her, but she held on to it and jabbed at it with her carrot. He leant over and read the name she was pointing at. 'William Frost!'

The first step in a case was to assemble the jigsaw pieces. Only then could you begin to fit them together. They had a lot of pieces.

'There's more!' Lucie was clearly enjoying herself. 'Not long after Glove Man was found, a boy came into Hammersmith Police Station and reported seeing a man and a woman going up there the year before. The timing fitted, but when a detective went to get his statement, the kiddy did an about-turn and claimed he'd got the location wrong, he'd meant Chiswick House grounds and he couldn't describe the pair. The policewoman ticked him off for wasting their time. Terry reckoned that the first story was true, so he went to see the boy, who was adamant it was Chiswick House grounds. The parents got antsy, said he had only been trying to help. Terry's hunch was that the boy had been warned off by someone, but with the mum and dad standing guard, he couldn't pursue it. So that was that.' She whacked the sheet of paper with her carrot, her e-cigarette bobbing between her lips. 'Brace yourself, Jackanory!'

Jack didn't need to brace himself: his nerves were taut piano wires. Like Lucie's secrets, he had tried to erase Simon from his mind, but he was alive. Simon was inside his mind.

'In 1988 the boy was ten. He'd be thirty-five now.' She clamped a hand on Jack's leg.

'Guess what?'

'What?' Jack obliged.

'The boy's name was Richard Frost!'

'Otherwise known as Rick Frost,' Jack exclaimed. 'Yes!'

Fifty-One

October 1988

'What did you say?'

Simon eased forward in the deckchair; then, feeling undignified, he struggled out of it and went to the supplies cupboard in the corner of the hut. He propped a foot on one of the packing cases that served as seats for foot soldiers. With Simon's promotion, there was only one foot soldier: the Captain who was now the Private.

The Private lingered in the doorway, his body angled as if he might turn and run, yet the dull lustreless look in his eyes belied this. His angular body was framed by the grey mausoleums, headstones and a manicured yew tree in the cemetery beyond.

'Come in, *Richard*!'

The boy flinched as if hearing his real name spoken had hurt. He stepped inside and, in a belated attempt at attention, clicked his heels together.

A shadow fell across the doorway.

'Who's there?' Simon shouted.

'It's me, Captain.' Nicky came in and, giving a sharp salute, fell in beside the boy.

These days it was a proper unit, Simon thought. Justin had never answered the note Simon had put through his door.

Why didn't you say I was your friend when he asked?

The question presented itself as it had repeatedly over the last year, since they had found Justin by the river.

Letting the others stand there, Simon inwardly reviewed the facts to himself. Justin and Nicky had been his friends and they had betrayed him. Mr Wilson had betrayed him, but he had been punished and, until two weeks ago, Simon had almost forgotten about him.

Simon could find no proper punishment for betrayal. Yet no one could get away with such a terrible crime. His mummy had betrayed him. Simon blinked away this thought.

'You must be punished,' he informed them.

'I did exactly as you told me.' The boy was pulling at his middle finger the way he used to do when he was imitating Simon. He was frightened, but Simon supposed he was mimicking him and it fuelled the inchoate fury that these days was always gnawing his insides. A sense of injustice was corrosive.

'I went to the police and told them that when I said I saw a man I had made a mistake.'

'He did. I went with him,' Nicky suddenly said.

'Did I say you could?'

She shook her head, whether in agreement that he hadn't said she could or because she found him too much, Simon couldn't be sure. He wanted to trust Nicky. He tried to explain to her, 'We are an undercover unit. We never show ourselves. Especially not to the police. You shouldn't have gone too. Neither of you should.'

'You ordered *me* to go.' The boy was distressed.

'I told you to go and undo the bad you did. You shouldn't have gone to the police in the first place. This unit stands together. You tried to get me put in jail. You are a traitor!' Simon fought to stay calm. 'You must be punished.'

'How?' The Captain was perhaps anxious to get the torture over with. 'I did what you said and I've been demoted.' He looked down at his chest as if to show there was nothing left of him.

'What would you do if it was me?' Simon hit on a method that would stay with him all his life: to punish people with their own demons.

'I d-don't...' the boy stammered.

'You'd have me court-martialled and shot.' Simon smiled, raising his eyebrows for confirmation. 'Remember?' He saw from her face that Nicky did. He saw her like him a tiny bit more.

'I didn't mean that.'

'I think you did and it's a good idea, don't you think, to set an example?'

Simon strolled past them to the door and cast a look across the cemetery. Dusk was falling. At this time of evening, the shadows shifted and it seemed that the statues moved. Simon wasn't afraid. Not any more.

He had brought the hut back into service as their HQ. The tower had been out of commission and now had police swarming all over it. The eyot had been occupied by the enemy. Simon knew he went there. He left him little signs: he moved the stones, he planted some bulbs, but had no idea if Justin had seen. Simon didn't pretend that Justin was his friend. When he had seen him on the eyot, he had looked right through Simon as if he was no one. He had denied that he knew him. The final betrayal.

Mr Wilson had told Simon that the disciple Peter denied knowing Jesus. Three times, it said in the Bible. He had said that by doing so Peter hadn't just betrayed Jesus, he had betrayed himself. Simon now understood what he meant. Justin was lost to him as a friend, but he was lost to himself too. Only Simon could save him.

'I didn't say I saw your mum going into the tower that day. I lied and said the people I saw were in Chiswick House grounds and were not a man and a lady. My brother even told them he had lost the glove. I did everything like you said.' Richard hiccoughed.

'You didn't lie. You never saw my mother,' Simon said. 'Why did you go to the police at all? You thought you were cleverer than me. If you go there again, I will tell them the truth. That you are a murderer and that your brother lied for you.'

'They told me off for wasting their time.' The boy scuffed his boot with the soft earth at his feet.

'You are not fit for this unit.' Simon echoed the Captain's own words.

'Give him his glove back, Simon. It's not even his, it's his brother's, so he's already been punished by him for taking it and getting him involved with the police. We all know Richard is innocent. This is a silly game. Let's stop.'

'Please let me go.' The boy made the mistake of nodding his thanks to Nicky.

'Please what?'

'Please, *Captain.*' The boy rubbed his nose on the sleeve of his windcheater. Simon had forbidden him to wear his Captain's jacket: he had seen that if he stripped him of the trappings of authority – uniform and rank – he could sap him of his strength, his identity. He could make him nothing.

Taking a bottle of Coca-Cola from the supplies cupboard, Simon put out a hand. Nicky tried to hand him the bottle opener, but Simon indicated the campaign table. Slowly she laid it down there as if giving up a gun. Simon snatched it up and, applying it to the bottle, prised off the cap. He didn't toss the cap away, as the Captain had done at their first meeting, he placed it with the opener on the table like the spoils of war.

'You see, the thing is, if either of you were to tell the police, or anyone about anything, you'd be put in prison. Your glove is evidence.' Simon was perfecting an imitation of his father: reasonable, always careful to explain a situation. His father, a psychiatrist, would be able to see right into their heads. Simon had convinced the unit that he could too.

'It's his brother's glove,' Nicky reminded him. She looked very pale, as if she had begun to guess there was more to the boys' exchange, that it was not a game.

'Have you told him?' Simon didn't address the question to her.

'No.'

'No what?'

'No, Captain.'

'See, if you did, I'd have to tell them you called my mother bad names. You lied to them – I'd have to tell them that too. I'd have to tell them everything that happened.'

The boy started nodding and didn't stop.

Simon had envisaged Nicky as official codebreaker, his

right-hand man. 'Did he tell you what he said about my mum?' he asked her.

'Ye-es.' She reddened. 'He shouldn't have, Simon, he knows that. It was mean.'

'Can I have my glove?'

The boy had no sense of timing or nuance. Of this, Simon, better able to read minds than his father, was openly scornful. 'You can go now,' he told Nicky.

'What are you going to do?' She was obviously frightened, but her sense of justice got the better of her. Perhaps the girl sensed that the time when Simon no longer valued her had not yet arrived.

'We are going to have a chat. You can go. Be back here tomorrow and we'll form a plan of action. We have much work to do. The police will be on the watch, so we have to resort to deep cover.' Simon was cheered by this prospect.

Nicky hesitated, looking at the Private. Then, with obvious reluctance, she retreated out of the door. Once outside she darted between the graves to the path. Simon waited until she had become another shifting shape in the cemetery, a trick of the light.

'What's going to happen?' The boy was quaking, his eyes – hazel flecked with green – never left Simon.

Simon let a silence fall before he answered, 'One day I'll come for you.' He addressed the Coke bottle. 'The thing is, you won't know what day that is until it comes.'

Outside, Simon kicked at a pile of leaves by the door that hadn't been there yesterday and, reaching in, shut the door. Zigzagging across the cemetery, he avoided uneven ground and toppled head-stones, on the lookout for Nicky, whom he wanted to trust. Until it was shrouded in gloom, he saw with satisfaction that the door was still closed. The Captain had done as he had commanded.

At the gate, in a pool of lamplight, Simon consulted his Timex watch. He noted that it was teatime: toast with honey and a mug of hot milk. As she always did these days, his mummy sat in the sitting-room window, watching for him. Or so he told himself.

Simon had noticed that since the day when he had tracked his mother to Stamford Brook station, she had reverted to how she used to be with him.

From now on, he decided, he would stop being nice. Everyone would have to be nicer to him.

Fifty-Two

Sunday, 27 October 2013

Jack shut his flat door. His clock said half past five. He had been with Lucie May for an hour. Walking there and back didn't count: he hadn't broken his promise to Stella, he imagined telling her.

Moonlight slanting in through the north window etched in silver his few bits of furniture – the bed, the cupboard, his desk and chair – like a photographic negative. Outside the beam of light everything was in deep shadow. Soon it would be dawn.

He flicked on the green lawyer's lamp on his desk and everything shrank to prosaic normality. He went into the kitchenette.

The twine, pebbles, sticks worn by the tides and bleached by the sun, and the flattened ballast were bathed in moonlight. The steam engine and the two carriages had gone.

Jack tore around the circular space, shoving aside books, papers, jumpers, shirts; he shook the duvet until the futility of his search caught up with him, a wolf snapping at his heels. He came back to the window and sat at the table. The binoculars lay where he had left them before going out to see Lucie. He snatched them up as if they might vanish too and looked out through the window.

Two lorries were on Hammersmith Bridge, heading into town. A centimetre adjustment took him several metres north. There was something by one of the buttresses. He twiddled with the focus although it was already sharp. It was only the barrier for buses. He combed the towpath either side of the river and arrived at the eyot. An area of pitch dark. He became accustomed to the lack of light and distinguished the swell of the tide and the gradual emergence of the causeway. He couldn't see anyone on

Chiswick Mall, or beneath the stone porch of the church, but he sensed a shift in atmosphere. Someone was there. Someone was watching him.

The same someone who had found their way into his tower and stolen his train.

Simon knew where he lived.

He ran to the window in the bathroom. He had told Stella there was no need to have frosted glass so high up.

The narrow walkway outside was well below the level of the windows. Only a high-wire artist would consider launching a ladder from it.

Yet Simon had got inside.

Jack could write to the landlords, ask for extra locks. He could have Stella's London bar and her many mortices. Jack stormed back to the main room. He pulled up the lid of his laptop and typed in his password. He changed his password every week. He chose set numbers from his timetable on random dates picked from his diary with his eyes shut to ensure they really were random.

If Simon could get into his mind, he could break the code.

Jack's fingers raced over the keys. He told Palmyra Associates there had been an intruder but that nothing was stolen. Strictly speaking, this was true: the train wasn't his. He said they must have been disturbed, but that he expected them to return. As he wrote this, he realized how upset he was. He had believed the tower to be impregnable, but it was not. He asked them to treat his request as urgent and pressed 'Send'. The message remained in his Outbox. He tried again and saw the problem.

CBruno. The other router had kicked in again.

He clicked on the drop-down list, but CBruno was the only router offered. He dived under the desk. His router was off. He clasped it in both hands and, clumsy and impatient, he indiscriminately pressed every button. At last it flashed with a series of lights that steadied to the required blue. Getting up, he heard the sink glug.

'No you don't!'

Frantically Jack ran to the sink and turned on the tap. Water thundered around the sink, splashing his chest, his face and the draining board. He turned it off and reached for a towel to mop his face. He glanced at the floor beneath the window.

The train was on the floor. The engine must have tumbled off the ballast and pulled the carriages after it. The stones had given way under the equivalent of a weight of over a hundred long tons. Jack had put artistic interpretation above accurate engineering. His father would never have done that.

He was relieved that, thanks to C. Bruno's router, he hadn't managed to send the email. Simon had not after all got into his tower. He was crediting him with too much power. Stella and Lucie had agreed on one thing: after all these years, Simon would have forgotten him.

Out of sight, out of mind.

Before going to bed, Jack confirmed that the outer door was secure. He went up to the top of the spiral staircase and confirmed that the skylight to the roof was locked and that the bolts were secure.

Inside the flat, he turned the mortice key and left it at an angle so that it couldn't be pushed out of the keyhole from the other side and then teased beneath the door, a trick he had used himself. The door fitted exactly within the aperture, so that not even gas could escape, but in the past Jack had achieved the impossible: he took no chances.

In bed, he was reluctant to turn out the light and lay looking at his books ranged on a shelf above the cupboard. His roving gaze halted at the purple-spined copy of *Strangers on a Train* by Patricia Highsmith. He jumped out of bed and pulled it out from the others.

When Guy Haines meets Charles Bruno on a train he cannot know that his life will change forever. Charles Bruno proposes a sinister deal – each will murder for the other – Guy assumes he's joking until Bruno calls and says he's kept his part of the 'bargain'. Now it's Guy's turn…

Charles Bruno. *CBruno.*

A search on Google Images netted at least five Charles Brunos: two black, three white; all but one were smiling. None looked mad. Or bad. Charles Bruno was just a name. Jack reconnected to his own router, deleted his email to Palmyra Associates and logged out. The C. Bruno who owned the router – Colin, Christopher perhaps – had doubtless never heard of *Strangers on a Train.* Stella would say he was over-complicating things. She would say none of it was to do with Jack's past; they were investigating a murder and the murderer was out there somewhere, trying to stop them.

Jack returned to bed and turned out the light. He heard creaks and cracks as heat ebbed from the cladding and floorboards settled. The Smiths' 'How Soon Is Now' began, increasing in volume, as his mind took over. Entering a dream, Jack told a sheeted figure that the words, the chords, the melody – such as it was – were embedded in the walls, in the body of the tower.

How Soon Is Now? was a message from the dead man.

Fifty-Three

'It's the letter I forwarded to Nicola earlier this month, it's been returned, I guess by the owner of the house. It seems she's moved.' Liz regarded an envelope lying between Stella's latte and her Americano with hot milk on the side. 'I didn't like to open it.'

They were seated in a coffee shop on Hammersmith Broadway. Liz had rung Stella when she was cleaning Terry's old office at Hammersmith Police Station and asked to see her 'as soon as possible'. Stella had opted for the only place she knew that was both close to the police station and allowed dogs. Stanley lay under the table, his head resting between his paws.

'So what do you think?' Liz asked.

'About—'

'Shall we open it?'

Two years after his death, a letter occasionally came for Terry. Stella disliked having to open them. But this letter might solve the case. Lucille May would have no compunction about ripping it open. Jack neither. Would Terry open it?

Nicola's London address was printed in capitals, small and neat. Stella had seen the handwriting before; Lulu had scoffed that her husband wrote like a twelve-year-old. 'This is from Rick Frost,' she exclaimed.

'I forwarded it last week, that doesn't make sense—'

'This is postmarked the sixteenth of September, the day he died.' All they had to do was open it. She had tried to take Jack in hand for not opening his post as soon as it arrived. Between his work at London Underground and Clean Slate, she was sure he earned well, so it couldn't be the worry of bills that put him off. As with so many things to do with Jack, Stella found she couldn't ask him why. 'If your friend Nicola is coming back, we can give it to her.' Stella found a solution.

'And if she doesn't?' Liz added milk to her coffee, holding the jug high so that it came out in a long thin stream. 'Isn't this the evidence your dad's policeman friend wanted?'

'Martin can't open mail on our say so – we might have stolen it. It's probably "interfering with the mail, intending to act to a person's detriment without reasonable excuse", or some such. And that neighbour down in Charbury saw Nicola, so she's not "missing".'

'We don't know where she is now,' Liz pointed out.

'We don't know where she was planning to go, so we can't say she didn't arrive,' Stella echoed Martin Cashman's line. She took out her phone. 'I'll call Lulu and ask exactly what the neighbour said.'

The phone rang and rang; Stella mouthed an apology to Liz. She was about to give up when Lulu answered. Stella asked for a blow-by-blow account. She was annoyed with herself for not asking for it the first time they spoke. Terry would have done.

'I was about to ring,' Lulu yelled. 'Nicky's landlady called!'

'What did she say?' Stella was ready with her Filofax.

'Her name's Chris Howland – for Christine, I suppose. Honestly, the things people mind, she was quite tetchy that Nicky went without saying goodbye.' A blast of air roared down the earpiece; Lulu bellowed over it, sounding as if she was at sea in a storm.

'Can you talk now? You sound as if you're outside,' Stella asked. She wrote down the name 'Christine' and underlined it and nodded to Liz, but Liz was looking at her phone and didn't see.

'Yes. Chiswick Cemetery. I'm weeding Mum's grave. It's her anniversary,' Lulu shouted.

There must be some moral code about talking on a mobile phone in the presence of the dead, Stella thought, and looking up saw scraps of rubbish flying across the Broadway like crazed birds. A newspaper had caught against the railings outside the Underground, held there by the force of the gale. Commuters scurried past the plate-glass windows, pushed and buffeted by the wind. When the café door opened, a strong gust blew napkins off the tables and scattered sugar sachets. The storm that forecasters were warning of was building.

'Christine was upset Nicky had typed the note!' Lulu bellowed.

'What's wrong with typing it?'

'She said it was too official. I told her: Nicky doesn't do "friends", if we don't count trying to steal my husband. And no, I didn't say that to her. I promised to call her if Nicky turns up – she wants to hand back some excess cash; Nicky had paid in advance – if she lets the house before the lease expires. I told her to think of it as compensation for the typing! The woman's a forensic specialist!' Lulu spoke as if this explained everything.

'You have Christine Howland's number?' *Detection wasn't just about asking questions – it was asking the right questions.* Lulu, scatty though she seemed, had been more thorough than Stella gave her credit for. Stella felt as if a fog had settled above her head, stopping her thinking straight. This came of having so little sleep over the last few days.

When she ended the call, Stella apologized again to Liz.

'Don't mind me. Justin's just texted, suggesting I visit him at home, that's a step forward!' Liz looked radiant.

Stella rang the number Lulu had given her.

'Chris Howland?' A woman answered with the preoccupied tone of someone too busy to talk.

'Stella Darnell here, I'm looking after Nicola Barwick's house in London.' Embarrassed by her fib, she flashed a look at Liz, but she was texting on her phone. 'You returned Nicola's letter.' She paused. Nothing. 'Nicola didn't mention leaving Charbury so, like you, we're surprised.' She went for a point of commonality.

'I should have kept it. She's coming back.'

'She called you?'

'No. I was doing a last tidy – incredibly I've got a new tenant

– and I found her purse and her passport in the kitchen bin of all places. She'll be back, she can't get far without her passport!'

After the call, Stella turned to Liz. 'Something isn't right. Why would Nicola throw her passport and money in the bin?' But Liz wasn't listening.

'Stella, could I just use your phone? I was in the middle of replying to Justin and my battery has gone. It would be simpler to ring him.'

Stella watched Liz weave her way through the café to the street. Her coat billowed out when she stepped on to the Broadway. Whoever this Justin was, he was making her smile. Jackie said that was her definition of 'Mr Right'.

'He sounds nice,' Stella remarked when Liz returned. 'What's his second name?' She felt suddenly duplicitous; Liz might not be inclined to answer if she knew the true reason for her interest.

'It's rather Mills and Boon. Venus. Justin Venus. Lovely, don't you think?'

'Yes.' And familiar. But with so many clients, most names struck a chord. Although Stella did think she might remember someone named after a planet.

'Confession, Stell! I've done that thing we did when we were girls – I practised writing Elizabeth Venus!' Liz gave a harsh laugh. 'It's not like I want to marry him and if I did, I'd keep my name. Don't say a thing!'

Stella didn't have a memory of doing this at school or whose name it had been if she had. She came to a decision. 'Hold on to the letter. If you see Nicola, tell her Christine Howland's got her purse and passport. If she doesn't turn up in the next twenty-four hours, I'll tell Martin Cashman.'

Outside the café, Stella texted Jackie to say she was running late for their catch-up meeting. Afterwards, she watched Liz crossing the Broadway at the pedestrian lights, her light eager walk unchanged since they were sixteen. Liz had always been optimistic. To her, good things had happened before, and they would again. Liz would put Justin Venus in this bracket. Stella should feel happy for her, yet she didn't.

Had Stella watched her old friend a moment longer, she might have noticed a man in a long dark coat with pale features step from the shadows of the arcade and follow Liz into Hammersmith Underground station.

When Stella returned to the police station compound where she had left her van, she received two texts. Jackie wanted to shift their meeting to later in the week and Suzie wanted her to come to her flat as soon as she got the text. With no meeting, Stella now had time.

Ten minutes later she parked outside her mother's flat. Her phone rang, but she didn't recognize the number on the screen.

'I've lost my phone. I'm in a call box.' It was Jack.

'Can you remember where you last had it?' The sort of annoying question Suzie would ask; if Stella had lost something she never knew where or when.

'My flat. This morning at eight thirteen.'

'Have you given it a thorough search?' Suzie again. Stella glanced up to the top floor of the mansion block, almost expecting to see Suzie and Dale framed there. There was no one at the window. 'I'm sure you have. It'll turn up, it's a small space.' She was conciliatory.

'I'm not so sure, it's like I'm living in a vortex. I've lost that paper with the numbers on it too.'

Stella was surprised, despite his floaty way of being, Jack was always good with actual objects, he never lost things. He sounded distressed, but it was usually she who assumed the worst. It occurred to Stella that he was quite like Liz: he had faith that something good would happen, although his optimism couldn't be based on what had gone before.

'I'll get you to ring when I'm in the tower so I can trace it. That's if the battery hasn't drained.'

'What about that "Find my phone" app?' It was rare for Stella to offer Jack technical advice.

'Never thought I'd need it; I've never lost it before.' He did sound upset.

Stella told him about her conversation with Chris Howland and her decision about the letter. He said nothing about the letter; she knew he would have opened it there and then. She guessed he'd have no trouble opening other people's post if required.

'Is he a relation of Alice?' he asked.

'Who?'

'A girl in Charbury went missing in the sixties. Big case at the time. Lucie May did a follow-up on it. He *must* be related to the girl. Things come full circle; in the end there's only one story, although we always hope for a different ending.'

'Chris Howland is a "she". She's a forensic scientist,' Stella added for no good reason. Lucie May filled Jack's head with unpleasant stories; Stella brought him back to the present. 'It means Nicola Barwick's alive. It also means she's still a suspect for murdering Rick Frost.'

'She's in trouble.' Jack was grave.

There was a series of beeps.

'Jack?' Stella looked at the phone screen. The call was still live.

'Here I am. I've fed in more coins.'

'I'll call you.' Stella swept the glove box for loose change before realizing how absurd she was being; it wasn't her that needed the coins. Lack of sleep did not agree with her.

'No need, I've got plenty.'

'How do you make out she's in trouble? Doesn't this imply Nicola Barwick has something to hide?'

'Chris Howland didn't actually speak to Nicola. She's right – a typed note is official. It's easier to trot out a message with a ballpoint on the back of a circular. Howland thought they had a rapport so the typing jarred.'

'Suzie types faster than she writes – her handwriting is unreadable. I wish she would type the lists she leaves for me.' Suzie hadn't left one of her lists since she went to Sydney.

'A typed note might be written by anyone.'

'She signed it. Odd, though, when I did the cleaning estimate for Liz, I saw a laptop on the desk in Nicola Barwick's study. Liz said it was Barwick's, so what did she use to type it on?'

'She could have had a tablet. But did she have a printer? I vote we get that letter and steam it open. Please can I be the one who does it? I love doing that. Or I think I would,' he added quickly.

Stella raised her eyebrows. Jack would steam open his own post – if he could bring himself to open it.

'No, it's illegal. I've told Liz we'll wait for Nicola Barwick to call her. Why would she throw her purse and passport into the bin? It's like the man who sat the wrong way in the photo booth. How could she do that by accident?'

'Accidents don't happen. She wanted Howland to find them. She *hid* them in the bin. The note was intended to make us think Nicola Barwick had gone abroad. The passport and purse are signs that she hasn't.'

'Are you saying she's been kidnapped?'

'Maybe not bundled unconscious into a car boot. She probably walked out of the cottage, but found a pretext to go back into the house and that's when she dropped them in the bin. Clever.'

'A risk. Christine Howland mightn't have seen them.'

'She had to act quickly. You said Howland is in forensics; Barwick guessed she'd check the bin. I'd know you'd check through the contents of my rubbish bin.'

'I'll call Martin. He said to if we had proof.' Jack knew how she would behave. Stella liked that.

'The note isn't' "proof" – the opposite in fact – so he won't be impressed.'

Stella could imagine Martin telling her that it added up to sweet nothing. When he had promised Terry to be there for his daughter, he hadn't bargained on nuisance calls from her.

'Where are you?' Jack asked suddenly.

'I've just got to my mum's. She wants to talk about me. It'll be about investing in Dale's business.' Strange question, Jack never asked where she was.

'Are you going to invest in it?' He sounded far away.

'The guy can cook, it might work.'

'Stella, those photos you found in that passport booth at Stamford—'

Jack's voice was drowned out by more beeping. Stella waited for him to drop in some coins. When the beeps stopped, she remembered. 'Does Justin Venus mean anything to you?'

Her question fell into phone silence.

Fifty-Four

Please may we meet? We need to discuss Stanley.

Stella reread the text. David had softened his request by implying he would negotiate. When he had asked her to look after his dog, she had refused, relenting only when the alternative was kennels. A dog required endless walks and tireless games with tuggy rope spiders and squeaky toys. Months on, she had built into her routine the blowy strides on Wormwood Scrubs common or Richmond Park with Suzie, and now with Dale too. Her mum had advised training classes: Stanley needed discipline. After weeks of these, it baffled Stella that he would 'sit' and 'stay' at her command and come when she called. She began to take care of his toys, restoring Mr Ratty – the stuffed rat he took to bed with him – to his original cream colour with sluice washes.

Stella had brought Stanley for their afternoon outing to Wormwood Scrubs common. Dale hadn't been at Suzie's that morning. Stella wondered if he was in on Suzie's proposal, typed and bound, 'ready for the bank'. The document was in her rucksack. Suzie seemed to have forgotten that she had advised Stella to stick to the core activity of cleaning and not risk ruin.

In her old bedroom, Stella had seen an album like the one displaying the history of Dale's business. She guessed that Suzie had bought it for volume two of his life story. No doubt she was going to put herself and Terry – his lost parents – in it.

Some women might have been upset by their mother's obsession with a long-lost son. Stella, ever practical and expecting little, took it in her stride. She hoped, though, that her mum would at some point return to her job at Clean Slate.

Stanley was bounding around on the grass with a stick three times his size, desperate to impress her. She pressed the 'rapid shutter' button on her phone and took pictures – although she wondered if she would want to look at them after she had handed him over.

Stella realized she didn't want to give Stanley back. Then she revisited her earlier observation; despite David's text, there was no room for negotiation.

S will be at the police memorial in Braybrook Street on Friday @ 2pm. She pressed 'Send' before she could cancel the text. It was two o'clock now, she had four days to pack Stanley's things. Tonight she would wash Mr Ratty.

The text had dented her good mood. An hour ago Jack had emailed an account of his findings. Although heartened that he had laid out all the information gathered so far, Stella was worried too: a typed report wasn't Jack's method. She had some sympathy with Christine Howland's response to Nicola Barwick's typing. Maybe talking about his school friend and finding the toy train had shaken Jack up more than he had let on. Jack had been about to say something about the photo-booth pictures when he was cut off, but had put nothing about them in his report. She opened it again. He had used the Courier font as if he'd written it on a typewriter.

```
Update Report for Clean Slate Investigative
Agency (CSIA)
Jack Harmon (agent) 28/10/13

• A boy called Richard Frost reported a man
  and woman entering the tower on the night
  of the 1987 hurricane. When police followed
  up, he said it was two men in Chiswick
  House grounds. (Source: Lucie May – Terry
  thought first story true.)
```

- A boy, William Frost, was interviewed about missing glove. Glove Stanley took has crown motif like first one. Police failed to connect WF to RF - see first bullet point. (Source: Lucie again.)

- After Rick Frost's inquest William and Lulu rowed in street then kissed. Proper kissing. (Source: Lucie.)

- Darryl Clark - Piccadilly line driver of train that hit Rick Frost thought I was on platform. (Link: Station inspector and Simon Carrington.)

- Meant to say that the den where you found 2nd carriage was used by Frost's gang in the eighties. (Lucie told me.)

- To do:

- Ask William Frost about his relationship with Lulu C. It changes everything.

- Ask William Frost about Rick F's childhood gang. Who was in it? Ask him for advance on expenses. (Jackie said about expenses. I've just thought about gang.)

- Ask Liz Hunter the name of Nicola's friend.

- Check out Rick Frost's study at his home - ask Lulu Carr (Frost-whatever) for access to his computer.

Jack x

Stella pictured Jack in rolled shirt sleeves, glasses on the end of his nose, pecking the keyboard with two fingers like a private investigator, around him a semi-circle of screwed-up balls of earlier drafts. A good image, although he could touch-type and didn't have a printer in his tower. Without having been to his house, Jack assumed that Rick Frost had an office in his home; he thought like a detective, she thought. On the other hand, it was a safe assumption that a man involved in surveillance had a computer.

Stella looked up. A man was under the trees. Stanley was heading towards him. She blew on her whistle. Stanley hesitated and then trotted with renewed purpose towards the man. The man didn't have a dog with him. Not everyone liked dogs. Since minding Stanley, Stella had become suspicious of anyone walking on commons or in parks without a dog. She whipped the lead from around her neck and hurried over the grass.

'Stanley!'

In the failing light of the impending storm, Stella saw the man was wearing a black coat. It was Jack. Jackie must have told him where she was.

Stanley halted and crouched low on the grass. Stella felt a twinge of guilt that he made his distrust of Jack obvious. She blew her whistle again and the recall training paid off; abandoning the stick, Stanley belted back to her. She rewarded him with a morsel of chicken and, straightening, splayed out an arm in semaphore greeting to Jack. There was no one there.

It was dangerous to shelter under the trees in a storm; surely Jack knew that. Stella set off at a pace across the grass towards where he had been. The wind was back in force and the sky threatened rain. Stanley trotted in front, stopping to make sure she was behind him.

Far off she heard the rumble of thunder and looked around. She was alone on the common.

She reached the trees and it was as if dusk had fallen. The mesh of branches above cut out what little light there was.

'Jack?' She felt awkward calling out his name. It might be like the other night, when he hadn't got together the courage to admit he was nervous of the tower. Her boots loudly crunched over a bed of beech-nut shells.

She took out her phone to see if he had texted. Nothing. She was about to put it away when she saw a symbol at the top of her screen. She peered at it. It was a pair of staring eyes.

Stalker Boy. The logo of Rick Frost's app. William Frost again. 'Stell-ah!'

Confused by the wind, Stella had no idea where the voice came from. She retreated deeper into the trees. She had to find Jack.

Over the two years she had known him, Stella had learnt to put up with Jack's odd behaviour. His sudden departures out of the back door, a propensity to sing nursery rhymes and recite poetry, and above all his night-time searches for his 'True Hosts', those with a mind like his own, intent on eliminating those who got in their way. She had made him promise to stop walking the streets at night. Yet Jackie advised it was best not to try to change people, to let them be.

'Stella!'

Stella crept around a tree trunk and looked out across the common to Braybrook Street. There was someone by her van. She took a few steps over the grass. It was William Frost.

'You've been stalking me!' she exploded at him. Walking past him, she fired her key at the van.

'I wouldn't go as far as calling it that, though I confess my brother's app got me here.' As if the app had transported him to her against his will. It explained the watching eyes on her screen. Stella felt her heart rate slow down.

Tempted to tell him where to go, she thought of Jack's report and said, 'We need to talk.'

'That's why I'm here.'

She strapped Stanley into his seat, thinking fleetingly that after she had given him back there would be no use for the seat; she would get it removed. She climbed in the driver's side.

'I've got questions.' This wasn't how Terry did it: no tape machine, no plain-walled room and no second interviewer. No Jack. In fact she did have a tape recorder. 'Are you OK if I record this?' She showed him her phone.

'Am I under caution, Detective Darnell?'

She fitted the phone into the cradle on the dashboard and, preventing herself from saying 'For the benefit of the tape', flipped to her notes in her Filofax.

'The police interviewed you in the eighties about a lost black glove. Where did you lose it?'

'I didn't lose it.'

'You told the police you had.'

'My brother stole both my gloves; he lost them. A glove was found on some man who died in that tower by the river. I told the police that I'd lost my gloves in the park. Christ knows why I covered for him, but Rick was scared stiff of heights, he couldn't climb a stepladder, certainly not a tower, so it was a harmless fib.'

Stella fumbled in her pocket. 'Is this your glove?' She thrust it at him, hoping Jack's hunch was right.

William took it off her and turned back the cuff. 'There's a "W" inside, the "F" has worn away. My mum and her labels! But where did you get this?'

'Do you know Nicola Barwick?' She heard Terry in her head: *You ask the questions. Don't give away what you know.*

'She was a friend of my brother's. Did she have this glove? Nicky wouldn't have killed him, if that's your theory. She was a kind girl.'

'Why "was"?'

'*Is* then. What is this, am I under the spotlight now?'

'Do you know where Nicola is now?' *Don't be led by the interviewee.*

'Not at this moment.'

'What were you arguing about with Lulu – with Tallulah Frost – in the street after your brother's inquest?' *Surprise them with your questions, give them no chance to anticipate or rehearse.*

Stella clicked her ballpoint on and off to agitate him, then remembered the microphone and stopped.

'I told her I thought that Rick had been murdered. She refused to believe me.'

Safety first: avoid being trapped with a person you suspect of murder. Don't ask questions likely to inflame. The houses in Braybrook Street were dark; if she shouted for help, no one would hear.

'Why didn't you tell us you were having an affair with Tallulah?' *Avoid open questions and tackling a point head on.*

'Because I'm not. Any more,' William said after too long a pause.

'You didn't think it pertinent to tell us this?' *Know when to be silent.*

He loosened his shirt collar, although the top two buttons were undone. 'It's over.'

'Why is it over?'

'Tallulah – or Lulu as she'd restyled herself – promised she'd leave my brother, but kept putting it off. When Rick was killed, I ended it, the whole thing had got out of hand. I couldn't live with the guilt. I had betrayed my brother. I was having a relationship with his wife and when he asked for help, I wasn't right there. I missed his call. But listen, I didn't want this to divert you. I didn't kill my brother and nor did Lulu, or at least—'

'You hinted we should talk to her. Was that out of revenge? Did you plan to frame her?'

'No! It was me that ended it, so it would be stupid to take revenge on her.'

Stella momentarily lost the thread of her argument. Was this what it was like for Terry? *Stain by stain.*

'You said you ended it because she wouldn't leave. Presumably if she had left her husband, then you'd still be with her.'

'I don't know. I thought I knew her, but I'm not so sure.'

'Meaning?'

'I have a feeling that someone's following me.'

'Like your feeling that your brother was murdered?'

'If you like, yes.'

'Why do you think it's Lulu?'

'She has the most to gain from Rick not being around. Simple.' He gave a shrug.

'Are you sure it was her?' Stella remembered Lulu arriving back, excitedly telling her and Dale that she had seen her husband in the street with his mistress. Had the 'husband' been William, not Rick? William had left her.

'With this app I can check where someone is. It was definitely her following me.'

'You were with Nicola Barwick.' Stella was gratified by his look of surprise. Like a boxer she must concentrate on one area and then suddenly go for another part of the body – mix it up.

'That's why I was coming to see you. I think that whoever was threatening my brother is after me.'

Rain pattered on the roof of the van. Black clouds made a false dusk that merged with the trees where Jack had stood. Stella hoped he wasn't still out there.

'Where were you the night your brother died?' *Stick to the basics.*

'I already told the police, I was at home alone, working, so yes, no alibi, it could have been me.'

He turned sideways in his seat to look at her as he had done the night she had taken him to Gunnersbury station. Then she had supposed he was one of Jackie's Mr Rights. How simple that problem seemed now.

'But it wasn't me.' He leant forward and touched her arm. 'Stella, you have to believe me.'

Stella's phone buzzed with a text. Excusing herself, she turned off the recorder.

Can't see you tonight. Driving. Jack had found his phone.

If Jack was out there, he could see her with William. She dialled his number.

'This is Jack, who are you? Tell me after the beep.' Her patience evaporated.

'Could I use your brother's app?'

'I should have told you sooner.'

'Your app?'

'Tallulah or Lulu's at home, if that's who you want, I checked.'

319

'It isn't.

Stella submitted to William's instructions – she couldn't say she had used the app before. When she put in Jack's number, up came the *Seek and destroy* icon. The cross hairs zeroed and found the target. Her heart thumped. Jack was on Du Cane Road, passing Wormwood Scrubs prison; if she went now she might catch up with him.

'I have to go.'

'Stella, I—'

'Now!'

She leant over and pushed open the door for William to get out. 'I'll call you,' she shouted back to him as she drove down Braybrook Street.

Fifty-Five

'Where's Jackie?' Stella burst into the office.

'Gone home. She got a text from Jack. She's put me in charge!' Beverly was Jackie's assistant. She was in her mid twenties, dressed immaculately in a short black dress with precise make-up, a precision that didn't extend to her work. Kneeling amidst piles of papers on the floor, Beverly tackled the filing as if searching for something. 'Shall I make you a cup of tea or coffee?' Beverly made perfect tea.

'No thanks.' Stella had the urge to say 'yes', to sit at her desk and plan next week's rota, scrutinize application forms, fix visits with prospective clients and prepare quotes. She could not. She had a case to solve.

'What did Jack want?'

'He told Jackie he was passing her house and noticed a window open. She's gone home to close it. When she got there, she found it was closed! She thinks Jack got the wrong house.'

'When was this?'

'An hour ago. She asked me to lock up. I've done it before.'

Stella couldn't absorb the detail. By the time she had got to Du Cane Road, there was no sign of Jack. The wind was blowing and it had been raining hard and in his dark coat he was as good as invisible. How had he got to Corney Road so quickly?

'I was going to drop Stanley off with Jackie, but, um—'

'She said to say I can look after him,' Beverly said.

'Are you any good with dogs?' Stella only trusted Jackie with Stanley.

'My mum breeds poodles, and I help out.'

'OK then.'

'We're old friends. Actually, I was about to say, I think he needs a drink.'

When she looked back through the wired glass in the office door, Beverly was putting a document into a drawer in one of the filing cabinets. Stanley was snoozing in his bed by her desk. He was more at home in the office than she was.

'You didn't tell me about William Frost?' Stella said as soon as Lulu Carr opened her front door.

'Sorry, is that your business?' Lulu eyed Stella coldly, no longer the scatty woman who Stella had assured Jack wasn't capable of murder.

Establish who has the most to gain by a person's death: usually the spouse, partner or close relative. 'Gain' doesn't have to be financial.

'I'm investigating your husband's death, so yes, it is my business.' Stella stepped into the hall and, closing the door, leant on it. This wasn't how she talked to her cleaning clients. 'I think it's time you started telling me the truth.'

'You weren't truthful. You pretended to be a cleaner when all the time you were spying on me.'

'I didn't know who you were until I found your husband's driving licence.' To Stella's surprise – she had expected her to brazen it out – Lulu appeared to accept this.

'My husband killed himself. They said so at the inquest, but William said it was murder, that Rick would never kill himself. William was just looking for a way to dump me. He behaved as if *I* killed him. Well, I've proved him wrong!'

'How?'

'Come with me.'

Lulu went up the stairs, so Stella had to follow her. On the way up, she tried Jack again.

'This is Jack, who are—'

'I've found out who killed my husband.' Lulu went into Rick Frost's study. She sat down in the black swivel chair and scooted the mouse about. The computer screen awoke.

Stella was looking at the picture of a room, taken from above. It showed a black chair, a desk and filing cabinets. It was the room they were standing in. There was a man sitting in the chair. With a shock, Stella realized she had seen the back of his head before. She looked behind her. Above the door, a camera was fitted to the wall. A red light blinked. It was on.

'I cracked Rick's password. My brother suggested I try his company registration number and he was right. This is who Rick told William was a threat.' She jabbed at the screen. 'He killed my husband.'

Lulu moved the cursor and the man on the screen came to life.

He opened a drawer in the desk, shut it and opened it again. He took something out. Stella moved closer. It was a belt with bullets in it. As she saw this, Lulu opened the same drawer in the desk and pulled out the same belt. She put it back and shut the drawer. The man put the belt back.

He sat so still that Stella thought the film had stopped. Then he leant forward and seemed to be peering at the desk. He took something from his jacket and scribbled on it as if crossing something out. Then, as if startled, he got up and went to the door. Stella saw his face. It was Jack.

She grabbed the mouse off Lulu and paused the film. She read the date and time at the bottom of the screen. It was the day she'd found the driving licence. The time was eleven minutes past eleven. The time when Stanley had barked outside the landing cupboard. Now she knew why. Jack had been in there.

'This man didn't kill your husband,' Stella said firmly.

She bent forward and looked along the desk, as Jack had done in the film. She ran her finger over faint indentations in the veneer.

'Is this the password?'

'No, his password isn't that long!'

'I wonder if it's the serial number for his phone.' She rummaged in her anorak pocket and pulled out the plastic bag with Rick Frost's phone that Jack had given her on Stamford Brook station, the night they visited it together. She pulled off the silver cover and squinted at the tiny lettering on the back. There wasn't a serial number.

'Whose phone is that?' Lulu Carr asked impatiently.

'Your husband's.' Too late Stella realized that the police would have given the phone to Rick Frost's next of kin, his wife, not his brother. William must have taken it from Lulu without her knowing.

She shook her head. 'No, it's not.'

'What do you mean?' Lulu never said what Stella expected her to. In that respect she was rather like Jack.

'He scratched his initials on the back of his phone. So worried about people stealing it. That doesn't have any scratches on it.'

'Are you sure?' Stella looked at the smooth shiny black surface. Not a scratch in sight. The phone in fact looked brand new.

'Of course I'm sure. The man was obsessed with holding on to his stuff. That's not his phone.'

'So who has his phone then?' Stella asked. And, she thought to herself, who left a brand new phone with no data on it where the police would find it?

'Good question. I suggest we start with the man in this film. What's he looking at?'

Stella crouched down and examined the numbers on the surface of the desk. Jack had left the paper with the numbers on in his flat and it had disappeared. She drew open the desk and found the bullet belt that was on the film. She also found a block of sticky notes and a bundle of Bic ballpoints bound with an elastic band. Typical of Jack to take a pencil rubbing when he could have written them down. Then Stella remembered Jack's dictum about leaving no trace and inwardly apologized. Except Jack had left a trace: he had left a film of himself.

She began scribbling down the numbers on a sticky note and then stopped. Jack did nothing for effect or as part of some fantasy. He honed his skills. He had taken a rubbing because he wanted not only to reproduce the numbers, but to see how they were written.

She looked again at the laminated surface of the desk. Jack had noticed that the distance between the numbers varied. He had guessed Frost – it was safe to assume the numbers were carved there by Rick Frost – had been in a hurry.

'19 9 13 15 14   19 8 21 20   20 15 23 5 18   4 15 15 18'.

When she had looked at the numbers on the paper with Jack, before he said he lost the rubbing, he had suggested it was a serial number of a computer. She had thought it was the IP address of a computer, although the latter didn't fit. Now she saw that the gaps between the numbers were irregular. Some greater than others. They were regularly irregular.

'Lulu, I wonder if Rick left this as a message for you,' she said slowly.

'He was always leaving me messages. Stuck them all over the house. Cryptic notes letting me know he knew I'd seen my brother, or where I'd been. The man was mad.' Lulu began to cry.

Stella ripped open a handy pack of tissues from her rucksack and passed Lulu one.

'I think it might be a warning.' Stella was feeling her way; the thought had come from nowhere. 'If these gaps are to distinguish the numbers, then the first five are nineteen, nine, thirteen, fifteen and fourteen. Do they mean anything to you?'

'No, they do not!' Lulu flapped at the air with her tissue.

'If it's not a serial number, it might be a code.' Stella heard herself sounding like Jack. 'Did you have a code, you know, a secret thing between you both?' A question she had never asked a client. Thinking of Jack, she must tell him about Rick's phone. She dialled him again and got his answer machine. When they were looking at the pencilled rubbing, Jack had commented that Rick Frost only had one computer in his study. She had supposed he had special detective powers so she hadn't asked how he knew. He knew because he had been here. Jack had lied to her. Stella made herself concentrate on Lulu.

'We had nothing between us. Unless you count a wall when he slept in here.' Lulu gave a hooting snort into the tissue.

'If it was a code, it'd have to be something you'd easily get.' Stella found a tactful way to say that Rick Frost would allow for Lulu not being used to codes and computer languages.

'Rick lived in a fantasy world. I should have listened to Simon, he warned me that "the Captain will betray you",' Lulu wailed.

'The Captain? Do you mean William?' Stella folded the sticky note into her anorak pocket. No point in pushing Lulu once she was upset.

'Rick. Simon called him the Captain because of their idiotic army games. It was bad enough when they were kids, but Rick never grew up.' Lulu's eyes swam with tears. 'My brother says Rick only married me to spite him; he used to bully my brother when they were boys. I wonder sometimes if Simon has ever forgiven me for marrying Rick.'

'Why would Rick have wanted to hurt your brother?' Stella didn't like the sound of the brother. At least Dale wasn't like that.

'Rick hated my brother and I think Simon was right, he hated me too. Rick watched me from this computer. There are cameras all over the house, haven't you noticed?'

Stella had noticed. She had thought they were burglar alarms.

'Rick wrote "Activity Reports" detailing where I had been, what I had been doing and who with. I found them all on the computer. Whom, I mean,' Lulu added.

'Whom.'

'Sorry?' Stella roused herself.

'Grammar. My brother's always correcting me, a horrid habit that I've caught off him.'

Stella wasn't listening. She ran her finger over the marks on the desk. Perhaps they hadn't been scratched directly on to the laminate, but were indentations from pressing too hard on paper with a ballpoint. Frost hadn't written them for Lulu; if he had, he would have taken a less subtle approach and left her notes all over the house. He had written the numbers down and sent them somewhere, but whom had he sent them to?

'If he watched you constantly, then Rick must have known

about William.' Stella didn't know whom to believe, Lulu or William. Neither. She got a feeling in her solar plexus. It was one of Terry's hunches. 'Lulu, don't take this the wrong way, but do you think your brother could have had anything to do with Rick's death?'

'You've been talking to William! No I do *not*. My brother looks out for me. When I told him about the Captain and Nicky, he reminded me that he'd promised to protect me. William's only jealous; he says I don't need protecting. All those boys think Nicky is Miss Perfect.' She dabbed at her nose with the tissue. 'This code-thingy was probably for her, she was Enigma Woman!'

'She was what?' Stella fought to keep bafflement at bay.

'In their unit, Nicky-Perfect was the Official Codebreaker. I can't imagine there were many codes to break for a bunch of kids sneaking about a graveyard wearing flower pots and shooting insects!' She balled up her tissue and tossed it at the scratches on the desk.

'Who was Nicola Barwick with when you saw her in Chiswick Mall that time? It can't have been Rick, as you told me then – he was dead.' Stella tried to keep on track.

'My brother,' Lulu muttered. 'He said he'd stopped seeing her, that I was right not to trust her. He had her by her arm, holding her tight, all over her like a rash. He lied to me!'

Stella examined the numbers she had copied on to the sticky note. The most obvious code was to swap out numbers for letters, but that was too easy. Then again, while Rick Frost had been hot on surveillance, it seemed he was a kid at heart. He mightn't have been a genius with codes. The one and the nine were together – so nineteen – then a gap followed by a nine and another gap, then thirteen, fifteen and fourteen and a bigger gap. She calculated out loud, 'The nineteenth letter in the alphabet is "S" and the ninth is "I". The thirteen is "M" and—'

'Simon,' Lulu whispered.

'Simon what?'

'Carrington.'

'Isn't your maiden name Carr?' Stella quelled frustration.

'My father wasn't my real dad. Mum had an affair and I'm the result. I don't know my real father's name so I shortened Carrington to Carr. Like I said, I wanted a "fresh start".'

Stella doubted that lopping off a bit of your surname amounted to a fresh start. 'If we assume the numbers closer together are one word, then this could be a message. Four words starting with Simon.' Stella put a line between each word. 'This next one has four letters. Another "S" and eight is—'

'I told William that I guessed Rick had found out about us and he killed himself. It proved he loved me after all.' Lulu's words were blurred with sobs. She snatched up her tissue from the desk.

'It's an "H",' Stella exclaimed. 'The two and the one are close together so "twenty-one", which is "U", and then twenty. That's a "T". "Shut"! "Simon shut". What did he "shut"?'

'How should I know?' Lulu huffed. 'A case, his mouth, my mouth, a door—'

'A door! Yes, this last grouping has four numbers. The first is "four". A, B, C, D. "Simon shut something door". To make sense it should be "the", but there are five letters. We know twenty is a "T", then we've got fifteen and a twenty-three.' Stella counted out the letters on her fingers. She got lost and started again.

'Tower,' Lulu offered dully.

'"Simon shut tower door".' Stella folded her arms. 'What kind of sentence is that? Is it another code?'

Lulu had stopped crying.

'Lulu, where is your brother now?' Stella demanded.

'Simon was so sweet to me when I was small. When Dad was cross with me, he would say I wasn't his daughter. Simon would take me out for walks by the river and tell me not to listen to him. We went to his HQ in the cemetery where he was the Captain. He once gave me a bottle of Coca-Cola. It tasted of blood, but he told me it was a magic potion to keep me safe. He'd say, "It's you and me, Lulu, against the world." When we were first married, Rick hated me seeing Simon and told me not to trust him. William once

328

said he loved me. No one had said that to me before, but after Rick died, William became like him and Simon. They were always checking up on me.' She tossed her hair back. 'My brother's got this thing on his phone; he can find me wherever I go. To protect me, he says.' She slumped back in the chair. 'So has William. Rick gave it to him.'

Stalker Boy. Stella said nothing.

'Does your brother protect you?' Lulu suddenly asked.

'I don't need protecting.' As she spoke, Stella wasn't so sure.

'Who's that man?' Lulu nodded at the picture frozen on the computer screen.

Stella had hoped Lulu had forgotten about Jack. 'My colleague, he works undercover,' she said. 'So, exactly when did you tell Simon Carrington – your brother – about your affair with William?' Was this how Terry felt when all the disparate bits of information, subtle nuances and apparently random events started making sense?

'I can't remember. I told you they hated each other,' Lulu muttered.

Stella's eye fell on two framed pictures beside the monitor. They weren't in the paused film; Lulu must have put them there very recently. The photograph of Lulu's parents had been on the sitting-room mantelpiece downstairs.

The other one showed two people in their late twenties. Stella recognized Lulu and guessed that the man was her brother, he looked like the man in the picture with Lulu's mother, who it seemed was not her actual father.

Cleaners shouldn't have opinions about their clients' homes, while detectives should. Simon Carrington had delicate features framed by locks of dark hair. In black and white, she couldn't tell the colour of his eyes; they were light, almost ghostly. He was looking at the camera with such intensity that she felt he could see into her head. His gaze was empty, his face without expression. Stella considered again that Lulu didn't take after her mother. However, were it not for the stubble on his chin and lack of make-up, Simon Carrington might be his mother's double.

He looked like Jack.

Stella opened her phone and, fingers clumsy, swiped through her camera roll to the picture she had taken of Stanley dancing with his stick on the common. She tweaked it and enlarged the screen until it filled with the trees in the background. She manipulated the image until she found the man under the trees. He was out of focus, but his face was just about distinguishable.

Simon shut tower door.

'Is this your brother Simon?' Stella held up her phone to Lulu. Jack lived in a tower. She had to stop herself shouting at Lulu. 'Take a look.'

'How can I… Ye-es, I think so.' Lulu sniffed into the tissue. 'That doesn't mean anything. He goes for walks.'

But it did. Stella had seen the man before. He was the man standing on the lawn outside her flat. It wasn't Jack. He was the inspector at Stamford Brook station. *Stalker Boy.*

'Lulu, where is your brother now? Where is Simon?'

There was a creak on the stair. Both women shrank from the door. There was nowhere to hide. A faint buzz. Stella caught the camera lens tracking them. A red light was blinking.

'You left the front door open.' Warm and friendly.

Lulu pushed past Stella.

Stella stared at the man in the doorway.

'I was trying to tell you all this when you rushed off.' Holding Lulu close to his coat, he stroked her hair. William Frost looked over her head to Stella.

'Tell me what?' Thoughts, pictures, impressions. Stella tried to arrange them. *Stain by stain.* All the stains had joined up.

'When you asked me about the glove. I remembered that Rick had said it was to do with the glove. I ignored him. He was always coming out with stuff like that – the guy was paranoid, I know that. He had to control everything. But it got me thinking. After I told the police I had lost the glove in the park, Rick was nice to me, far nicer than necessary. Made me wonder, had I covered for him without intending to?'

'This isn't Rick's phone.' Stella waved the phone at William. 'Someone took his phone, swapped the case and left it for the police to find. You said Rick had the stalking app on his phone, didn't you?'

'Yes—'

'So whoever has his phone can find out where anyone they want is and stalk them?'

'If they have their number, yes.'

'Where is Simon now?' Stella shouted at Lulu. Simon was the name of the boy Jack said he had known at school. Jack said there was no such thing as coincidence.

'I don't know.'

'Where does he live? You must know!'

'I don't.' Lulu sobbed, waving her hands in front of her face as if clearing away cobwebs. 'He's very private. He takes me out for meals. I don't go to where he lives. His father left the house in trust to my mother – he cut me out of his will because I wasn't his. Simon gave me half the value of the house. He's a fair man, you see. The other day I walked past the house and saw it's up for sale.'

'They used to live next door to Jackie, in Corney Road,' William said quietly.

'Why didn't you say?' Stella demanded

'Why would I? I didn't think it was anything to do with who killed Rick.'

'There were two children next door, a sweet boy as thin as a rail and his cute sister, think her name was Lulu, something like that. Their parents' marriage was on the rocks, the dad was a psychiatrist with a fancy car, chap never passed up a chance to be sarcastic about his wife – talk about airing dirty linen! The boy was playing substitute husband, protective little mite. I made Graham promise that those parents wouldn't be us one day. I think we've succeeded! The boy – or man – moved out years ago, he rented the house out and is only selling it now. We're holding our breath as to who buys it. Good neighbours are gold.'

Stella remembered Jackie's words. She let the information fall into place.

'Stay here! Lock the windows, don't answer the door to anyone! If he has Rick's phone, he'll be using his app and will know you're both here. He knows we're all here.' She looked at her phone. There was a pair of staring eyes at the top of the screen. 'Turn off your phones!'

Stella snatched up the framed photographs and, shoving them into her rucksack, ran down the stairs and out of the house. Despite her instruction, she didn't think to turn off her own phone.

Fifty-Six

Monday, 28 October 2013

The wind whistled down Chiswick Mall, its screams and whines punctuated by bangs and smashes as flower pots, garden ornaments and benches were dislodged from window ledges and hurled on to the ground.

Shrouded in a billowing cagoule, hooded and shapeless, Liz Hunter could have been mistaken for being drunk or a passenger on the deck of a ship tossed and rolling in high waves. She swayed and staggered, to the left, to the right, into the gutter, stopped and set off again, quickening her pace. She kept close to garden walls and hedges. She paused every now and then and consulted her phone to reassure herself she was following Justin's directions. She looked up and saw the tower. She was here.

She checked her phone again; Stella hadn't replied to her text.

'Let's see the letter?'

She jumped. A man stepped out of an alley. It was Justin. She nearly hugged him, but he didn't like being hugged. He looked annoyed.

'Can we get out of this wind?' Liz shouldn't have texted Justin and told him about the returned letter. She had hoped he would have advice, but he seemed cross. Maybe he minded after all that she hadn't told him Nicola's address. She had been so pleased with herself for demonstrating to him she could be trusted to say nothing. She should have waited for Stella. She should have done what they agreed and waited to see if Nicola would come for it.

Although she had been looking forward to this, their first meeting in his home, Liz was suddenly sure she shouldn't have come.

333

'No need to worry about the letter. Indeed, from now on there's no need to worry at all,' Justin remarked pleasantly. His crossness apparently gone, he took her hand.

'That's marvellous!' She laughed, although she didn't feel in the least like laughing.

'This way.' He led them down a narrow passage that smelt of rotten leaves and urine. The bricks glistened in the lamp-lit dark.

'I feel bad, Justin. You see, I decided to open it. It's from the man who died at Stamford Brook station whom Nicola knew when she was little. It's a list of numbers. Twenty-seven altogether. Justin, are you any good at deciphering codes?'

'As you say, let's get out of the storm. I've brought us a bottle of champagne and cheese and biscuits. I hope you like brie. Come up to my tower!'

'This is *your* tower! How amazing!'

Fleetingly, Liz Hunter considered whether it was wise to have told no one where she was going. Then Justin drew her close and she breathed him in.

Fifty-Seven

Monday, 28 October 2013

A strong gust of wind buffeted the van. Forecasters were warning people to stay inside unless their journeys were strictly necessary. A storm called St Jude was going to hit southern Britain tonight. It was strictly necessary to find Jack.

Stella saw she had a text. Jack always contacted her in the end. It was from Liz. *Call me.*

Liz would have to wait.

In the dark, headlamps in her rear mirror dazzled her. She couldn't tell if she was being followed.

There was no point going to Jack's tower, he had told her he was driving. He didn't answer his phone when he was on the trains. She drove around Hammersmith Broadway twice to try to lose Carrington if he was out there, and then pulled off into Sussex Place. Immediately she saw her mistake: it was a dead end. She flung the van around and headed back towards the Apollo on the Broadway. She slowed down and checked her mirror again, although Carrington couldn't be behind her. She'd stopped in a parking bay opposite a mansion block, and confirmed the doors were locked. Just in case, she kept the engine running.

Stella forced herself to think rationally. If she called Martin Cashman, he would remind her he required evidence that Nicola Barwick was missing, that Rick Frost had been killed by Simon Carrington. If he had, Lulu Carr and William Frost would be unreliable witnesses at a trial. William had lied about his glove and not been honest about his relationship with Lulu. Even if the glove was matched to the one on the dead man, it wasn't a link to Simon.

Lulu didn't know truth from reality. The Piccadilly line driver might identify the photo of Simon, but his testimony wouldn't stand up in court because he had initially thought the man on the platform was Jack. Simon Carrington had been clever; he featured nowhere.

Simon. Stella's heart was palpitating. This was like a game of Patience: the cards were falling into place, with one card blocking a suit.

She reached into her bag and lifted out the pictures. In the light of the street lamp, Simon looked nothing like Jack. His mother was smiling off camera at someone to her left. Stella could see a snippet of shoulder. Someone had been cropped from the image.

Out of the blue, Stella smelled Dale's scones. She trusted her olfactory sense. She had seen the woman's face before. The sight of her mother holding Dale's album flashed up. Stella realized where she had seen the woman. She texted Suzie: *Send photo of first page of D's life story.*

There was one person who would help her get evidence for the police. Stella drummed on the steering wheel, dismissing the idea. The van was hit by a vicious squall, it lurched and she dropped her phone. She scrabbled for it in the passenger footwell.

She had run out of options. She brought up her contacts list and found the number. Against any better judgement Stella had ever had, she pressed 'Dial'.

'Stella Darnell here. Are you free?' She waited. Then: 'I'm on my way,' she said.

Fifty-Eight

There were no rattling casements or creaking joists. Jack couldn't hear loose tiles crashing off roofs or recycling bins and bottles clattering along empty streets, hurtling and twisting. The only sign of the storm were murky grey clouds that streamed across the sky, joining and re-forming, and flurries and blusters tearing at the surface of the Thames.

Jack sat in the Hammersmith Bridge window, resting his binoculars on the heel of his palms. A coil of steam rose from his mug of hot milk. The domestic scene belied his mood: he was full of foreboding.

He had been positive that he had lost his phone in the tower. But he had looked everywhere and not found it. He had tried to email Stella, but the storm must have caused his internet connection to break. He had decided to find a phone box and ring her, but when he stepped out on to the walkway, he was blown over to the rail by the force of the wind and admitted defeat.

Though Jack knew he was safe in the tower – if he couldn't get down, no one could come up, yet he didn't feel safe. When Stella had shown him the passport photo of the back of the man's head, he had said he didn't recognize him. He recalled the image. It wasn't so much the head, but the back of neck, above the shirt collar. It might be nearly thirty years, but Jack knew who it was. His senses attuned to the slightest sound or movement, he trained the binoculars on Chiswick Eyot.

Somewhere out there, Simon Carrington was alive and he was watching.

Fifty-Nine

Monday, 28 October 2013

'It's the Detective's Daughter!' An electronic cigarette cocked above her shoulder, Lucille May exhaled a cloud of vapour. Stella caught a whiff of peach.

Stella had expected this. Lucille May relied on sex appeal, she didn't relish female competition. Least of all from the daughter of the man who, Stella suspected, was the love of her life. Stella had convinced herself that Lucille May wasn't Terry's type, but she didn't know what his type was.

'Come in, since you're here.' Lucille waved the cigarette in vague invitation and sashayed on pink leather pumps to her sofa.

'Tea, coffee, water? If you're still off the booze.' Lucille twisted the top off a bottle of mineral water, gulped from it and flopped back, apparently exhausted, lending little weight to her offer.

'No thanks.' Stella ignored the jibe that was prompted by her refusing triple gin and tonics on previous visits. The water and the electronic cigarette suggested that Lucille May was on a health drive. Stella caught the buzz of a text. 'Excuse me.' She opened her messages.

'Social networking is vital these days. Not for me, of course, I'm established.' Lucille blew a peach-scented cloud towards Stella.

Suzie had photographed the whole newspaper cutting from Dale's album. Laboriously, moving the text into view on the small screen, Stella read:

FEARS MOUNT FOR MISSING TEACHER

Five years to the day since English teacher Nathan Wilson vanished, police say they have no clue to his whereabouts.

The forty-year-old bachelor, on a sabbatical from Menzies High in exclusive Vaucluse, set off last October on a three-month walking tour of New Zealand to 'feed his soul' and never came back.

Apart from a possible sighting in the NZ town of Wangherie and another on Manley's Shelley Beach early one morning, no one has seen or heard from Wilson, described by colleagues as a loner with no living relatives. Neighbour Byron Carter, who lived in the same apartment block in Cremorne, said Wilson introduced him to his fiancée (pictured left). 'The girl was quick to say he was "jumping the gun, they were just friends". Nat looked pretty crook, bloke was smitten.'

Inspector Todd Mangen of the NSW Police Force told a packed press conference at the Local Area Command on Pacific Highway this morning that Wilson's bank account has remained inactive and the mystery 'fiancée' has not come forward. They have no reason to suspect foul play, but with no contact from Wilson, they fear for his safety and welfare.

'We are in the dark,' Mangen said. 'It's as if Nathan stepped off the planet.' He appealed to anyone with information or who recognizes the woman to contact Harbourside LAC.

In the photo, the woman was resting her head on Wilson's shoulder. Some friend, Stella observed. Wilson was ducking to ensure he was in the frame.

'Don't mind me.' Lucille May regarded her nails.

'Read this.' Stella handed her the phone.

Amid a plume of steam, Lucie May languorously scrolled down the screen.

After what seemed to Stella a frustratingly long time, Lucille waved the phone, 'Jack said you knew, so why come to me?'

'Sorry?' Jack wasn't there when she was looking at Dale's album.

'The Prodigal Son! Doesn't Darnell Junior look like Simon Le

Bon. What a dish!' She fanned herself with a hand. 'Get you, Miss Marple. First you solve Terry's biggest unsolved case and now you've found his long-lost son.'

'What do you mean?' Stella's windpipe constricted.

'Terry went to his grave without finding his boy. I pulled strings like a crazed puppeteer, but nothing – and Mr By-the-Book wouldn't bend police rules. He dies and the Cleaner flies in on her magic broomstick and conjures up the lovely Dale!'

'Dad knew about Dale?' The words battered Stella's skull like brick bats.

'Mrs Darnell says to Terry, "Here's your new daughter, oh and by the way I gave away our son!"' She swigged some water. 'Sorry, I know it's your ma!'

'I meant the article next to it.' *Stick to the basics.* 'The one about the missing teacher.' Her dad didn't come to see his newborn baby daughter in the hospital for three days. He had always said it was because he was called up to hunt for the killer of the three police officers in Braybrook Street. Was it because Suzie had told him he already had a son?

Lucille May scrabbled under a cushion, retrieved a pair of black-framed glasses and jammed them on her face with one hand. Gone was the flaky manner; she studied the article with a frown, e-cigarette held aloft.

Terry had known about Dale. Stella looked about the room and made herself do a cleaning estimate, although there would be nothing to do. Lucille cleaned like a pro. Was that why Terry liked coming here? Was it in this room that he told her he had a son and swore her to secrecy because his daughter didn't know?

'She killed him.' Lucille May whipped off her glasses. 'Country as big as Australia, she could bury him in the outback and get on with her life.' She puffed on an arm of her spectacles, scowled and swapped it for the cigarette. 'So, you and Jackanory ride again!'

'He didn't die in Australia.' She gave May Lulu's photograph. 'This is Madeleine Carrington. Her daughter was married to Rick Frost, the man who died under that train in September. You covered the inquest.' She had to trust the journalist, even if it wasn't two-way.

Lucille May narrowed one eye and exhaled a plume of steam. She regarded the picture as if weighing up whether or not to believe Stella.

'It's the same photo as in the Australian article.' Stella pointed at the phone. 'You can see that the man cut out from the picture is the missing teacher, Nathan Wilson.'

'You're saying he did a John Stonehouse and faked his death?'

'Who?' Stella asked.

'Before your time, kiddo.'

'He covered his tracks. He wanted to start again. A fresh start.' Stella thought of the Clean Slate strapline.

'Some fresh start, he rotted in a tower!' May spoke with some relish. 'Let me get this straight, Madeleine Carrington killed her son-in-law, is that your theory?' Lucille asked.

'The framer's details are on the back; it's dated this September. Madeleine Carrington died a year ago. The date on the back is a week or so after Frost died under the train. Looks like someone else other than Madeleine cut Wilson from the picture.'

'Madeleine Carrington also went under a train at Stamford Brook. I wanted the headline "Station of Death" when Rick Frost died there too. My wimp of an editor vetoed it. She did it in front of her son. Riddled with cancer, she'd obviously had enough, but selfish all the same.' Lucille replaced the cartridge in her cigarette. 'I should have spotted the connection!'

'What if her son murdered her?' It was falling into place. Stella outlined the points to Lucille May. Simon Carrington had promised his sister it was her and him against the world. He hadn't forgiven her for countermanding his advice and marrying his sworn enemy; it was the last straw when he found out she was having an affair with the Captain's brother. To deflect him while not really understanding the level of threat she was deflecting, Lulu had suggested her husband was also having an affair with Nicola, the woman Simon had loved since he was a boy.

341

And then there was Jack.

'That's a hell of a leap!' Lucille pulled a face at her pun.

'Simon and Lulu's mother had an affair with Nathan Wilson. The date on that Australian article is in the eighties. Carrington was married with a son by then.'

'So when shy "boy next door" Nathan Wilson was crowing to his neighbour in Sydney about his fiancée, she was leading a double life.'

Lucille May finished her bottle of mineral water, rammed the bottle down until the neck met the base and screwed the top on. She tossed the crushed plastic at a waste bin on the other side of the room. It glanced against the rim and rolled away. Scrunched paper and wrappers around the bin testified to earlier misses.

'Time to take stock.' Lucille clambered over the top of the sofa. 'Grab an end.' She dragged a whiteboard out from the back of the sofa. 'Lean it against the fireplace.' She produced a pen from a packet under a sofa cushion, yanked the lid off with her teeth and knelt by the board.

'We'll start with Madeleine Carrington.' She wrote the name on the board. 'At some point she went to Australia either to see Wilson or she met him out there. Easy to verify and it doesn't matter for now. She is connected to Rick Frost, how?'

'He married her daughter Tallulah, now called Lulu.'

Lucille wrote 'Lulu' and drew a line between the names.

'Madeleine has a son.' Stella liked whiteboards and was at her best with flow charts.

'Name?' Lucille tapped the board.

'Simon. He is now our prime suspect.' Stella felt mildly silly using the phrase, but Lucille dashed down 'Prime Suspect' and underlined it.

'Does he know you suspect him?'

'Not as such…' Stella began.

'Meaning?'

'I spoke to a man I assumed was surveying on Stamford Brook station last week. I think now he was Simon Carrington.'

'What makes you think he wasn't a surveyor?'

'It was dark and he had no equipment.'

'Now you're talking like a 'tec!' Lucille drew a box around Simon's name.

'Jack went to school with a boy called Simon—'

'I thought I knew the name!' Lucille May flung down the pen and began to rifle through a heap of files on the coffee table. She detached a fat manila folder. 'Here we are. I found this after Jack had gone. Simon Carrington's the name of the CEO of the company that redeveloped the water tower. He's an engineer. I tried to interview him, but he never replied to my emails.'

'Simon is the only person who knows Jack liked trains when he was a boy. Jack thought he was dead.'

'So did his family. Another missed connection: I should have seen that. Carrington was the boy who didn't die at Charing Cross Hospital. I need a database.' She underlined 'Prime Suspect'.

Stella reached down to stroke Stanley; her hand swept the air. She had forgotten he was with Beverly. By now she would have taken him to Jackie's as arranged. When he was away from her, she had no means of communicating with him, rather like Jack. At the end of the week Stanley would be gone and she would never see him again. Jackie hadn't texted to say he was there. Stella forced herself to concentrate. Her head ached as if there were cogs turning slowly. 'As you told Jack, Rick Frost was the name of the boy who reported the couple near the tower. It must have been Madeleine Carrington and Nathan Wilson. My guess is he recognized Simon's mother and went to the police, and then Simon forced him to withdraw his statement.'

'There's a motive.' Lucille scribbled. 'Motive: tell police about Mum' next to 'Prime Suspect'. She tossed down the pen and clambered back on to the sofa, thumping a cushion for Stella to join her. Unearthing a Windows tablet from under the files, she opened it and, swiping at the screen, brought up Google.

'Teacher's name?' she barked.

'Nathan Wilson.'

'Nath-an Wil-son.' Lucille May typed with two fingers as Stella had imagined Jack doing for his report.

There were many Nathan Wilsons. Lucille skipped the offers to link in with Nat Wilson or be Facebook friends with Nathan of Idaho or of Bermondsey. She put in 'missing', 'teacher' and 'Australia'. Up came the Australian Federal Police website for missing people.

'Here we go.' She switched off her e-cigarette and handed it to Stella. She read out the wording on the masthead. '*One person goes missing every fifteen minutes.* That's two since you arrived here.' She shot a look at Stella as if she was responsible, angling the screen so Stella could read it.

According to the profile for *Wilson, Nathan Bertram*, he was last seen on Saturday, 22 November 1986, the year of his birth was 1947, his gender male. His complexion was described as pale, his hair and eyes were brown and build slim. Under *Circumstances* she read that Nathan Wilson was last seen at Vaucluse High School, Vaucluse, Sydney, NSW. He had told colleagues he was flying to Auckland the next day. It said: *The above photograph was taken in 1986. Police reported his passport missing from his Cremorne apartment. He never flew to Auckland. Grave fears are held for his safety and welfare.*

The man in the picture looked like Lulu Carr.

Lucille May scrolled through a gallery of photographs of missing people. Some were grainy or out of focus, others cropped from a group pose like in Wilson's picture, with disembodied hands on shoulders; the missing ranged from teenagers to older people. Jack believed there was a finite number of faces. If you lived long enough, you saw them all. Vaucluse was where Dale lived. Sometimes there had to be coincidences.

The types of photographs differed too. Some, Stella guessed, were scrambled out of a shoebox by a distraught relative. Passport-booth portraits, one black-and-white shot of a man not seen since 1966, the year Stella was born. Holiday snaps, a man in strong sunlight with a background of blue sea who had gone out to buy breakfast and never returned. Stella vaguely expected the pictures to betray some sign that the person was about to slip through the net of life. A faraway look in their eyes, a troubled expression, but none gave a hint of what lay ahead. They might have been her clients.

A banner on the website announced that 96 per cent of people are found within a week. Cashman had expected Nicola Barwick to return. She roused herself: 'Go to the UK Missing Persons' site.'

'Shut your eyes if you're squeamish,' Lucille warned. 'This is a gallery of dead people.' Deftly she resized the two missing person websites, the UK and Australian, on to a split screen.

'Bingo!' Lucille said under her breath. On the screen was Wilson's Australian profile, with the UK entry that Stella recognized as the one Jack had shown her.

Stella reread the list of clothes and items found with the body. The bottle of champagne and the child's glove. When she had looked at it with Jack, she had dismissed the sketch of the dead man. With only brown hair and a bone structure to go on, it couldn't be realistic. Comparing it to the photograph of missing teacher Nathan Bertram Wilson, she saw it was a good likeness. In the picture, Wilson was wearing a light blue jumper. A turquoise crew-neck jumper was listed among the clothes found on the body in the tower.

'Stella, you have matched a name to a face, or a skull!' Lucille was enveloped in a peachy fug. 'Nathan Wilson is Glove Man!' She handed Stella the tablet and returned to the whiteboard. 'So, when Simon was a boy, he locked Wilson in Chiswick Tower. The guy died. Carrington went back and planted Rick Frost's glove on the corpse, presumably to frame him. Is it possible he still held it over Frost when he was an adult? Surely Frost could have gone to the police and explained? Wait a minute.'

Lucille May scooted over to the coffee table on her knees and shuffled the files around until she found a file labelled 'One Unders'. Stella was grateful Jack wasn't there to see.

'Yes! I checked out the clients Rick Frost's company had. Only one by the end. Guess what they were called. Palmyra Associates!'

'So?' Stella was losing it. Again she tried to stroke Stanley. Jackie had promised to text when Beverly brought him. That was hours ago.

'Palmyra Associates are civil engineers. They do most of their work abroad. No website, but I looked at their listing at Companies

House and, wait for it! The most recent UK project is Palmyra Tower and, winding back, who is the CEO?'

'Simon Carrington.' Stella could not hide her own triumph.

'Right! Looks like Simon C. had Frost by the short and whatsits!'

'Rick Frost bullied Carrington when they were boys, his sister told me.' She didn't say that Jack had said he had been unkind to Carrington.

'This is one cool story!' Lucille May waved her e-cigarette like a conductor's baton. 'One less missing person for the Australian police and one identified Misper for our guys. Shame Terry isn't here to celebrate.' She took a long vape and, it seemed to Stella, a shadow passed over her face. 'I owe you, Officer Darnell.'

A true reporter, Lucille was interested only in her story. Stella didn't share her excitement. Stella remembered Jack's expression when he told her about Simon. He had been afraid.

'Here we are.' Lucille pulled out another manila folder from the stack on the coffee table. She sat down next to Stella on the sofa and spread a huge sheet of paper across their laps.

Stella's phone rang. Jackie.

'Don't want to alarm you, Stella.'

Stella became alarmed.

'Beverly gave Stanley to a man who came to the office. He said he was Jack's brother and that I'd sent him. Foolish, and she knows it, but apparently he was the spitting image of Jack, so she had no doubts. She did take up his suggestion she call Jack to confirm it, but he didn't answer his phone. If only she'd called me.'

'Jack doesn't have a brother.' Stella was numb.

'I know that. Beverly does too, now. She's distraught. I said it wasn't her fault. I did wonder if it was David?'

When Stella rang off, she couldn't think or speak.

'Read this.' Lucille May tapped the sheet with her e-cigarette.

Stella tried to make sense of tiny printed text within a vast diagram.

Discrete entrances ensure that tenants in either residence rarely meet. Each has the experience of being a sole occupant. An internal staircase utilizes the pre-existing pipe cavity in the central shaft, giving both dwellings access to the roof. There was a signature at the bottom next to a printed name. It was Jack's father's name.

'What is this?' she demanded.

'It's a plan of Palmyra Tower.'

'Jack never said his father was the architect!' Stella couldn't hide a sense of betrayal. She stared at the technical rendition of spiralling staircases, steel supports and intricate pipework.

'Hold your horses! He doesn't know.' Lucille rattled the sheet. 'The first developers were faithful to the original use of the building as a water tower. They hired an engineer – Jack's dad – rather than an architect. He incorporated the pipe cavities into the new design, but when they went bust, he wasn't paid. The poor guy was shafted, he should have known better, but after his wife died I suspect he took what he could get.'

'My dog has been stolen—' Stella stopped, a stolen dog was not a 'cool' story. David hadn't trusted her to hand Stanley back on Friday, he had gone to the office and taken him. Stella let herself breathe. David wouldn't hurt Stanley. 'But Jack's flat is the only one in the tower,' she said instead.

'Oh no, it isn't! No guesses as to who lives downstairs. Call Jack!' Lucille May leapt to her feet, sending the engineering drawing flying up.

'Jack's lost it.' The fluttering in Stella's stomach became a frantic beating of wings.

'He can still talk on the phone.'

'He's lost his phone. I thought he'd found it, but I think—' What did she think? David looked like David Bowie; he was nothing like Jack. Jackie had left the office because she had got a text from Jack saying the window was open. He had not got the wrong house – he hadn't sent the text.

'Simon Carrington's got Jack's phone,' Stella shouted.

'Come on!' Lucille was already in the hall.

'Where are we going?'

'To find your dog and to save Jack!'

Sixty

'Come out, come out, wherever you are,' Jack whispered with false bravado.

On the eyot something was moving amongst the bushes and stunted trees. The tide was out, the beach between the eyot and the shore was discernible only by an absence of light. It was like a great chasm.

Jack trained the lens on the brushwood and reed clumps and saw he hadn't been mistaken. Nosing along what, at high tide, was the perimeter of the eyot, he saw a creature. A fox.

Jack slumped back in his chair, his face slick with perspiration. It was past midnight and the wind was strong. It didn't only disrupt humans, it blew birds off course and, stunning them, caused them to 'crash'. Guillemots who lived by the sea would tomorrow be found dead on the streets of London. He raised his binoculars and scoured the beach with them. The creature lacked the prowling fluidity of a fox, it was trotting about with no awareness of a predator. It was Stanley.

Where was Stella? Jack dropped the binoculars, flung on his coat and rushed out of the flat. He leapt recklessly down the spiral staircase and heaved open the lower door.

On the walkway, he was again blasted by the wind: it lashed at him and pushed him centimetres shy of the edge. He inched along, paying the slender rail through his hands like a rope, his skin burned by the ice-cold metal. At last he reached the cage. Wind harassed the grille, shaking it violently.

'Stella!'

348

His shout was whipped up and away. As he struggled down the stairways, Jack was bounced against the sides of the cage. Stella had come to the tower, but with no means of telling him she was outside, she must have gone away. She had gone to his Garden of the Dead. She had missed her footing and been washed out into the river. A vicious current had pulled her down. Stanley was searching for her. This dreadful narrative could not be true, Jack told himself.

'Stella!'

On Chiswick Mall the wind roared about his ears; it scooped tiny stones and flung them at him. Head down, he slithered down the steps and on to the foreshore. His shoes sank into the mud. He raced along to stop it pulling him down, using rubbish strewn at his feet as crude stepping stones. He knew the terrain; forcing himself to calm down, he found the causeway.

He reached the steep bank of concrete-moulded sandbags and pulled himself up to the path. Without his phone he had no torch. He felt his way over the land, touching the branches, the reeds. At last he arrived at the place where he had seen Stella's pet. The dog wasn't there.

'Stanley? Here, boy.' Stella said that dogs sensed uncertainty; it made them less likely to respond. He lowered his voice and commanded, 'Here, Stanley.'

In his hurry, Jack hadn't brought any food. He had nothing with which to entice the dog. He was overtaken by tingling panic. *Where was Stella?* The river was oily black; he could see nothing.

'Stanley?' The sound was parcelled away by the wind. The St Jude storm had arrived.

He reached the place where Rick Frost had tried to throw Simon Carrington into the river. He had stopped him. Did Simon remember that Jack had saved his life? Jack clambered up the bank into his garden.

The line of white stones had light of their own. To him, disorientated by the storm, the place was strange. The rush of reeds and the scrape and rasp of leafless trees, their branches lashed by the storm, were not the sounds of his garden.

Jack tripped and fell. A remorseless squall tore at his shirt.

'Stella!' he sobbed, kneeling in his Garden of the Dead as if in prayer.

Something pushed at his pocket, and then tugged. He felt a cold snout and, peering down, found Stanley beside him. The dog nuzzled up to him and licked his cheek with a warm tongue.

Jack grasped the dog around the waist. Struggling to his feet, he grabbed at flailing branches. He couldn't go back the same way, he might fall into the river. He risked the inner path where he might meet Simon. He inched forward, feeling for compacted ground that defined the path. He pushed through reeds and brambles and emerged opposite Chiswick Mall. The street lamps were out – there was a power cut. He couldn't see his tower.

The dog was quaking, his woolly coat sodden. He had been in the river. Had Stella tried to save him? Jack lowered the little dog to the ground.

'Go find Stella!' he whispered. Like his mistress, Stanley had a powerful sense of smell. He would lead Jack to her.

Stanley stood at his feet shivering, unclear what Jack wanted from him.

'Go find!' Jack shouted.

A gust of wind hit the dog and he tottered against Jack's legs. He hadn't sniffed a scent. Jack picked him up and the dog burrowed into his neck. Stella couldn't be out there. Jack began a perilous journey across the mud.

Had anyone looked out from a window in one of the houses, their eyes accustomed to the dark, they might have made out two figures, tall and of similar build, wending their way over the mud. An onlooker might have assumed them to be of one party, for their pace was synchronized as if their walk was choreographed. When the man in front paused to locate a stepping stone, the other, twenty yards behind, paused. He moved only when the first man resumed his journey to the shore.

No one was watching.

*

The storm was deafening, wind whistled about his ears, the banging and crashing of loosened casements was underpinned by the relentless thud of a barge smashing against its mooring.

Jack regained the camber and, slipping and sliding over debris chucked up by the river, the wind swirling around him, struggled past St Nicholas' church. A clanging jangled in his head, like discordant bells, although the actual bells were silent. He ducked into the alley and saw he had left the cage door open. It swung back and forth, the clanking resounding in his ears.

In the dark Jack couldn't see his feet. Numb with cold, he was in a dream where limbs are lead and air is water. He chose his moment between the furious slamming of the gate and pushed into the cage, clutching the dog.

On the third stairway, Stanley cocked his head. Jack made it to the platform and looked down. A shadow moved. It was his imagination. There were shifting shapes and shadows everywhere. Nevertheless: 'Who's there?' He couldn't bring himself to say the name, to admit his existence.

You denied you knew me. Three times.

A splitting tore the air. One of the rivets on the cage sheared. The structure was adrift from the wall. Jack ran up the last two stairways and flung himself on to the metal walkway.

Time telescoped twenty-six years to the night in 1987 when the man had been trapped in this tower. Scared and alone, his voice drowned by the roar of the wind. Jack imagined that the wind he heard now was a scream of terror. He pressed his back to the cold concrete as the walkway lurched like the deck of a ship pitching on stormy waters.

London was chaotic. The storm battered trees and tore up fences, tossing them like kindling. On King Street, a 27 bus rocked and tilted against a shop front, wheels a metre from the road, a ship on a reef. On Hammersmith Broadway, a lorry slewed into a railing and coarse sand spilled over the road. Cars and houses were crushed by branches and blocks of masonry. No planes flew in the sky; no trains travelled along tracks engulfed by soil when embankments gave way. Drains blocked and roads flooded. Power lines came down.

Jack saw there was no point in turning the clock back. Wherever it stopped, someone would die.

You denied you knew me. Three times.

His tower had survived over seventy years; it would withstand the storm. He pushed his way inside the little lobby. Simon couldn't reach him here. He held tight to Stanley and navigated the spiral stairs. He whispered to the trembling animal:

'This is the house that Jack built.
This is the malt
That lay in the house that Jack built.'

Jack placed Stanley on his bed. The dog's saturated fur soaked into the duvet and a damp patch spread around him. Streaks of mud flattened his whiskers and plastered down his chest. He was a scrap of a thing, his button-brown eyes wide with fear. Intermittently he was gripped by an immense shiver; like a Mexican wave it travelled from his head to his toes. Stella said it was threatening to stare at dogs so, affecting nonchalance, Jack sauntered into the kitchen and filled his cereal bowl with water.

He studied the meagre contents of his fridge for something Stanley might like. There was a lump of stale cheddar on the top shelf. Jack felt shame he had so little to offer. Stella would want him to feed Stanley. His throat caught: he was thinking as if she would never come back. He pulled himself together and pared off the hard rind and the top of the cheese and cut it up. Cupping the cubes in his palm, he returned to the front room.

'Here you are, Stan—'

Stanley was beside the bed, sitting bolt upright. Jack chucked him a bit of cheese and resumed his rhyme.

'This is the rat,
That ate the malt
That lay in the house that Jack built.'

Stanley didn't move.

'Yeah, good boy, no reason you should trust me.' Jack tried a bright tone. The dog was circumspect. Like his mistress.

'This is the cat,
That killed the rat,
That ate the malt
That lay in the house that Jack built.'

He tossed a cube of cheese a little closer to the dog. Stanley looked at the cheese and then at the partition wall as if choosing between them. Jack threw another cube, further away from him this time. The dog looked at the wall. The dead man had been found on the other side of the room, by the door. Why was Stanley here?

The dog began to dig furiously at the partition wall as he had on the boards where the body was found. The animal was distressed; he was missing Stella. Confounded by the wind, he had confused the wall with the door. Jack couldn't make it better – he too missed Stella. He should not have come up here; he should have gone to the police.

Jack squatted down to see what Stanley was fixated by. A line had been drawn, straight as if with a ruler, but it was so faint that, if it weren't for the dog's fuss, he wouldn't have seen it. It did a right-angle turn and went vertically up the wall and stopped centimetres above his head. It continued horizontally a metre and came down again. It was the outline of a doorway.

Jack strode around the partition wall to the kitchenette. The wall came out in a 'v', about sixty centimetres at its widest point. Diverted by the curving walls, Jack hadn't noticed that the wall was on a slant.

Jack had always wanted to live in a panopticon like Jeremy Bentham's nineteenth-century concept: a tower that observed prisoners from behind slatted windows. The prisoner could never be sure how many officers were up there. There need be none.

Thinking they were being observed, the prisoners, Bentham believed, would behave.

When pipes hissed or the sink glugged or his internet connection switched to a router labelled CBruno, Jack had found explanations for the anomalies. 'How Soon Is Now?' was only his mind soothing him, as his mother used to do. Simon had sent him signs, clues and messages, but, intent on keeping watch on the city, Jack had dismissed them.

Simon didn't want to be his friend any more. Of all the places Jack could be, the tower felt the least safe.

Stanley shrank away from the wall. Jack picked him up. Cold air drifted into the room. The line was a crack. The crack was widening. Jack heard a whisper:

'This is the dog,
That worried the cat,
That killed the rat,
That ate the malt
That lay in the house that Jack built.'

Sixty-One

Tuesday, 29 October 2013

'Come on, Stella.' Lucie May was wrestling into a red woolly coat that covered her like a tent. She wound a yellow scarf around her face, muffling her voice. 'Would you mind doing the driving? I never learnt.' She asked as if Stella had an option.

Outside the storm was wild. Wind hit the windows and roared about their ears. As soon as Lucie was in the van, Stella accelerated away from the kerb. The passenger door swung out.

'Steady on, Officer Darnell. If we are the cavalry, can we at least stay on our damned horse!'

Neither woman spoke as, keeping to the speed limit, Stella drove through deserted streets, littered with smashed fascias, glass, sheets of roof felting, tiles and branches. The wind rocked the van as if it was being attacked by an angry crowd.

On King Street, Stella swerved to avoid a car's exhaust pipe and slammed into a recycling bin, dragging it several metres under her fender. Jack was in the tower believing he was safe from Simon, but instead he was a lamb to the slaughter. Simon had taken Stanley.

Overwhelmed by a hopelessness that was unfamiliar to her, Stella drove under Hammersmith flyover and on to the Great West Road. Her phone lit up with a text.

'What does it say?' she shouted at Lucie.

Lucie fished her glasses out from a voluminous leather handbag, taking a maddeningly long time to extract them from the case and fit them on to her face. She extracted the phone from the dashboard cradle and frowned at the screen.

'It's from Jack!'

'What does it say?' Stella yelled, her foot squeezed the accelerator pedal.

'*The cock has crowed.* Oh Lordy-lou, that boy!'

'What does that mean?' For once Stella was inclined to agree with Lucie about Jack.

'No idea. Does he have a pet hen?'

'He has an owl – no, that's a door knocker.'

'You're worrying me, darling.'

'Is it in the Bible?' Stella didn't know where her question had come from.

'Damn right! It's the Last Supper. Jesus says that Peter will disown him three times, before or after the cock crowed, can't remember. Anyway, Peter's adamant he won't betray Jesus, but he does. Three times!'

'Jack wouldn't betray anyone.'

'Jack refused to be Carrington's friend. I think in this scenario, Carrington is Jesus.' Lucie May pulled her scarf away from her mouth. 'We're dealing with a madman!'

'Simon sent this text. He's got Jack's phone!' She smacked the dashboard. It occurred to her that Jack put a kiss after a message and this one had no kiss. She berated herself for dwelling on irrelevant detail while missing the key issue. Simon Carrington had Jack's phone. What would he do next?

She signalled left into Church Street, bumping the van over debris strewn over the road from bin bags and chucked up from the riverbed, and braked opposite the passage to the tower. She tried to open the van door. It was stuck.

'It's the force of the storm.' Lucie made no move to get out. 'Do a three-point turn so we're facing the other way.'

'That's ridiculous!' Stella pushed harder and opened the door five centimetres, then stuck her arm into the gap to stop it closing. Excruciating pain took her breath away. She was caught in a giant vice. She pushed with all her might and managed to release her arm.

Lucie was puffing placidly on her e-cigarette. Giving in, Stella started the engine and did what amounted to a ten-point turn, revving the engine and stamping on the brake.

With the wind blowing against the back of the van, the door was snatched from Stella's grasp when she opened it. They both clambered out of the van easily, sheltered from the gale by the bonnet. Only then did Stella notice Lucie's shoes. Slip-on pink high heels.

'You can't wear those, you'll fall,' she shouted against the wind.

Lucie delved into the huge handbag and produced a pair of pink Hunters. Leaning on Stella's arm, she hopped about on each foot and swapped her high heels for the boots.

Stella pulled her phone out of her pocket, looking in vain for a text – any sign – from Jack. All she saw was a pair of staring eyes at the top of the screen.

Stalker Boy.

Who was watching her?

Stella stepped out of the shelter of the van, and a powerful rush of wind felt as if it would rip her hair from her scalp. She reached up to pull up her hood and saw the tower.

Someone was on the roof.

'JACK!' she yelled. She tried to point him out to Lucie, but the journalist had crossed the road and was stomping off down the passage.

The cage door crashed open and then shut, harassed by the wind. Above the clamour of the storm, Stella heard a high-pitched humming as if some choir was singing. It was the wind whistling through the grille. She wrenched open the door. Her little finger bent back; distantly she registered that it might be broken. She hustled Lucie into the cage and on to the first stairway. As they climbed, the frame shook, the force of the wind increasing with each step. Fixed on Lucie a few steps above her, Stella had no sense of making headway.

Lucie staggered on to the walkway and leant recklessly on the flimsy guard rail. All that stood between her and a plummet of several hundred metres was a length of rusting iron. Stella waved at her to come away, but Lucie was shouting and gesturing. Stella turned and saw what she was pointing at. In a freak lull in the storm, she heard Lucie: 'Rivets. Gone! If rest go, it's curtains!' Her telegrammatic words rang out above the wind.

As if to illustrate this, the frame swayed out from the wall: another rivet had snapped. The walkway shook. Stella took Lucie's hand and lunged at the door. Already open, it gave way and they fell inside, stumbling at the foot of the spiral staircase. Lucie shut the door.

In the sudden quiet, Stella heard music. She recognized the Smiths.

'I never could bear that band. Enough to send you back to take a jump.' Lucie stuffed her cigarette in her coat pocket and clutched her handbag.

'It's Jack's favourite,' Stella said.

'Get away!'

'It's a sign.' Stella clattered up the staircase, shouting, 'Jack, it's me, Stella!' Her words reverberated against the concrete wall. 'And Lucie.'

Jack's flat door was closed.

'He's on the roof.' Stella continued up the staircase.

'We're coming!' Lucie's tone implied she was playing hide and seek.

At the top of the spiral staircase was a flat ceiling in which was a glass hatch of a metre square. Stella stretched up to slide the bolts. It was open. Of course it was – Jack was up there – but why shut the skylight?

Stella slammed her hands against the glass, but it didn't shift. She pushed harder but it made no difference – she lacked the strength to lift it; the glass alone must weigh thirty kilos.

Stella went up to the penultimate step, until she was so close to the skylight that she had to crouch. She flattened herself against the curving glass, her feet either side of the stair, grasped the handrails and, pushing, manoeuvred herself to half standing. The hatch didn't shift.

'Wait!' Lucie inserted herself into the gap between the top step and the skylight above Stella. She raised her hands above her head and splayed her fingers on the section of glass beside Stella's back. 'Say "when"!' she gasped.

'One, two, three. Push!'

Stella and Lucie began to straighten their bodies, the action like two levers. There was the crack as the rubber seals parted and the frame lifted a centimetre, three, five centimetres. It stopped.

'Keep going!' Stella spoke through clenched teeth.

'I'm a bloody short arse, that's my lot,' Lucie gasped. She was standing up, her arms were extended to their limit. 'It's down to you, Officer.'

Stella felt the weight increase as the frame went beyond Lucie's reach. A blinding pain shot down her back. She stood on tiptoe and gained a fraction more height; the weight was on the back of her head – her neck must break. She had stopped the lid closing, but lacked the height to raise it further.

She dared not move.

'Move over,' Lucie whispered. Keeping the frame in place, Stella shuffled along. Lucie's pink high heels appeared on the step above her. Forcing herself to ignore the agony, Stella concentrated on them: patent leather, pointy toes, stiletto heels. This was not the time to dress up. Lucie fitted them on and Stella thought of Cinderella, her thought cut off by a bolt of pain like a flame travelling from her head down her spine. The lid was closing.

'Stay with it, Officer,' Lucie spluttered as she eased her foot into the second shoe.

Stella stopped breathing. If she let it drop, she would not be able to lift it again.

'One, two, three!' Lucie raised herself up, standing taller in her shoes, the narrow heels wobbling on the metal tread. Stella gave one last push.

The skylight tipped as the angle activated the pneumatic hinge. The lid stopped when it was vertical. Stella crawled out of the aperture on to the roof. Ahead of her was a garden shed. She blinked, sure she was seeing things.

The wind howled. Across London the air was frantic with a cacophony of alarms: house alarms, car alarms; emergency service sirens whooped. She struggled around the shed. No one was there.

The roof was empty.

Stella strained out over the parapet.

Jack!

Sixty-Two

Tuesday, 29 October 2013

'Stanley!'

An echo – from above or below – in the dark. Jack's perception was skewed.

'Stanley,' he whispered again.

Stanley!

The dog's claws skittered on the iron treads. He was close by. Jack let himself breathe. The air was dank and chill like a tomb. His nerves screamed at him to go back to the safety of his flat. Nowhere was safe.

He put out a hand and felt concrete, cold and crumbling. He shuffled down another step, tip-tapping his shoe, testing for the next one. He was on a spiral staircase. The treads were narrow and steep and the angle of the rail told him it spiralled like a corkscrew.

Humpty Dumpty sat on the wall,
Humpty Dumpty had a great fall.

Simon was inside his mind. The dog had slipped behind him. Even without light, Jack sensed that the animal was hanging back; he too was scared. Jack had no choice but to go on. He must face Simon. He could not deny him again.

The central column in the tower wasn't a key supporting stanchion. It was a shaft, built to carry pipes and give access to the roof. Lucie's article had said Simon studied engineering at university. Simon had outwitted him.

With each step the metal vibrated, accumulating to an insidious thrum. It was the sound he had attributed to the Glove Man's ghost.

Simon had waited until he was asleep and then he'd crept up the shaft, opened the wall beside Jack's bed and entered his flat. The tower was no refuge. Like Icarus, Jack would pay for his hubris.

Faint light spilled through slits in the concrete. Inside his flat there were slits high up in the partition wall and in the kitchen. Jack had believed that they provided a free flow of air between the two rooms but there was no door between the spaces, so air could flow without vents. Drunk with the power of living in the watch tower commanding a view of London, he had made basic engineering errors. He had ignored Simon's signs. His wings were aflame.

The meagre light increased with each step. Nerves electric, Jack paused. Should he go up or down?

You choose!

He detected a change in the atmosphere. The walls whispered, 'Truly I say to you, this very night, before the cock crows, you will deny me three times.'

The dog wasn't behind him. Jack clattered down the steps and found him bunched in the corner of a cramped space, eyes black in light that leaked in from a porthole. Jack gathered the little animal up and folded him into his waistcoat.

The Smiths track filled his head.

Jack had seen the porthole from the outside. It was beyond the reach of the walkway that circled half of the tower. Stupidly he hadn't considered where it was inside the tower. He returned to the staircase.

Running away is no escape if you don't know which direction is 'away'.

He swept his hand over the concrete wall, the rough patina grazing his fingertips, and found a door.

'Good boy.' He whispered Stella's mantra to soothe the dog. 'It's all right,' he breathed into Stanley's ear. A warm tongue slathered his cheek, soothing him instead.

With a click the door swung inwards. The music swelled.

'Hello, Justin. Here I am.'

Sixty-Three

Tuesday, 29 October 2013

Dazed, Jack shifted Stanley on to his shoulder and walked into a semi-circular space. Shapes resolved into a bed, a cupboard, a desk with a chair. It was identical to his flat above.

> *'I'll tell you a story*
> *About Jack-a-Nory,*
> *And now my story's begun;*
> *I'll tell you another of Jack and his brother,*
> *And now my story is done.'*

Jack couldn't see the source of the voice.

'Welcome!' Low laughter.

'You'll frighten the dog.' Jack shouldn't have drawn attention to Stanley.

'Why did you save me from drowning if you wouldn't be my friend?' No laughter now.

'Where is Stella?' Jack demanded. The voice was coming from the corner of the room, which was in shadow. It had broken since he last heard it, but, like eyes, voices don't alter.

'Don't disappoint me with silly questions.'

Outside, the St Jude storm was raging, but in here, but for the Smiths music, it was quiet.

You are trespassing. This is out of bounds.

Jack clasped his forehead with his free hand as a faint throbbing in his temples increased to hammer blows. The words were inside and outside his head.

The light in the room was increasing incrementally, like a sunrise. Shadows dwindled as ambient light washed over the curving concrete walls. There were no windows.

A quarter of a century had passed since Jack had seen Simon. He was wearing a long black coat with a baseball cap low over his eyes. He snatched it off and flung it on the bed. His face was smooth as if experience hadn't touched him. But for this, Jack was looking at a version of himself. Simon flicked his fringe from his forehead in the manner of Jack.

'I've called the police. They'll be here soon,' Jack said.

He distinguished pictures on the partition wall behind the bed. As the light brightened, he made out close-ups of men and women. Their faces were different, varying hairstyles and ages, black, Asian, white, but each had the impassive expression Jack knew from those waiting on platforms when he pulled into stations. Their unregistering gaze, like that of the dead, would slide over him as he brought his train to a stop. The faces on the wall were his passengers. There was the man with large ears and wispy hair, and the jittery woman in her forties who he suspected was a drinker. She stood on the same spot at Ravenscourt Park station every evening. The young woman so like his mother that Jack could believe she had returned from the dead. And the woman at Ealing Broadway station the night his train broke down.

The end photograph was not a face. Silver tracks glinted in the headlamps of an approaching train. Just visible, insubstantial as a ghost, was the driver. Jack recognized himself.

'Silly Justin.' With a half-finger, Simon waved something at him. Thinking it was a weapon, Jack stepped back against the wall. The door had shut. There was no handle. Simon didn't have a gun. He was holding Jack's mobile phone.

'The Cleaner is here. Redoubtable, isn't she! We did have a nice chat on the station while she did her best to hide her fear. Yes, I was the "inspector" at Stamford Brook station. I'm disappointed it took you so long to work that out.'

'What were you doing there?'

'Another silly question. Where you go, I go. *Justin*. Thanks to the handy little "stalker" app on Rick Frost's phone. He was quite clever, all said and done, you know!' He tugged on his half finger and continued.

'But for the soundproofing, you'd hear the Cleaner and the Reporter blundering about on the roof. They think you've jumped. Poor Justin, his past caught up with him and, unable to bear the shame, he jumped. The Reporter will relish writing that.'

'They won't think that. There's no body.'

'By the time they ask themselves that question, it will be too late. They'll find your body soon enough.'

Jack had never been alone in his tower. Simon had been there. Simon was the man on the bus outside Stamford Brook station; he was the man on Hammersmith Bridge. Simon had delivered the fliers about the tower through his door. He was the man in the crowd.

Jack had been Simon's Host. He hadn't read the signs.

'More disappointment, I thought you'd read them sooner.' Simon spoke soothingly, as if he could follow his thoughts.

Into Jack's mind came the thought that if his own mother had lived, he might have wanted Simon as his friend. But had she lived, he wouldn't have been sent away to school and he wouldn't have met Simon.

'You betrayed me.' Simon spoke in a kindly tone. 'More than three times, you denied you knew me. What did Mr Wilson teach us? There was a man who didn't practise what he preached. By now the Cleaner and the Reporter will have worked it out, but I hoped you'd get there before them. You recognized his Timex watch. I supposed it would be plain sailing for you after that.'

'Mr Wilson was the man trapped in the tower.' Jack nodded as he got it. He had recognized the Timex watch. Stanley tensed; he stroked him. 'You were the one who shut the door on him.'

'At last!' Simon tossed Jack's phone back and forth between his hands. 'Mr Wilson was the only person who bothered with me. He

365

found me in the basement after you locked me in that last time at school.'

'So why kill him?'

'He betrayed me, like everyone else. Like you did, Justin.'

'You killed him because he betrayed you?'

'Do you consider betrayal a minor transgression? Your Cleaner puts a high price on loyalty. That was one thing in her favour. You and she are haphazard detectives, but you get there in the end! Shame for you it is the end.'

'So why Mr Wilson?' Jack asked again.

'My mother, the lovely Madeleine, met Wilson when she was on a business trip to Australia. She left me for a month to go to a banking conference in Sydney. She was at the conference all right but, as my dad in one of his rather cruder moods once shouted at her, she did less banking than bonking!' Simon raised his eyebrows. 'She met Wilson in a bar. He did his disappearing act and followed her over here. That man took my mother away from me.' He smiled brightly. 'Mr Wilson had to pay for his sins.'

'So you killed him?' Jack repeated.

'Call it the wrath of God. A week after the hurricane, I went back to the tower to warn him to stay away from her, intending that he'd have learnt his lesson. He was on the floor by the door, stiff and cold and dead.'

'The post-mortem thought it likely that Wilson had a heart attack.' Jack had thought the sketch of Glove Man on the Missing Persons' site was familiar. He had assumed it was because he saw so many faces, some of which were on the wall before him. The main reason he had dismissed it was because he had blotted out that time at school. He had blotted out Simon.

'Your mother may be dead, Justin, but it's no excuse for cruelty. Simon tried to care for you. He only wanted to be your friend. Now you have no friends.' The man tapped the Bible. *'One day you'll understand what you have done. God watches over us all.'*

'I shut the door on him.' Simon tapped his lips with Jack's phone. 'I killed him just as that train driver you bought coffee for the other day killed the Captain. It should have been me standing him a cup of coffee. I have much to thank him for. He was my amanuensis. The Captain knew his day had come.'

Jack had sensed a presence on the balcony overlooking Earl's Court station. He should have trusted his instinct that he was being watched. Simon had been there.

'Mr Wilson thought my mother was joking. When he realized he was trapped in the tower, he called her names, he shouted unforgivable things about her and about me. When I got outside, the hurricane was raging. I had to go – it was dangerous to be out.'

'Where is Nicola Barwick?' Jack interrupted him.

'In good time, Justin.' Simon ran a coin over his fingers, tumbling it over the top of his hand, his half-finger bobbing. At school, Simon had done it to impress him; Jack knew he was doing it now to mark time.

'Tell me my nickname at school?' Simon said.

'Stumpy.' Jack had made it up.

Simon flicked the pen into the air, caught it and continued his trick. His hand resembled a giant insect. The boys had called the teacher a stick insect. Jack's past was flooding back.

Stanley struggled to be let down. Jack lowered him to the ground and he ran across to the bed, leapt upon it and settled down. So much for dogs sensing danger. Perhaps that was exactly what Stanley had done: he had gone to Simon, the little boy who had only tried to help and was lonely.

'You have known what it's like to be shunned. To see people's eyes glaze over, that flash of disappointment, even panic, when they hear you're on their football team. They tell you a chair is taken when you try to sit down – all the empty chairs in the class are taken. You were my blood brother, but you did nothing. You told me my mother didn't love me.'

'I was unhappy. No one wanted to talk to a boy touched by death.' Jack had had blackness in his soul. Mr Wilson had intoned: *'And then if anyone says to you, "Look, here is the Christ!" or, "Look there he is!" do not believe it. False Christs and false prophets*

*will arise and show signs and wonders, to lead astray, if possible, the
elect.'*

'I don't have friends,' Jack said. Stella and Jackie invited him to
their houses. Clean Slate's cleaning team and Beverly in the office
had bought a cake in the shape of an engine on his birthday.
Dariusz in the mini-mart beneath the office and Cheryl in the dry
cleaner's checked he had eaten recently. There was Lucie May and,
before Dale turned up, there had been Suzie. Isabel Ramsay was
commemorated in his Garden of the Dead. He did have friends.

*Then Jesus said to the chief priests and captains of the temple
and elders, who had come out against him, 'Have you come out
as against a robber, with swords and clubs? When I was with
you day after day in the temple, you did not lay hands on me.
But this is your hour, and the power of darkness.'*

Jack rubbed at his forehead to stop the voice.

'Quite a contact list for a man with no friends!' Simon was
looking at Jack's phone. 'Hmm, I don't see myself here.'

'I didn't want a friend. I wanted my mum and my toys. I wanted
my bedroom and the tree in our garden. I wanted to make tunnels
and bridges like my dad. I wanted to go home. I didn't want a
friend!' Jack's voice reverberated off the concrete.

'You told the Captain you didn't know me. The cooks called me
greedy when I asked for seconds, but you got thirds because your
mummy was dead.'

Abruptly the music stopped.

'I am the engineer, not you.' Simon raised his voice. 'It's me that
builds bridges and tunnels. You only drive in them and wonder
about how long they are. This is my tower, not yours. As you know,
the best way to vanquish your enemy is to become him. Look for
the person with a mind like your own. All those True Hosts – and
for what? Time and time again the Cleaner has to save you from
yourself, but not this time.'

'How do you know about the Hosts?'

'Oh, Justin! You can do better than that. You and me, we know how to make ourselves invisible, how to garner facts about those we shadow. You taught me surveillance tactics. You told me that, unless they've done wrong, most people don't think they're being watched. I wanted you to see me, but even when you did, you looked through me and failed to read the signs. You promised the Cleaner to stay in at nights. She's made you soft!'

He tapped at the screen on Jack's phone with his stubby finger. 'Look, the Cleaner's sent you a text. *Stella mob*! Stella mop, perhaps!'

Beware the jokes of those with no sense of humour.

'*Simon is alive. Stay where you are, I'm coming.* She's ahead of you, Justin! So you're happy to be her friend, or would you like to be more than friends? Is that why you hate Dale, the Brand-new Brother? What shall we reply to her? *Too late, he's dead?* or *Leave or the dog dies!* Shall we tell her you have betrayed her? That you were hiding in the house when she was there? They say anger helps assuage grief. My sister should know, although it's guilt at her own betrayal she has to assuage, not grief. She's in with the Captain's brother. She lied to me. She is Wilson's daughter – betrayal's in the blood.'

'Wilson wasn't in a relationship. He was in love with your mother. Who did he betray?'

'Me.' Simon might have been a small boy, his face untouched by the years. 'Really, Justin, did Jesus really die for the likes of all of you?'

'I can't turn the clock back.' But Jack had tried to.

'I have looked for myself inside your head, but I'm not there, am I? I was dead to you.'

'I told you your mother was having an affair with Mr Wilson. I saw them in the car park at school.'

'You weren't being kind, if I remember. You laughed.'

'Yes, I did.' Jack had wanted someone else to have a reason to cry. He had felt a thrill of cruelty as he told the boy that his mummy had kissed the RE teacher.

'Knowledge is power,' Simon said. 'It did at least mean I was no longer in the dark.'

'I was jealous your mother was alive. I wanted you to think she loved Mr Wilson more than you so that you'd be alone like me.' Jack had blotted out this self of his.

'I overheard him asking my mother to come away with him. She went to meet him at Stamford Brook station. I followed her. When he didn't come, she would have assumed he had betrayed her. Until I found him dead in the tower, I did too. When they found him, she must have guessed that it was Wilson's body in the tower, but she kept it to herself. She let his family wonder where he was for all those years. His mother died not knowing what happened to him. My mother knew. Perhaps she kidded herself it wasn't his body up there because she never stopped looking out for him. She kept the living-room curtains open at night. She would follow men in the street and then see they were strangers. She knew I didn't believe her lies about where she was. She knew why I was at Stamford Brook that day. She may have suspected I shut that door. We became strangers. I waited for the right time and then I killed her. Just a little push. You see, betrayal is unforgivable.'

'She didn't betray you.' Jack spoke mechanically.

'Only because he didn't come to the station. It's intention that counts. She was going to take my sister because she was his child. She was going to leave me.'

'Did she take bags with her to the station?' Jack asked.

'No, that would have given her away.'

'So she didn't plan to leave you.' Jack snatched at a sliver of hope, but Simon wasn't listening. 'Simon—' Jack saw what he had done to Simon. Not just him – he recognized he was not solely to blame – but he had played his part in changing Simon. It was no excuse that he had been unhappy; he had destroyed Simon's faith in people. Jack wanted to plead, not for his life, but for forgiveness, but it had been too late a long time ago.

'The day I found Mr Wilson lying dead on the floor of the tower, I learnt that if you dislike someone, they don't have to live.'

Simon jumped up. 'Did you get all my signs? I'm Charles Bruno and you're Guy Haines. Like Bruno in *Strangers on a Train*, remember I told you? I see loyalty in reciprocity. I do your murder, you do mine.'

'They aren't real. It's a story.' Jack heard his mistake. He could neither placate nor argue with Simon.

'Fiction is a way of being alive. Or dead.' Simon looked about him. 'I wonder if my treacherous mother let her mind drift to those walls in your flat while she had sex with Mr Wilson. Is the concrete stained with her passion?' He faltered briefly.

'Where is Nicola Barwick?' Jack dreaded the answer.

'Nicky tried to be clever, but lucky for me, my sister, thinking only of her own feelings, told me what Nicky had done with her passport. That she had betrayed me. Up until then, I had still hoped she was my friend.'

'Where is she?' Jack pushed past Simon into a kitchen the same as the one in his own flat. A train was on the window sill, set on top of stones and strands of twine. A pair of binoculars sat on the table by the 'Hammersmith Bridge' window. Simon had replicated everything. He had known what Jack was thinking because he had a mind like his own. He could follow him in all senses of the word.

Simon slid back the partition panel to the shower room and went inside. Gingerly, sensing a trap, Jack stayed in the doorway.

'Nicola Barwick, this is John Justin Harmon.'

A woman was seated on a chair by the partition. Long hair straggling down her shoulders, she was dressed in a loose-fitting fleece jacket and jeans. She had the dull-eyed look of the passengers' faces in the other room. Jack could see no gag, no ropes restricting her, but she seemed unable to move.

'Are you alright?' He heard how lame his question was. He recognized her. 'You were on my train, the one that broke down at Ealing Broadway last month,' he said. 'You got off before I cleared it.' Her face was one of the pictures.

'I thought you were *him*.' She was matter of fact.

Jack stepped towards her.

'Don't come closer or he will kill us all.' She didn't move.

Jack saw that Nicola wasn't alone. A woman sat on a stool in the shower cubicle, as if entombed in a huge glass case. Unlike Barwick, she was dressed smartly in black bootleg trousers tucked into knee-high leather boots, with a wool jacket over an ironed shirt. She too wore no gag and wasn't visibly restricted. Simon entered people's minds; he had no need of physical fetters.

'She's right.' Simon paced about Nicola as he might an exhibit. 'Nicky only pretended to be my friend. She left her house without telling me where she was going. Friends don't do that.'

'My mother will call the police. I'm due there to cook her supper. My brothers will come looking.' The woman in the shower cubicle spoke with authority. Jack felt a frisson of reassurance that vanished as quickly as it had come. Her threats were impotent: Simon didn't care.

'I *was* your friend.' Nicola Barwick sounded weary as if she had repeated this many times. 'Until you made Richard climb up here. He was a cruel boy and he became an unkind man. But you have become worse. You took revenge on him and on all those around you. He even married your sister because he was frightened you would report him for murder. You took over his company and threatened to bankrupt him. He lived in fear of you. In the end he went to William for help, but you were there first.'

'Running away is no escape if you don't know which direction is "away".' Simon laughed. 'We know that, don't we, Justin! He married my sister because he thought it was the best way to hurt me. He wasn't frightened of me, he wanted to destroy me.'

'Are you Liz?' Jack asked the woman in the shower. She nodded.

'Liz was my friend too until she started talking to the Cleaner,' Simon explained. 'She broke her promise. She told her about me.'

'I only promised not to tell anyone about where Nicola was!' Liz's voice trembled, and Jack saw that, behind the bravura, she was frightened. There was nothing he could do; Simon had planned it meticulously. In a locked tower, there was no way out. Or in.

'Did you call him Justin?' Jack asked Liz, remembering something Stella had said. Another missed sign.

'He said his name was Justin Venus.' She spat out the words.

'That's my grandfather.' Jack exclaimed. Simon knew everything.

'Come on, Justin.' Simon beckoned with his half-finger. 'You two will be OK here, I've shut the windows to keep out the storm so you won't hear a thing.' He gave a low laugh. 'Nor will you be heard.'

'The police are on their way,' Jack said stoutly, but his tone lacked conviction.

'This is how it is.' Simon addressed them all. 'The Reporter and the Cleaner are here. The Cleaner spotted me on the roof so they have gone up there and now they can't get down. They will be shouting, but in this wind… it's a pity, but no one will hear them. Today, or rather yesterday, since it's after midnight, was St Jude's feast day, so the gods have named this storm after him. Mr Wilson told us that St Jude carried the image of Christ. Some think St Jude the brother of Christ. We were blood brothers, weren't we, Justin? Or shall I call you Jude!'

Jack heard the prattling small boy, eager to cheer him up, whom he had put out of his mind. Nicola Barwick had liked Simon. That boy had gone.

Returning to the front room, Simon lifted Stanley from the truckle bed. Jack expected him to attack Simon, but he nestled on his shoulder. There was a flash of silver; Simon had a knife. He opened the door. They were at the foot of the spiral staircase that led up to Jack's flat.

'Stella!' Jack yelled. This was his only chance.

The silence was profound. No Smiths, no sink noise, no storm. The soundproofing was effective.

'Effective soundproofing.' Simon pulled open the door and a powerful gust of wind hit them, bringing with it the cloying odour of river mud.

'After you, *Guy*!' Still holding Stanley, Simon stepped out on to the walkway and, his bad hand clasping the knife, he said, 'Come with me.'

For the first time in his life, Jack did as Simon said.

In sudden squalls, freezing rain hit them from every direction. Soon, despite his coat, Jack was soaked through. Simon was walking ahead of him over the causeway to the eyot. He never looked to see if Jack was behind him. He had slung Stanley over his shoulder and, in occasional gleams of light, Jack saw Stanley's eyes watching him; like Liz Hunter's they showed fear. The dog wasn't fickle, he was playing it safe; his gaze willed Jack to do the same.

The tide was out, but already, beneath the wailing and moaning of the wind, Jack heard the trickling of water filling miniature creeks and gullies in between debris on the beach. Pools were spreading and joining up.

Jack saw that Simon walked with no hesitation. Not once did he stumble; like Jack he must know every stone, every jutting slab of concrete embedded in the mud. Adroitly he avoided the viscous mud that, like shifting sands, threatened to pull them below the glistening surface.

Jack couldn't think of escaping because Simon would read his mind and stop him.

On the eyot, Simon stopped and, shining his torch into Jack's face, said, 'You're the Captain, you lead the way.'

Obediently Jack took them along his hidden path deeper into the undergrowth. Jack tried to keep his mind blank, to keep Simon out. He forced himself to think of the calculation of the West Hill Tunnel: 266.66 recurring. Recurring. *Recurring*.

Jack hoped Simon was taking him to Stella. He trod heavily, deliberately snapping branches and reeds to warn her of their approach.

'The Cleaner won't hear you,' Simon said.

They arrived in his Garden of the Dead, out of sight of Chiswick Mall and of the tower, and hidden by a screen of reeds and willow fronds from any boats on the Thames. Jack couldn't see Stella.

Simon's voice broke into his thoughts: 'I've done my murder. Now it's your turn.'

They were standing by the gap in the reeds where, nearly thirty years before, Jack had stopped Rick Frost – the Captain – from pushing Simon into the Thames. Below, the river raced on: oily, turbid, toxic; the rain shattered reflections to nothing. Were he to fall, within seconds the current would drag him down. Shocked by the icy cold, Jack knew he would not struggle. Simon would watch until the black water closed over him, then he would walk away.

Sixty-Four

Tuesday, 29 October 2013

The perimeter wall was chest-high with no footholds. Stella couldn't see directly down without clambering on to the edge. She peered into the darkness. The triumph of opening the skylight was long gone. Rapid crosswinds battered the trees and bushes on the eyot. A finger of stony ground leading out from Chiswick Mall was fractured as water rushed over the stones.

'There he is!' Lucie exclaimed.

Jack, hair wild and straggling, his coat billowing, was moving in a zigzag along the fringe of the island. He changed direction, changed again. Whipped up by the wind, the river was rife with conflicting currents, their strength measured by the speed at which wood, scum and rubbish, churned up from the river's bed, streamed past. Waves rolled and crashed, driven by the force of the storm. A sack floated past. Even in the dark and from high up, Stella could see it was a dog, lifeless and bloated.

'Jack!' She waved both arms, but he was too far away and the wind was too loud.

'He's trying to get back, the tide's turning!' Stella yelled to Lucie. Lucie, puffing on her e-cigarette, nodded.

From their vantage point, Stella could see that Jack was going the wrong way. He should continue to the western tip of the island where, although it was shrinking, a scrap of land offered a safer route to Chiswick Mall. He was taking the most obvious way, but already the river was rising.

Something hit Stella in the eye, as hard and sharp as a stone. She wheeled away and rubbed it with her palm. A raindrop. Water thundered down, drops coming from all directions as the wind battered them. In seconds she was soaked. The island was a blur. Hands over her face, she peeped through her fingers.

Jack was picking his way across the stony ridge, but already the end nearest Chiswick Mall was submerged. He could go no further.

'Go back!' Stella jumped up and down, flailing her arms. There was still a path, narrow and already broken, at the other end of the island. Water stung her eyes: she couldn't see him properly. She heard a clap of thunder.

Turning around, she saw that the skylight had slammed shut.

She heard a shout, faint about the roar of the wind. Lucie was scrabbling at the parapet wall.

Stella rushed over and, cupping her hands over her forehead to protect her eyes from the pounding rain, looked to where Lucie was pointing.

At last Jack was making for the far shore of the island. Already the eyot was officially an island, the path was disappearing as the stretch of water widened. Cold rain pelted her head like hail, but Stella didn't put up her hood. She fixed on Jack as he struggled across the ground, flailing at reeds to prevent himself slipping into the river. She could see he wouldn't get to the other path in time. He had left it too late.

'Jack!' Stella yelled. There was more water than land. 'We have to stop him!' she bellowed at Lucie, while aware that they could do nothing.

Jack reached where the beach had been and teetered on the edge of the water. Waves broke around his ankles. He stepped in and began to wade. At first he made good progress, but then he floundered; he held his arms above his head to keep them clear of the water and waded deeper in.

'He should wait,' Lucie bellowed in Stella's ear. 'He should stay where he is.'

Jack pulled his coat tight, the water now up to his waist. He gave into the water and pushed himself along in an awkward upright crawl. He slipped and went up to his neck, then regained his footing.

'Take off your coat!'

Although she guessed what Lucie had said, Stella only heard 'coat'. Jack's coat was like a second skin; he wouldn't take it off. Saturated, it would be hampering him. He went under, came up and, struggling against a current, went under again.

Through the rain, Stella stared at the river. Jack had told her once that he couldn't swim.

Sixty-Five

Tuesday, 29 October 2013

'We need to find some way out. We can't just sit here and do nothing.' Liz Hunter slid back the shower screen and stumbled out on to the metal floor.

'He's locked us in and, as he said, no one will hear us in here. I've been shouting and no one has come. You don't know Simon. He's thought of everything. There is nothing we can do.'

'We can't give up,' Liz protested. 'He's not thought of everything – he hasn't even bothered to tie us up.'

'That's because he knows we can't get out. He let a man die in here and blamed another boy for it. He murdered his brother-in-law and his mother. He's a cold-blooded killer.'

'I'm not prepared just to sit here and wait for him to come back and kill us. What is this hold he has over you, Nicola? Over everyone?' Liz glared at Nicola Barwick sitting stock still on the chair.

'He gets into every corner. Nowhere is safe. Even if we escape, he'll find us.'

'We have to try!' Liz dragged Nicola to her feet. 'That man just got in and it wasn't through the door. Come on, Justin – Simon – will be back any minute.'

They ran through the little kitchen to the main room. Ahead was a door of galvanized metal. Liz Hunter banged and kicked it, making only dull thuds. There was no handle.

Nicola pulled aside a cupboard and examined the wall behind. Nothing. She ran to the bed and, sitting on the floor, pushed it back with her legs. It shifted a few centimetres.

'Here, let me.' Liz joined her. Together, the women pushed the bed several metres out into the room and stared at the exposed partition wall. Liz saw the same hairline cracks that, unknown to her, Jack had seen in his own flat earlier. 'That's it!' She ran against it and fell back nursing her shoulder.

'It must have a secret mechanism.' Nicola got down on her knees and crawled along the skirting.

'Out of the way.' Liz lugged the black swivel chair over and prepared to use it as a battering ram.

'Simon is an engineer, he doesn't work with brute force.'

'He's a killer,' Liz retorted.

'He doesn't use violence, he relies on leverage and coercion. He deals in stress and load bearings.' Nicola had reached the end of the skirting.

'There's money on the floor.' Liz tried to pick up the ten-pence piece lying where the bed had been. 'It's stuck.'

'Try pushing instead of pulling!' Nicola was beside her.

Liz pressed on the coin with the flat of her thumb and, with a rumbling, the wall slid aside.

Two women stepped into the room. One of them, billowing in a bright red coat, had a gun.

'Don't move!' she shouted.

'Stella!' Liz exclaimed.

'Do you know them?' the woman in the huge red coat asked Stella. Water was pooling into the room from their clothes. Liz saw that they were soaking wet. The 'gun' was an electronic cigarette.

'Stella, this is Nicola Barwick,' Liz said.

'Where's Simon Carrington?' the woman in the red coat asked.

'He's gone with your friend, Jack. That was ages ago – he could be back any minute. Stella, I think he was going to—' She couldn't use the word 'kill'.

'This way!' The woman with the cigarette dipped back into the darkness beyond the wall. 'We've found the way out. A shed is not always a shed.'

Stella was stony and unresponsive. Liz knew it was because she had realized that her friend Jack would be dead.

Sixty-Six

Tuesday, 29 October 2013

The tea was warm and sweet, not how Stella liked it, but she didn't care. She pulled the foil blanket tighter around her. The liquid warmed her, but did nothing for the profound numbness that made her feel she was floating above her body. Hazily she hoped she would always feel this way.

Jack wouldn't feel the wind or the rain. He couldn't feel the cold. *Jack.*

If Jack had heard her ask him about Justin Venus from the pay phone before his money ran out, he could have told her it was his grandfather's name. She had seen the headstone herself. Lucie May had known instantly when Liz told her. But then Lucie May made it her business to remember names and faces. Stella was a cleaner.

Stella heard a ping and looked at her phone as if Jack might have texted. It was from Liz Hunter. She had texted an hour earlier, but everything was disrupted by the storm. Liz had opened Rick Frost's letter to Nicola Barwick. Attached was a picture of it: '19 9 13 15 14   19 8 21 20   20 15 23 5 18   4 15 15 18'. If I die, tell the police about Simon.' Unable to reach Stella, Liz had told the man calling himself Justin Venus. The very last person she should have told.

If they had read the letter in the café, Jack would be alive.

'Stella, I'm sorry.' Martin Cashman climbed into the ambulance and sat down on the bed beside her.

'It's OK,' she said because she couldn't say just how much it wasn't OK.

'Lucie May says you're the next of kin,' Cashman said.

Stella was grateful he was being businesslike. She didn't want sympathy. She didn't want to feel anything.

'We're not related.' Stella shook her head. 'Jack doesn't have any living relatives.'

'You can nominate a person who isn't a blood relative as next of kin. Lucie May says Jack Harmon nominated you.'

'How would she know?'

'What doesn't Lucie know!' He smiled briefly.

A cordon of police tape and cars had been set up along the mall. The plastic smacked in the wind. Through the rain, the flashing lights of emergency vehicles were like stars falling. Stella was thinking like Jack. No, she wasn't; no one thought like Jack. Through the open doors Stella could see her van. It was inside the cordon. She had parked it in another life, the one where Jack was alive.

Jack.

'Clean Slate for a fresh start!' Why did they offer that? She didn't want a fresh start. When someone dies, you want the old life back. You want everything to stay the same. A fresh start was like dying all over again.

'Jack.'

'Sorry?' Martin Cashman said.

'Nothing.'

Cashman extracted Stella's empty cup from between her hands.

'What about Jack. Have you found him?' Stella hadn't meant to ask.

'We think so.'

'What do you mean?'

'Stella, I need you to—' He got up, putting his arms out as if she might fall. 'We have found a male, white Cauca—' He stopped, evidently remembering who he was talking to. 'I asked Lucie May, but she says she can't face it. I've seen her at dozens of PMs, but I guess this is different. It's different for you too, but—'

'I'll do it.' Stella got off the bed and jumped down out of the ambulance, the blanket around her like a cape.

Chiswick Mall was impassable; the river covered the camber. Waves, lashed up by the wind, pushed it up the street.

'Where is he?' she asked.

'This way.'

A group of people were huddled on the slipway. In slick black rainwear they looked like crows picking at carrion. Stella was thinking like Jack. He would know the word for a collection of crows.

Jack.

A long black roll of carpet lay at their feet. A body bag, sleek and black and zipped up, looked like rubbish in the storm-littered street.

The first dead person Stella had ever seen was Terry. The strain gone from his face, he had looked better than when she had given him his Christmas aftershave weeks earlier. The next two bodies she saw involved blood. After the third one, Stella had believed herself inured to the sight of death.

Jack.

If she saw him dead, it would be true.

She walked away. The wind roared about her ears. She reached her van and flung open the passenger door.

Lucie May nearly fell out on to the pavement. She kept hold of her tablet, the screen casting a glow over the wet flags.

'You have to come with me!'

Lucie struggled upright.

'I can't do it by myself,' Stella said.

'I told Cashman, I've got to file the story. It's an exclusive with the *Mirror*!'

'Now!' Stella leant in and switched off Lucie's tablet.

'I look a fright, but I suppose he won't...' Lucie patted at her hair.

'Jack won't know!' Stella said.

'No, of course.' Lucie took Stella's arm.

Something grabbed her leg. She lashed out, dislodging it. It happened again; she shook it off and kicked harder.

Lucie was gesticulating. Stella wheeled around, fists ready. A creature cowered by the slipway. Stella stared unbelieving. Then it was rushing to her and swarming around her legs. Stanley was alive and she had nearly killed him.

Stella snatched him up and buried her face in his chest. His coat was damp and matted with mud. He smelled of the river, of dank undergrowth. She sniffed again. Shampoo, washing powder – biological – honey soap… Stanley smelled of Jack.

Martin Cashman escorted them down the slipway. Someone stepped into the lamplight.

'Martin, I'll do it,' Jackie said. 'Jack Harmon was like another son to me.'

'Thank you.' Martin began to lead her to the 'roll of carpet'.

Jack had been there for her dad's funeral. He had stopped her from driving away before it began. If it were Stella in a zip-up bag on a wet pavement in the dead of night, he would see she came to no harm. Jack would insist that if someone had to identify her – to see her dead – it should be him.

'Let me.' Stanley on her shoulder, Stella strode down the ramp. A man introduced himself. She heard 'pathologist'.

'Ready?' he asked.

'Yes.' No.

A crumpling of plastic, a zip buzzed. Someone shone a torch above the exposed face, keeping it clear of the body to soften the light.

Stella forced herself to look down. The eyes were shut, the lips so pale the skin hardly showed. A straggle of hair smeared across the forehead. Although effort had been made to clean his face, there were streaks of mud on his cheeks. The bag had been opened to his chest, the hands folded. Stella found she couldn't speak.

'This man has been pronounced dead before, so let's get it right this time, folks!' Lucie May was by her side, around her an aura of steam. 'This is the man who owns that tower over there. He refused to give me an interview.' She nodded at the pale hands. 'That's Simon Carrington. Distinguishing mark? The man has two joints missing on his left middle finger. There's a sister: she can do the formal thing; but one thing I can say, this is *not* Jack Harmon!'

There was a shout from the direction of the river. The rain had abated, but the wind was stronger. There were no lights on the opposite bank. The Thames was in darkness.

A movement. A light moving towards them over the water. The chugging of a motor. Stella made out a boat with two figures hunched at the stern. As it got closer, she saw it was a police launch. Carrying Stanley, she walked down the slipway. She started to run.

The blood pounded in her ears and the dog felt lighter as he moved with her. She waded into the river oblivious to the ice-cold water up to her calves and fell against the boat. Hands pulled at the sides and dragged it up the cobbles.

People were all around her, police and paramedics. Jackie was by her side, Stanley tucked into her neck. The paramedics were lifting something out of the boat. Against the wind, Stella heard Lucie: 'This is Jack Harmon. His middle name is Justin. John Justin Harmon.'

Stella felt her legs go from under her and was supported from each side. Jackie and Martin Cashman held her up.

A shout.

Scrambling, footsteps, an engine revved. Stella was dazzled by headlights from the slipway. She was steered out of the way of two women with a stretcher. Stanley began to bark. Shrill and informative.

John Justin Harmon.

In the glare of the ambulance lights, Stella was aware of Lucie May coming away from the river, talking into her phone. She took Stella's hand and shook it up and down as, speaking into the mouthpiece, she yelled, 'He's breathing!'

Sixty-Seven

Tuesday, 29 October 2013

'So when did Terry find out he had a son?' Stella fixed on the flickering television screen in the 'Relatives' Room'. An old episode of *Dad's Army* was showing; she watched the platoon pass the camera one by one. The volume was down, but – whether it was not quite off or she was imagining it – she could hear the theme tune in her head. The men stumbling across some common made her think of Simon and the Captain, Captain Mainwarings both.

Lucie and Stella had been sitting on the plastic bucket chairs in Charing Cross Hospital for two hours while Jack – who had been in the river, clinging to a clump of reeds and fighting against the current – was treated for hypothermia and a strained arm.

Two hours gave ample time for Lucie May to spill every bean on Terry that she had.

'On the day he came to see you in Hammersmith Hospital, three days after you were born, he'd been on that search for Harry Roberts who killed the policemen.' Lucie sucked on her cigarette even though it was switched off. Her tablet was on her lap. She had been in busy email contact with more than one newspaper, but in the last half an hour there had been a respite. It was then that Stella asked her about Terry. Lucie was the one person she could rely on for the unvarnished truth. Lucie wouldn't restrain herself with concern for Stella's feelings and for this Stella was grateful.

'How did he find out?' Stella didn't need to ask.

'Suzanne told him. He reckoned she was fed up that he had put an armed man before a newborn daughter. To be honest, I'm inclined to agree. He was working around the clock, but all it took

386

was two minutes. Terry wasn't great on multi-tasking unless he'd had a drink and we—'

Stella put up a hand: the unvarnished truth had limits. 'He never told me,' she said.

'He thought you'd be jealous, that if you knew you had a brother you'd assume he loved him more. Terry was always scared you wouldn't love him. Cock-eyed thinking, if you ask me, and I said as much. Dale became the skeleton in your family's cupboard.'

Stella had had enough of skeletons, and cupboards for that matter.

On the television screen, the titles for Hitchcock's *Strangers on a Train* were showing. This reminded Stella of Simon Carrington's train, left at Underground stations and in the cemetery for Jack and her to find. Jack had a copy of the novel on his shelf; it was one of the few he had brought with him to the tower.

Looking at the television, Stella asked, 'Did you love Terry?'

Puffing on her dead cigarette, Lucie concentrated on the screen. 'This is Jack's favourite film.' She reached for the remote and turned up the volume.

'Did you?' Stella repeated.

'Yes, stupid mare that I am, I did.'

Sixty-Eight

Friday, 1 November 2013

Dale and Suzie were on the step when Jack opened the door of Terry's house. Beside them on the path were two enormous suitcases. Dale was holding a picnic hamper. Jack was tempted to find a reason to flee back to the tower, but since Stella had come and collected him from his overnight stay in Charing Cross Hospital she hadn't let him out of her sight. Jackie and Stella had made up a bed for him in what had been Terry's bedroom. Dale had sent over a vat of soup that Jack had to admit was an elixir, its effects instantly curative, not that he'd let it cloud his judgement about the Bounty-hunting Brother.

He'd promised Stella to take her to the airport and mind Stanley while Stella and Suzie went with Dale to the departure gate. Later that day Stella was handing Stanley back to his owner. She hadn't said, but Jack guessed she wanted the dog with her up until the last moment.

Stella also wanted Jack to help with Suzie after Dale had gone and Suzie lost her son for a second time.

'I've brought us a Heffernan starter-pack!' Dale grinned.

Jack caught the smell of freshly baked bread. Stella had told him that while he was staying with Suzie, Dale had treated them both to bagels, dark rye toast and honey, flatbreads with hummus, fruit loaves with sultanas and currants and lashings of butter. Jack could have told Dale that, apart from a cheese sandwich from the mini-mart beneath the office that she forgot to eat, Stella barely touched bread. In a few hours Heffernan was flying home to Sydney, then there would be no more cooking.

The house was as warm and bright as it had been on the evening that Dale had made lamb stew. Jack had filled the cafetière, and a rich smell of dark-roast coffee wafted down the hall. Stella had asked him to lay the table. Now Jack felt a wash of alarm. Heffernan's deadly weapon was his skill in whipping up delicious concoctions – potions – to gain Stella's trust. Against all odds, it had worked.

'Welcome back to the land of the living, Jack. Tuck in!' Heffernan ushered him into his usual seat, facing the kitchen door. 'When I did the cleaning with Stella, I thought that Lulu was weird about the man she'd seen in the street. I couldn't work out if she meant her brother or her husband was with the other woman. Beware of brothers!' Dale handed Jack a plate on which grilled bacon, tomatoes with scrambled egg, garnished with parsley, were tastefully arranged.

Jack had to be alert to protect Stella from her brother's underhand intentions. Australia might be the other side of the world, but the internet wiped out the distance. Money could be wired from London to Sydney in seconds.

'So, Jack, we're lucky to have you, mate! Your old school friend tried to drown you. How come that wasn't in the paper?' Dale asked.

Stella came to the rescue. 'We want Jack working undercover.'

In her syndicated article for the *Mirror*, Lucie May had described Simon's campaign of revenge on his mother's lover, Nathan Wilson, his RE teacher at school. The boy had believed the Australian had only wormed his way into his confidence to reach his beloved mother. As Jack considered this, he thought of Dale and was struck with the idea that history was repeating itself.

As a stand-in for an unloving husband, Simon's role was usurped by the teacher. Over thirty years he had planned careful vengeance on his betrayers. His brother-in-law, Rick Frost, whom Simon still called the Captain, was a long-standing enemy. His sister Tallulah was the love child of his mother and Wilson, but Simon cared for her and protected her. When she began an illicit affair with William, she truly betrayed him. He could convince himself that Rick had married her out of spite and she was 'innocent', but when he found out she was in love with William, he was appalled and could find no refuge. He saw it as a final betrayal: it was tantamount to nullifying him. Nicola Barwick, the third member of the children's gang, sided with Rick Frost against Simon. Simon fell for his sister's unfounded suspicion that Barwick was having an affair with the Captain. From then on, she wasn't safe.

Lucie May hadn't told the story of Simon's obsession with a boy who refused to be his friend and how, growing up, he had adopted Justin's mannerisms and ambitions. How he had spied on him, tracked him through the streets and ultimately got inside his head.

Jack had told no one that Simon hadn't tried to drown him. He had wanted Jack to kill him. He had planned to turn Jack into a murderer like himself. A true blood brother. That would remain his secret.

'Here's a taste of "Sixty-Four" until you all make it there!' Dale's tactic was upfront. It had worked on Suzie; it was working on Stella. Even on Stanley, busy with his helping of scrambled egg.

'Tuck in, guys.' Heffernan handed Jack a mug of hot milk and slid a pot of manuka honey over to him. He gave him a look, a flick of the head, like a private signal. Jack wouldn't be drawn into some joke at the expense of Stella and her mum.

'I'm going to miss our cosy meals around the fire,' Dale said to Suzie.

'Me too.' Suzie was smiling bravely. Jack felt a pang of sorrow. Whatever else, Heffernan was Suzie's son. He couldn't imagine what it would be like to give a son away and then have him come back. Even if he planned to fleece you for all you were worth.

Stella finished and laid her cutlery together. 'I've considered Mum's proposal.' She got up and collected the plates.

Jack gripped the sides of his chair. Stella hadn't talked to him about it – not that it would have made any difference; when Stella decided on something, that was that.

'I can't invest in another business. Two is enough.' Stella carried the plates over to the sink.

Jack nearly shouted with joy.

'I don't want investment, we sorted that,' Dale protested.

'You run one business,' Suzie corrected Stella, her lips pursed.

'I run a cleaning company and...' Stella took a breath, '...a detective agency.'

Jack hadn't expected that. When Stella took a risk, she did it in style. He tried to catch her eye.

'Wow!' Dale broke the silence.

Jack took another croissant and slathered it with honey. Containing his triumph, he detected well-concealed disappointment in Heffernan; Dale would be a practised con man.

'We should be going soon,' Jack said, although they had another half an hour. No one answered. He finished the croissant.

'I've always advised sticking to your core activity,' Suzie reminded Stella.

'I know, but—'

'Detection is what you do.' Suzie folded her napkin. 'You find dirt and wipe it away – you clean up. Clean Slate is turning a healthy profit, but you must reinvest to grow. The company needs to develop. A static company is a shrinking company. It's right to diversify within your core activity.' She poured herself the rest of the coffee and raised her mug. 'To Clean Slate Detectives!'

Jack snatched up a roll and ate it. Suzie, like her daughter, could deal out surprises. Stella would have expected her to argue, to have sound reasons why the idea was a bad one, but she had supported her.

'So, Terry knew he had a son.' Stella nodded to her mother.

The mood in the room dropped.

Terry and Suzie had kept their secret from their daughter. Simon would call it betrayal. Jack smeared the last of the crumbs off his plate. Simon would be right.

Terry had compounded the betrayal by confiding in Lucie May. Apart from Terry, Suzie at least had told no one.

'Terry could have used his position in the police to find you, but he respected the law, so he didn't,' Stella said to Dale.

Dale rolled his shoulders. 'I never came looking for you guys.' Jack could see that his confidence had ebbed.

'Stella, he thought of you as his only child, that's why he left you everything,' said Suzie.

'No, Mum, he didn't think that.' Stella squeezed out detergent into the bowl and snapped on rubber gloves. 'Terry didn't make a will, so as his only surviving heir, in the eyes of the law, I inherited everything. This place has never felt mine. I didn't work to get it.' Stella rinsed the plates under the tap.

'Terry worked so you could have it,' Suzie said. Jack had never heard her speak in such a conciliatory way about Terry before. It must be the 'Dale effect'.

'Terry would have been there at the airport to meet you. I gather he considered a trip to Australia, but couldn't get insurance because of his heart,' Stella added. Jack guessed Lucie May had told her. It seemed she had told Stella a lot of things. He thought he was pleased.

Suzie threw down her napkin. 'Are you saying Terry knew about his heart?'

'Terry knew a lot of things he kept to himself.' Stella turned to Dale. 'Terry liked good plain food and after Mum left he lived on ready meals. He would have liked your lamb stew, providing you ditched the garlic.' She gave a quick smile and stacked the plates on the dish rack. Jack saw that Terry's bowl and spoon and cup had gone. 'If Terry had met you, he would have put you in his will,' she added.

'You don't know that, Stella.' Suzie was fierce.

'I do.' Stella repacked the hamper. Everyone sat back as she wiped the table. She turned to Dale. 'Half of this house is yours.'

For Jack, what happened next was a blur. There was a knock at the door. No one moved to answer it. Stanley started barking and ran down the passage. Jack went with him. There was a taxi at the gate and a man was on the path, already walking away. He turned around and Jack saw him like an identikit: pronounced cheekbones, glittering eyes, an elegant green serge suit. He was a double of David Bowie.

He was Stella's ex and he had come to get his dog. Jack guessed this wouldn't have been the arrangement or Stella would have told them. The man must have broken their agreement. With these thoughts whizzing through his mind, Jack forgot about Stanley until the dog whisked through his legs and leapt at David Bowie.

'Good boy!' David – that was his actual name – crouched down and buried his face in the dog's coat. Jack conceded that the man had a right to the dog's enthusiastic greeting. Stanley was his dog.

He was distracted by another black cab pulling up behind the one that had brought 'David Bowie'.

'Fare for Heathrow?' the driver called through the cab's open window.

Jack spread his hands in apology. 'We don't need a taxi.' Who had called him?

'Please give Stella this letter.' The 'David Bowie' ex thrust Stanley into Jack's arms. 'Tell her she can keep him. He's hers now.'

'It's for me.' Dale was on the doorstep.

The man called David was in the first taxi and being driven away before Jack found he was holding an envelope as well as Stanley. He stuffed the envelope in his pocket and held on to Stanley tightly.

'Stella's taking you to the airport,' he reminded Dale. 'We all are.'

'Change of plan. I hate goodbyes, I get choked. Do me a favour, Jack, help me with this stuff.' Dale heaved two suitcases and a carrier bag out on to the path. He left the carrier bag on the path and struggled down to the taxi with the cases. The driver came to meet him.

Jack grabbed the bag and, still holding Stanley, went after him. Vaguely he noticed it was the bag Suzie had arrived with.

Dale climbed into the taxi. 'The girls think I'm in the bathroom.'

'I don't like goodbyes either,' Jack heard himself say.

'I thought you'd get it. I kept trying to catch your eye to let you in on it, but you were eating for all of us!'

'They'll be upset that you've gone.'

'Listen, Jack, I have a sister in Sydney and if some joker rocked up claiming to be her brother, I'd give him the evil eye. You are right to be wary of me.' He was seated in the back of the cab. 'I wanted to meet Stella, my biological sister, and see where I might have grown up. It's not great to know you were given away, even if you get the reason, but this way, I might get closure.' He clipped on his safety belt. 'My adoptive parents were happy and I had a great childhood, even though there was no spare cash and the Parramatta Road's not quite as salubrious as this bit of Hammersmith. If I'd stayed here, then I too would have been trundled between two homes like Stella – but at least there would have been two of us. I could have been there for Stella. I mind that.' He shuffled along the seat closer to the window. 'At least Stella's got you.'

'I'm not her brother.' Jack had got it wrong. While he had been thinking of himself, Dale had been thinking of Stella.

'No, mate, you are not!' Dale reached through the open window and grasped Jack's hand in his. 'Tell the world's best cleaner that Old Man Darnell's will must stand as it is. For obvious reasons, she'll listen to you.' He let go of Jack's hand.

'I'll support Stella with whatever she decides.' Jack stepped away from the car, holding tight to Stanley.

'Course you will, Jacko!' He grinned at him. 'Oh, and Jack?'

'What?' Jack heard himself sounding gruff and tried to smile.

'How come you knew exactly where in Sydney I grew up? You said Crows Nest when you met me. You were right on the mark. How could you know that? Did you check me out? Wouldn't blame you if you did.'

'I lived in Sydney once.' Jack looked up at the sky. Clear blue, the storm had gone. 'I moved there in 1988 and lived there for some years until my father got work back in the UK.' His father had worked on a bridge over the Hawksbury River outside Sydney that was never built – typical of most of his projects.

'Fair dinkum!' Dale ramped up his accent. 'What suburb?'

'Crows Nest, then Manly.'

'Good on you, you're an Aussie after all! Get yourself there again and I'll shout you more than a drink! Bring Stella.'

As Jack stepped away from the taxi, he heard the echo of Dale's earlier words. 'What did you mean, "for obvious reasons"?' he asked.

'Jack, for a smart guy, you are one dillbrain around women!' Dale leant forward and tapped on the glass partition. 'We're good,' he called to the driver. The car drew away from the kerb.

St Peter's church clock struck eight.

Jack watched it round the corner into St Peter's Square. *Bring Stella*. He thought again how close Simon had come to making Stella his fourth victim. She had shown him the picture of Simon under the trees at Wormwood Scrubs common. If William hadn't come when he did, Simon would have lured her further in. He had planned to hurt the woman who mattered to Jack more than anyone in the world. Or worse.

'For obvious reasons, she'll listen to you.'

The clock finished striking.

Dale was mistaken. There was no obvious reason why Stella would listen to him.

The first thing he saw when he went back into the house was Dale's album on the stairs. He must have put it by his suitcases and forgotten to pick it up. Jack grabbed it and flung open the front door, but the taxi had long gone.

'Did he get off all right?' Suzie asked. She and Stella were sitting at the table sipping freshly made coffee.

'You knew?' Jack exclaimed.

'I heard him booking it.' Suzie tore a scrap off Dale's last crois-sant. 'I think he wanted to spare me. I'd said I hated goodbyes.'

'I didn't know that.' Stella pushed a mug of hot milk towards Jack.

'Because it's not true. I *love* them, but when Dale confessed he needed diazepam to make it to his dad's funeral, I guessed that he wouldn't handle us waving him off to his plane! Me, I'm all for waving goodbye, doing a good tidy, then getting back to the old routine!'

'I'll have to go to the airport. He's left this.' Jack laid the album on the table.

'I asked him to hide it in the hall.' Suzie picked it up and, shifting her chair to make room for Stella, she asked her, 'Are you sitting comfortably?'

'I should get to the office.' Stella shot Jack a look; he could guess her thoughts. Dale Heffernan had not entirely gone; he had left them with episode two of his life story.

'Stella Darnell, this is your life!' Suzie handed the album to her daughter.

Stanley on his lap, Jack read the heading over her shoulder. 'Clean Slate: the Story so Far'.

Suzie had pasted the pages with testimonies from clients, before and after photographs of carpets and worktops, the changing logo over the decades. There was Stella in the late nineties, modelling the first uniform. A section headed 'Staff' featured group photos of cleaners, starting with Stella as the only one. Cuttings from trade magazines of Stella at gala ceremonies collecting awards: one for excellence in disaster restoration; several for excellent customer service and low staff turnover. An article by Lucie May described how Stella had built up a cleaning empire single-handed.

'Thanks, Mum.' Stella's voice was thick. 'How did you find all this?'

'I've been collecting it since the beginning. I never thought of making an album!' Suzie shut Dale's breakfast hamper and did up the straps. 'Shows you all that you've done. That's my daughter!' She ate the last bit of croissant.

Stella hefted the hamper out to the hall. Jack caught up with her by the front door.

'I forgot to say, that guy you went out with, who Stanley belongs to?' He heard himself imitating Dale's upward inflection.

'I'm handing him over at two p.m. this afternoon. Actually, Jack, I was going to—'

'He said you could keep him,' Jack finished.

'Until when?'

'Um, well, until he die— Forever. He said he doesn't want him back.'

Stella started to smile. Still smiling she returned to the kitchen. He heard her saying, 'Mum, I'm taking Stanley for a walk, do you fancy coming?'

It wasn't until Jack got out the key to unlock the tower that he found he still had the envelope 'David Bowie' had handed him. He was about to text Stella, but she would be walking Stanley. He was seeing her that evening. He would give it to her then.

Epilogue

Mist hung over the eyot. The tide had ebbed, exposing the causeway. The river flowed fast, the water murky and unforgiving. The beach was dotted with smashed glass, plastic and wood. Last Tuesday morning St Jude's storm had left in its wake a trail of devastation across southern Britain. Four people were dead.

On the eyot a snapped reed, a crushed leaf and one footprint were signs of the route he'd taken with Simon. He paused by the gap in the reeds where Simon had tried to make Jack kill him.

'Why did you save me that time if you wouldn't be my friend?'

'I would save anyone.'

'I'm not anyone.'

'No, you are not.'

'You won't save me this time, Jack. Justin. It's your turn to murder.'

He stared through the gap in the reeds at the rushing water below, thinking that the spangles of sunlight would join up and become Simon's face rising out of the blue-grey water. Right until the end, Jack had refused to do what Simon had wanted. It was his turn to murder and he had refused.

The white stones in his Garden of the Dead glowed in stippled sunlight. Jack took four more stones from his coat and, one by one, added them to the circle.

'Nathan Wilson. Madeleine Carrington. Rick Frost.'

He held the last stone in his palm.

'Simon Carrington,' he whispered as he laid the stone within the circle.

'As I walked by myself,
And I talked to myself,
Myself said unto me:
"Look to thyself,
Take care of thyself,
For nobody cares for thee."'

'What do you call a group of crows?'

'A murder.'

Stella seemed satisfied by his answer, although he doubted she believed him. She held up the front page of the *Chronicle*.

'*Detective's Daughter Does It Again!*'

'We didn't actually solve the case.' She was squatting on the floor in the main room of the tower, where his desk had been. The removers had taken everything back to his parents' house, leaving the space as bare as it was when Mr Wilson had come here with Simon's mother.

Stella spread the *Chronicle* on the floor. She had popped in on her way back from the office.

'We worked it out, but more by luck than ingenuity. We didn't realize it was Simon until he had captured you. We'll have to get better at this business if we're going to offer it as a service. We missed all sorts of clues. Dale saw that Lulu Frost wasn't what she said she was, but I ignored him. He texted Mum and me to say he'd landed safely.'

Jack saw a cloud briefly pass across her face. He suspected Stella of missing her brother.

'We did solve it. We discovered it was murder by suicide. We gave the police new evidence.' Jack was at the north window. He picked up the binoculars from the sill.

'I still don't see why Rick Frost ran when he saw Simon. It can't have been the first time – he was married to his sister after all,' Stella said.

'Remember what Nicola Barwick told us? She hid behind the hut one night when they were kids and overheard Simon telling

399

Richard Frost that one day he'd punish him. Richard would know when that day came. The boy was in Simon's grip: Simon had his glove and over time his threat gained potency. Rick knew Simon was closing in. Something impelled him to text William and go to see him. He saw Simon in the dark at the end of the platform and panicked. Simon didn't have to do anything. He simply had to be there. Over time he had become a potent threat to Rick, the embodiment of his darker side, the boy who had bullied and humiliated Simon.'

'Martin Cashman said we should have called him in earlier,' Stella said.

'You tried and he said he needed evidence.'

'He said Nicola putting her passport in the bin was evidence.'

'Maybe he should have listened to William Frost when he came to him in the first place. The main thing is we fulfilled William's brief and he's paid us. By hook and by crook we've done our first job. Your staff manual says do what the client wants and no more. We've closed Terry's "Glove Man" case too,' Jack reminded her.

'Clients don't ask us to clean and expect us to guess where.'

'Like we do with cleaning, we'll improve the more crimes we solve.' Jack trained the binoculars on one of the plane trees in St Peter's Square. The St Jude storm had denuded it of leaves. He added, 'Lucie's happy. She might never write that book, but she's done a spread for the *Observer* magazine and been read all over the world. She's back in the mainstream!'

'Lulu still loves Simon, even though he killed her real father and her mother. Simon never appreciated his sister's loyalty,' Stella said.

'Actually I think he did. His mother betrayed him, as did his teacher, and by refusing to be his friend, so did I. It poisoned his soul.' Jack couldn't bring himself to tell Stella the things he had said to Simon when they were boys.

'His mother having an affair wasn't betrayal, she was still his mother,' Stella said.

'She lied to her son. If you can't trust your parents to tell you the truth, whom can you trust?' Too late Jack thought of Terry and Suzie. They hadn't lied to Stella; they had avoided telling her truth.

'Parents don't have to tell their kids everything,' Stella replied.

Jack didn't say that having a brother *was* Stella's business. She had her own way of squaring things.

'Rick Frost looked at me before he jumped off the platform because he recognized me. We had met only once, when we were boys. I never forgot his eyes, hazel flecked with green, without a glimmer of warmth or life in them. That night on the station, they were full of fear. I did forget where I'd seen them before.' *You are trespassing*. He had erased the memory.

'He wasn't a nice man, but he didn't deserve to die,' Stella said. 'What was that about you denying him three times? Lucie said it's in the Bible. I didn't have you down as religious.'

'I learnt early that if you deny something or someone, you can wipe them away. I didn't want things to be the way they were. I didn't want to go away to school and I didn't want Simon to be my friend. By denying he was, I meant him to go away.'

'No reason you should have been Simon's friend. We choose who we like.' Stella was looking at the photographs in the *Chronicle*. Lucie's editor had printed the passport-booth pictures of Simon facing the wrong way. Jack had refused to look at them properly when she had tried to show him. Another sign he had passed up.

'Simon was an engineer. He calculated every stress point, every weakness; he covered every eventuality. When Nicola Barwick slipped through his net, he befriended Liz Hunter. He hadn't reckoned on William bringing us the case, but his plan was like water: regardless of obstacles, it found a path. He had watched me for decades, biding his time.' At walking pace, Jack shifted the binoculars out of the square and up to the church on the corner of Black Lion Lane.

'How could he know where you were?'

'From up here. Simon delivered those fliers; he knew I wouldn't be able to resist the chance to live in a tower, my own panopticon. He organised the removers, he made sure everything was exactly where I would have put it. He knew everything about me. Once I moved here, I became his True Host. Simon had stolen Rick's phone and replaced it with a decoy one for the police to find. William told me Rick had invented an app that tracks wherever you are. Simon stalked you and me. He knew where we were all the time. Chilling thought, isn't it?'

'Yes.'

Jack saw that the idea made Stella uncomfortable. He tried to reassure her. 'Not any more, though.'

He focused on St Peter's Church as the bells chimed five times. He had noticed that when he looked at places through the binoculars, even in the soundproofed tower, he heard the local sounds. He shifted to Terry's house on Rose Gardens North and gave a start.

'There's a massive white pantechnicon outside your dad's house!'

'You're not the only one moving.' Stella wandered out to the kitchen. She called back, 'I'm selling the flat and moving into Terry's. The garden will be good for Stanley.'

'That's great.' Jack was stunned. Stella was giving up her high-security flat with its three mortices and London bar for a house on a street with neighbours. He saw that it was fair that Stella give Dale half of the value of Terry's house, but hadn't expected her to take action so soon – and not this action. While he was retreating to his childhood house – returning to the ghosts – Stella was moving on. He murmured:

'I answered myself,
And said to myself
In the self-same repartee:
"Look to thyself,
Or not look to thyself,
The self-same thing will be."'

It wasn't all about ghosts. He had missed the short-eared owl knocker on his door and wondered if she had missed him.

'Can you see how they're doing?' Stella was back.

'They're going.' Jack put down the binoculars.

'I'll go down.' Stella was zipping up her anorak. 'Listen, I bought sparkling wine to celebrate the end of the case – cases – and that we're keeping Stanley.' She gave Stanley a fishy treat. 'Fancy coming over? I've taken Dale's stew out of the freezer. It just needs a flash in the microwave.'

'I'll do a last check and meet you at the van.' Jack hid his delight.

Stella was on the spiral staircase when he remembered the envelope David had given him.

'I'm sorry! I totally forgot – Dale going put it out of my mind!' Jack hung over the railing and handed the letter to Stella. 'I hope it doesn't matter that it's late.'

Stella took it from him. Seconds later, Jack heard the thud of the main door closing.

She had said '*We're* keeping Stanley'. He stopped himself doing a little skip.

Dear Stella,

When I asked you to mind Stanley, you weren't keen, but you do things properly. You will have cared for him and he will have become attached to you – and I think you to him too, so it is best if you keep him.

I'm going to live far away – somewhere where I won't see a Clean Slate van in the street and feel sad. I would like to say a proper goodbye. I know you hate them, but maybe just this once you might make an exception.

If you are willing, I'll be at Stamford Brook station tomorrow at 3 p.m. Please come without Stanley – I couldn't bear to see him. I'll wait fifteen minutes, then, if you don't come, I'll suppose you didn't want to see me. Here's to a Tabula Rasa!

Love,
David

PS You might want to change Stanley's name because you didn't choose it.

The letter was dated last Friday. By 'tomorrow' he had meant Saturday.

Leading Stanley across the road, Stella walked past her van on down to Chiswick Mall and leant against the railings overlooking the eyot. She folded up the letter and tucked it into her anorak pocket. Once again she reminded herself that 'Mr Right' didn't exist. Her phone beeped. *David*. She snatched it out of her pocket, registering that there were no staring eyes at the top of the screen.

Fancy a drink tonight? x. It was Liz.

When they were young, Liz had sent her letters to suggest they meet. She never rang Stella. She gave her space to decide. Stella had said she was cleaning or had left it a while before replying and then not replied at all. Liz knew what Stella was like. She didn't try to change her.

Can't tonight, tomorrow? You OK? Liz had liked 'Justin Venus'.

Nicola Barwick was moving back into her house in Chiswick. Liz was going to buy Stella's flat in Brentford. Stella had been reluctant to do a deal with a friend, but Liz had persuaded her. The flat was quiet with a view over the river and, with its locks and pass-codes, secure. Liz had said she trusted Stella. Stella's phone pinged again.

See you at the Ram on Black Lion Lane? Yes I am OK, thanks to you, 'tec! Lxx.

Stella shuddered to think what Simon Carrington might have done if he had not drowned before he could make it back to the tower where he had left Liz and Nicola Barwick. Nicola had said that Simon Carrington was once a nice little boy. Stella found that hard to believe.

Jack hadn't told Stella what had happened between him and Carrington on the eyot and she wouldn't ask him. There was a lot about Jack that she didn't know and didn't want to know. When he came down from his tower, she would say that she had been wrong to ask him to promise not to walk in London at night. Jack must walk where and when he liked.

Stella couldn't bring herself to admit to Jack that she had used

Rick Frost's stalking app to locate him. She couldn't bear that she hadn't trusted him.

If Jack asked her why she had changed her mind about him walking at night, she wouldn't be able to explain, except that if she had to make a promise not to clean, she would find it hard to keep.

'You will always be called Stanley,' she told the dog. 'It's who you are.'

Jack put the binoculars back in their case. He would keep them. Simon had given them to him as a present, he wouldn't reject them. He slotted them back into his bag alongside Simon's toy train.

He had lived with the darkness of own unkindness to Simon. Like Rick Frost, he had lived with threat, if vague and amorphous. Even though he had assumed Simon was dead. Simon's death did not lessen the feeling. Jack knew he would always live with the darkness.

Stella was the light. While she could be awkward and insensitive, she would never set out to cause hurt. If someone hurt her, she absorbed it and carried on. She never sought revenge. She hadn't held it against Suzie, or Terry, that they had kept so important a secret from her. She had accepted Dale into her life. Stella did what was right.

He listened. No glugging sink, no vibration on the spiral staircase and no music seeped from the curving grey concrete walls that had witnessed death and silence.

His mind was his own.

The Tower card had turned up in his Tarot reading on his birthday. It was a sign. He had ignored it. Simon had forced him to experience the chaos and destruction that the card might be said to herald. He had made him face the darkness in his soul. The tower – the card and the building itself – had made Jack see himself. To have posted it through his door, Simon must have been inside his house and taken the card from the pack on the hall table. He was a True Host in more ways than one.

Jack returned to the eyot window. Light sparkled on the Thames, the calm before the ebb tide. A plump seagull perched on the tide marker on the eyot. On the beach at the western tip of the island were two figures. A woman, hands on hips, was watching a little boy pushing what looked like a steam engine down a plank of wood into the water. A dart of sunlight dazzled Jack and he blinked. Thinking to get the binoculars, he looked again and saw that, but for the gull preening itself on the tide marker, the beach was deserted.

On Chiswick Mall, Stella and Stanley stood by the railings facing the river.

They were waiting for him.

Acknowledgements

In the course of researching and writing *The Detective's Secret*, many people have been generous with their knowledge, experiences and time.

The help of Frank Pacifico, Test Train Operator for the London Underground, has been invaluable. Although he's nothing like Jack in character, Frank has succeeded in imagining Jack's preoccupations and, as we travelled the District line, he offered me fitting 'driver' observations that enabled me to see through Jack's eyes. Any mistakes or errors regarding detail of the London Underground are mine.

Jack isn't a believer in coincidences, so I wonder what explanation he would have for my finding that the information from brothers of two childhood friends proved to be key to my research. My thanks to them both.

The designer Tom Dixon is the brother of my beloved old friend Vikasini. Tom kindly lent me his water tower and I spent one hot summer morning wandering through it. I looked out at London from the roof and imagined Jack's panopticon. In this novel I have taken the liberty of moving Tom's tower across London from North Kensington and relocating it beside the River Thames at Chiswick.

I grew up in Hammersmith, up the road from Tanya Bocking and her brother Nat. While trawling the internet, I landed on the Water Tower Appreciation Society's website and found that the writer and photographer Nat Bocking is its secretary. I am grateful to Nat for sending me links and a reading list, which included *Water Towers of Britain* by Barry Barton, a fascinating account of their use and construction.

As always, my thanks go to Detective Superintendent Stephen

Cassidy, retired from the Metropolitan Police. Again, any factual errors regarding the police are mine.

Thanks to: Emeritus Professor Jenny Bourne Taylor of the University of Sussex for her recommended reading from the nineteenth century – the spirit of this century haunts this story.

My partner, Melanie Lockett, listens to and gives discerning comments on my unfolding ideas. When words arrive on the page, she is my first reader. Thank you.

Stella's dog Stanley was 'trained' courtesy of Michelle Garvey at Essentially Paws. Any of Stanley's wayward behaviour is my responsibility.

Lisa Holloway, Creative Industries consultant and lecturer, has given me valuable advice.

Thanks to: Tasmin Barnett, Domenica de Rosa, Marianne Dixon (aka Vikasini), Juliet Eve, Hilary Fairclough, Christine Harris, Kay and Nigel Heather and Alysoun Tomkins, who, in varying ways, gave me encouragement along the way.

West Dean College in Chichester was accommodating and supportive during the writing of this novel; my thanks in particular to Rebecca Labram, Francine Norris and Martine McDonagh. Thank you to my agents, Capel and Land. My agent Philippa Brewster is exceptional. Much gratitude goes to Georgina Capel, Rachel Conway and Romily Withington.

Laura Palmer is the best of editors and a joy to work with. Big thanks to all at Head of Zeus, in particular Nic Cheetham, Kaz Harrison, Mathilda Imlah, Clémence Jacquinet, Madeleine O'Shea, Vicki Reed and Becci Sharpe. Once again, my thanks to Jane Robertson and Richenda Todd, who have given the text unremitting scrutiny, proofing and copy-editing respectively.

How to get your free eBook

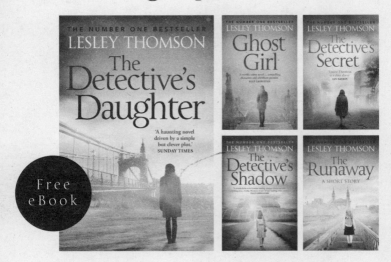

Free
eBook

For readers using a kindle or kindle app:

1. Email us at promotion@headofzeus.com with the subject line THE DETECTIVE'S DAUGHTER KINDLE

2. We'll email you the ebook of THE DETECTIVE'S DAUGHTER, the first book in the series

3. Follow the instructions to download the ebook to your kindle

For all other reading devices / reading apps:

1. Email us at promotion@headofzeus.com with the subject line THE DETECTIVE'S DAUGHTER OTHER

2. We'll email you the ebook of THE DETECTIVE'S DAUGHTER, the first book in the series

3. Follow the instructions to download the ebook to your device